19/1/19
24 8.19
13/12

KT-559-150

Please return/renew this item by the last date shown
on this label, or on your self-service receipt.

To renew this item, visit **www.librarieswest.org.uk**
or contact your library

Your borrower number and PIN are required.

4 4 0007360 9

Dilly Court

The River Maid

HarperCollins*Publishers*

HarperCollins*Publishers*
The News Building,
1 London Bridge Street,
London SE1 9GF

www.harpercollins.co.uk

First published by HarperCollins*Publishers* 2018
1

A catalogue record for this book
is available from the British Library

PB ISBN: 978-0-00-819960-9
HB ISBN: 978-0-00-819959-3

Set in Sabon Lt Std by Palimpsest Book Production Limited,
Falkirk, Stirlingshire

Printed and bound in Great Britain by CPI Group (UK) Ltd,
Croydon CR0 4YY

MIX
Paper from
responsible sources
FSC
www.fsc.org   FSC™ C007454

This book is produced from independently certified FSC™ paper
to ensure responsible forest management.

For more information visit: **www.harpercollins.co.uk/green**

Chapter One

Limehouse Hole, London, 1854

Essie Chapman pulled hard on the sculls as she rowed her father's boat towards Duke Shore Dock. It was dark and the lantern on the stern of the small, clinker-built craft bobbed up and down, shedding its light on the turbulent waters of the River Thames. Essie fought against the tide and the treacherous undercurrents, but she was cold, wet and close to exhaustion. Her mysterious passenger had not spoken a word since she had collected him from the foreign vessel moored downriver. The task would normally have fallen to her father, Jacob, but he was laid up, having slipped on the watermen's steps the previous evening. He had fallen badly and had been carried home to White's Rents on an old door, the only form of stretcher available to the wharfinger's men at the time. He had lain on the sofa like a dead man for twenty-four hours and when he awakened he could barely move a muscle.

'You'll have to do my next job for me, Essie, love. It's a matter of life and death.'

His words echoed in her mind as she battled against the elements. By day Jacob's small craft scurried up and down the river doing errands considered too small by the lightermen and watermen, but by night things were different. Sometimes it was the odd barrel or two of brandy that had to be sneaked ashore before the revenue men laid hands on it, or packets wrapped in oilskin, the contents of which would forever remain a mystery. There was always a messenger waiting on the shore to grab the cargo and spirit it off into the darkness. Money changed hands and Jacob would spend most of it in the Bunch of Grapes, coming home reeking of rum and tobacco smoke. Sometimes, when he felt generous, he would give Essie twopence to spend on herself, but the money was usually spent on necessities like bread, coal and candles.

The tide would turn very soon and Essie was anxious to reach the shore before the current took her downriver. She shot a furtive glance at her passenger, who was wrapped in a boat cloak that made him merge into the darkness. His face was concealed by the hood and she could not tell whether he was young or old, although his lithe movements when he had climbed down the ship's ladder and boarded her boat suggested that he was in the prime of life. Getting him to dry land was uppermost in her mind and she put every ounce of strength into a last supreme effort to reach the wharf. The sound of the keel grating on gravel was like music to her ears, although it was as much as she could do to rise from her cramped position. Then, to her surprise, her passenger was on his feet and had stepped over the side, wading ankle deep in water as he dragged the craft effortlessly onto the mud and shingle.

The top of the wharf towered above them, menacing even by moonlight. The great skeletal iron-work of the cranes was silhouetted against the black velvet sky, and an eerie silence hung in the still air, punctuated only by the slapping and sucking of the water against the wooden stanchions. It had to be well after midnight and yet the river was still alive with wherries, barges and larger vessels heading for the wharves and docks further upstream. It was slack water and soon the tide would turn and the river would churn and boil as it flowed towards the coast. Jacob always said that river water ran in his veins instead of blood, and as a child Essie had believed every word her father said, but now she was a grown woman of twenty and she was not so gullible.

She stood up, but before she had a chance to

clamber ashore the stranger leaned over and lifted her from the boat as easily as if she were a feather-weight. She was acutely aware of his body heat and the scent of spicy cologne mixed with the salty tang of the sea. Most men of her acquaintance stank of sweat, tar and tobacco, but this was altogether different and oddly exciting. She had barely had time to catch her breath when he set her down on the ground, pressed a small leather pouch into her hand, and, without a word of thanks, he strode off, heading in the direction of the stone steps.

Driven by curiosity, Essie hurried after him, although her progress was hampered by her damp skirts and flannel petticoat. She reached the top of the steps in time to see him climb into a waiting cab and it drove off into the night, leaving her alone on the wharf amongst the idle machinery. The brief moment of quiet was shattered when the door of a pub in Fore Street opened, spilling out a group of drunken men, who cavorted and sang in good-natured tipsiness until someone landed a punch, which started a brawl.

She weighed the purse in her hand and it was heavy – this had been no ordinary job. The tall stranger with strong arms and gallant manner was not a common seaman, and if he was carrying contraband, it was something small that could be easily concealed beneath his cloak. There was nothing more she could do and she was tired. She might never know the identity of the man who smelled of the sea and spice. What his mission was must remain a mystery – but she was chilled to the bone and the thought of her warm bed was uppermost in her mind.

Essie started walking. Home was a small terraced house in White's Rents, a narrow alley leading to Ropemaker's Fields. It was a poor area with several families crowded into the two-up, two-down dwellings. Chimney sweeps, brewery workers, dockers, street sweepers and sailmakers lived cheek by jowl with the families who raised ten or more children in the tiny houses, with a shared privy at the end of the street. The constant reminder of what fate might have in store for the less fortunate inhabitants was Limehouse Workhouse, just a short walk away.

Essie quickened her pace, but all the time she was aware of the deep shadows where danger lurked at any time of the day or night. The yellow eyes of feral cats blinked at her as they slunk along the gutters in the constant search for food, and skinny curs prepared to fight for survival. Drunks, drug addicts and thieves on the prowl might lurk in the shadows to attack the unwary, and it was a relief to arrive home unmolested.

'Is that you, my duck?' Her father's voice boomed out like a foghorn from the sofa as she opened the front door, which led straight into the front parlour.

'Yes, Pa.'

'Is the job done?'

'Yes, Pa.' Essie trod carefully as she made her way across the floor in almost complete darkness. The curtains remained drawn back but there were no streetlights in White's Rents, and clouds had obscured the moon. 'Do you want anything, Pa?'

He reached out to feel for her hand. 'A cup of water would go down well, Esther. I've drunk all the ale, but it didn't do much to help the pain in my back.'

'We should get a doctor to look at you.'

'You know we can't afford it, love. I'll be all right in a day or two.' Jacob shifted his position and groaned. 'Did he pay up?'

Essie tightened her grip on the purse. 'Who was he, Pa?'

'It's not for us to know. Where's the money?'

'I have it safe.'

'Give it here, there's a good girl.'

'We'll talk about it in the morning, Pa. Right now I'm tired and I'm going to bed.' Essie opened the door that concealed a narrow staircase, and she closed it behind her, cutting off her father's protests. She would give him the money, but not before she had taken out enough to pay the rent collector and buy food. She had not eaten anything since a slice of bread and a scrape of dripping for breakfast, but she had gone past feeling hungry. Pa might be content with a couple of bottles of beer, but Essie could not remember the last time they had sat down to a proper meal. She climbed the stairs to her room where she undressed and laid her damp skirt over the back of a wooden chair, the only piece of furniture in the tiny room apart from a truckle bed. She slipped her cotton nightgown over her head and lay down, pulling the coverlet up to her chin, but through the thin walls she could hear the infant next door howling for his night feed. The organ grinder who lived at number three was drunk again, and, judging by the screams and shouts, was beating his poor wife. Someone was singing drunkenly as he staggered along the pavement below, banging on doors and laughing as he made his way back to the dosshouse in Thomas's Rents, an alleyway situated on the far side of the brewery.

Essie leaped out of bed and went to close the window, shutting out the noise. Clouds of steam billowed into the sky above the brewery, filling the air with the smell of hops and malt, which was infinitely better than the stench from the river and the chemical works. She returned to her bed and lay down again, closing her eyes but, tired as she was, she could not sleep. There was no saying where the next job was coming from and the money in the pouch would not last long. Her father was well known on the river and work was put his way, but it was a man's world and she was little more than a girl. She was tolerated because she was Jacob

Chapman's daughter, but on her own she might as well be invisible. For both their sakes, she could only hope that his injury was not serious.

Next morning, having made sure that her father was ready for another long day on the sofa, Essie set off with money in her pocket. Her first stop was at the pharmacy to purchase a pennyworth of laudanum. That done, she visited various shops in Fore Street to buy enough food to last for a day or two only, as it was summer and milk went sour overnight, cheese grew soft and oily, and flies feasted on meat, leaving their eggs to develop into squirming maggots. Essie bought bread, dripping, two meat pies and a small amount of tea. Then, as a treat, she added a few lumps of sugar. It was an extravagance, but she felt she had earned it.

'Hold on, Essie. What's the hurry?'

She glanced over her shoulder and saw her friend walking towards her. 'Haven't you any work today, Ben Potter?'

'I'm just about to start now.' He lengthened his stride, slowing down as he fell into step beside her. 'How's Jacob? I heard about his accident.'

'Not very good. I've got some laudanum to dull his pain, but I think he ought to be in hospital, or at least see a doctor.'

'What about the bonesetter?'

'I hadn't thought of that,' Essie said, frowning.

'But I'll see how Pa is by this evening. We really can't afford to throw money about unless it's going to do some good.'

Ben nodded, pushing his cap to the back of his head. 'I've got to go or I'll be late and the guvnor will dock my wages. Old Diggory used to knock me for six when I first started my apprenticeship, but I'm bigger than him now and he's a bit more respectful.'

Essie shot him a sideways glance. She had known Ben all her life and when they were children they had roamed the muddy foreshore together, searching for valuables or coins that lay hidden beneath the surface. When he was fourteen Ben had been apprenticed to Diggory Tyce, a waterman who had won the Doggett's Coat and Badge in his youth, and whose knowledge of the River Thames was second to none. Ben was ambitious, and Essie admired that in a man.

She smiled. 'They say that wherries will soon be replaced by steamboats.'

'Aye, they do, and that's the future as far as I'm concerned, but the guvnor will take a lot of convincing.' Ben came to a halt at the top of Duke Shore Stairs. 'I'll call round tonight when I finish, if that's all right with you, Essie.'

'Yes, but I can't promise to be there. It all depends if I can find work.'

'You shouldn't be working the river on your own.

It's hard enough for a man, but it's dangerous for a slip of a girl like you, especially after dark.'

'I can beat you at rowing any day of the week.' Essie blew him a kiss and he waved cheerily as he made his way down the stone steps to the foreshore where Tyce's wherry was about to be launched. The passengers were already seated, and judging by their appearance they were seamen returning to their vessel from a night ashore, some of them very much the worse for wear. One had a black eye and another had his head bandaged, blood seeping through the grubby dressing.

Essie sighed, hoping that someone would offer her employment, although it seemed unlikely. She walked on, heading for home. It was still early but White's Rents was alive with activity. Small, barefoot children had been turned out to amuse themselves in the street, and the boys were rolling around in the dirt, scrapping and testing each other's strengths like playful fox cubs. The older girls sat round plaiting each other's hair and chatting while they kept an eye on the babies.

On the other side of the road Miss Flower was bent double, using her little trowel to pick up deposits left by feral dogs. The smell added to the general stench, but she seemed oblivious to it and trudged on her way, heading in the direction of the tannery where the contents of her wooden pail would be used in the tanning of leather. She said that, on a good day, she could get a shilling for her efforts, but Essie would not have traded places with her for a king's ransom. Miss Flower's occupation was almost as unenviable as that of Josser the tosher, who earned his living by venturing into the sewers in search of valuables that had been washed down the drain. Josser and Miss Flower lived at number ten, sharing the house with the night-soil collector, several railway workers and a succession of Irish navvies. Essie wondered how anyone could exist in such conditions, but the poor had to make do in order to survive. She hurried past a group of slatternly women, who stopped talking to look her up and down and went on to whisper and giggle like schoolchildren. Essie was used to this and she walked on, ignoring their taunts.

As she entered the front parlour she was surprised to find her father sitting up.

'Did you bring beer, Essie?'

'No, Pa. I spent the money on food. I'll light the fire so that I can boil the kettle.'

He slumped back against the worn cushions. 'I need something for the pain.'

'I bought some laudanum, but you're obviously a lot better. At least you can sit up now – you couldn't do that last evening.'

'Give me the bottle and I'll dose meself, Essie, love.' Jacob's tone changed and he gave her a persuasive smile. 'Help your poor old pa, there's a good girl.'

She snatched up the basket and headed for the kitchen. 'I'll mix some laudanum in water and then I'll get the fire going. I'm dying for a cup of tea.'

'I'm dying for a sip of ale. You could have bought a couple of bottles. What if I give you the money and you take a jug to the pub and get it filled?'

Essie hesitated in the kitchen doorway. 'What if you give me more money so that I can pay the rent on time every week, Pa?

'You're an ungrateful child, Esther Chapman. Your poor mother would turn in her grave if she could see how you treat me.'

'That's not fair,' Essie said angrily. 'I do my best.' She closed the door on him and busied herself unpacking the contents of the basket. Her memories of her mother were hazy, and probably enhanced by time, but everyone said that Nell Chapman had been a remarkably pretty young woman. She had come from a good family and had married Jacob to spite her father, who had tried to come between her and the penniless boatman who had captured her heart. The only thing that Essie could recall clearly was the sound of voices raised in anger, and her mother's tears when Jacob came home from the pub the worse for drink. The sickness that had taken her ma to live with the angels had almost claimed her own life, but Essie had survived, largely thanks to the care of her brother, George. She dashed her hand across her eyes – George had left home after a furious row with their father. She had been only six years old, but that day was etched in her heart for ever.

But there was no point dwelling on the past. Essie heaved a sigh and returned to the parlour where she used the last of the coal and kindling to light the fire.

'Where's me tea, Essie?' Jacob demanded crossly. 'I'm parched.'

'All in good time, Pa. I've only got one pair of hands.' Essie sighed and scrambled to her feet. The pail, which was normally filled with water, was empty and that meant a short walk to the communal pump at the end of the street. Jacob normally undertook this, although it was done under protest. She left by the back door and went out through the tiny yard to the narrow passageway that separated White's Rents from the ropeyard, the tarring house and the other buildings associated with rope making. The smell of hot tar lingered in the air, filling her lungs and making her cough, but she hurried to the pump and joined the queue of ragged women and barefoot children.

'Looks as if it's come straight from the river,' the woman in front of Essie complained. 'I dunno why we don't just dip our buckets in Limehouse Hole and hope to catch a few fish as well.'

'This water's got legs.' Her companion sniffed and wiped her nose on the back of her hand as she stared at the murky water in her bucket. 'Fish can't live in this stuff.'

Essie knew better than to join in the conversation, but she had no intention of drinking the water in its present state. An old woman who had survived the cholera epidemic of 1848 had told her to boil water before drinking it, and she had done so ever since. Pa had said much the same thing, only he used it as an excuse to sup more ale. Essie filled her bucket and returned home, but as she entered through the back door she heard the sound of male voices coming from the parlour.

She stopped to fill the kettle before going to investigate, but the front door closed as she entered the room. 'Who was that, Pa?'

Jacob gave her a gap-toothed grin. 'The answer to our problems, girl. We've got a lodger and he's willing to pay handsomely for a room, with no questions asked.'

'We haven't got a spare room, for a start, and who is this mysterious person?'

'It's only temporary, and I can't get up the stairs while I'm like this, so I told him he can have mine. You'd best see to it. Put clean sheets on the bed, or whatever you need to do to make it comfortable.'

'All right,' Essie said slowly. 'But I'd like to know who it is who'll be sleeping in the room next to mine. I might be murdered in my bed, or worse.'

'You don't need to know his name, and you won't

be seeing anything of him. He'll sleep all day and go out at night. It's only for a short while, so don't ask questions. Anyway, he's paying good money for the privilege, so leave it at that.' Jacob shifted on his seat and pulled a face, uttering a loud groan. 'Where's that laudanum? I'm in agony.'

Essie returned to the kitchen and poured the last of yesterday's boiled water into a tin mug, adding a few drops of laudanum. She took it to her father, holding it just out of his reach.

'Don't tease me, Essie. I'm in agony.'

'I'll give it to you when you tell me who this "lodger" is and why he's hiding here.'

Jacob glared at her, licking his dry lips and grimacing with pain. 'His name is his own business, and that's all you need to know. I'm not telling you anything else, girl, so give me my medicine.'

Essie could see that this was getting her nowhere and she handed him the mug. 'When do we expect him to arrive, Pa?'

'Just leave the back door unlocked. He'll come and go as he pleases. You don't have to do anything other than keep out of his way.'

'I dislike him already,' Essie said bitterly. 'He must be a criminal if he has to creep about in the darkness. I don't like it, Pa. I really don't.'

'Here, take this.' Jacob pulled a leather pouch from his pocket and placed it in her outstretched hand. 'Maybe that will change your mind. Pay off that bloodsucking rent collector and get some proper food in, and some ale. What our friend does is none of our business.'

'Friend!' Essie tossed her head. 'I'll go along with it because there's nothing else I can do, but I hope you know what you're doing.'

That night Essie lay in her bed, listening to every creak and groan of the old timbers as they contracted after the heat of the day. The background noise from overcrowded dwellings, street fights and infants wailing was always the same, whether it was noon or the early hours of the morning, but tonight was different. She had tried to elicit more information about their mysterious lodger from her father, but he had refused to be drawn, and now her mind was buzzing with questions and she was apprehensive. Life was difficult enough without getting directly involved in criminal activities. The night runs she had done with Pa had been testing, but work was hard to find and they had to eat. She dozed and eventually drifted into an uneasy sleep, but was awakened suddenly.

She sat up, straining her ears. The hinges on the back door were rusty and she was certain she had heard the scrape of boots on the flagstones in the kitchen. She swung her legs over the side of the bed and seized her wrap, slipping it around her as she stood up and went to open her bedroom door. Her heart was pounding and she hesitated as she heard the door at the foot of the stairs open and close again, as softly as a whisper. Then the shadowy outline of a man filled the narrow space and he was ascending the stairs, two steps at a time.

'Stop.' Essie barred his way. 'Who are you?'

He came to a halt, raising his head but in the darkness his face was a pale blur. 'You were told to ignore my presence.' His voice was little more than a hoarse whisper, and she could not tell if he was young or old, but it was obvious from the way he spoke that this was no ordinary criminal.

'You are in my home,' Essie said boldly, although her knees were trembling and she was poised ready to retreat into her room and slam the door in his face. 'I have the right to know your name at least, and what sort of business you have that can only be done by night.'

'You ask a lot of questions.' There was a hint of amusement in his voice.

'Your name, sir. I refuse to share my house with someone who is afraid to make himself known to me.'

'And what do you propose to do about it, Miss Chapman? Your father has agreed to this.'

'But I have not.' Essie folded her arms, staring down at him. 'You might be a murderer, for all I know.'

He mounted the last of the steps so that they were standing close together on the small landing. 'Then perhaps you should be afraid. Your father is sound asleep – drugged with laudanum and ale, I should imagine from the smell downstairs. We are alone and I have you at my mercy. What do you intend to do about it?'

The blood was drumming in her ears in a deafening tattoo, but she was not going to let him see that she was afraid. 'You don't frighten me, sir. My father has made an agreement with you, which I must honour for now, but if I discover that you are engaged in criminal activities I will have no hesitation in reporting you to the police.'

'Which is my room?' he asked, stifling a yawn. 'I'm tired and I need to sleep.'

'You haven't answered any of my questions.'

'And I don't intend to. There are things that you don't need to know.' He stepped past her and opened the door to Jacob's room. 'The bed has not been slept in so I assume this must be mine.'

As he pushed past her Essie had felt the warmth and a scent that was unforgettable. 'I recognise you now. I brought you ashore from the foreign ship yesterday evening.'

He glanced over his shoulder as he was about to enter Jacob's room. 'Very clever of you, but I'd advise you to put it from your mind.'

'Who are you? You might do me the courtesy of telling me your name.'

'You may call me Raven,' he murmured, and shut the door.

'Raven?' she repeated dazedly. 'What sort of name is Raven?'

'You shouldn't have done that,' Jacob said crossly. 'It's better that you know nothing about our friend.'

'He's not my friend,' Essie countered. 'I don't like it, Pa.'

'Just get on with your work, girl. I want you to go to the wharfinger's office and see if he's got any jobs that you can do. I don't know how long our guest will be staying or how long I'm going to be laid up. Don't think I'm enjoying this, because I'm not.'

Essie relented. Her father's face was lined with suffering and he looked pale and ill. 'All right, Pa. I'll go out and get some fresh bread for breakfast and some coffee from the stall in Nightingale Lane.'

'I haven't got money to burn,' Jacobs muttered. 'You ought to make up the fire and put the kettle on.'

Essie took a deep breath, praying for patience. 'I would, Pa. But we've run out of coal and kindling.'

'Oh, well, do what you must, girl.' Jacob lay back and closed his eyes. 'I can't sleep properly on this thing. I miss my bed.'

Essie snatched up her shawl and wrapped it around her shoulders, biting back the sharp words that threatened to tumble from her lips. 'I'll be back soon, Pa.'

She let herself out of the house and hurried down the street, nodding to Gaffer Wiggins, the chimney sweep, who was mustering his gang of small apprentices ready for the day's work. Essie smiled at the boys, all of them tiny, undernourished and very young, but they did not respond. She saw them nearly every day and, had it been in her power, she would have taken them home, given them a bath in the tin tub in front of the fire and fed them nourishing food. But they belonged to their master and the many attempts by those in power to improve their lot had been largely ignored.

Essie sighed and walked on, heading for the wharfinger's office. Maybe one day she would find herself in a position to help the poor and downtrodden, but now the need to find work was uppermost in her mind. And she did not trust the man who called himself Raven.

Chapter Two

Essie heaved the boat across the stony foreshore and secured it to an iron ring above the high-water mark. She had just returned from taking a junior dock official to Limehouse Hole Pier, a job too small to be considered worthwhile by the watermen, but there had been a degree of urgency from Saul Hoskins, who was afraid he might face the sack if he was late for work yet again. Saul lived in Thomas's Rents and Essie knew his young wife, Marie, who was the mother of twin girls and had recently given birth to a boy. If Saul lost his job the family would face an uncertain future and Essie had been only too glad to help, even if Saul could only afford to reward her with a penny for her efforts. Rowing fiercely against the tide was exhausting work, but she had got him to work on time.

It was a week since Raven, their mysterious lodger, had moved into Jacob's room. Very little had changed in number seven White's Rents, but Essie had to admit that Raven's contribution to the housekeeping had made their lives easier. They had paid off the arrears on the rent and had eaten well every day, although Essie had kept some of the money aside, hiding it beneath a loose floorboard in her bedroom. Their lodger would move on soon, or so she hoped, but Jacob was not yet fit to return to the river and she would have to earn enough money to keep them both until he was strong enough to work. She was still curious and not a little worried about Raven's activities, but he kept himself to himself and neither she nor her father had seen him to speak to since that first night.

Essie hitched up her damp skirts, wishing that she could wear breeches like the men, but it was difficult enough for a girl to find gainful employment, without shocking the male population and antagonising them. She had many acquaintances on the wharves and amongst the lightermen and watermen, but she knew that they tolerated her for her father's sake, although he came in for a certain amount of criticism for allowing his daughter to take his place. She did not want to be an object of pity, but she was realistic enough to know her limitations when it came to physical strength. She had always thought of the turbulent River Thames as an entity in its own right, with a throbbing heart that would go on for ever: the river was to be respected, feared and never taken for granted. She climbed Duke Shore Stairs and had just reached the wharf when she spotted Ben, who was chatting to one of the crane operators. He broke off his conversation and hurried to meet her, dodging between piles of crates and coils of rope.

'You're looking very serious. Is anything wrong, Essie?'

She shook her head. 'No, I'm fine, thanks.'

'I'm sorry I haven't managed to come round to see your pa, but we've been working day and night for the last week.'

'That's all right. Pa doesn't feel up to having visitors.'

'How is he doing? It's going about that he might not walk again.'

'Whoever is spreading such lies should mind their own business,' Essie said sharply. 'Pa's improving every day. He's moving about the house, although he can't make the stairs yet, but he'll be back to work soon.'

'All right, don't bite my head off. I was only asking.'

'I'm sorry, Ben. I'm not having an easy time. It's just hard to make a living with such a small boat. I've taken Saul to work again this morning, and he could only afford to give me a penny.'

'If you're short of money I might be able to help.'

Ben's weather-beaten features creased into a worried frown. 'You've only got to ask.'

'Thank you, but we'll manage.' Essie glanced round, hoping to spot a likely customer. 'Why are you here, anyway? Shouldn't you be working?'

'Engine trouble. These new-fangled steam engines break down too often. Sometimes I think we were better rowing the wherries, even if it was hard work.'

'Will it take long to fix it?'

'I dunno, but the guvnor told me to take the morning off, or what's left of it.' Ben gave her a searching look. 'Have you eaten today?'

'Not yet. I was hoping to find another job, but it looks a bit quiet.'

'There's a pie seller in Shoulder of Mutton Alley. Come on, Essie. I'll treat you to a pork pie and a cup of coffee.'

It was an offer that was too good to refuse. Someone had eaten the last crust of bread and had scraped out what remained of the dripping. Essie had two suspects in mind, but her father was sound asleep on the sofa and there was no sound of movement from Raven's bedroom. She had heard him come in at dawn, but she had given up trying to find out anything more about him, and so far his stay in their house had been uneventful. It was not his fault that the milk had gone off, although he was guilty for using the last of the tea. She would have to go shopping later, but that could wait.

'That sounds wonderful.' Essie linked arms with Ben. 'I'm starving after all that rowing. The river is in a funny mood today, full of eddies and cross-currents. It's behaving like a grumpy old man.'

Ben threw back his head and laughed. 'The things you say, Essie Chapman. It's a river, it can't think. It just does what it has to do and flows down to the sea.'

'You say that, Ben, but I grew up in Limehouse like you, and I know the river. It's the heart and soul of London and despite its moods and tantrums, I love it.'

He patted her hand as it lay on his sleeve. 'You need food inside you, love. You're light-headed.'

The pies contained more gristle than meat, but the pastry was thick and filling, and the coffee was hot and comforting. With a full stomach Essie felt more optimistic as she parted from Ben and walked to the wharfinger's office.

Riley, the wharfinger, a stocky man with a broken nose and grizzled grey hair, had once been a bare-knuckle fighter. What he lacked in stature he made up for with lightness of foot and dogged aggression. He had floored many a would-be champion, and the dockers, crane operators and watermen all treated him with respect.

Riley looked up from the ledger he had been studying and his lined face crumpled into a smile. 'Essie, me darling, how are you today?'

'I'm well, thank you, Mr Riley. Have you any work for me?'

'Is that father of yours still not able to work?'

'He's getting better each day,' Essie said firmly. 'He doesn't like being idle.'

'It's true I haven't seen him in the Grapes recently, so he must be poorly.'

'But I can take his place, Mr Riley. I'm as good at rowing as any man and I know the river better than most.'

''Tis also true, me darling, but you have to admit that you cannot match the men for strength.' Riley leafed through a pile of paperwork. 'Nothing today, I'm afraid. Go home, Essie, there's a good girl.' He bent his head over the book on his desk and she was effectively dismissed.

Essie knew what he said was true but it still rankled. 'Thank you, Mr Riley. I'll pop in this afternoon, just in case anything turns up.' He did not look up and she left the office, acknowledging the cheery waves from one or two of the men on the wharf and ignoring the salacious comments of those who regarded her as fair game, Diggory Tyce being one such person. If it were not for Ben's watchful eye and strong arm, Diggory might have become a nuisance, but Essie knew of the waterman's reputation with women and she kept out of his way as much as possible. Not that it was easy in the relatively small world of the river people at Limehouse, where brawn ruled and the strongest came out on top. Essie knew from past experience when to stand up for herself and when it was better to back away. Women's work, according to almost all the men of her acquaintance, was to stay at home, marry, keep house, bring up children and cook and clean. Whether it was their father or their husband, men were their masters and it was a woman's duty to do as she was told. Essie refused to believe this. She was certain that there must be more to life than drudgery and giving birth every year. She made her way to the grocer's shop and purchased a few necessities before making her way home.

She had just reached the door of number seven when it opened and she was almost bowled over by a tall man wearing a reefer jacket. His cap was pulled down over his brow but she was aware of a pair of intelligent, startlingly blue eyes set beneath straight black brows. The lower half of his face was covered by a small moustache and neatly clipped beard, but even though she had only seen him in the dark she knew it was the man who called himself Raven. For a brief moment their eyes met and then he tipped his cap and strode off.

'Wait a minute.' Essie followed him, although she had to run to keep up with his long strides. 'Are you leaving? I thought you weren't supposed to be seen in daytime.'

He came to a sudden halt, rounding on her. 'You

were told to mind your own business. Please go home and tend to your father.' He walked off, cutting a swathe through the curious neighbours who had gathered on their doorsteps, and the children playing on the pavement.

'What are you looking at?' Essie demanded, turning her back on the women who were chattering, giggling and pointing at her. She reached the house and let herself in to find her father propped up on a couple of pillows. Judging by the tipsy smile on his face he had supped one too many bottles of ale, and the evidence lay around him on the floor. The smell of alcohol filled the front parlour.

'I suppose he bought these for you,' Essie said angrily as she put her basket down and bent over to pick up the empty bottles. 'You'll only fall again if you get drunk, Pa. You know you can't take your ale like you used to.'

'Stop fussing, girl, it was only a little tumble.'

It was at that moment Essie noticed a large lump on her father's forehead and the beginnings of a bruise. 'I'll soon put a stop to this.'

She abandoned the task of tidying up and ran from the house, determined to catch up with Raven. Dodging passers-by and leaping over infants who were crawling about in the filth, Essie chased after their errant lodger. He had been heading towards Fore Street, and, as she rounded the corner, she caught sight of him striding along, but he stopped suddenly as a carriage drew to a halt at the kerb. The door opened and he climbed in. Essie hesitated, waiting for the vehicle to continue on its way, but it remained stationary and this made her even more curious. She approached cautiously, pretending to study the contents of the shop windows, but as she drew level the carriage door opened and Raven leaped out.

'What do you think you're doing?' He grabbed her by the arm. 'Why are you following me?'

'Let me go, you're hurting me.'

He tightened his grip. 'Who put you up to this?'

'No one. I don't know what you're talking about.'

'What's going on, Raven?' A fashionably dressed young woman leaned out of the carriage, staring curiously at Essie. 'Who is that?'

'Get in. We're drawing attention to ourselves.' Without a by-your-leave Raven lifted Essie off her feet and tossed her into the vehicle. He climbed in and closed the door. 'Now then, I want an explanation.'

'My dear, you're scaring the poor creature.' The young woman turned to Essie with a beguiling smile. 'Who are you? And why were you following this man?'

'She is the boatman's daughter,' Raven said angrily. 'Unfortunately our paths crossed just as I was leaving White's Rents in answer to your note, Alice. I wasn't to know the silly little fool would follow me.'

'I am not a fool,' Essie protested. 'And I'm capable of speaking up for myself, sir.'

'Aha, a young lady of spirit.' Alice leaned back against the padded velvet squabs, putting her head on one side as she eyed Essie with renewed interest. 'Tell me about yourself. What's your name?'

'I might ask the same of you, ma'am,' Essie said stiffly. 'I didn't ask to be pitched into your carriage. I was merely following this man because I want to know what he's up to.'

'Let's start with who you are, shall we?'

'My name is Esther Chapman and I brought this fellow ashore from a foreign vessel, with very little thanks for my trouble and a good deal of inconvenience, I might add.'

'Really? I'm impressed, and I apologise for Raven's treatment of you, but he is rather anxious to keep his presence in London a secret, as you might have guessed. And you are quite correct, introductions should have been made first. I am Alice Crozier.'

'Lady Alice Crozier,' Raven added with a wry smile. 'Daughter of the Earl of Dawlish.'

'I'm sure that has little interest for Esther,' Alice said sweetly. 'I'll thank you to mind your own business, Raven.'

'You are very much my concern, Alice.' Raven's smile faded as he turned to Essie. 'You will keep this to yourself.'

She nodded. 'I just want to know what you're up

to, and what business you have that keeps you out all night. Times are hard enough without dragging my pa into something shady.'

Alice raised her eyebrows, fixing Raven with a questioning glance. 'Well? What do you say to that?'

He eyed Essie thoughtfully. 'How trustworthy are you, Esther?'

'It all depends what you mean by trustworthy. My main concern is for Pa and myself. We're struggling as it is and we don't want any trouble.'

'But you've taken my money,' Raven said smoothly. 'That might implicate you in my crime, or whatever you imagine my misdeeds to be.'

Alice laid her mittened hand on his arm. 'Stop teasing the poor girl, Raven. I think Esther could be trusted, and anyway she knows too much to fob her off with threats or platitudes.'

He leaned back in his seat, fixing his intense gaze on Essie. 'I am a convicted felon,' he said slowly. 'I was transported to Australia five years ago.'

Essie, for once, was speechless – she could only stare at him in amazement. He was obviously an educated man, and not the sort she associated with the crimes that could be punished by transportation to the colonies.

'That surprises you,' Raven continued. 'I suppose I should be flattered, but I was accused of obstructing officers of the Crown and sentenced to seven years' penal servitude.'

'Were you guilty?' Essie demanded, finding her voice at last. 'What did you do?'

'That doesn't matter.' Raven turned his head away, staring out into the street. It had started to rain and the passers-by were scurrying for shelter.

'He was protecting his brother.' Alice leaned towards Essie. 'Raven did not deserve such a harsh sentence. He was punished because he came from a privileged background and was supposed to set an example to his inferiors, or so the judge said.'

'Seven years sounds a bit harsh,' Essie said thoughtfully. 'I don't know what your brother did, but surely he should have been punished, not you.'

'My brother was young and irresponsible. He got away.'

'You saved him from himself,' Alice said severely. 'Frederick was your mother's spoiled darling, and he thought he could do as he pleased. But for you he would have been sent to a penal colony instead of living a life of luxury abroad.'

'A monastery in Italy is hardly the most thrilling place for someone like Freddie to spend the rest of his days.' Raven shook his head. 'I intend to clear both our names, but I'm no hero. If I'm discovered I'll be thrown into jail and will probably face the death penalty.'

'Then why have you risked everything to return to London?' Essie demanded.

'It's a matter of trust and honour, but I don't want you to be involved.'

'But she is already,' Alice said gently. 'And you are risking everything by being seen in daylight. We will all be in trouble if you're recognised.'

'I know that, Alice. But I have to see Gilfoyle today – it's taking too much time with all this creeping about at night. I need to go to his office and have it out with him.'

Alice's green eyes widened and her mouth turned down at the corners. 'That's insanity.'

'Nevertheless, I must see him in person. I have to sort out my affairs before the *Santa Gabriella* sails. I have to be on that ship.'

Essie shifted uncomfortably on the padded velvet seat. 'I shouldn't be here. Perhaps I ought to go home. I have to find work anyway.'

Alice reached out to grasp Essie's wrist. 'Don't go yet. I have an idea that might save us all from a great deal of trouble and heartache.'

'You always were the clever one in the family,' Raven said with a wry smile. 'What do you suggest?'

Alice ignored him, concentrating her attention on Essie. 'How do you earn your living, Esther?'

'It's Essie, my lady. No one calls me Esther unless I'm in trouble.'

'All right then, Essie – what work are you looking for?'

'My pa fell and hurt his back. He's works the river and I've taken over his job while he's poorly.'

'Forgive me, but I don't know what that entails.'

'We have a boat and we do trips that are too small for the watermen and lightermen to take on. As I told you, I brought Mr Raven ashore the other night, and it was blooming difficult, rowing against wind and tide.'

'We need a go-between, Essie,' Alice said earnestly. 'Raven is risking everything simply by returning to London, but he has important business to transact.'

Essie looked from one to the other. Raven was frowning thoughtfully, but he made no comment. 'You're an escaped convict,' she said slowly. 'I'd be in trouble too, if you were caught.'

He nodded. 'Yes, you would. I don't want you going into this blindly.'

'But we would pay you well,' Alice insisted. 'You're involved now anyway.'

'Don't tell the girl that,' Raven said angrily. 'She can still walk away. I won't be responsible for ruining a young life.' He fixed Essie with an intense look. 'You aren't under any obligation to me or my cousin. If you're unhappy with this you are free to go now, and nothing more will be said.'

Essie held his gaze and saw a man she could trust. 'I will help you,' she said slowly. 'Just tell me what you want me to do.'

Raven was about to reply, but Alice laid her hand

on his arm. 'Leave this to me.' She turned a brilliant smile on Essie and the sun seemed to shine inside the luxurious carriage, even though the rain was drumming on the roof. 'We will take you home and you can tell your papa that you have been offered work in the house of a respectable lady, which will give you an excuse for visiting me in Hill Street.'

'Take me home?' Essie shook her head. 'Are you mad? Begging your pardon, my lady, but if this carriage arrived in White's Rents it would cause a sensation.'

'She's right, Alice.' Raven's tense expression melted into a smile. He opened the door. 'Go home, Essie. I'll see you later.'

Essie visited Riley on the way, but he had no work for her and she spent the day cleaning the house, attempting to ignore her father's constant carping. In the end she went to the pub and had a jug filled with ale, which kept him happy. He was soon sound asleep and snoring loudly, and Essie was sitting by a desultory fire in the kitchen, waiting for the kettle to boil, when Raven entered the room.

She jumped to her feet. 'I thought they'd got you,' she said crossly. 'I've been waiting all day for you to return.'

He took off his cap and reefer jacket, shaking droplets of rainwater on to the tiled floor. 'You sound like a nagging wife.'

'I don't know who would want to marry a man like you,' Essie countered. 'You asked me to help you and I need to know exactly what I'm supposed to do.'

He pulled up a chair and sat down, stretching his long legs towards the fire. 'Haven't you got any more coal? That's a pitiful excuse for a blaze.'

'No, I haven't. I bought a bag yesterday and put it out in the yard but someone pinched it.'

'I'm sorry, I know I've put you to a lot of trouble, but you'll be handsomely recompensed.'

'If I'm not sent to jail first.'

A smile curved his lips and he nodded. '*Touché*. But I'll take great care that doesn't happen.' He leaned forward and took the poker from her hand. 'That really is a poor apology for a fire.'

Essie sat back in her chair, eyeing him thoughtfully. 'Why aren't you staying with Lady Alice? You'd be a lot more comfortable in her house. She'll have a servant or two to take care of you, and I'm sure she has coal fires in every room.'

'My cousin has a large house in Hill Street, as you'll discover, and she has a small army of servants. Most of them are trustworthy, but there's always someone with a loose tongue.' He put the poker down with a sigh. 'I can't afford to be caught, Essie. This isn't a game, which is why I want you to visit Hill Street daily and return with whatever information Alice has for me.'

'What do you hope to gain from all this?' Essie asked boldly. 'And don't say it's none of my business, because you've involved me and my pa whether we like it or not. Why would you risk everything to return to London now, when you only have to wait for another two years and you could be a free man?'

'Free, but still a convicted criminal.' He stared into the pale flames that licked around the damp nuggets of coal. 'Have you heard of a place called Ballarat?'

'No, can't say I have.'

'You know that fortunes are being made from the goldfields?'

'I suppose I must have seen something about it in the old newspapers that people leave about, but Australia is on the other side of the world. What has that got to do with us here?'

Raven put his hand in his pocket and took out a gold nugget, which gleamed dully in the firelight. 'This is what it's all about, Essie.'

'You've struck gold?'

'Let's just say that I've found enough to buy back my good name and that of my brother.'

'It's hard to believe that something so small can be of such value.'

'This is not the whole of my find. There's more.' He put the nugget back in his pocket. 'You mustn't breathe a word of this. People become savages when there is so much money at stake.'

She laughed, despite the seriousness of the situation. 'Round here they'd kill you for a silver sixpence, let alone a lump of gold.'

'Which is why no one must find out.'

'I will help you, but what did Frederick do that caused you both so much trouble?'

'I suppose it will do no harm to tell you.' Raven leaned back in his chair with a faraway expression in his eyes as if seeing a world quite different from the poorly furnished kitchen with damp staining the walls and cracked windowpanes. 'Our family home is in Devon. Freddie had just come down from Cambridge and, for whatever reason, he got involved with some undesirables. Despite the efforts of the preventive officers, smuggling still goes on along the coast and probably always will. Freddie was caught aiding the gang to unload their illicit cargo onto the beach.'

'What happened then?' Essie asked anxiously. She could almost smell the salty air and hear the waves crashing on the shingle as the boat laden with contraband was hauled ashore.

'Freddie escaped and came home, but the revenue officers followed him. I did what anyone would do when their younger brother was in trouble and I said he was doing my bidding. I thought, quite wrongly, that my privileged position could keep me out of trouble.'

'But you said he's in Italy. I don't understand why you were punished instead of him.'

'We were both put on bail, but I knew that Freddie would admit his culpability and I arranged for him to leave the country. I stood trial and I was punished for my stupidity and arrogance. It was too late to tell the truth and that's why I'm here now, paving the way for freedom for both myself and Freddie.'

'But your brother is guilty and he's escaped punishment. That doesn't seem fair.'

'Freddie was young and stupid, but he's no criminal. You would do the same for a brother if you had one, I'm sure.'

Essie's eyes filled with tears. Memories of long ago flooded back on a tide of emotion – a smiling face, a playful tug at her hair, a paper poke filled with shards of toffee, a piggyback when her little legs were too tired to walk another step – the older brother ousted from the family home when she was a small child. She gulped and swallowed, turning away so that Raven would not see her tears.

'What's the matter?' he demanded. 'What have I said to upset you?'

Chapter Three

The need to tell him was too strong. It was a forbidden subject as far as her father was concerned, but love did not fade away on command, and she had loved George. She had hero-worshipped her elder brother, who had alternately teased and spoiled her, but the feeling ran deep. 'I have a brother, too,' she murmured, half-afraid to speak his name in case Pa should hear.

'You have a brother? Where is this fellow? He ought to be taking care of you now.'

'I should have said that I *had* a brother, but George left home when I was very young. Pa won't allow his name to be spoken, and he blames George for my mother's death. He says he broke her heart and that's why she died.' Essie wiped her eyes on her apron. 'But I know that's not true. She died of the fever that she caught from me. I am to blame for her death, not George.'

'That's ridiculous, Essie. You couldn't help being ill, and you certainly weren't responsible for your mother's death.'

'I try to believe that, but George left anyway.'

'To lose your mother and your brother at such a young age must have been hard for you to bear.'

'It was – it still is – which is why I will help you. Just tell me what to do, and I'll try my hardest to help you and your brother.'

Next morning Raven gave Essie the money for a cab and she walked to Commercial Road, waiting until she was safely out of sight of prying eyes before she hailed a passing hansom. The cabby looked askance when she gave him the address and demanded to see her money, but the sight of a silver shilling was enough to convince him that she could pay her way.

'Hop in, but I hope you know what you're doing, miss. The toffs don't take kindly to the likes of you knocking on their door, begging for work.'

'Drive on, please.' Essie picked up her skirts and climbed in with as much dignity as she could muster. The cab pulled away from the kerb and she settled down to enjoy the luxury of being driven through the city, but the cabby's words still rankled, and she was beginning to feel apprehensive, especially when they reached the exclusive world of the West End.

The elegant terraced house in Hill Street was as far removed from Essie's home in White's Rents as was possible: both were constructed of bricks and mortar with slate roofs, but here the similarity ended. There were no beggars hanging around in doorways or ragged urchins picking pockets. The street sweepers were hard at work keeping the thorough-fare free from the horse dung, straw and the general detritus that buried the East End roads beneath layers of filth. Maidservants wearing black dresses, spotless white aprons and white mobcaps, were busy buffing up the brass door furniture and shaking dusters out of upstairs windows. Even the air Essie breathed seemed different in this part of London, although the smell of fresh paint and polish did not quite mask the stench from the river on a hot summer day. It was like entering another world and Essie's hand shook as she raised the gleaming doorknocker and let it fall. Moments later the door was opened by a liveried footman.

He looked her up and down. 'Tradesman's entrance is down the area steps.'

She put her foot over the threshold as he was about to close the door. 'You don't understand. I am expected. Please tell Lady Alice that Essie Chapman is here.'

He hesitated for a moment, but then he relented

and stood aside. 'You'd better come in. Wait there and don't move.' He stalked off, leaving her standing in the marble-tiled vestibule. Shallow steps led into a wide entrance hall with a grand staircase sweeping up to a galleried first floor. From the outside the house did not look enormous, but inside it seemed vast and magnificent. Scantily clad marble statues in artistic poses graced the hall, and frosty-eyed dignitaries stared down at Essie from oil paintings in ornate gilt frames. Long mirrors reflected the dancing prisms of light from crystal chandeliers, and slender plant stands supported urns filled with exotic flowers. Essie felt dwarfed and out of place amongst such opulence and grandeur. She was beginning to think that her offer to help Raven had been a huge mistake, and was about to make her escape when the footman reappeared.

'Lady Alice will see you in the morning parlour.'

Essie followed him across the black and white tiled floor, stifling a sudden childish impulse to slide on the polished marble as if skating on ice. She managed to restrain herself and was ushered into the morning parlour. If she had been unsure of her welcome her doubts were immediately dispelled when Lady Alice rose from her seat by the window.

'How good of you to come, Essie. I realise this must be difficult for you. You must be in need of refreshment after that tedious journey from the other side of the city.' She turned to the footman who was still standing stiffly to attention in the doorway. 'Bring coffee and cake for Miss Chapman, Fielding.'

'Yes, my lady.' Fielding remained stony-faced as he bowed and backed out of the room, closing the door behind him.

'Now we may speak freely.' Lady Alice's smile was replaced by a serious expression, and she motioned Essie to take a seat. 'I have two appointments today, both of them on Raven's behalf. The first one is with his lawyer, and the second with his bank. All of this is strictly between you and me, and my servants know nothing of what is going on, and it must be kept that way.'

'How do I fit in, my lady?' Essie asked anxiously. 'I'm sure my presence here must raise questions.'

'I've thought of that. I used to employ a sewing woman but she retired recently. Her eyesight had been failing for some time and her work was quite unacceptable. The sewing room is upstairs on the third floor.' Lady Alice paused, giving Essie a searching look. 'You can sew, I suppose?'

'I can darn a sock, my lady. I can mend a tear, but I can't do anything fancy.'

'That will suffice. It's only the servants' uniforms that occasionally need a stitch or two, and I don't really know what Moffatt did all day, but she seemed to keep busy.'

'I see,' Essie said slowly, although she was not convinced. 'Won't the servants think it's odd that you're employing someone like me to do a bit of mending?'

'It doesn't matter what they think, the main thing is that they don't find out the real reason for your being here. I trust you not to gossip, Essie.'

'I wouldn't dream of it, my lady. But is that all I have to do?'

'Your main task will be to take the information I gather to Raven. It might be in the form of documents for him to sign, or written notes from me, but secrecy is the most important thing.' She broke off at the sound of approaching footsteps and the rattle of cups and saucers. Forgetting that she was a guest in Lady Alice's house, Essie jumped up to open the door. A young maidservant staggered into the room carrying a tray laden with crockery and a silver coffee set. Fielding was close behind bearing a cake stand, and it was obvious from the superior expression on his face that he was above helping the girl, who was little more than a skinny child.

'That's far too heavy for a girl like you.' Essie took the tray from her and placed it on a rosewood tea table next to the cake stand. She glared at Fielding, but he remained aloof and impassive.

The maid's pale eyes filled with tears and her lips trembled. 'Please, miss. That's my job.'

'I'm a servant here, too,' Essie said boldly. 'Lady Alice has just taken me on to work in the sewing room, so it's all right if I give you a hand.' She turned to Fielding. 'You might have helped her.'

'Sit down, Essie,' Lady Alice said in a bored tone. 'And Fielding, that child should be working below stairs. I expect better from you.'

Fielding bowed and backed towards the door. 'Be careful, Miss Chapman,' he said in an undertone. 'I've got your mark, and yours, too, Dixon.'

'What is going on?' Lady Alice demanded angrily.

Fielding stood to attention. 'My apologies for Dixon, my lady. I'll report her behaviour to Mrs Dent. She'll deal with the girl.'

'It wasn't her fault,' Essie protested. 'This man is a bully.'

'That's enough.' Lady Alice said coldly. 'If anyone is to speak to my housekeeper it will be me. Tell Mrs Dent I want to have a word with her, Fielding.' She dismissed him with a wave of her hand and he shooed Dixon out of the room, closing the door behind them.

Essie had a feeling that Fielding would make the poor child suffer, but there was nothing she could do to protect Dixon from his wrath.

'That young man needs a lesson in manners. This would never have happened if I hadn't sent my butler to the country house.' Lady Alice picked up the coffee pot. 'I won't allow bullying in any shape or form amongst my servants, but you would be wise to hold your tongue, Essie. You need to be invisible as far as the rest of my staff are concerned.'

'Yes, my lady. I'm sorry.'

Lady Alice reached up to tug on a silk-tasselled bell pull. 'I'll send for someone to show you where to go and give you instructions, Essie. You can say that you're a distant relative of Moffatt's, and it was she who recommended you. There's no need to elaborate, just try not to offend Mrs Dent when you meet her. I can't afford to have a rebellion in the servants' hall.'

Essie glanced longingly at the tiny cakes and pastries that were arranged so prettily on the cake stand, but she did not like to take one, and Lady Alice had apparently forgotten about food. Essie had barely sat down again when a maid answered her summons.

'Take Miss Chapman to the sewing room, Morrison. She'll be replacing Miss Moffatt.'

'Yes, my lady.' Morrison eyed Essie curiously. 'Follow me, miss.'

The sewing room on the third floor of the town house overlooked the garden and the mews. Flies wandered tiredly up and down the glass panes, as if giving up all hope of escaping from their prison. Dust had settled on the work table and the seat of the upright wooden chair where Essie was to sit. The small space was hot and stuffy and she opened the window, releasing the captive insects. A waft of fresh air filled the room with the smell of the stables mingled with the scent of flowers from the well-tended beds below. A gardener was scything the grass into a velvety lawn, and in the small back yard a housemaid was beating a rug as if punishing it for disobedience. The household seemed to run on well-oiled wheels and Essie felt like an interloper. Morrison had been less than friendly and Fielding had been suspicious of her from the start, and now he held a grudge against her. Life in Hill Street was not going to be easy.

She turned with a start as the door opened and a middle-aged woman dressed in black bombazine entered the room. Even the smallest movement was accompanied by the jingling of a large bunch of keys attached to a chatelaine at her waist. She looked Essie up and down.

'I am Mrs Dent, Lady Alice's housekeeper.'

Remembering her manners, Essie bobbed a curtsey. 'Good morning, ma'am.'

A shadow of a smile flickered across the housekeeper's even features. Her smooth skin was unrelieved by laughter lines or furrows on her brow, but it was obvious from her shrewd expression that she missed nothing, and her firm chin suggested a steadiness of purpose and a stubborn nature. She placed a bundle of cloth on the table. 'These garments need mending. I hope you're more competent than poor Miss Moffatt. She should have retired years ago.'

'I'll do my best, ma'am.'

'I hope so.' Mrs Dent folded her arms, head on one side. 'I gather you won't be living in.'

'No, ma'am. I'll return home when I've finished my duties here.'

'And where is home?'

Essie realised that she was being gently cross-examined and she did not want to give too much away. 'I live in Limehouse, Mrs Dent.'

'That's a long way to travel each day. Why would you do that?'

'My pa injured himself in a fall,' Essie said truthfully. 'I have to go home to look after him, and we need the money.'

'I see.' Mrs Dent turned as if to leave the room, but she paused in the doorway. 'You won't earn very much here. I wouldn't have thought it worth your while. The cab fare would be very expensive, more than you could hope to make for a few hours' work.'

'I walk part of the way and then I catch a bus,' Essie said, improvising wildly. She had no idea how much the fare would be, but it sounded reasonable and it seemed to convince Mrs Dent, who smiled vaguely and left, closing the door quietly.

Left to her own devices, Essie found needles and thread in a chest of drawers and a pair of scissors, and she settled down to work. Sewing was not her most favoured occupation, but it was easier than working the river in all weathers. It was the silence that was hardest to bear, used as she was to the constant noise both at home and at work. The house in Hill Street might have been deserted for all the sounds that could be heard on the third floor. No doubt the kitchen was buzzing with activity and chatter, but even the birdsong was muted at this level and the neighbours might have been a million miles away, not yelling and bawling at each other at the tops of their voices, as they did at home. If there were babies in the nurseries their nannies kept them from crying, and older children must be fully occupied in their school rooms, or perhaps taken out for long walks in Hyde Park by their tutors and governesses. Essie found herself in a different world – one where she did not feel at all comfortable.

She had no idea of the time, but judging by the position of the sun, it was well past noon and she was feeling hungry. The memory of the cake stand, laden with dainties, came back to haunt her and she wished that she had had the forethought to tuck one in her pocket before Morrison spirited her away. If this was how things were Up West, Essie decided that she preferred the rough and tumble, privation and poverty of the East End. At least you knew where you were with Miss Flower – you could smell her bucket of pure a mile off, but she always had a kind word and a smile. Josser the tosher was also less than fragrant, but he would give you his last farthing, if he had one, and Ben would be wondering where she was. Essie tried to forget her rumbling belly and stitched away, storing all her experiences up to tell Ben when she saw him next.

A timid tap on the door brought her back to earth and she jumped, pricking her finger and yelping as a tiny bead of blood broke surface. 'Come in,' she murmured.

Dixon put her head round the door. 'I brought you some grub, miss. I think they must have forgot you below stairs.' She glanced over her shoulder as if to ensure that the coast was clear before slipping into the room. She had her apron folded into a bundle, from which she produced a chunk of bread and a couple of slices of ham. 'I managed to nick this off the kitchen table.' She put her hand in her pocket and took out an apple and a piece of cheese. 'Sorry it ain't much, but you was kind to me earlier. No one has ever stood up for me before, so I wanted to do something for you.'

'You are very kind, Dixon.' Essie stared at the girl, frowning. 'I can't keep calling you that. I'm Essie – what's your name?'

'It's Sadie, Miss Essie.'

'Just Essie will do nicely.' Essie gazed at the food and her mouth watered. 'I hope this won't get you into trouble downstairs.'

'I'm used to it, miss. I gets the blame for everything from sour milk to Mr Fielding losing money on the horses. He's a one for betting, is Mr Fielding, but he don't tell Mrs Dent how he spends his afternoons off, or where he goes to on a Sunday when everyone else attends church.'

'Where does he go?' Essie made an effort to keep a straight face, but Sadie's childish prattle made her want to laugh, if only for the sheer relief of speaking to someone friendly.

'He's sweet on Iris Morrison,' Sadie whispered. 'Only don't tell no one I said so. Iris will lose her job if Mrs Dent finds out they're stepping out together, but Mr Fielding will deny it and Morrison will get the sack. It ain't fair, but that's how it is.'

This was too much for Essie and she chuckled. 'I'm sorry, I know it's not funny, but I was beginning to think that everyone here was stuck up and unapproachable. You are a breath of fresh air.'

Sadie's pale blue eyes widened. 'I ain't never been called that before, either.' She was suddenly alert, like a small animal that sensed a fox was on the prowl. 'I got to go or I'll be in even more bother. I was supposed to be scouring out the pans in the scullery.'

'Well, I'm truly grateful for the food,' Essie said earnestly. 'But you mustn't risk your job for me, Sadie, dear. I'll brave the servants' hall later on and make myself known to everyone. I'm sure someone will tell me what I'm supposed to do about meals.'

'Cook is all right, miss. But she gets a bit upset when she burns things, and then you got to watch out for flying pans, and she can't half swear when she's in a state. Mr Barton ain't here at the moment, but he's a stickler for behaviour and clean fingernails. The kitchen maids are a funny lot. Sometimes they're friendly and at other times they're scratching each other's eyes out like a lot of alley cats.'

'It sounds a dreadful place to work,' Essie said thoughtfully. 'Can't you go home to your family?'

'Ain't got one, miss. I was raised in the Foundling Home. There's lots of us kids around. I suppose I'm lucky to have a roof over me head and three meals a day. It could be worse.' She backed out onto the landing and her footsteps grew fainter as she raced towards the back stairs.

Having eaten every last scrap of food, Essie worked with renewed energy, and by late afternoon she had almost finished the pile of mending. Her back ached and her fingers were sore, having pricked them on the needle more times than she could remember, but there was a certain satisfaction in seeing the neatly patched and darned garments ready for wear. She had almost forgotten the reason for her being in Hill Street when Lady Alice breezed into the room.

'I didn't send for you, Essie, because it would arouse curiosity in the servants' hall. I want you to be as inconspicuous as possible.'

'I understand, my lady. Have you anything for me?'

Lady Alice nodded and handed her a sealed document. 'Give this to Raven and tell him that the money is deposited in the bank. He knows which one, and I've arranged another meeting with his lawyer tomorrow at eleven o'clock, but this time he has to attend without me.'

'I'll tell him that, my lady.'

'Good. We're trusting you, Essie. This is extremely important – you might say a matter of life and death – so nothing must go wrong. Do you understand?'

'Yes, my lady.'

'Then I'll say no more.' Lady Alice took a leather purse from her reticule and placed it on the table. 'There's enough money to pay your cab fares. I'll expect you here after Raven's appointment with his lawyer. It's not safe for me to be seen with him, so you will take my place. Go now and I'll see you tomorrow.'

Essie walked part of the way, but it was hot and she grew weary of being jostled on the crowded pavements. Eventually she hailed a cab, alighting in Fore Street, and made her way along the wharves, hoping to bump into Ben. She owed him an explanation, but that might prove difficult without giving away her new position in Hill Street. She was deep in thought when she was accosted by Diggory Tyce. He loomed out of the shadow of a large crane.

'So, you've returned to us, Essie Chapman.

Where've you been all day? I believe Riley has been looking for you.'

'It's none of your business, Mr Tyce.' Essie tried to sidestep him but Diggory Tyce was a big man and nimble for his size. He grabbed her by the arm.

'Don't try to humbug me, miss. I know there's something going on. I saw the man you brought ashore the other night. What has that father of yours got you into now?'

'I don't know what you're talking about.' Essie struggled but he only tightened his grip on her arm. 'Let me go or I'll scream.' She looked for a familiar face, but it was unusually quiet for the time of day.

He leaned over so that his face was close to hers. 'Give us a kiss, little girl. I've a fancy for you and now your dad is out of action there's no one to stand up for you.'

'That's where you're wrong.' Ben came striding towards them, his hands clenched into fists. 'Let her go, guvnor.'

'Or what?' Diggory demanded, grinning. 'You depend on me for your livelihood, boy. You're bound over to me for another year and I can make or break you, so go away and leave me to enjoy meself for a change.'

Essie wrenched her arm free. 'You're a disgrace, Diggory Tyce. Leave Ben out of this, but my pa will hear of it, you may depend on that. He won't be laid up for ever and then you'd best watch out.'

Diggory backed away, his face contorted with rage. 'You little slut. You toss your head and you're all smiles when you want something, but you don't want to give anything in return. There's a name for girls like you.'

Ben took a step towards him but Essie held him back. 'No, Ben. Don't get into bother because of me. I can take care of myself.'

Reluctantly Ben dropped his hands to his sides. 'I'll see you safely home, Essie.'

'No, you won't. There's still work to do and you work for me.' Diggory turned on his heel and stomped away in the direction of the wharfinger's office. 'You'll be sorry for this, Essie Chapman.'

She shook her head. 'He's a brute. I wonder I didn't see it before, but he's never behaved like that until now.'

'I'm sorry, Essie. I should have flattened him while I had the chance.' Ben shoved his hands in his pockets, shoulders hunched as if he carried the weight of the world on them. 'But he's right. I'm bound to him until I finish my apprenticeship. Sometimes I wish I'd gone to sea or joined the army.'

'Let's walk on. I don't want to give him the chance to tell you off for shirking.' Essie tucked her hand in the crook of his arm. 'If you had done any of those things it would have been my loss, Ben. I really appreciate what you did just now.'

'I just made it worse.'

'No, you didn't. He might have gone further if you hadn't intervened, and I'm grateful.'

He came to a halt at the top of the steps leading down to the foreshore, where mudlarks were picking over the detritus left by the ebb tide. 'Where have you been all day? Riley asked me where you were and I didn't know what to say. Your boat is still where you left it, so I knew you weren't working on the river.'

'I can't tell you, Ben. I went on an errand for someone, that's all I can say, but I'm going home now.' She backed away. 'But first I'd better go and make peace with Riley.' She hurried off before he had a chance to question her further. Keeping a secret from her friends was not going to be easy, and she could only hope that Raven would finish his business quickly and leave them in peace.

Riley looked up as she entered his office, but his grim expression was not encouraging. 'Nice of you to call in, Miss Chapman. I suppose you know that I've been looking for you all day?'

'Yes, and I'm truly sorry, Mr Riley. I had work in a different part of the city.'

'I thought you were a good girl, Essie. There's only one sort of occupation that springs to mind.'

'I don't have to explain myself to you.'

'Then you won't care that I've found someone else to do the work that I'd normally put your way. You let me down, Essie Chapman, and your pa will

hear about this. I dare say you've been keeping
company with some young fellow who's taken your
fancy, but be warned it'll bring you nothing but
trouble. You may think you're pretty, with your big
hazel eyes and your long dark curls, but you girls
are all the same, trollops at heart, leading men on.'

'You have a very poor opinion of woman, Mr
Riley. Maybe you were crossed in love or something,
but I'm a respectable girl and I don't have to stand
here and listen to your insults.'

'Get out of my office and don't come knocking
on my door when you're desperate for employment,
because you're finished. Now clear off before I throw
you out.'

Chapter Four

Essie did not dare tell her father what had happened in the wharfinger's office, and she did not mention Diggory Tyce. Pa might have his faults, but he would be furious if he knew that she had been accosted in the street, and even in his weakened condition he might go roaring off, ready for a fight. There were some things that were better kept secret, and this was one of them.

She did not see Raven until next morning. He came downstairs looking tired but purposeful. 'I'll leave by the back door,' he said firmly when she had given him Lady Alice's message. 'Give me a couple of minutes and then you go out as if you were going about your daily business. I'll have a cab waiting at the far end of Fore Street.'

'What are you two talking about?' Jacob limped

into the kitchen. 'What's going on between you?'

'Nothing, Pa,' Essie said hastily. 'Mr Raven has found me employment in a big house Up West. The money will keep us going until you're fit enough to return to work.'

Jacob glared at Raven, lowering his brow in a scowl. 'I won't have you taking advantage of my daughter, sir.'

'I promise you that there's nothing untoward in my dealings with Miss Chapman.' Raven dropped a leather pouch onto the kitchen table with a clink of coins. 'You'll be well recompensed, Chapman. I always pay my debts.'

Jacob snatched up the money before Essie had a chance to make a move. 'Pa, I'll need some of that,' she protested.

'You abandoned me in favour of your new friends. I can manage very well on my own.' Jacob tucked the pouch into his pocket and returned to the front parlour, slamming the door behind him.

Essie sighed. 'He'll spend all of it in the Grapes, treating his friends to rum punch.'

'You don't have to put up with a life like this,' Raven said earnestly. 'I'm sure my cousin would take you on permanently, should you wish to leave Limehouse.'

'This is my home. The river and the people round here are part of me and this is where I belong.'

'It's a shame to have such a limited outlook at your age. There's a whole world out there, if you chose to embrace it.'

Essie placed her teacup in the stone sink. 'Maybe I ought to commit a crime so that I get transported to Australia like you. Would that broaden my horizon, Mr Raven?'

'I wouldn't go so far as that,' he said, laughing. 'But you're a pretty young woman and you're bright. You deserve more than this.'

Essie had a sudden vision of herself married to Ben, living in rented rooms further down the street with a new baby arriving like clockwork every year. It was the fate of most women in Limehouse – either that or working until they dropped with exhaustion, starvation or succumbing to one of the many diseases that were rife amongst the poor.

'Isn't it time we were gone?' she said briskly. 'The sooner you get your affairs sorted out the sooner you can return to your goldmine and leave us all in peace.'

Essie sat in the clerk's office waiting for Raven to emerge. The clock on the wall opposite ticked noisily, accompanied by the scratching of the clerk's pen as he wrote laboriously, the tip of his tongue clamped between two rows of yellowed teeth. Essie shifted her position on the hard seat of the wooden chair, which was not designed for comfort. Every so often the clerk sniffed and gave her a sideways glance before returning to the ledger in front of him. The sound of a door opening and closing followed by footsteps made them both sit up.

Raven strode past Essie. 'Come along. It's time to go.'

She leaped to her feet and followed him out of the building into Lincoln's Inn. 'What happened?' she demanded. 'Where are we going now?'

He walked on until they were in the relative seclusion of the sunlit gardens, and he came to a halt. Taking a document from his inside pocket he placed it in her hand. 'Take this to Hill Street and give it to Lady Alice in person.'

Essie tucked it into her reticule. 'I will, of course, but can you tell me what this is all about?'

He shook his head. 'Remember that I'm an escaped convict and aiding me is a crime, so the less you know, the better, for your own sake.'

'But you were just standing up for your brother. You're the injured party because you took his punishment. I still don't understand why you did that.'

'If it were your brother, George, who had got himself in a fix, wouldn't you do your utmost to help him?'

'Yes, of course, but surely you've suffered enough?'

Raven smiled a charming, crooked smile that made him look infinitely more approachable and gave him an almost boyish appearance. 'I'm tough – I can take hardship and come out on top. I've made a fortune in Australia and I intend to share it with those nearest and dearest to me. By investing wisely I'll have something to come home to when I'm a free man, but what I really want is to appeal against the sentence in the hope of acquittal.'

'You're taking a terrible risk.'

'The ship that brought me here is due to sail tomorrow and I'll be leaving then. My mission is accomplished, almost.'

'Almost?'

He held up his hand to hail a passing cab. 'You ask too many questions. Take this to Alice and soon you'll be rid of me.' He bundled her into the cab, barely waiting for it to stop. 'Hill Street, cabby.'

Lady Alice took the sealed document from Essie. 'You've done well, thank you.'

'Am I finished here now, my lady?'

'I think we'd best wait until my cousin is safely on board ship and on his way back to Australia before we make any rash decisions. The sooner he leaves the better for all of us.'

Essie hesitated, waiting for further instructions. 'Shall I continue to work in the sewing room, my lady?'

Lady Alice broke the seal and studied the contents, frowning. 'Yes, continue as you did yesterday. I don't want the servants to suspect anything. You'd best keep to your room and I'll have Dixon bring your meals to you. I don't want a whispering game to start in the servants' hall.'

'Yes, my lady.' Realising that she had been dismissed, Essie left Lady Alice poring over the document. She closed the door and was making for the back stairs when she bumped into Sadie.

'Oh, you've come back,' Sadie cried joyfully. 'They was laying bets below stairs that you wouldn't last another day.'

'I don't know why,' Essie said warily. 'It's quite an easy, pleasant sort of job.'

'Mrs Dent told Cook that she didn't think you was the sort who would settle down to such mundane tasks. She said you was probably flighty and good-looking girls was always trouble.'

'I don't know whether to be annoyed or flattered,' Essie laughed, but the memory of Diggory Tyce's attempt to kiss her had haunted her dreams and she had awakened that morning feeling sick and angry.

'You won't say nothing, will you?' Sadie asked anxiously. 'I'll get me ears boxed for certain if you tell on me.'

'Don't worry, I won't say a word. Anyway, Lady Alice said you were to bring me my meals so I won't be mixing with the servants below stairs.'

Sadie's eyes rounded in surprise and her mouth dropped open. 'Lawks, who would have thought it? She don't normally interfere with the running of things – Mrs Dent does that. Her majesty below stairs won't be best pleased.'

Essie left Sadie standing at the foot of the narrow

staircase, muttering to herself. There was enough intrigue going on without involving the servants in Hill Street, and she doubted if Sadie could resist the temptation to pass on a juicy piece of gossip sparked off by a careless word.

There was a fresh pile of mending in the sewing room and Essie set to work with a will. At least she could enjoy the peace and quiet up here above the trees tops, although she had a feeling that a storm was brewing. There was no particular reason for alarm but Essie had seen the expression of Lady Alice's face when she read the document, and it was one of puzzlement followed by a tightening of the lips and a furrowed brow.

When the sun was high in the sky at midday Sadie arrived with a bowl of soup and a chunk of bread. After a brief greeting she disappeared again, returning minutes later with a tea tray. 'Her ladyship said you was to be treated well.' She dumped the tray on the table with an expressive sigh. 'You ought to be a fly on the wall in the kitchen, miss. They don't know who you are or where you came from, and it's driving them all mad. Mr Fielding is the worst. He says you're up to no good and her ladyship should be warned, and then Mrs Dent told him to hold his tongue and he didn't like that one bit. Then Cook stood up for him and she got a mouthful from Mrs Dent, because she won't take cheek from no one. It's better than a trip to the circus down there.'

Essie tasted the soup. 'Tell Cook the soup is delicious, but don't say anything else, Sadie. I'll get on with my work and you must try to keep out of trouble.'

Sadie tapped the side of her nose, winking and grinning. 'I ain't enjoyed meself so much since the matron at the Foundling Hospital got bit on the bum by her pet dog. It clung on for dear life, and it served her right for beating it with a cane just the same as she whacked us nippers whenever she felt like it. You only had to look at her the wrong way and she'd get that stinger off the wall and come at you with her face all screwed up with rage, and the tips of her ears flaming red.' Sadie left the room and Essie could hear her giggling all the way to the stairs.

The rest of the day passed uneventfully, but Essie was restless and the afternoon dragged. Curiosity as to the information she had passed on to Lady Alice was nagging at her like a sore tooth, but she knew she would have to wait until she had a chance to speak to Raven, although there was no guarantee that he would tell her anything. She longed to know more about Freddie and his exile in Italy, and Raven himself was a mystery that she found both intriguing and exasperating.

Sadie brought her a cup of tea late in the afternoon. She was more subdued this time, having been in trouble with Cook for breaking a plate, the cost of which would be deducted from her wages that quarter, which meant that she had worked for almost nothing. 'I'd rather have a beating.' Sadie's bottom lip quivered and her eyes filled with tears. 'I was going to buy meself a pair of boots with me wages. I saw a pair in the popshop in Shepherd Market. They was red leather with little heels what would have made me look taller, and that would make me look more grown up. If people thought I was older they'd treat me better.'

'Red leather,' Essie said thoughtfully. 'Not very practical for work, Sadie. I doubt if Mrs Dent would approve.'

'But I would look like a princess. I'd only wear them for best, and I'd keep them in a box under me bed so that I could take them out at night and put them on. I bet I could move light as a fairy in them boots, and no one would laugh at me.'

'I don't doubt it,' Essie said, smiling. 'I'm sure you'll get your red boots once day.' She drank the rapidly cooling tea and handed the cup to Sadie, who was gazing out of the window with a rapt expression on her small features as if she was in a delightful daydream. 'Ahem,' Essie cleared her throat in an attempt to bring Sadie back to the present. 'I need to speak to her ladyship before I go home. Do you know where I might find her?'

Sadie blinked and stared at her as if she had just awakened from a nap. 'I took a tray of tea to the drawing room before I come up here. But you can't go barging in on her – it ain't done. You have to go through Mrs Dent.'

Essie reached for her bonnet and shawl. 'Don't worry, I know what I'm doing.'

Essie knocked on the drawing-room door and waited impatiently. She had finished her work and was eager to get away from the stultifying atmosphere of the house in Hill Street, where the servants seemed to rule supreme, leaving Lady Alice vulnerable and alone. When there was no reply Essie opened the door and stepped inside, but the sight that met her eyes made her come to a halt. For a moment it was not clear if her ladyship was enjoying the advances of the man who held her in his arms, or if she was struggling to get free.

'Oh, excuse me. I'm sorry.' Essie was about to retreat, but a cry from Lady Alice made her stand her ground. 'Are you all right, my lady?'

'Give me that document, Henry.' Lady Alice held out her hand. 'Give it to me this instant. It has nothing to do with you.'

He tossed at her. 'Take it, Alice.' He turned to Essie. 'Who the devil are you?' The man, who was dressed like a gentleman even if he was not behaving like one, advanced on Essie with a grim look on his handsome features. 'How dare you burst into her ladyship's drawing room like this? Get out of here.'

'No, wait.' Lady Alice clutched the piece of parchment in her hands. 'Sir Henry was just leaving. I need to speak to you, Chapman.' Her pale cheeks flushed with colour as she fixed him with a steady look. 'You were mistaken in your assumption, Henry. I am not in the least bit interested in what you have to offer or your threat to expose my cousin.'

'We'll see about that, Alice.'

'You have my answer, and now I want you to leave.'

He bowed, but it was a mocking gesture. 'My lady.' He strode past Essie, giving her a thunderous look as he left the room, slamming the door behind him.

Essie rushed forward to support Lady Alice, who had paled suddenly and was swaying on her feet as if about to faint. 'Are you all right, my lady?'

'I just need a minute.' Alice sank down on the sofa, fanning herself with her hand. 'Sir Henry Bearwood is not the sort of man to cross.'

'Men are all the same, if you ask me,' Essie said boldly. 'Diggory Tyce is another one. They think they can take liberties and get away with it.'

'Quite so,' Lady Alice said vaguely. 'But this is quite different.' She raised her hand to her forehead and closed her eyes as if in pain.

Essie glanced around and spotted a table laden with decanters and crystal glasses. This seemed to be the right time for a tot of something stronger than tea, and she picked one at random, pulled out the stopper and sniffed. Pa only drank brandy on special occasions, but this was purely medicinal and she poured a small measure into a goblet and pressed it into Lady Alice's cold hand. 'Sip this, ma'am. It will make you feel better.'

'Thank you, Essie. I'll be fine in a moment. He caught me unawares, and unfortunately he saw the paper from the solicitor's office.' Lady Alice sipped the brandy and colour flooded her thin cheeks. 'I don't know how much he read, but it was enough to alert him to the fact that Raven is in the country. If only I'd had the sense to set light to it and turn it to ash.'

'He had no right to read your private correspondence, my lady. He's no gentleman.'

A faint smile curved Lady Alice's lips. 'Sir Henry is one of the richest men in England, so he behaves as he pleases and gets away with it, or at least that's what he thinks.'

'But you don't like him.'

'I used to find him amusing and he can be very charming, but I enjoy my life. I don't need a man to make it complete, but Henry isn't the sort of man to take no for an answer.'

'My pa has his faults, but he would kill any man who took advantage of me.'

'My father died several years ago, and my only male relatives are Raven and Freddie. I can take care of myself, or so I thought, but Henry Bearwood is another matter.'

'Do you want me to tell Raven, my lady? He'll come to your aid, I know he will.'

A smile flitted across Lady Alice's face and she

swallowed another mouthful of brandy. 'I can normally handle Sir Henry, but this is a different matter altogether. You must go now and warn Raven to be extra careful. You mustn't come here again unless it's absolutely vital. I don't think Henry would stoop so low as to have my movements watched, but he's a very determined man.'

'He must love you very much,' Essie said thoughtfully.

'He loves my pedigree more than he loves me. His family fortune was made in the sugar trade and that means it was founded on the misery of others. I abhor slavery, as any sane person must.'

'Surely he doesn't have slaves now.'

'Of course not, but Henry has a reputation with women, and I don't intend to be one of his conquests. The fact is that he's reached the age of thirty-five, he's decided to settle down and he wants a son and heir to carry on the family name. That is where I come in, or at least that's what he wants.'

'But you don't?'

Lady Alice shook her head, holding out her empty glass. 'I do not. Anyway, I shouldn't be telling you all this. Pour me another drink and go home. Warn Raven that Sir Henry knows that he plans to appeal, although I doubt if Henry will do anything about it. Tell Raven I said *bon voyage*. I won't see him again until he returns a free man, and I hope still to be a free woman.'

Essie added another small measure of brandy to the glass and placed it on a table by the sofa. 'Will you be all right?'

'Of course. I'm used to looking after myself, Essie. Get along home and thank you for everything you've done.'

Essie arrived home to find Raven and her father seated in the front parlour sharing a jug of ale. Raven looked up and smiled. 'How did my cousin take the news?'

Baffled, Essie stared at him. 'What news?'

'I don't suppose she would have shared it with you, come to that. Did she give you a message for me?'

'She said to say *bon voyage,* whatever that means. She won't be coming here and I'm not to return to Hill Street.'

'Such goings-on,' Jacob said crossly. 'You should know your place, Esther. It's here in White's Rents with the rest of us. I need you to help me on the river, so don't get ideas above your station.'

'Hold on a minute, Jacob.' Raven fixed Essie with a penetrating look. 'Why the sudden change, Essie? Not that I think there will be any need for you to continue to work for Alice, but I can see you're disturbed. What is it?'

'Nonsense!' Jacob reached for the jug and refilled his glass. 'Girls like to make a fuss about things.

That's what they do, leaving it to us men to sort out the mess they make.'

'I'm going to put the kettle on.' Essie curbed her tongue with difficulty. Sometimes Pa was impossible to deal with, and this was one of them. She went into the kitchen and slipped off her shawl, placing it on the back of a chair before taking off her bonnet. She was hot and thirsty after walking the length of Fore Street and Lady Alice's predicament was still fresh in her mind. She picked up a bucket and opened the back door, intent on visiting the communal pump, when Raven emerged from the parlour. He took in the situation with a single glance.

'Give that to me and I'll fetch the water for you.'

'No, certainly not. You mustn't be seen outside. You know that.'

He pulled up a chair and sat down at the table. 'All right. Now tell me what's happened to upset you? Have the servants been difficult? I can't imagine that Alice would have said anything untoward.'

Essie was silent for a moment, wondering how much to tell him. 'Do you know Sir Henry Bearwood?'

'He's not the sort of man I'd associate with normally, but how do you know him?'

'I don't. It's just that he was trying to take advantage of Lady Alice and she was having none of it.'

'The devil he was! But on the other hand I'd like to meet the man who could get the better of my cousin.' Raven's smile faded. 'What are you trying to tell me?'

'I'm not supposed to say anything,' Essie said slowly.

'But you're dying to tell me, so out with it.'

'Lady Alice wants you to leave the country as soon as possible and you're not to try to see her.'

'That wasn't what you were going to say. You're hiding something. What is it?'

Essie noted his set expression and the hard lines of his jaw and she knew that he was not about to give up until he knew the truth. 'Sir Henry was making a nuisance of himself, if you know what I mean. He wants to marry Lady Alice and she isn't interested, but he saw the document you sent her.'

Raven stood up abruptly, pushing back the chair so that it almost toppled over. 'I'll soon sort him out.'

'No, you mustn't,' Essie cried anxiously. 'I shouldn't have told you about him. Lady Alice will be furious with me, and you'll only get yourself into trouble. She doesn't think he'll let on that you're here.' She clutched Raven's arm and she could feel his muscles tensed beneath the sleeve of his well-cut jacket. 'Please sit down. I'll go and fetch some water and make a pot of tea.'

His grim laughter echoed round the small kitchen. 'Tea – the panacea for all ills.'

'I think Lady Alice can take care of herself,' Essie

said firmly. 'She was clear about one thing, and that was for you to keep away from Hill Street. You've only got another day and then you'll be on your way back to Australia.'

'I came home to make things better for my family and I don't intend to leave Alice in a fix. She's risked a lot helping me and I'm going to sort out Bearwood for once and all.' He stood up and made for the back door, pushing past Essie as he stepped outside into the back yard.

Essie hurried after him. 'Please stop. You'll only make more trouble this way.'

He shook off her restraining hand. 'Don't interfere, Essie. You've done your bit, now go indoors and look after your father.'

Essie knew that nothing she could say or do would prevent him from seeking out Sir Henry Bearwood, and she wished with all her heart that she had said nothing. Lady Alice must have known that this was how Raven would react, and now Raven was heading for trouble. Essie clenched her hands at her sides, inwardly fuming at her own stupidity. Nothing good could come of this. She toyed with the idea of rushing over to Hill Street to warn Lady Alice, but that was not the answer. She bent down to pick up the bucket and headed out of the yard to the pump. A cup of tea would not solve her problems, but making it would give her something to do.

Time seemed to have stood still as Essie waited

for Raven to return. She occupied herself as best she could with household chores. She made her father a simple supper of bread and cheese, but the ale he had drunk combined with a dose of laudanum sent him to sleep soon afterwards and Essie was left to wait and worry on her own. Outside the business of the street went on as usual with the constant sound of raised voices, hurried footsteps and the ever-present background noise of the river traffic. Hoots, sirens, bells and the grinding of cranes still at work unloading vessels moored alongside the wharfs went on all day and for most of the night.

The light faded and Essie paced the floor, accompanied by the rhythmic snores emanating from her father's slack lips. He had drunk a copious amount of ale and had taken a hefty dose of laudanum before falling into a stupor. She lit a candle and placed it in the window, but still there was no word from Raven. In an attempt to calm her nerves she opened the front door and stood on the step, but retreated quickly. Late at night it was not a good idea to loiter in the street and she went to sit in the kitchen and wait.

The candle had burned down and Essie was about to go to her room when she heard a scrabbling sound on the front door. 'Who's there?' she demanded nervously.

Chapter Five

Essie wrenched the door open and stepped aside as Raven practically fell into the room supported on either side by Lady Alice and Sadie.

'What happened?' Essie demanded, closing the door and bolting it. There did not seem to be anyone following them, but she was taking no chances. 'What happened?' She picked up the candlestick and in its flickering light she saw a dark stain that look suspiciously like blood on Raven's jacket. 'Take him through to the kitchen,' she said, glancing anxiously at her father, who had slept through everything so far; disturbing him was the last thing she wanted.

'I'm all right,' Raven whispered. 'I can make it on my own.'

'Stop talking and save your strength.' Lady Alice steered him towards the kitchen, but Sadie appeared to be flagging and Essie took her place. Together they managed to get him onto a chair at the table and, combining their efforts, they relieved him of his jacket.

'He's bleeding to death,' Sadie cried, collapsing onto another chair. 'I can't stand the sight of blood. I've come over faint.'

'Make yourself useful,' Essie said sharply. 'There's a bowl in the cupboard – fill it with water from the kettle and pass me that towel.'

Sadie jumped to her feet, seemingly forgetting that she was about to faint and obeyed Essie's instructions without another word.

'It's just a scratch. Stop fussing.' Raven tried to get up but sank back on the chair, his face pale beneath his tan.

'Stop talking,' Lady Alice said firmly. 'I'm going to ease your shirt off, Raven. I need to take a look at that wound.'

'So you're a nurse now, are you?' Raven's lips curved in a wry smile, but he winced as she peeled the blood-soaked cotton away from the gaping hole in his left shoulder.

Essie could see by Lady's Alice's expression that she was revolted by the sight of blood, and she stepped forward. 'I've dealt with a good number of injuries. Maybe I can help.' Essie held the candle closer so that she could examine the wound. 'He was shot?' She turned to Lady Alice, eyebrows raised.

'It's all right, Essie. I'll deal with this. It wouldn't

have happened if Raven hadn't come barging into my house,' Lady Alice said bitterly. 'I was dealing with Henry. He'd been drinking and was getting amorous, but Raven had to act like a hero.'

'He was drunk,' Raven murmured.

'I had taken Papa's duelling pistol from its case, although I had no intention of shooting Bearwood. I just wanted to show him that I meant what I said. Henry tried to take it from me and it went off. Papa always said it had a hair trigger and that proves it.' Lady Alice took the cloth and bathed the wound, ignoring Raven's protests. 'Bearwood was about to leave when you came bursting in like a knight of old, and you took the bullet, which otherwise would have merely made a hole in the door. It serves you right for interfering.' She frowned anxiously. 'It's bleeding faster. What should I do?'

Essie folded the towel and pressed it on the injured shoulder. 'We have to stop the blood flowing by pressing on the wound.'

'I am going to faint now,' Sadie said weakly and collapsed onto the floor.

'We should fetch a doctor.' Lady Alice stood back, clasping her blood-stained hands together. 'Is he going to die?'

'Not if I can help it.' Essie jerked her head in the direction of the cupboard. 'There's an old sheet that we can tear into strips. We need to bind the wound as tightly as we can.'

Lady Alice stepped over Sadie's prostrate figure and returned seconds later with the neatly folded sheet. 'Trust you to complicate things, Raven. Henry would have gone peacefully. Now he'll tell everyone that you're in London, if he hasn't done so already.'

'I have to get on board ship for all our sakes.' Raven's head lolled to one side and his eyes closed.

'He's passed out. That's good because we can bandage his shoulder without him struggling.' Essie took the strips of cloth from Lady Alice and proceeded to wind them round Raven's torso. 'I'm not very good at this, but it will have to do until we can get him to a doctor.'

'He has to be on the *Santa Gabriella* tonight.' Lady Alice sank down on the nearest chair. 'Sir Henry might notify the authorities and the police will be looking for Raven.'

Sadie scrambled to her feet. 'What happened?'

'You fainted,' Essie said tersely. 'Sit down and take deep breaths. You'll be fine and we need your help.'

'What do you propose?' Lady Alice demanded warily. 'We don't want to involve anyone else.'

'It'll be low tide. If we can get Raven down the steps to the foreshore I can row him out to the ship. I've done it before and it should be slack water now, so the current will take me downstream. We just have to get him to my boat.'

'How do we do that without being seen?' Lady Alice demanded.

'There are plenty of drunken men staggering around the streets of Limehouse every night,' Essie said drily. 'And we haven't much choice. Help me get his jacket on and we'd better set off as soon as he regains consciousness.'

Raven was weak from loss of blood but he was able to walk, albeit slowly, and Sadie danced on ahead clearing the way and poking fun at Raven, telling the other drunks that he was her dad who had been boozing in the pub all day, and they were taking him home. Essie had been wary about drawing attention to themselves, but oddly enough it seemed to work, and Sadie was in her element. Negotiating the steep, slippery steps proved to be more difficult and it was a considerable drop to the stony foreshore. As they hesitated on the wharf Essie was beginning to think that their efforts had been in vain when she spotted Ben walking towards them. At first she was inclined to hide behind Raven, but she could see the outline of the ship anchored in Limehouse Reach, and she knew it was only a matter of time before the vessel sailed. She left Lady Alice and Sadie supporting Raven, who was drifting in and out of consciousness, and she hurried to meet Ben.

'I'm glad it's you,' she said breathlessly. 'We're in desperate need of help.'

He took in the scene with a single glance. 'Who are these people?'

Essie could see that he was not going to be fobbed

off with fairy tales and she gave him a brief outline of
the events since she had brought Raven ashore.

'Well, I'll be damned. What have you got yourself
into, Essie? You could end up in jail for this.'

'I know that, Ben. I didn't choose to be involved
and I wouldn't have been if Pa hadn't had the accident. Anyway, it's too late now and I simply have
to get Raven on board the *Santa Gabriella*.'

'What about the woman and the kid? Are they
going, too?'

'No, but we must move quickly. Will you carry
him down the steps? It's our only chance.'

He hesitated, as if weighing up the consequences
of such an action, and then he nodded. 'All right. I'd
offer to row him out to the ship, but I'm working.'

'I just need to get him into my boat. I can manage
after that.'

'I'll have words with your pa, Essie. I saw him
walking to the Grapes earlier today and he wasn't
even limping. I reckon he's fit enough to return to
work, but it suits him to loaf around the house, drinking
ale.' He walked off and Essie hurried after him.

'I've got you, cully.' Ben hoisted Raven over his
shoulders like a sack of coal and descended the steep
steps, disappearing into the darkness.

'I'll see he gets safely on board,' Essie said hastily.
'You'd best go home.'

'I'm coming with you.' Lady Alice hitched up her
skirts and made her way down the steep stone stairs

until all that could be seen of her was the tip of the ostrich feathers waving from the crown of her bonnet. Essie followed with a reckless disregard for safety and Sadie was close behind. It was very dark on this unlit part of the foreshore and the river looked eerily calm and menacing. Ben helped Raven into the boat and steadied it as Lady Alice climbed in to sit beside him, followed less elegantly by Sadie, who landed in a heap.

'You ought to go home, my lady,' Essie said urgently. 'I'll make sure he reaches the ship safely.'

Lady Alice's face was a pale oval, her eyes dark shadows in the dim light. 'No, I won't rest until I know that he's being looked after properly. I want to see the captain and pay him well.'

'And I got to stick with her ladyship. I ain't staying here on me own and that's for certain,' Sadie added, although there was a tremor in her voice and she sounded close to tears.

'You'd best get going,' Ben said urgently. 'The tide is on the turn and if you delay the ship might sail without him.'

Essie reached up to kiss him on the cheek. 'Thank you, Ben. I'm very grateful.'

'I'll call round when I finish, just to make sure you're all right.'

'I will be. Don't worry about me.'

'Let's get this boat into the water.' Ben untied the painter and Essie helped him drag the boat to the water's edge. 'Get in and I'll give you a push.'

Essie bundled up her skirts and leaped on board, settling quickly and taking up the oars as she had done on countless occasions when she was with her father. She began to row, heading into Limehouse Reach and using every last ounce of strength in an attempt to reach the *Santa Gabriella*, but the small, overloaded craft was low in the water and the wake created by a passing paddle steamer spilled over the gunwales, leaving them ankle-deep and in imminent danger of sinking. Essie hailed the *Gabriella* and a rope ladder was flung over the side, but getting Raven on board was no mean feat. He managed to haul himself painfully step by step until willing hands reached out to drag him on board. Lady Alice followed but Sadie cowered in the rapidly sinking boat, refusing to move.

'I can't swim. I'll fall in and get drowned,' she moaned, covering her face with her hands.

'We'll both drown if we stay here,' Essie said urgently. 'I can't bail out fast enough so you'd better grab the ladder and jump for it.'

Sadie dropped her hands, gazing at Essie in horror. 'I can't.'

'Yes, you can, and if you don't go now it'll be too late.' Essie reached out to grasp the ladder. 'Hold on to me. We'll go together.'

Sadie clutched her round the waist and Essie took a deep breath. 'Now!' she cried, clinging onto the rope with both hands as the boat sank beneath them.

Shouts from above encouraged her to hold tight and they were hauled up the side of the ship, inch by inch until they were dragged over the side. Essie landed on the deck with Sadie falling on top of her.

'Pa will kill me,' Essie murmured.

When she opened her eyes she was lying on a narrow wooden bunk in a tiny cabin. A lantern hung from the ceiling and it swayed to and fro with the movement of the ship.

'Are you all right, miss?' Sadie jumped to her feet and leaned over Essie, peering into her face. 'You fainted dead away.'

Essie raised herself on her elbow. 'What's happening? Are they going to put us ashore?' She looked down at her bare arm and realised that beneath the coarse blanket she was stark naked. Sadie was wrapped in what looked like a sheet. 'Where are my clothes?'

Sadie sank back on the chair, which appeared to be the only other item of furniture in the cabin. 'I undressed you, miss. Our duds were soaked and they've taken them away to dry.'

'But we must get off this vessel at the first opportunity,' Essie said urgently. She sat up, wrapping the coarse blanket around her. 'I have to go home and look after Pa. Where is Lady Alice? What does she say to all this?'

Sadie shook her head. 'I dunno, miss. I was put

in here with you and I've been sitting here for ages, waiting for you to wake up, and I'm frozen.'

'Give me your sheet.' Essie swung her legs over the side of the bunk. 'You can have the blanket.'

Reluctantly, Sadie unwrapped the cotton sheet and handed it to Essie, snatching the blanket to cover her bare flesh. 'What are you going to do?'

'I'm going to find someone who can give me some answers. You'd better wait here.' Essie opened the door and stepped outside into a narrow passage. She could feel the engine pulsating beneath the deck as her bare feet padded along the corridor to the next cabin. She knocked on the door.

'Who's there?'

Essie breathed a sigh of relief as she recognised Lady Alice's cultured tones. 'It's me, my lady. Essie Chapman.'

The door opened and Lady Alice stood aside to let her in. She was wearing a man's velvet dressing robe and her long blonde hair hung loosely about her shoulders. 'Are you all right, Essie? I was afraid you had injured yourself.'

'I've got a sore head, but that's all. I want my clothes and I must get home before Pa wakes up.'

'I'm going to find the captain and order him to put us ashore, but first I need to make certain that Raven is being cared for. You can come with me because I don't want to wander round this ship on my own and in a state of undress. It's highly improper.'

The sudden desire to laugh took Essie by surprise. They were in a dire situation, having aided a felon to escape the law, very nearly drowning in the attempt, and now they were on a ship, bound for heaven knows where. It was utterly ridiculous, but she could see the funny side even if they were in serious trouble. 'I'm sorry, my lady. I know I shouldn't find it amusing.'

Lady Alice stared at her, frowning. 'No, it most certainly isn't the least bit comical. Raven might die from blood loss, and I've put myself beyond the law by helping him to escape. I don't know what I was thinking.'

'You said you wanted to pay the captain to look after him, my lady. Did you lose the money when my boat sank?'

A slow smile curved Lady Alice's lips. 'I had it concealed around my waist.' She moved to the bunk and drew back the coverlet to reveal two large leather pouches. 'These are filled with gold. If I'd gone overboard I would have sunk to the bottom of the river.'

'Were you going to give it all to the captain?'

'Don't be so naïve, Esther. Of course not – I'll treat him generously, but this is for Freddie. He sent word some time ago that he's ill and in desperate need, and this will help him in more ways than one. He'll be able to hire a good lawyer to plead his case and he'll be able to live well until he's free to return home.'

'But it's Raven's money, isn't it?'

'Yes, it's a small part of his fortune. His solicitor,

Watkin Gilfoyle, has invested the rest and no doubt taken a large fee for representing Raven and Freddie, but then he's the best solicitor in London.'

'And will he continue to plead their case, even though they're absent?'

'Of course he will. That's what he's paid for. Anyway, I'm going to find the captain. I want a word with that gentleman.' Lady Alice opened the door and, wrapping the robe more tightly around her slender figure, she marched along the passage, knocked and entered a cabin at the far end without waiting for a response.

Essie hurried after her. Wearing nothing but a thin sheet made her feel vulnerable and extremely uncomfortable, but she forgot her own problems when she saw Raven prostrate on a bunk with a strange man standing over him.

'How is he, Capitano Falco?' Lady Alice asked anxiously.

'I am not a doctor, my lady. All I can say is that he is a strong man, and I have seen worse injuries. By the time we reach Brindisi he should be able to leave the ship.' He spoke perfect English, with a strong accent that Essie found very attractive, and with his dark good looks he had the romantic appeal of a corsair.

'But you will put us ashore as soon as possible, Capitano.' Lady Alice gave him a direct look. 'And we need our clothes, whether or not they are dry.'

'Alas, I cannot put into port along the river, my

lady. If what you said is true, the authorities will have been alerted and the police will be looking for him. We make our way full speed to the Channel where we will be safe.'

'But you must allow me to go ashore,' Lady Alice protested. 'I will be missed and you will be accused of kidnapping me and my maid, not to mention this poor girl.' She waved her hand in Essie's direction. 'Her father will be distraught.'

Falco shrugged his shoulders. 'Perhaps you should have thought of that before you boarded my ship, my lady. I am not responsible for you or your companions. Now, please go back to your cabin. Your clothes will be returned to you when they are dry.'

For a moment Essie thought that Lady Alice was going to argue, but she merely nodded and walked out of the cabin with her head held high. 'Come with me, Esther. I know where I'm not wanted.' She marched out and headed for her own cabin, swaying with the movement of the ship as it met the opposition of the incoming tide.

'What are we to do?' Essie asked anxiously.

'Come inside and close the door.' Lady Alice slumped down on the bunk. 'There must be a place where Capitano Falco could put us ashore. I refuse to accept his decision, but perhaps a little tact and a few charming smiles might do the trick.'

'Pa won't notice I'm missing until morning, but I'm afraid he will call a constable and report me as lost, stolen or strayed – like a pet dog.' An irrepressible giggle bubbled to the surface and Essie covered her mouth with her hand. 'I'm sorry – I know it isn't funny, but our predicament is so unbelievable that any minute I think I might wake up and find it was all a dream.'

'A nightmare, more like.' Lady Alice ran her hand through her hair. 'I really don't understand you, Esther. This isn't at all funny – I haven't got a hairbrush or a mirror, let alone a change of clothes. When I'm dressed I'll speak to the captain again, and this time I'll back my demands with money. It never fails to work; everyone has a price.'

Next morning, seated in the small saloon where the captain and officers ate and took their brief moments of leisure, Lady Alice was even more downcast. Sadie seemed to be the only one of them who was enjoying the experience, and she chattered endlessly until Lady Alice silenced her with a searing glance. Sadie subsided, eyeing her mistress nervously, and Essie felt sorry for her. None of them had had a good night's sleep, and, as there was not a spare cabin for Sadie, she had slept on the floor in Essie's cabin. Her groans and the sound of thuds as she turned over and bumped herself on the bulkhead had kept Essie awake until the small hours, and even then she had slept fitfully. The movement of the vessel and the rhythmic throbbing of the engine created an alien environment, and she could not help worrying about Raven, whose life might hang in the balance. Captain Falco had insisted that he would be cared for by the first mate, who had a smattering of medical knowledge, but Essie had met the man at supper and she was not impressed. She had come across many seafarers during her days on the river, and the officers and crew of the *Santa Gabriella* were more like her idea of Barbary pirates than a disciplined bunch of professional mariners.

Lady Alice toyed with a slice of stale bread and rancid butter. 'If this is their daily fare no wonder the crew look like rabid dogs. What possessed Raven to hire the captain's services is beyond me.' She pushed her plate away and sipped her coffee, pulling a face. 'This is so strong it tastes like tar. Maybe it's what they use to caulk the ship, but it's filthy stuff. Just wait until I get a chance to speak to Falco. I'll tell him what I think of him and his vessel.'

'And what is that, my lady?' Captain Falco strolled into the saloon and pulled up a chair. 'You wish to speak to me?'

Essie shifted uncomfortably in her seat, wondering exactly how much he had heard of Lady Alice's candid opinion, and Sadie shrank into a corner, eyeing the master of the ship as if she expected him to rant and rave, even though he appeared to be mildly amused. Lady Alice's cheeks flushed rosily but she met his quizzical look with a defiant stare.

'Yes, Capitano. I could complain about the food and this disgusting brew you call coffee, but as we will only be on board for a short while, I will refrain from doing so. However, I demand to be put ashore at the first possible opportunity. Keeping us here amounts to kidnapping and that is against the law here, as I am certain it must be in Italy.'

'You boarded my vessel of your own free will, my lady,' Captain Falco said smoothly. 'As to the food, I can only say that the crew have never complained.'

'They wouldn't dare,' Lady Alice countered. 'And as to the accommodation, I am speechless.'

Captain Falco rose to his feet. 'Then that is the end of our conversation. Now if you will excuse me I have work to do.'

'Just a moment,' Essie said boldly. 'You've ignored my lady's request, which is perfectly reasonable. Circumstances forced us to come on board, and the least you could do is to set us back on dry land as soon as possible.'

His wolfish smile revealed canine teeth that looked suspiciously like fangs. 'And your wish will be granted – in a week or so, when we reach Brindisi.'

'But that's ridiculous,' Lady Alice protested. 'I don't want to go to Italy. For one thing, I haven't any clothes to wear, and for another, I will be missed. The police will already be looking for me.'

'They won't find you unless they hire a faster ship than the *Santa Gabriella*.' Falco bowed and backed out of the small saloon, still smiling.

'He thinks this is a joke,' Lady Alice said angrily.

'Maybe Raven can help,' Essie suggested. 'Surely getting him better is the most important thing to do now. I've never sailed as far as the estuary, but I know it's a long way off.'

'You're right.' Lady Alice rose to her feet. 'Come with me, Esther. I might need your help.'

'What about me?' Sadie asked anxiously.

'You could give our cabin a clean.' Essie stood up, swaying with the movement of the ship as she gained her balance. 'It looks as if we might be on board for some time yet.'

'Not if I can help it.' Lady Alice steadied herself by grasping the door handle. 'Come along, Esther. Don't dawdle.'

Raven was propped up on grubby pillows and fully conscious. He looked pale, and dark circles underlined his eyes, but he was awake and alert. There was no sign of the man who had been assigned to tend to his needs and last night's bloodied dressings had been left to congeal in an enamel bowl.

'How are you feeling?' Lady Alice glanced round the cabin, wrinkling her small nose. 'It smells foul in here.'

'I'm all right, Alice. You needn't worry about me. I'd get up, but I'm not dressed.'

She laid her hand on his forehead. 'You feel cool enough. Thank heavens for that, at least.'

'I'm sore but I don't seem to have a fever. I'll rise as soon as Hooper returns my clothes.'

'Esther, I want you to examine the wound,' Lady Alice said imperiously. 'You'll have to do the necessary. I'm sure you're a born nurse, whereas I am not.'

Essie edged past her, but she hesitated, eyeing Raven warily. 'Do you mind?'

'No, go ahead,' he said, closing his eyes. 'I suppose you'll do as you wish, whatever I say.'

His grudging attitude was uncalled for and unfair. Essie folded her arms, glaring at him. 'You are a very ungrateful man. If it weren't for me you might be in prison at this moment instead of lying there like a lord, while the rest of us are virtual prisoners on this rusty old bucket of a ship.'

His eyes opened and he stared at her in surprise. 'Well now, so you can stand up for yourself, Essie Chapman. I was beginning to think that your father had bullied the spirit out of you.'

'Stop fidgeting or this might hurt.' Essie unwound the bandage and eased off the blood-soaked pad.

'I'm going to my cabin,' Lady Alice said, backing out of the door. 'Call the girl in if you need assistance, Esther.'

'Alice never could stand the sight of blood,' Raven said with a wry smile. 'Do your worst, Essie. I can take it.'

Hooper, the first mate, had left a pile of torn cotton sheeting, presumably intending to change the dressing at some point. Essie did not think the material looked too clean, but there was no alternative. She worked quickly and was relieved to find that the bleeding had stopped and there was, as yet, no sign of putrefaction.

'It looks as if you've been lucky,' she said as she secured the bandage in position. 'But you must rest or you might start bleeding again.'

'I need to see Falco. I want you and my cousin put ashore as soon as possible.'

Essie met his gaze with a steady look. 'He says he won't put into port until we reach Brindisi. Was that your plan?'

'For myself, yes, but I didn't know that Alice and her maid would be on board, let alone you, Essie. You helped me, and for that I'm grateful, but I didn't intend for you to become so involved. This is my business.'

She piled the soiled dressings into the bowl. 'It's become mine as well, and short of jumping overboard I don't see how we're going to get ashore.'

His eyes lit with a smile. 'Don't do that, you might drown and then I'd feel really guilty.'

'I'm serious, Raven.' Until this moment Essie had never called him by name, but the time for observing the rules of etiquette was past, and she faced him angrily. 'You seem to think this is a joke, and I can see the funny side of most things, but this has gone too far. You must make the captain put into port before we leave England.'

His smile faded. 'You're right. Send Falco to me. I'll put an end to this charade.'

Chapter Six

They disembarked in Brindisi after what seemed like a lifetime on board the *Santa Gabriella*. Despite Raven's alternate pleas and attempts at bribery, Captain Falco had refused to put ashore in England. Lady Alice had tried everything from tears and tantrums to mild seduction, all of which were ignored, leaving them no alternative but to accept their fate.

If she were to be truthful, Essie had enjoyed some aspects of life at sea. The sunrises and sunsets over the water had been magical and she had seen dolphins playing in the bow waves, a sight that filled her with joy despite the dire conditions on board. The sanitary arrangements left everything to be desired and the food was awful, but, for the most part, the crew were friendly and cheerful, and

Captain Falco was not only an entertaining host but was also a talented singer with a beautiful tenor voice that could move Essie to tears. Lady Alice was frequently at loggerheads with him, but even she had to resort to her crumpled handkerchief when the captain came to the end of a particularly passionate rendition of a love song.

The voyage had ended now and it was good to step onto dry land at last. Essie breathed in the scents of Italy. The tantalising aroma of cooking floated on the gentle breeze, mingling with the scent of wild thyme and marjoram from the surrounding countryside, and Essie's mouth watered at the thought of good food. The air was surprisingly sweet and clean, even allowing for the fact that they were still in the docks and vast catches of fish were being landed nearby, but the heat was stifling, and Essie was in desperate need of a change of clothes. Lady Alice looked pale and tired, probably due to the fact that she had never stopped moaning about her lack of wardrobe and the insanitary conditions on board ship, where fresh water was too precious a commodity to waste on laundering clothes.

'Find us a hotel, Raven.' Lady Alice stood on the quay wall, refusing to move. She glanced round, shaking her head. 'I doubt if they have any decent shops in a place like this, but I must have new garments. We're all in desperate need of a bath, including you.'

'I look a hundred times worse than any of you ladies,' Raven said gallantly. 'Hooper tried to get the blood out of my jacket, but nothing can disguise the damage.'

'Yes, you look quite disreputable, so please go and find somewhere for us to stay.'

'But we are supposed to be looking for the monastery, Alice. The sooner we find Freddie, the better.'

Essie laid her hand on Raven's sleeve. 'Another day or two isn't going to make any difference, and we do look like a band of didicoys.'

A reluctant smile curved his lips. 'You're right, of course. I'll make enquiries in the dock office. They're bound to know everything. Wait here and I'll be as quick as I can.'

'I'm hungry.' Sadie clutched her belly, which was rumbling loud enough for all to hear.

'I'm sure we'll eat soon,' Essie said vaguely as she watched Raven stride off with a feeling of relief. Her most pressing need was to have food that wasn't boiled to a pulp or mouldy, and then the luxury of a tin tub filled with warm water and a bar of soap seemed like heaven on earth. Worries about her father and what was happening at home had long since taken second place to the act of survival, but relief was within her grasp and she experienced a surge of optimism. How she was going to get home was another matter, and one that she pushed to the back of her mind. Damp, cloudy London seemed a million miles away from the brilliant sunlight and blue skies of Italy.

Minutes later Raven returned with news that he had found an inn that could cater for their immediate needs and it was only a short walk from the harbour. Lady Alice fanned herself with her hand. 'Aren't there any cabs in this place? It's far too hot to walk any distance.'

'It's half a mile at most, Alice. Surely you can manage that?'

'Just think how nice it will be when we get there,' Essie said with an encouraging smile. 'Maybe we could find someone to wash our clothes. They'll dry quickly in this heat.'

Lady Alice seemed about to argue when Captain Falco joined them. 'How may I help you, my lady? You look a little perplexed.'

'My cousin wants me to walk to the inn.'

Captain Falco's dark eyes gleamed with amusement, but he put his head on one side, giving her a sympathetic smile. 'Perhaps it would help if you took my arm, my lady. I have business with the landlord. I will make sure that you are given the respect due to an English lady.'

Essie held her breath, half expecting Lady Alice to brush his offer aside, but she seemed to revive a little and she laid her hand on his arm.

'Thank you, Captain. You are a gentleman.' Lady Alice shot a resentful look at Raven. 'Captain Falco understands a lady's sensibilities.'

Raven shrugged and walked on. 'Come along, Essie. You too, Sadie. Or do I have to carry you both?'

Essie and Sadie fell into step behind him, leaving Captain Falco to assist Lady Alice.

The inn was a squat, square building, whitewashed and cool-looking beneath a terracotta-tiled roof. Hens pecked busily in the dust and goats roamed around freely, looking for anything remotely edible. The cockerel stalked about, fixing his beady eye on each of them in turn, and it seemed to Essie that he was eyeing the feathers on Lady Alice's bonnet with suspicion, perhaps seeing them as a possible rival. Lady Alice herself was visibly wilting in the unaccustomed heat, but Captain Falco was being very solicitous, and his undivided attention seemed to please her. They were met in the doorway by the landlord, who bowed and smiled, welcoming them with gestures as if he were performing in a pantomime. He then embraced Captain Falco, speaking to him in rapid Italian. Essie had picked up a few words from the crew, but not enough to understand what he was saying.

Captain Falco slapped their host on the back. 'Giacomo welcomes you all to his humble hostelry,' he said grandly. 'Unfortunately he does not speak English, but you will find him very accommodating.'

Lady Alice was suddenly all smiles. 'Thank you so much, Capitano. You've been very kind, but we must not detain you. I'm sure you have much more important things to do than looking after us.'

'There is nothing more important than taking care of a beautiful lady,' Captain Falco said, taking her hand and raising it to his lips. 'We will be in port for several days and I hope to see you again.'

Essie glanced at Sadie, who was watching open-mouthed. 'Perhaps we ought to see our rooms,' she suggested tentatively. Raven was looking bored and frankly sceptical and she was afraid he might say something to offend the captain, and then they would lose the help of the only person who spoke English fluently. She tapped Lady Alice on the shoulder. 'You should go inside, my lady. The sun will ruin your complexion.'

'Indeed it will.' Lady Alice clicked her fingers to attract the landlord's attention. 'I want a bath tub filled with hot water, my good man. And I need the services of a dressmaker who can work quickly.'

The landlord turned to the captain, shrugging and holding his hands palm upwards with a bemused look on his plump face. Captain Falco drew him aside and after a brief conversation the landlord went indoors shouting orders to his employees.

'Come along Alice,' Raven said impatiently.

'You've caused enough of a stir amongst these good people. Let's go inside and I'll order a meal.'

'Bath first, food later.' Lady Alice marched into the inn, her fatigue apparently forgotten, and Essie hurried after her with Sadie following close behind.

The interior was dark but surprisingly cool, and a flustered maid led them up a narrow wooden staircase to the first floor. The rooms were small, clean and sparsely furnished but after enduring the confines of a tiny cabin for over a week it seemed like heaven to Essie, even though she still had to share with Sadie. There were two beds, set against opposite walls with a chest of drawers beneath a window that overlooked the harbour. A rag rug was the only splash of colour in the room where everything was white, including the bedspreads.

'I wonder if Lady Alice has got her bath,' Sadie said, grinning. 'I hope she lets us use it because I know I smell something chronic.'

'Me, too.' Essie sat down on the bed and took off her boots, wriggling her toes. 'I think Lady Alice is used to getting her own way. She's probably got a dressmaker in her room as we speak, and I wouldn't be surprised if she had a new gown by this evening.'

'I feel like a ragbag.' Sadie glanced down at her grimy skirt with its frayed hem and a small tear where she had caught it on a nail. 'Mrs Dent wouldn't approve at all.'

'Stay here,' Essie said firmly. 'I'll go and speak to her ladyship. I know she said we could have new clothes, but I need to remind her.' Essie left the room and marched along the corridor to knock on Lady Alice's door.

'Enter.'

Essie opened the door and stepped into the room, which was larger than the one she shared with Sadie. It was furnished with a brass bedstead, covered with a multi-coloured patchwork quilt, a painted wooden washstand and a clothes press. A large window overlooked countryside and distant hills. A bathtub had been placed in the centre of the floor and it was already half full.

'Unbutton my gown, Essie. I can't reach.' Lady Alice stood stiffly to attention while Essie undid the tiny, fabric-covered fastenings. 'I believe I have a dressmaker coming shortly.' Lady Alice glanced over her shoulder. 'Maybe she can do something for you and the girl as well. I can't be seen with servants who look as though they've been dragged through a hedge backwards.'

'I'm not your servant, my lady.'

'You work for me, don't you?'

'That was different. I was helping you and Raven, and I became embroiled in your affairs, but it wasn't my choice to be here.'

'Nor mine, come to that.' Lady Alice stepped out of her gown. 'You can unlace me while you're here. What did you want, anyway?'

'It was to ask if we might have the bath water after you, and I was going to remind you that both Sadie and I are desperate for new clothes.'

Lady Alice turned to face her and her petulant expression melted into a charming smile. 'Of course you may have the bath after me, in fact I insist upon it. I just hope they have some decent soap because I have a sensitive skin. As to clothes, if this woman is any good with her needle we will all have new gowns, although Sadie's will be suitable for a child of her age, and mine will be grander than yours, which is only fitting.'

Essie threw back her head and laughed. 'You are priceless, my lady. Here we are, miles from home, on the run from the law, which makes us equals, but you still think you're better than us.'

Apparently unabashed, Lady Alice raised a delicate eyebrow. 'And I am, naturally. My late father was the Earl of Dawlish and we can trace our family tree back to William the Conqueror. Your papa is a boatman.'

'And you can't dress yourself without someone to help you. Maybe there's a lesson to be learned there somewhere.'

Lady Alice recoiled and for a brief moment her smile faded, then a gurgle of laughter escaped her lips. 'All right, Essie. Given our situation perhaps we are equals, but that will change when we get back to England.'

'When we return home we will probably be thrown into jail.'

'But I will have a better cell, and I can afford to hire a good lawyer.'

Essie was saved from replying by a knock on the door and she went to open it. A flustered maidservant stepped into the room carrying a ewer filled with steaming water, which she emptied into the tub. She bobbed a curtsey and hurried from the room.

'Enjoy your bath, my lady, and please don't allow the water to get cold.' Essie left the room, chuckling to herself. Title or no title, money or lack of it, they were sisters under the skin.

It was only later, when she was bathed and had washed the salt from her hair, that the reality of her situation came crashing in on Essie. She was alone in her room, sitting on the bed, wrapped in a skimpy towel, when she had a sudden vision of her father pacing the floor at home. He would be wondering what had happened to her, or more likely, he was in the bar at the Grapes, drowning his sorrows in rum punch. Then there was Ben. She could not begin to imagine what he must be thinking, but one thing was for certain, Ben would be distressed by her sudden disappearance. The boat had sunk, and Pa would be out of a job – but there was nothing she could do about it now. Her fate and Sadie's seemed to be inextricably tangled up with that of Raven and Lady Alice, and there was nothing to be done other than to see the adventure through to the bitter end. Essie combed her hair, staring out of the window at the sun-bleached scene. During the sea voyage Captain Falco had provided them with necessities from a seemingly limitless supply of combs, hairbrushes and hand mirrors, which led Essie to suspect that they were not the first female passengers he had entertained on the *Santa Gabriella*. If he had produced a gown or two it would not have come as a surprise.

Essie jumped at the sound of someone tapping on the door. 'Come in.'

The maid who had supplied the bath water entered the room, this time carrying a bundle of garments. She dropped them on Sadie's bed. '*Capitano Falco*.' She stood, arms akimbo, eyeing Essie curiously.

'*Capitano Falco?*' Essie repeated dazedly.

'*Sì, Capitano Falco*.' The maid nodded, pointing at the clothes and then at Essie.

'For me?' Essie studied the young woman's face, liking what she saw. Olive-skinned and dark-eyed with glossy black hair and plump cheeks, the maid was handsome rather than beautiful, and she was obviously curious. '*Grazie,*' Essie said, recalling the word from her attempts to converse with the crew of the *Santa Gabriella*.

A wide smile almost split the young woman's face in two. '*Prego*.'

Essie seized the opportunity to introduce herself.

'I am Essie,' she said, indicating herself with a hand gesture. 'Essie.'

'Filomena.'

Essie smiled and held out her hand. '*Buon giorno, Filomena.*'

'*Buon giorno, Essie.*'

They shook hands solemnly and then, as if by mutual consent, they broke down in giggles. Filomena was still laughing as she left the room, and Essie let the towel fall to the floor as she stood up to examine the clothes. No doubt the captain had conjured them up from somewhere; she had complete confidence in his ability to handle any situation, having seen him as master of the ship and its crew. But Captain Falco aside, the thought of wearing clean clothes was almost too much to bear without shouting for joy. There were two cotton print gowns, both well-worn and faded from many washes, but spotlessly clean. One was smaller and that would be suitable for Sadie, and the other, when slipped over Essie's head, was a near-perfect fit. Essie could not help wondering if Captain Falco had chosen the dresses himself and she felt the blood rush to her cheeks. It was one thing for a man to be gallant and charming as the captain was, when in a good mood, but quite another for a gentleman to gauge a woman's size by merely looking at her. However, the dress was cool and comfortable, and for that she could only be grateful. What it looked like was another matter, as there was no mirror in the room, but that was the least of her worries. What to do next was more important.

Essie had just tied the sash about her waist when Sadie burst into the room, pink-cheeked and smiling.

'Oh, my,' she said, coming to a sudden halt. 'You do look pretty, Essie. That dress really suits you.' Her eyes lit up as she spotted the garment left on her bed. 'And there's one for me, too. I ain't had a new frock since I started working in Hill Street.' She allowed the towel to drop to the floor, exposing her skinny body still dripping wetly after her bath, which Essie was certain must have been cold and scummy. Such details did not seem to bother Sadie and she slipped the simple shift over her head. 'Ain't this just the prettiest thing you ever did see?'

Essie nodded wordlessly. The summery garment suited Sadie's childish form, and with her damp golden hair curling wildly around her shoulders she looked like a water sprite who had risen from the deep to dance and twirl in the sunlight. For the first time Essie saw a hint of beauty yet to make its stamp on a young face and figure, and more importantly, Sadie was happy and excited. Essie gave her a hug. 'You look very nice.'

'I feel good,' Sadie said, beaming. 'I almost forgot – Lady Alice wants you.'

Essie left Sadie combing the tangles from her hair, and she went knock on Lady Alice's door, entering when she heard a muffled response. 'You wanted me, my lady?'

'Look at me. Who does he think I am?' Lady Alice stood stiffly to attention, holding her arms out like a scarecrow. 'This is the ugliest gown I have ever seen and the material is cheap. I wouldn't dress a servant in this.' She looked Essie up and down. 'Your gown isn't much better, but then you're a—' she broke off, blushing. 'I mean, you don't have a position to keep up.'

'It's all right,' Essie said, shrugging. 'You don't have to explain, but it's not too bad. At least it's clean and tidy.'

Lady Alice held out the skimpy skirt. 'It's a peasant's dress. I expect Captain Falco thinks it's funny – well, it isn't. I won't leave this room looking like a serving wench.'

'I dare say these garments were hard to come by.' Essie eyed Lady Alice critically. 'Our own clothes should be ready soon. They'll dry quickly in this heat and you've sent for a dressmaker, so it's just a matter of time and you'll feel like yourself again.'

'Stop being sensible, Esther.' Lady Alice threw up her hands. 'I can't face Falco looking like this, and I'm hungry. I need food, so you'll have to go downstairs and order something to be sent to my room. I intend to remain here until my clothes are dry.'

'Of course I'll do that, but first I need to know what is to become of me. I'm here by accident, as are you, I suppose. But I want to return to London. My pa will be frantic with worry.'

'Neither of us intended to travel to Italy, but now I'm here I want to make sure that Freddie is all right. At least I'll see that he gets the money that Raven intended him to have.'

'Where does that leave me, my lady? I haven't a penny to my name.'

Lady Alice sat down suddenly. She reached for her hairbrush and began using it with a faraway expression on her face. 'I should be in my home in Devonshire, walking my dogs on the cliff top and meeting up with old friends. Dinner parties, soirées, card games, dancing and listening to beautiful music with like-minded people. Instead of which I am here in a poky little room with a bath full of disgusting dirty water, and I'm wearing a gown that is unfit for the lowest menial in my employ.'

Essie's patience was stretched to its limit. 'Yes, my lady, but that doesn't answer my question. If you intend to remain in Italy will you pay my passage home, and Sadie's, too? Assuming that there is a ship in the harbour that might be sailing for England.'

'You can't abandon me,' Lady Alice protested. 'I cannot travel in the company of gentlemen without a female companion.'

'But Raven is your cousin. Isn't that respectable enough?'

'No, it is not. You must see this through with me,

and Sadie is my maid, so naturally she will remain with me.' Lady Alice narrowed her eyes, gazing speculatively at Essie. 'I will make it worth your while, but only if you promise not to leave me in the lurch.'

Essie thought quickly. She did not relish the thought of travelling home on her own, and it was not every day that a girl from Limehouse was given the opportunity to see a bit of the world. 'All right,' she said slowly. 'But I need to send a message to my father, letting him know that I am safe.'

'I'm sure Raven could organise that. Do I have your word that you won't abandon me?'

'I promise to stay with you until we return home.'

Lady Alice uttered a sigh of relief. 'Thank you. Now, please, do as I asked and fetch me something to eat or I might faint from lack of nourishment.'

Essie collected Sadie on her way downstairs and they found Raven and Falco seated at one of the large pine tables, which was spread with a selection of foreign-looking cheeses, sliced sausage, bowls of glistening black olives and crusty loaves. Green and black grapes spilled over the side of a terracotta platter, which was filled with oranges, lemons and purple figs.

'Come and join us,' Raven said, raising a glass of red wine to them. 'Where is my cousin?'

'Lady Alice would like to eat in her room,' Essie said tactfully. She turned to Captain Falco. 'Maybe you could ask the maid to take her something?'

'Why won't she leave her room? She was not so shy on board my ship.'

Essie could see that he already knew the answer and was enjoying Lady Alice's dilemma. Perhaps he had deliberately chosen the ugly gown, although Essie could not think why he would want to humiliate Lady Alice. 'I think you know why, Captain.'

He rose to his feet. 'We can't have the beautiful lady eating on her own. Leave it to me.'

'Can't you do something?' Essie demanded, glaring at Raven, who was refilling his glass from a carafe.

'Alice can look after herself. It's time she met someone who could get the better of her in an argument. Sit down, both of you, and eat. The food is very good indeed.'

Sadie had been eyeing the food hungrily and she threw herself down on the bench, making a grab for a chunk of sausage and a slice of bread. Essie hesitated, wondering if she ought to go to Lady Alice's aid, but she decided against it and took a seat beside Sadie.

Minutes later Falco reappeared, rubbing the side of his face. 'That lady is a wild cat.'

'I warned you,' Raven said smugly. 'You're lucky to have escaped with a slapped face. Alice has claws and she's not afraid to use them when she's really angry.'

Falco resumed his place at table. 'I've sent Filomena upstairs with a tray of food. Perhaps her ladyship will be in a better humour when she's had something to eat.'

Raven shook his head. 'You'll learn, my friend.'

'I am ready to take on the challenge. There isn't a woman alive who can resist Enrico Falco when he sets out to charm.'

Essie gave him a withering glance. 'You think a lot of yourself, Captain. Maybe you've met your match.'

He shrugged, smiled and raised his glass to her. 'We will find out on our way to the monastery. I am to be your guide.'

'We're going to a monastery?' Essie looked to Raven for confirmation.

'My purpose for coming here was to see Freddie. I want to make certain that he's being treated well and that he has everything he needs.' Raven downed the last of his drink and stood up. 'I'm going to have a word with Alice. We'll be leaving early in the morning, but she can remain here if she doesn't feel like travelling on.'

'What happens then?' Essie asked anxiously. 'Will we return to England?'

'That's a decision my cousin has to make.' Raven headed for the stairs, taking them two at a time.

Essie turned to Falco. 'What does he mean by that?'

'Don't ask me, I am merely the captain of the ship. Raven hired my vessel to take him to London and back to Australia, with a stop here in my native Puglia.'

Essie stared at him nonplussed. 'But Lady Alice lives in England. We have to return home.'

'That is for Lady Alice to decide.'

Essie leaned across the table. 'Are you telling me that we will be taken to Australia, whether we like it or not?'

Captain Falco shrugged, holding his hands palms facing upwards. 'Who knows?'

Chapter Seven

The journey along the coast to the monastery was undertaken on sure-footed donkeys with Falco at the head of the small procession, followed by Raven and Lady Alice, who was still in a sulk and refusing to speak to anyone. Her argument with Raven had resounded throughout the inn. Essie had been able to make out the odd word, but it was obvious that her ladyship was not happy.

'What's happening?' Sadie asked, drawing her donkey alongside Essie's as the path widened. 'Why is everyone so cross?'

'It's probably the heat,' Essie said vaguely.

'But the captain said he was taking us to Australia. It's on the other side of the world, where convicts go. That can't be right.'

'Yes, he did, but Lady Alice wants to return to

London, and I'm sure she'll make alternative arrangements for us as well as for herself.'

'I want to go home,' Sadie whispered. 'It's too hot here and I don't like the food. I miss London.'

'I suppose I do, too. Although it is beautiful here and the sea is such a wonderful colour, and the air is fresh and clean, but London is home.'

'Stop chatting and keep up, or you'll get left behind.' Raven turned in the saddle, beckoning to them. 'That goes for you, too, Alice. And you can take that look off your face. We're not school children now, and you can't expect to have everything your way.'

Lady Alice responded by urging her sturdy little animal to a trot so that she passed Raven and was second in line to Falco. She glanced over her shoulder. 'The same to you, Raven. If you think you can ride roughshod over me, you're very much mistaken.'

Essie and Sadie exchanged knowing looks and encouraged their donkeys to walk on a little faster.

It was midday and the sun blazed down from a clear sky that was so blue it hurt Essie's eyes to look into its azure depths. There was not a cloud in sight and silence was broken only by the sound of the donkeys' hoofs on the hard-baked ground, and the gentle swish of the waves on the shore. The tussocky grass was burned brown in places, but clumps of pink and white rockrose and blue bellflowers had managed to survive, adding welcome bursts of colour to the sun-bleached landscape. It was hard going on the rough terrain, even riding animals that were used to such conditions, but the sight of the monastery perched high on the cliff top, gleaming golden white in the sunshine, was more than welcome. The donkeys seemed to realise that rest and shade were near and they raised their heads and quickened their pace.

As they drew nearer Essie was confused to see that half the building appeared to have collapsed into the sea, but a plume of white smoke rose high into the sky, confirming that what remained of the monastery was inhabited. An olive grove straddled the hillside and trees studded with bright yellow lemons softened the harshness of the landscape. As they neared the high stone walls there were goats tethered by the roadside, munching on anything within their reach, and hens scratched in the reddish brown soil of the open courtyard.

Falco reached up to tug at a rope and the metallic peal of a large bell rang out as if announcing the angelus. A monk came towards them, walking at a leisurely pace, and exchanged words with Falco. He motioned them to follow him and they were ushered into the cool and echoing silence of a cloister, which surrounded a quadrangle spilling over with greenery. Grapevines clambered up the stonework and in the centre a large fig tree was laden with purple fruit, but even more surprising was the fact that one section of the cloister had been demolished, leaving the building open to the elements. Beyond its fractured walls Essie could see the cliff top and a wide expanse of the Adriatic Sea.

'Barbary pirates,' Falco said as if reading her thoughts. 'They raided and sacked all along the Mediterranean coast and beyond, capturing vast numbers of people and selling them as slaves. The monks resisted and the pirates subjected the monastery to an intense cannonade before they moved on to a more profitable area.'

Raven studied the ruins, shaking his head. 'They could have rebuilt, or at least made an attempt.'

'It's a poor order,' Falco said grimly. 'They live a simple life devoted to prayer.'

'You sound as if you envy them.' Lady Alice eyed him curiously. 'What a strange man you are, Captain.'

He bowed from the waist. 'I am not a barbarian, whatever you might think, Lady Alice.' He turned to the monk, speaking in rapid Italian. 'I've just asked Brother Ignacio if we might see Frederick, but apparently he is still unwell.'

'I want to see him right away,' Raven said impatiently. 'Maybe you ought to stay here, Alice.'

She gave him a withering look. 'If you think I've travelled all this way on a dirty little screw steamer without the benefit of a change of clothes, only to be told I cannot see Freddie, then you have another think coming, Lord Starcross.'

Essie stared at him open-mouthed. She had not given a thought as to whether Raven was his first or last name, but hearing him addressed in such a manner made him seem like a different person. He gave her a sideways glance and a wry smile curved his lips.

'Forget the title, Essie. It carries no weight in the Antipodes. Muscle and tenacity are all that is called for in the goldfields of Victoria.'

'Utter nonsense,' Lady Alice snapped. 'Don't believe anything my cousin says, Esther. He likes to hide the fact that he inherited an earldom and a large country estate.'

'Add convicted criminal to my names and there you have it,' Raven said sharply. 'Now stop all this, Alice. The reason we're here is to see Freddie. Lead on, Brother Ignacio.'

Brother Ignacio looked to Falco, who nodded, adding a few words in Italian, and the monk led them along the cloister to a doorway that opened onto a narrow spiral staircase. He said something to Falco as they came to a sudden halt.

'Brother Ignacio and I will remain here while you go and see your cousin. There is not much room for all of us, according to the holy man.'

The tower, complete with arrow slits, seemed to have been built many centuries earlier as a defence against marauders from the sea, and it had survived against the odds. It was dark and the stone stairs were worn by the passage of time and constant use.

Small white moths flitted about their heads and Sadie's cries of distress bounced back off the limestone walls in a wailing chorus. Eventually, just when she thought her knees were going to give way beneath her, Essie arrived at the top, finding herself in a circular room with tall, unglazed windows on all sides. It was bright and breezy with views of the surrounding countryside as well as an uninterrupted view of the coast and a vast expanse of sea.

Raven and Lady Alice went to the bed where a young man lay propped up on pillows. Essie stood back, holding Sadie's hand. She could feel her trembling and whether from fear or exhaustion it made little difference, and she gave her an encouraging smile.

'You see,' she whispered. 'That must be Raven's brother, Freddie. He looks a bit poorly.'

'How are you, old chap?' Raven went down on his knees at his brother's bedside. 'What's laid you so low?'

Lady Alice perched on the edge of the bed. 'How would he know?' she demanded angrily. 'Have you seen a physician, Freddie?'

'Still arguing? Now I know I'm on my way home.' Freddie smiled feebly.

'I'm afraid not,' Raven said softly. 'Not yet anyway, Freddie. I've got my solicitor working on the case. He's going to appeal against both our sentences, although I don't hold out much hope.'

Freddie turned his head away. 'Then why have you come here?'

'You sent word that you were ill and needed funds,' Alice said impatiently. 'Good heavens, Freddie. Have you any idea what you've put us all through? Raven risked his neck to return to London in an attempt to clear your name as well as his own. It wasn't my intention to come all this way, but I didn't have much choice in the matter.'

'I'm sorry.' Freddie's thin fingers plucked at the faded coverlet. 'I didn't mean to cause trouble. I've been sick with fever.'

Essie released Sadie's hand and moved closer to the bed. She had seen many cases of typhoid, dysentery and cholera in Limehouse and she had treated her father for countless attacks of the ague. 'You're obviously over the worst,' she said boldly.

He gave her a curious look. 'Who the devil are you? And who's the child standing by the door? She looks scared stiff.'

Essie kneeled down at his bedside. 'My name is Essie and my friend is called Sadie. We were in the boat with Lady Alice when it sank, and we had to climb on board Captain Falco's ship.'

'And we might all have drowned,' Sadie added. 'But we ended up here.'

Freddie's blue eyes, so like those of his brother, lit up with amusement. 'I'd like to hear the story.'

'And so you shall, but not at this moment.' Raven

patted his brother's hand. 'We've brought funds so the brothers will have plenty of money to buy food and anything you need.' He rose to his feet. 'We will stay here tonight. I've spoken to Brother Ignacio and arranged it, but we will have to leave tomorrow morning.'

'No, don't go so soon. You've only just come,' Freddie protested weakly. 'You can't abandon me again, Raven. I'll die if I have to stay here any longer.'

'Don't be silly, Freddie.' Lady Alice took his hand in hers and stroked it gently. 'You can't return to England unless you get a full pardon, and that's going to take time. I thought you were happy here. Surely there's everything you could possibly want. You're free to take your paints and go into the countryside, and live a quiet life away from temptation.'

'That's just it, Alice. I've been in Italy since I was twenty, and that's five long years ago. It was all right until I ran out of money, and that was why I came to the monastery. They took me in and let me stay here for next to nothing. I helped them till the land and I picked fruit and made myself useful, but I missed life in the town.'

'Surely you could visit Brindisi occasionally?' Raven said, frowning. 'The monks must go into the town, if only to purchase absolute necessities.'

'I made a few mistakes when I was living in my studio. I was popular amongst the locals while I had money to buy drinks, and I painted portraits of their wives and children. I even painted a parrot once, for a retired sea captain.'

'Would your mistakes have anything to do with young Italian women?' Lady Alice said bluntly. 'I know you of old, Freddie. You always had an eye for the girls.'

A faint smile lit his eyes. 'There were a few, Alice. Such dark-haired beauties as you can only imagine, and they were eager to please me. They all wanted their likenesses saved for posterity, but then their fathers began making their presence felt. I had to leave town in a hurry, and that's when the monks found me, collapsed on the cliff top a mile or so from here.'

'You are a magnet for trouble, Freddie,' Raven said, laughing. 'How long have you been living in the monastery?'

'A year or two, I think. Nothing much happens and I've lost count of time. Everything is ruled by that damned bell. They get up in the middle of the night for prayers and it goes on all day and well into the evening. Sometimes I think they want me to join their order, but the life of a monk is not for me.'

Essie had been listening intently, but cramp and sore knees forced her to stand. She gazed down at the pale, handsome young man whose long dark hair curled around his head and shoulders in a way that would make any woman jealous. 'It seems to

me you got your comeuppance,' she said unsympa-
thetically. 'You led those girls on, so it serves you
right.'

'Enough of the moralising, Esther.' Lady Alice
leaned over to kiss Freddie's cheek. 'I dare say she's
right, but it's hardly helpful in the circumstances.
We'll have to decide what's best for you, cousin. I'm
not even sure how I'm going to get home.'

'We'll sort that out, Alice,' Raven said firmly. 'But
you haven't much choice, Freddie, old chap. You
can't return to England yet, and it seems that you've
burned your boats as far as the townsfolk are
concerned. I can give you money, but knowing you
it will soon be gone. I don't know what I'm going
to do with you.'

'Think of something, Raven,' Freddie pleaded. 'I
will die if I have to remain here. There's no doubt
about that.'

Lady Alice eased herself to a standing position.
'That bed is very uncomfortable. The monks obvi-
ously believe that suffering is good for the soul.
Anyway, I'm starving so I'll go downstairs and ask
Falco to arrange food for us.'

'Falco?' Freddie asked dazedly. 'Who is he?'

'He's the captain of the ship I chartered in Geelong
to take me back to England, and he brought us here.
Falco takes work wherever he can find it, and as
long as I can pay he'll do anything I ask, within
reason.' Raven turned to Essie and Sadie, who was

still hovering by the door. 'You girls had better go downstairs first. I'll follow.'

'I'd like to stay and talk to your brother, if you don't mind,' Essie said boldly. 'I might be able to make a concoction of herbs that will help him, but I need to ask him more questions.'

'Good God! Are you a witch, Esther Chapman?'

'No, sir, but in Limehouse people can't afford to send for a doctor every time they have bellyache or the squits. I can't pretend to cure cholera or typhoid but I can help relieve the symptoms and maybe speed a patient's recovery. The rest is in the hands of the Almighty, but I'd say that your brother is on the mend.'

'Well, well.' Raven stared at her as if seeing her properly for the first time. 'You are a young woman full of surprises. All right, I'll have some food sent up for you and Freddie.' He turned to his brother, smiling. 'You seem to have a volunteer nurse, so I'll leave her to it. Be nice to her, Freddie. She's been a great help to me in London.'

Essie waited until they were alone and she pulled up the only chair in the room and sat down. She felt Freddie's forehead and it was cool to the touch. 'How long have you been like this, Mr Dorincourt?'

'Call me Freddie, please.'

'All right, Freddie. Suppose you tell me when the fever started and what the monks have done for you.'

He fixed her with a curious stare. 'Who are you, Esther Chapman? How do you come to be here? You said something about a boat sinking? Where was that and how did it happen?'

'Why do you want to know? We'll be leaving tomorrow and I doubt if we'll ever meet again.'

'You are as spiky as a cactus. Humour me, Esther. I've been up here in the tower, mostly on my own, for what seems like weeks. Tell me your story.'

Essie was about to answer when she heard heavy footsteps on the stone stairs and Brother Ignacio staggered into the room carrying a heavy tray, which he placed on a small table close to the bed.

'*Grazie,*' Essie said, receiving a curt nod in response as Brother Ignacio retraced his steps and left them to their food. She peered into one of the two bowls and sniffed. 'Soup,' she said, turning to Freddie. 'It smells good. Are you hungry?'

He shook his head. 'I haven't much appetite. I'd rather listen to you than eat.'

She dipped the spoon into the vegetable broth, thickened with little strips of pasta. 'I'll talk, but only if you promise to eat.'

He opened his mouth as obligingly as a small child and Essie told him of her first meeting with Raven, and the complications arising from his visit to London. Freddie listened with a rapt expression on his handsome features, supping the broth without seeming to notice that he was taking nourishment.

When the bowl was empty, Essie peeled a peach and fed him slivers until he lay back, protesting that he could eat no more.

'Your soup will be cold,' he said severely. 'Now you eat, and I'll lie here and watch you. It's good to be in the company of a pretty girl again. I'm sick of seeing male faces and listening to their deep voices. You look and sound like an angel from heaven.'

Essie almost choked on a spoonful of rapidly cooling broth. 'Now I know how you charmed the young ladies in the town,' she said, laughing. 'I'm hungry so I'm in no danger of losing my appetite, but you can tell me about yourself. For instance, how did you get involved with the gang of smugglers in the first place?'

'Someone has been talking,' Freddie said with a rueful smile. 'I suppose Alice has told you about my wild ways. Most of it I suspect is true, but when I came down from Cambridge I found life in Devon much too quiet. I'm not one for hunting and fishing and pursuits like that, and I used to frequent the village pub, where I met the boys I grew up with. When we were young we used to roam the countryside and get into all manner of scrapes.'

'But you'd grown out of that, surely?' Essie broke off a piece of bread and dipped it in the soup. 'Go on.'

'There's not much choice for young men born and bred in the country. They either work in the fields or they fish for a living and those occupations pay very little. My boyhood friends had chosen to flout the law in order to earn a little extra money. I did accompany them on one of their sorties, but on the night in question I just happened to be on hand when they beached. Unfortunately someone had informed the revenue men and they were there, waiting to pounce.'

'I'm sorry you were caught, but you must have known it was a dangerous pursuit.'

Freddie heaved a sigh. 'My main regret is that Raven became involved. He's taken the punishment that should have been mine.'

'You could have faced the gallows,' Essie said, placing her empty bowl back on the tray. 'The least you can do is to promise to be patient and wait until your appeal is heard. He risked his life by returning to London, and it was all for you.'

'I know that, Esther. There's no need to rub it in.'

'You can call me Essie. I think Lady Alice is the only person who's called me Esther since I left school, except for my pa when he's scolding me.'

Freddie reached out to hold her hand. 'I won't make things difficult for Raven. I'll promise to behave and wait patiently for the law to take its course.' He squeezed her fingers and his lips twisted in a mischievous grin. 'But I can't guarantee my behaviour if the appeal fails. I might book passage to Australia for myself. Raven hasn't said anything, but he must have struck gold to be able to afford to hire a ship.'

'That's something you'll have to discuss with your brother.' She turned her head to see Raven standing in the doorway.

'You two seem to have got on well,' he said casually. 'What is it to want to discuss with me, Freddie?'

Essie withdrew her hand and rose to her feet. 'I'll leave you two to talk.' She picked up the tray and made her way down the spiral staircase to the cloisters. The fragrant aroma of hot bread and soup led her to the refectory where she found Lady Alice seated at a long table with Sadie and Captain Falco. The monks sat at another table and they were intent on eating, but Essie could tell from their covert glances that they were fascinated by Lady Alice Crozier. Even clad in a plain peasant gown she was undoubtedly a beautiful woman and her vivacity lit up the dark refectory like a beacon. The monks might be holy, but they were men first, and it was obvious that they were falling under her spell.

'There you are, Esther,' Lady Alice said, frowning. 'Have you finished playing nursemaid to my cousin?'

Essie placed the tray at the end of the table and sat down. She had grown used to Lady Alice's moods during the sea voyage and had found it best to ignore her barbs. 'We had an interesting conversation, my lady,' she said calmly. 'But I think Mr Frederick's problem is caused more by boredom and loneliness than illness.'

'So you're a doctor now, are you?'

'No, my lady, of course not.'

Falco gave Essie a beaming smile. 'I think you may be right. A clever young lady like you would be an asset to my crew. Alas, Hooper only knows how to bandage a wound and give purges.'

Lady Alice rose to her feet, causing the monks to look up from their food, although they quickly bowed their heads when they caught the abbot's reproving glance.

'Tell them I need somewhere to rest my head tonight, Falco,' Lady Alice said imperiously. 'Esther and Sadie will sleep in my room, for their safety and my own.'

'I don't think you have anything to fear from the holy men,' Falco said, chuckling.

'Men are men, whether they wear a monk's habit or a priest's vestments.'

Falco crossed himself, casting his eyes heavenwards. 'May you be forgiven, my lady.'

'That's not funny.' Lady Alice met his amused look with a stony stare. 'If you had put me ashore in England I wouldn't be here now.'

He stood up and bowed from the waist. 'And I would have been denied the pleasure of your company, my lady.'

Essie held her breath. For a moment she thought that Lady Alice might throw something at Captain Falco, but a slow smile curved her lips and her laughter echoed off the vaulted ceiling.

'You are a rogue, Falco. I have a sneaking suspicion that you kept us on board for your entertainment only, so now you can return the favour and find me a comfortable place to sleep.'

Falco nodded and went to speak to the abbot, returning moments later. 'They only have one room to offer.'

Sadie tugged at Essie's sleeve. 'What's going on? Have we got to stay here tonight?'

'It appears so,' Essie said in a low voice.

Falco said something to Brother Ignacio, who replied, nodding and gesticulating. Falco turned to Lady Alice. 'I have explained the situation, and Brother Ignacio will show you to the cell.'

'It sounds like we're going to prison,' Sadie whispered.

Essie hushed her with a glance as they followed Lady Alice and Brother Ignacio from the refectory.

The cells were in a block that had escaped the fire from the Barbary pirate ships, but when Lady Alice saw where they were to sleep she threw up her hands. 'This really is a cell. It's as bad as the cabin on the *Santa Gabriella*.'

Brother Ignacio bowed and backed away. It was

obvious to Essie that he had had enough of the imperious foreign lady, and could not wait to return to his life of prayer and contemplation.

Lady Alice slumped down on the bed. 'This is so hard I might as well sleep on the floor.'

Essie glanced round the tiny room where the only furnishings were a small table, a single chair and the narrow bed. 'It look as though Sadie and I will have to do just that.'

'Oh, well. It's just for one night.' Lady Alice rose swiftly to her feet. 'I think I'll go up and spend the rest of the day with Freddie. You two can amuse yourselves as you please. But whatever happens, we're leaving first thing in the morning, and I'll insist that Raven books us a passage home. I can't wait to get back to England.'

Chapter Eight

That night, of necessity, as the cell allotted to Lady Alice was too small to take the three of them, Essie volunteered to sleep in the chair in Freddie's tower room. Falco and Raven sat drinking wine late into the evening, and the prospect of sleeping on the floor in the refectory did not appear to bother them. Essie, on the other hand, was glad to escape the constant ringing of the bells that summoned the brothers to prayers at all hours of the day and into the night. At least it was peaceful at the top of the tower and the air was sweet with the fragrance from the lemon grove and the herby aroma of the sun-warmed cliffs, tempered by the salty smell of the sea.

Just as she thought that Freddie had settled down to sleep, he sat up in bed and leaned over to touch her hand. 'I must leave with you tomorrow, Essie.'

She peered at him, trying to make out his features in the darkness. 'I thought you had to stay here for your own safety.'

'Raven is going to Australia. I want to go with him.'

'But he's returning to the penal colony. If they find out that he's been away he'll be in terrible trouble.'

'My brother is too smart to be caught, and he's made a fortune in the gold fields. I want to have that chance, too. Money can buy anything, even freedom.'

'That's why he risked everything,' Essie said patiently. 'He went to London for that purpose only.'

'And I'm grateful to him, but I'll die if I have to remain here another day on my own. You can understand that, can't you, Essie?'

'I think so, but you need to speak to your brother. He's the only one who can help you.'

'Yes, I will. First thing in the morning I want you to bring him to me.'

'I will,' Essie promised. 'Now go to sleep.'

Freddie heaved himself off the bed. 'I can't lie here in comfort while you're sitting in the chair. We'll swap places. You need your rest more than I do.'

She stared at him in horror. 'I can't do that. You're unwell.'

He took her by the hand and pulled her to her feet. 'I'm quite recovered from the fever. I need fresh air and something to do or I'll go mad. Now take my bed and let me sit in the chair. I insist upon it.'

Next morning, Essie awakened to find Freddie watching her with a smile on his face. 'It's a pleasure to watch you sleeping,' he said cheerfully. 'You looked as though you were having sweet dreams.'

She sat up, self-conscious and embarrassed. 'I can't remember. I hope you managed to doze off.'

'I cat-napped, but that's all I ever do. I don't need much sleep.' He leaned forward, his smile fading. 'Now, will you do as I asked you last night? Go and find my brother and tell him that I'm leaving with you.'

Essie shook out her tangled mop of hair. 'All right, but I can't go down looking like this. I don't suppose you have such a thing as a hairbrush or a comb?'

Freddie stood up and walked over to a chest of drawers, returning with a mirror and a brush. 'The brothers do allow such luxuries, but that's about all. I had to leave my few possessions when I abandoned my studio in town. Not that I brought much with me from home, as my departure was rather hurried.'

Essie winced as she tugged at a particularly knotty tangle, and to her surprise Freddie took the brush from her. 'I haven't finished,' she protested.

'Turn round and I'll do your hair. It's a long time

since I ran my fingers through a dark silky mane like yours. I've always loved women, and the monastic life isn't for me.'

'From what I heard it was your liking for a pretty face that brought you here in the first place,' Essie said, chuckling.

'My intentions were misunderstood, and I never had any complaints from the ladies in question. But you will do your best to convince Raven that I'm desperate to leave here, won't you?'

She closed her eyes, enjoying the rhythmic strokes as he brushed her long hair. 'I'll do my best, Frederick.'

'It's just Freddie. Standing on ceremony doesn't have a place here.' He stood back to admire his handiwork. 'You have beautiful hair, Essie. And the face of an angel, particularly when you're asleep.'

Essie felt the blood rush to her cheeks. 'Please don't say that in front of anyone else. Heaven knows what they'd think.' She moved to the top of the spiral stairs. 'I'll do what I can, Freddie.'

'I think I'm in love with you, Essie.' He blew her a kiss.

She smiled as she negotiated the stone steps. The Honourable Frederick Dorincourt was not so different from Ben, who was always declaring his love for her – she knew it was just words.

*   *   *

Raven and Falco were sprawled on chairs in the empty refectory. Essie tapped Raven on the shoulder. 'Wake up. I need to talk to you.'

He opened one bleary eye, staring at her as if he had never seen her before. 'What d'you want?'

'Your brother wants to go to Australia,' Essie said sharply. 'Wake up. Don't go back to sleep.'

He opened both eyes and raised himself to a sitting position. 'What did you say?'

'Freddie insists on leaving here. He says he's desperate and I believe him. He wants to go with you.'

Raven leaped to his feet. 'We'll see about that.' He strode off towards the tower, leaving Essie alone with Falco, who was slowly surfacing.

'What's happening?' he demanded, yawning. 'What is all the fuss about?'

At that moment the monks began to file into the refectory carrying baskets of bread and fruit, which they laid on the table together with jugs of water. Grace was said and they took their seats, ignoring Essie and Falco, who had moved away to a respectful distance.

'Freddie wants to leave with us,' Essie whispered. 'He says he'll throw himself out of the window if we go without him.'

Falco did not look impressed. 'I doubt if he'd go that far.'

'He wants to go to Australia with his brother,'

Essie insisted. 'I don't see why that should be impossible.'

Falco shrugged and reached for a carafe of wine, taking a swig from it and wiping his lips on the back of his hand. 'They make this concoction themselves, but it's terrible.'

'I'd better go and find her ladyship,' Essie said, backing away. 'Do you know what time we're leaving?'

'I am just the guide and interpreter,' Falco said with a glimmer of a smile. 'Raven is the one in charge. We'll have to wait and see what he decides.'

Essie knew that there was only one person who might influence Raven, and she went to find Lady Alice.

'What?' Lady Alice sat up in bed, staring at Essie. 'Surely you're mistaken? Freddie wouldn't want to go to a penal colony, even if Raven has struck gold.'

'That's what he said, my lady. He seemed determined.'

Lady Alice climbed stiffly from the bed. 'That was the most uncomfortable night I have ever had. The monks obviously believe in mortifying the flesh.' She prodded Sadie's sleeping form with her foot. 'Wake up, girl. We're leaving as soon as I'm ready, no matter what Raven says.'

Whatever passed between the two brothers that morning was never discussed openly, but Freddie said goodbye to the monks, thanking them for their hospitality, and the small party set off on the return journey to Brindisi. When they reached the inn a little after midday, a room was found for Freddie, who was plainly exhausted by the long ride. It was obvious that he had not fully recovered his strength, despite his refusal to acknowledge the fact that he was still recuperating from his illness.

Essie was relieved to find her clothes washed, dried and laid out neatly on her bed together with Sadie's garments, and later that afternoon the local dressmaker arrived to take Lady Alice's measurements for at least one new gown. Having satisfied her ladyship that she was perfectly capable, the dressmaker turned her attention to Essie and finally to Sadie, although she made it clear that their clothes would come second to those ordered by Lady Alice. Falco and Raven had gone down to the docks soon after they had arrived and returned in time for dinner that evening. Essie sensed a tense atmosphere, but neither of them was forthcoming and Lady Alice appeared to be oblivious to their change of mood. She seemed happy now that she was wearing her own clothes, even though they were well worn and faded, and Sadie had put up her ladyship's hair in a very becoming style.

'I hope you were getting the ship ready to sail for England.' Lady Alice took her seat at the table, spreading out her skirts and tilting her head in a coquettish manner, addressing Falco with a charming smile. 'You will see me safely home, won't you, Captain?'

Falco had risen gallantly, as had Raven, but they exchanged wary glances as they resumed their seats. 'I'm afraid that will be impossible, my lady,' Falco said smoothly. 'But I have had a word with the captain of another vessel, who will be setting off for Portsmouth in two days' time.'

'Oh!' Lady Alice pouted prettily. 'Surely you could go out of your way for me?'

'I don't think you understand the situation fully, Alice.' Raven spoke with a sharp edge in his voice. 'Falco risked everything when he took me to London. To return there would be foolhardy in the extreme.'

'I knew it,' Essie said softly. 'You are a pirate, Captain Falco.'

He shook his head. 'No, on my honour, I am not a corsair. On the other hand, I have sometimes flouted the law, just enough to make it impossible for me to remain here a moment longer than necessary.'

'So there's a price on your head as well as Raven's,' Lady Alice said crossly. 'And Freddie dare not show his face in this town for fear of being recognised by irate fathers. Is there such a thing as an honest and trustworthy man?'

Essie moved aside as Filomena placed a steaming bowl of pasta, glistening with a rich tomato sauce and studded with basil leaves, on the table in front of her. The savoury aroma made her mouth water and conversation ceased while they ate. The landlord brought wine to the table and this time Falco approved, going so far as to fill a glass for Essie and a small one for Sadie. The alcohol went straight to Essie's head, and Sadie was nodding off before she had finished her food. Aided by yet another bottle of wine, the tension eased and Falco entertained them with amusing anecdotes, although he could not be persuaded to give them a song. Essie was quick to note that Raven was still troubled, although he was making an effort to be lighthearted. She wondered what had occurred during their visit to the ship, but she was not in a position to ask questions.

She looked from one smiling face to another. 'Has anyone been upstairs to see Freddie recently?' she asked pointedly.

There was a brief lull in the conversation and a shaking of heads. Essie stood up and helped Sadie to her feet. 'I'll take Sadie upstairs and I'll check on Freddie.'

Lady Alice frowned. 'It's Mr Frederick to you, Esther. Remember your manners.'

'Nonsense,' Raven said sharply. 'We're all equal here, Alice. We rely on each other and social mores go by the board.' He turned to Essie with a grateful smile. 'Thank you, Essie. I'd be much obliged if you would. I'm afraid I forgot the poor chap.'

'Don't mention it.' Essie turned away quickly, afraid that her pink cheeks might be mistaken for a maidenly blush – it was the wine, of course, that had brought colour to her face. She guided Sadie to the staircase, and, having put Sadie to bed, Essie went to Freddie's room.

He raised himself on one elbow and smiled. 'You're the only one who's bothered to come to see me, Essie. Thank you.'

'I should have come sooner, but there was the dressmaker and then Falco and Raven came back from the docks.' She moved closer to the bed. 'Are you hungry?'

'Yes, for the first time in weeks I think I could eat a decent meal. If you'd be kind enough to pass me my clothes I'll get up and join them downstairs.'

She hesitated. 'Are you sure about that? I could bring you something from the kitchen?'

'No, I don't want you to do that. Give me my things and if you'd be kind enough to wait outside the door I might need a steadying hand to negotiate the stairs.'

She picked up his garments and laid them on the bed. 'I'll be outside. Just call if you need me.'

Essie left Freddie seated at the table with a plate of food in front of him before returning to her own room where she settled down on the floor, not wanting to disturb Sadie, who was sound asleep. A breeze floated in through the open window, bringing with it the sounds of ships' hooters and the flapping of canvas against masts and stays. The babble of voices was faint but audible as men lurched out of the inn, some of them bursting into song as they made their way home. It was all in complete contrast to the echoing silence at the monastery, but at least there were no bells to summon the faithful to prayer. Essie closed her eyes and drifted off to sleep.

She was awakened by someone shaking her. 'What's the matter?' She snapped into a sitting position, stretching her cramped limbs. The floor was not the most comfortable place to sleep.

'We have to leave now. Get up and get dressed and wake the child. We leave immediately.'

Essie pulled the thin sheet up to her throat, realising that it was Raven who had woken her, and it was not a dream. 'Why? Where are we going?'

'Don't waste time talking. Do as I say.' He left the room and his footsteps echoed eerily in the silent building.

Essie scrambled to her feet and slipped her gown over her head. The urgency in Raven's voice spurred her to hurry. She had suspected that all was not well earlier that evening, and now she was certain.

'Wake up, Sadie. We have to leave the inn now.'

Sadie stirred, moaned and curled up in a foetal position. 'Go away.'

Essie gave her a shake. 'I'm not joking. Get up or

you'll be left behind. I don't know what's happening, but we have to go.'

Reluctantly, Sadie allowed Essie to help her into her faded frock. They bundled their few possessions in their shawls and went to join the others in the bar. Falco and Raven were there, supporting Freddie, but they had to wait a few minutes for Lady Alice. Even in a crumpled gown, with her hair hanging loose around her shoulders, she managed to look beautiful and elegant. Essie might have been envious had she not been so anxious.

'What is going on, Raven?' Essie demanded in a stage whisper. 'Why are we running away?'

'We are all here now. We must leave at once.' Falco opened the door and stepped outside. 'The coast is clear. Hurry.'

'Have the fathers in the town discovered that I'm here?' Freddie asked with a wry grin.

'Don't flatter yourself, brother,' Raven said tersely. 'Lean on me, Freddie. We've got to get to the boat.'

'Are you taking me to England?' Lady Alice hurried after them.

'Are we really going home?' Sadie asked breathlessly as she tagged on behind Essie.

'Who knows?' Essie grabbed her by the hand and broke into a run, following the others as they sped down the hill into the darkness. Quite how they managed to get through the town and onto the *Santa Gabriella* was something of a miracle, considering that they were challenged outside the docks by men in uniform. Falco spoke to them briefly, and for a few minutes they waited while an official checked through a sheaf of documents, but then, to Essie's surprise, they were allowed to board the ship. A good head of steam had already been achieved and the crew were waiting to cast off.

'Just a moment, Falco.' Lady Alice caught him by the sleeve. 'I don't know what this is all about, but I want you to swear that we are on our way back to England.'

He stared down at her small white hand with her fingers clutching the coarse material of his jacket. 'You know that's impossible, my lady.'

Essie made a move towards Lady Alice, who was swaying on her feet as if about to faint. 'Maybe we ought to go below, my lady. Freddie needs you.'

'Don't interfere, Esther.' Lady Alice faced up to Falco. 'Are you, or are you not taking me home, Falco? I want a straight answer.'

Raven came up behind them and he put his arm round his cousin's waist. 'Steady on, Alice. You know we can't return to England, particularly now. Freddie would be arrested the moment he put foot ashore, as would I, and you'd be in trouble for aiding and abetting. We're all in this together, even the two girls.'

'You bastard!' The words spilled out of Lady Alice's mouth, more shocking because Essie had never heard her using such language.

Raven merely grinned and dropped a kiss on top of her golden head. 'I'm sorry, my love, but we're all bound for the Antipodes, unless you want to stop off in Malta or Cape Town. You could make a life for yourself there for the next two years.'

Lady Alice stared at him in dismay. 'I don't believe you're saying these things, Raven. You can't expect to take three women to the penal colony in Victoria. We might not survive the journey.'

'You are a great deal tougher than you look. I remember you climbing trees and swimming in Lyme Bay when we were young. You were as strong and agile as any of us.'

Freddie laid his hand on her shoulder. 'I am so sorry, Alice. This is all my fault. If I hadn't insisted on coming with you things might have been different.'

Falco took her hand and raised it to his lips. 'I apologise, too, my lady. As you can see, I am a wanted man in my native country, and this is partly my fault.'

'What did you say to those armed men, Captain?' Essie asked curiously. 'I thought they were going to arrest all of us.'

'I told them that my lady is an important English aristocrat, a relative of Her Majesty Queen Victoria, and she must be allowed immunity.'

'You are a good liar,' Lady Alice said with a reluctant smile. 'I admire your nerve and your cool head, but that doesn't excuse you for bringing me on this rusty old wreck.'

Falco held his hand to his heart. 'My lady, you're talking about the woman I love.'

'This isn't a game, Falco. You haven't heard the last of this, you reprobate. You will put me ashore in Malta and find me a vessel to take me home, or I will want to know the reason why.' Lady Alice stormed off in the direction of her cabin.

'What's a reprobate, Essie?' Sadie whispered.

'You may well ask.' Essie stifled a sigh. This promised to be an eventful voyage, over which she had no control. She wanted to go home, but a small part of her was excited by the prospect of travelling to the other side of the world. She had read about the goldfields in Australia and she had seen one of the nuggets that Raven had brought home. It would be so easy to catch gold fever – she could feel it pulsing through her veins – the adventure was about to become even more exciting.

The plan to dock in Malta was abandoned due to a sudden storm, which made landfall impossible, and Falco, having sighted a flotilla of British ships at anchor, refused to sit out the bad weather. He said he was in no hurry to meet up with the Royal Navy, and Raven was eager to get as far away from authority as possible. Lady Alice might have protested volubly, but she was laid low with seasickness, something she denied fiercely, blaming the poor food on board the *Santa Gabriella*. Sadie was also suffering, but Essie was not affected and it fell to her to act as their nurse.

They put into port in Gibraltar in order to take on supplies. Lady Alice was too weak to even consider going ashore, and she sent Essie to purchase soap, needles and thread and bolts of material, as well as a pair of scissors.

'I hired you as a seamstress,' she said curtly. 'You can show me how clever you are by making me a gown similar to the one I ordered from the woman in Brindisi. I cannot go on with a single change of clothes when we land in Cape Town, and I am determined to get home, one way or another.'

Time was limited as Falco was eager to set sail as soon as the stores were stowed away in the hold and the vessel had taken on coal and fresh water. Even so, Essie managed to purchase all the things on Lady Alice's list, including some towels and three bolts of cotton print as well as the necessary sewing materials. Then there were the three lace shawls and three straw bonnets that Raven insisted on buying. The prettiest bonnet trimmed with silk roses and a pink bow was for Lady Alice, the other two in plaited straw were for Essie and Sadie. Raven presented them to Essie with a wink and a smile.

'Alice is learning to be more democratic, but we have to let her down easily. She'll have a shock when we disembark in Geelong, even more so when we get to Ballarat.' He shouldered the bolts of material.

'Come on, Essie. Let's get back to the ship before Falco sails off without us. You'd think the devil was on his heels.'

Essie fell into step beside him, clutching the wicker basket containing her purchases. 'But you said we would be put ashore in Cape Town where we could get a passage back to England.'

He gave her a quizzical look. 'If you think the weather was rough in the Mediterranean, you just wait until we round the Cape. My cousin is a brave woman, but even she might balk at repeating the journey so soon, especially at this time of the year when the storms are at their worst. However, we'll wait and see. I think Falco might be able to persuade her to stay with us until we reach Australia. You can all travel home from there, or you could stay until I am a free man in two years' time.'

'Would you want us to do that?'

'Why not? There are plenty of women who have stuck it out, mostly because they have no alternative, but there are the wives of the military and a few genuine settlers.'

'I might find gold for myself,' Essie said thoughtfully. 'Then I could go home with enough money to buy a house in a nicer area, and maybe George would come home.'

Raven hitched the heavy bolt of material onto his other shoulder. 'Tell me about him. What was George like?'

'Why do you want to know?'

'Because I do, that's all. I'm curious about your family background. For instance, what sort of man sends his daughter out into the night, rowing a small craft to meet a stranger from a foreign ship? That stretch of the river is notoriously dangerous.'

Stung by the unfairness of this remark, when Raven knew that the reason she had been sent out was because of her father's injury, Essie glared at him. 'You know why I had to do Pa's work. He wouldn't have let me go out at night on my own in the normal run of things.'

Raven shrugged and quickened his pace. 'If you say so, Essie.'

She would have hurried after him, but she was still annoyed by his criticism of Pa, who was not a model father, but he did love her in his own way. Life had been hard since Ma died and George had left home. In his continued absence it was Essie who had had to be housekeeper and general helper. It had done her no harm and, if anything, it had made her more independent.

Back on board, Essie leaned on the ship's rail, gazing out to sea as they started to make headway, and yet again she was in awe of the magnificence of the ocean and its mighty power. The crew had set the sails and they were scudding along, and, yet again, dolphins were playing in the bow waves. It was a sight that never failed to thrill and excite her as she watched the playful animals cavorting and streaming along as if life was good and filled with fun. Surely there was a lesson to be learned from such beautiful creatures. Essie turned with a start as someone tapped her on the shoulder and her feeling of euphoria evaporated.

'Lady Alice wants you,' Sadie muttered, gazing down at the white-crested waves with a green tinge to her pale skin. 'I want to go home, Essie.'

'And so you shall, all in good time.' Essie turned away from the view and wrapped her arms around Sadie's skinny body in a warm hug. 'Maybe we'll be put ashore in Cape Town. I know that's what Lady Alice wants, in spite of what Raven says.'

'Do you really think so?' Sadie gazed at her with tears in her eyes. 'Will they let us go back to London?

'I hope so, but let's get you back to the cabin and then I'll attend to her ladyship.' Essie guided her to the companionway. 'I'm going to speak to Raven and Falco. I won't allow them to treat us like children. They must put us ashore and arrange our passage home.'

Chapter Nine

Despite her bold words, Essie did not find it easy to pin Raven down, and the same went for Falco, who was charming and urbane, but refused to be drawn on their immediate plans. During a period of calm seas and light winds Lady Alice began to recover from her bout of *mal de mer*, and Freddie was getting stronger every day. Essie found herself with spare time and she tried her hand at dressmaking. Sadie was her model and Essie's first attempt left much to be desired, but Sadie was delighted with the result and wore the frock with pride. Essie used the experience to create a gown for Lady Alice, and this time she was much happier with the end product. Lady Alice was grudging with her praise, but she brightened perceptibly when Raven and Falco complimented her on her appearance. Essie's final attempt before they reached Cape Town was to make a skirt and blouse for herself, but the weather had deteriorated and the *Santa Gabriella* pitched and tossed on wild waves, making it almost impossible to thread a needle, let alone sew a straight seam. Lady Alice retired to her cabin once again and succumbed to another bout of seasickness.

They put into Cape Town battered and bruised after rounding the Cape, but Lady Alice did not ask to be put ashore. She was pale and weak after a long bout of sickness and unusually compliant. Essie had expected tears and tantrums when Falco said that they would be stopping only to take on fresh food and water, and there was no question of staying in port long enough to arrange their passage home. Raven backed him up, as did Freddie, and, faced with such strong opposition, Lady Alice gave up without a fight. Essie was surprised, but secretly relieved. As the days went by she had been dreaming of striking gold and now they were well on their way to Australia she could think of little else.

As before, the food was awful and Lady Alice complained about every meal. In the end it was Freddie who came to the rescue. He invaded the tiny ship's galley and ousted the cook, who was only too willing to accept other duties.

'But, Freddie, you don't know how to cook.' Lady Alice stared down at her plate in disbelief as they sat in the saloon at suppertime.

Essie sniffed appreciatively. The pasta had been tossed in olive oil with the addition of dried herbs, fresh tomatoes and grated cheese. 'This smells wonderful, Freddie.'

'Where did you learn to do this?' Raven demanded, staring at his plateful of food in disbelief.

'I was on my own for four years,' Freddie said, shrugging. 'I couldn't afford to eat in the cafés and bars all the time, so I had to learn how to feed myself, and then I found that I enjoyed cooking and the father of one of my lady friends taught me how to make pasta.'

'I'm sorry, Freddie, but you were always so useless, and now it seems you've found your true calling in life.' Lady Alice subsided into a fit of the giggles that was so infectious it made everyone laugh, even Freddie.

'You can poke fun, Alice, but I made that pasta from scratch. If you don't like it I can always call the cook back—'

'No!' They all spoke in unison.

'And before you ask,' Freddie said defensively, 'the crew loved it, although Hooper, being a Londoner born and bred, said he wanted boiled beef and carrots. I pointed out that we'd used up our supply of salt beef, so he'll have to wait until we take on fresh supplies.'

Essie met Freddie's triumphant gaze with an encouraging smile. She had a feeling his cooking talent would make the final stage of their voyage a more enjoyable experience, and the sails had been set in order to take advantage of the Roaring Forties, the strong westerly winds that would speed them across the Indian Ocean to their final destination. Keeping boredom at bay was the main problem, but Essie busied herself with her sewing and she taught Sadie how to stitch a seam. Lady Alice, who had recovered fully, began to take an interest in the new dresses that Essie had made for her. She added a few frills, using scraps of material and ribbon, and they sat on deck plying their needles and drinking tea, much to the amusement of Raven, who teased Lady Alice mercilessly. However, he changed his tune when he ripped a hole in his shirt, having caught it on a rusty nail, and he had to persuade someone to mend it as neatly as possible. Lady Alice refused, but Essie took pity on him and spent a whole evening working by the light of a paraffin lamp, using tiny stitches to patch the tear.

She took the mended garment up on deck where Raven was leaning on the rail, staring into the darkness. 'There you are,' she said, handing him the shirt. 'It's as good as new, well, almost.'

'Thank you, Essie. It was kind of you to bother. Alice would have torn it up for rags, if she thought about it at all. We were very spoilt as children – I realise that now.'

'Which must have made it harder for you when

everything went wrong,' Essie said softly. 'At least growing up with nothing makes you appreciate good fortune.'

He turned to give her a searching look, his face pale in the moonlight. 'You haven't had an easy time of it.'

'Maybe not, but I was happy enough, except when Ma died and George left home. That was bad.'

'Have you any idea where your brother might have gone?'

'No, but I think he might have stowed away on a ship. I've nothing to base it on other than the fact that he always wanted to join the navy.'

'Why didn't he?'

'Pa wouldn't allow it. He said that it was a hard life and only toffs became officers. I'm sorry to say so, but it's how Pa thinks.'

Raven nodded, his expression serious. 'Your father's right, but I suspect that your brother went his own way. Maybe he's sailing the seven seas as we speak.'

'I like to think that he's happy, wherever he is. George was a good brother, even if he did tease me a lot.'

'That's what brothers do. I was just as bad when I was young. Freddie will vouch for that.'

'I'm sure that's an exaggeration. You couldn't have done more for him.'

'Maybe not, but now we've involved you in our

family troubles.' He laid his hand over hers as it rested on the ship's rail. 'I'm sorry, Essie. You didn't deserve to be involved with outlaws like us, and now we're dragging you to the other side of the world without a by-your-leave. It's unforgiveable.'

The pressure of his fingers and the warmth of his hand made any anger she might have felt against the Dorincourt brothers and Lady Alice Crozier melt into the infinity of space. The sky was a dark indigo bowl, studded with diamond-bright stars and a silver moon that formed a pathway on the surface of the oily black sea. It looked so solid that Essie imagined she might walk across the Indian Ocean and step onto land without getting her feet wet. She came back to earth with a jolt as Raven withdrew his hand.

'I am sorry, Essie,' he said earnestly. 'I'll do my best to atone somehow.'

She clasped her hands together in an attempt to retain the warmth of his touch and failing miserably. 'You don't need to do any such thing. Just show me how to find gold and I can return home with my head held high.'

'You really mean that, don't you?'

'Yes, I do. It's a gamble I'm prepared to take if it means that I can make a better life for myself and my pa.'

'You never fail to surprise me, Essie Chapman. You're a girl after my own heart.'

She laughed and turned away. He was so near to the truth that it hurt – she would have given her soul for a chance to win the love of the Earl of Starcross, but that was as impossible as walking to Australia on a path created by moonlight.

'I'd better go below,' she said awkwardly. For a moment she thought he might try to detain her, but he merely nodded and rested his arms on the rail, gazing out into the inky darkness. Essie stifled a heartfelt sigh and went to join Lady Alice and Sadie.

The sound of Falco singing a snatch of 'The Last Rose of Summer', wafted from the open door. It always brought tears to Essie's eyes, and was usually followed by the equally sad 'Long, Long Ago'. She waited until he had come to the end before entering the saloon.

'You took your time,' Lady Alice said, frowning. 'Sadie was certain you'd fallen overboard.'

'I was enjoying the night air.' Essie tried to sound casual, but she knew that she was blushing. She could only hope that they would think her heightened colour was due to the salty breeze.

Freddie was lounging in a chair with his feet up on a stool. 'Come and sit down. I've had a go at making a cake, which is a feat in itself in the galley stove, and I don't think Cook would give me top marks.'

Sadie seized a knife and cut a slice. 'It's nice, Essie. I can't remember the last time I had cake.'

Falco leaned over and helped himself. 'Not bad, Freddie. But a little more sugar, perhaps?'

Freddie tossed a spoon at him, which Falco caught and placed on the table. 'It's lucky you are not in the habit of throwing knives, my friend.' He eyed Essie with a smile curving his lips. 'You look prettily pink, Signorina Esther.'

'It's breezy on deck,' Essie said hastily. 'I'm going to make a pot of tea. Would anyone like some?' She left the saloon and made her way to the tiny galley on the port side of the vessel, where the kettle was simmering on the embers of the fire in the brick-built oven. She looked round to see Freddie standing in the doorway. 'Would you like a cup?'

'Yes, although I'm not sure if there's milk left in the jug. That goat is a nasty beast – she tried to butt me when I was talking to Hooper. He can do anything with the animal but she's taken a dislike to me.'

'It's your imagination,' Essie said, smiling. It was true, Graciela the goat had a mind of her own and a mean temperament. She disliked everyone except Hooper, whom she tolerated. He had bought her in Brindisi so that they would have milk during the last half of their voyage, but Essie suspected that the person who sold Graciela had been glad to get rid of her. It was an odd friendship, but one that produced fresh milk daily. Hooper, although a terrible cook, knew how to make the excess into a creamy cheese, which was a welcome addition to their diet.

'Is there anything wrong, Essie?' Freddie leaned against the door jamb. 'You seemed uneasy just now, so I thought I'd come and make sure you were all right.'

She managed a tight little smile. 'Thanks, Freddie, but I'm fine. It's just that Australia is so far away from home and I'm worried about my pa. He won't know what's happened to me. In fact he probably thinks I drowned when the boat sank, and there's nothing I can do about it.'

'That's unfortunate and I'm sorry. I hope Raven appreciates what you've done for us.'

'I'm sure he does, and it wasn't his intention to bring us with him. You could call it a stroke of fate.' She concentrated on making the tea, avoiding his penetrating gaze. Freddie might appear to have a casual attitude to life, but he was more sensitive and perceptive than almost everyone on board. She knew that Raven was well aware of the sacrifice she had made, but he was single-minded in his intention to return to Australia before the authorities discovered his absence.

'Here,' Freddie said, taking the teapot from her hand. 'Let me do this. You look as though you need to sit down. It's only natural that you should be concerned about your father, Essie. My brother and I have no close relatives, apart from Alice, so we don't have that problem, but I can see that it's hard for you.'

Essie accepted a tin mug filled to the brim with tea. 'Thank you, Freddie. I suppose it will all work out in the end, especially if I can strike it rich.'

'Not you as well.' He cast his eyes heavenwards. 'Gold fever is catching.'

In the ensuing weeks it seemed that the lust for gold was the wind that filled the sails and fuelled the boilers, giving them full steam ahead as the *Santa Gabriella* ploughed her way across the Indian Ocean. It infected the crew as well as the captain and his passengers. Lady Alice was beginning to take an interest, although she feigned boredom whenever the subject was mentioned, and Sadie was already planning how she would spend the money when she struck gold. Her cupboard would be filled with red leather boots and shoes, and she would have as much cake as she could eat. Essie kept her dreams to herself, but the first thing she would do when she returned to London a rich woman would be to purchase a house in a more respectable street, with a privy in the back yard and their own pump, so that she did not have to walk down the street to fetch water. Such luxuries were truly the stuff of wild imaginings, but at sea there was plenty of time to allow her mind to wander into the realms of fantasy.

The one person she banished from her daydreams was Raven, and she avoided his company as much as was possible in the confines of a relatively small vessel. Freddie was her friend and confidant. He had recovered from his illness and was a different person from the sick young man they had found in the monastery. Raven spent most of his time alone on deck or else he was in Falco's cabin poring over maps, while Falco himself was entertaining Lady Alice. He left Hooper to navigate, with a crewman at the wheel, and Falco sang and charmed his way across the Indian Ocean. Lady Alice appeared to enjoy his company, but Essie suspected that her ladyship's interest in Falco was driven by boredom rather than any romantic feelings. It was impossible to know what Falco thought or felt, but he appeared to be enjoying himself. Maybe they were simply using each other to alleviate the tedium of a long sea voyage. Essie wondered what would happen when they eventually made landfall in Australia.

It was dark when they arrived in Corio Bay. The *Santa Gabriella* was at anchor and they were rowed ashore in relays. Left standing on the jetty in Geelong, Essie shivered and clutched Sadie's hand. The suffocating darkness was relieved by a few tiny pinpoints of light.

'What sort of place is this?' Lady Alice demanded

angrily. 'It seems they've brought us to the back of beyond.'

Essie shrugged and shivered. It was chilly and she had only a thin shawl wrapped around her shoulders. 'It's impossible to tell until daybreak.'

'Well, I wish they'd done as I asked and put us ashore before we left England. Now we're stuck on the other side of the world, and we'll probably be arrested because we're here under false pretences.'

'I don't understand,' Essie said, mystified.

'We haven't committed a crime.' Lady Alice shuddered dramatically. 'We've landed amongst convicts, some of them murderers, and we're defenceless.'

Raven had gone to find some sort of conveyance to take them to Ballarat, but he rejoined them smiling broadly. 'You? Defenceless? Alice, my love, I would place bets on your ability to stun a man with a single glance. You don't need pistols or fists.'

'You're just saying that to ease your conscience, you villain. Anyway, have you found us a carriage, or is there a railway station nearby?'

'They're only just starting out here, Alice,' Raven said patiently. 'It's pretty basic, as you'll find out in the morning, but it's not safe to travel at night. I've booked us into the only hotel in town. We'll leave first thing when I've had a chance to hire some horses.'

'But I haven't brought my riding costume,' Lady Alice protested.

Raven threw back his head and laughed. The sound echoed eerily across the dark water of Corio Bay.

Alice turned to Falco, who had come ashore on the last boat. 'I can't stay here. You will take me to England, won't you, Captain? You said you would.'

He took her hand and raised it to his lips. 'I would do anything for you, beautiful lady, but you don't seem to understand that I have to earn my living.'

Lady Alice stared at him in dismay. 'I thought that I could trust you.'

'And you can, my lady. I would give my life for you, but this is where I must be until I can return home to Italy.'

'But you brought Raven to London,' she insisted angrily. 'You could do that again.'

'Leave him alone, Alice,' Raven said sharply. 'Falco's work is here now, transporting people from Geelong to Melbourne or round the coast to Sydney.'

Falco nodded gravely. 'I wish I could oblige, but you must understand that I cannot. We spend one night ashore and tomorrow I pick up passengers bound for Melbourne. I would like to stay by your side, but I have to think of my crew. We all have to live, my lady.'

'You are a wicked man and a philanderer,' Lady Alice cried angrily. 'You led me to believe that you would do anything I asked.'

Falco bowed and backed away. 'You don't know how much it pains me to leave you here, my lady.'

'But not enough to save me from certain death in this benighted land.' Lady Alice made to follow him but Essie caught her by the sleeve.

'Let him go, my lady,' Essie said urgently. 'You can see that this is hard for him.'

Lady Alice pushed her away. 'Don't tell me what to do, Esther. Remember your place.'

'That's enough of that talk, Alice. We are all equal here.' Raven proffered his arm to Essie. 'Come along, I'll take you to the hotel.' He turned to Sadie with a grin. 'And you, child. You look dead on your feet.'

'What about me?' Lady Alice said sulkily. 'Have you forgotten family loyalty, Raven?'

Freddie stepped forward and linked her hand through the crook of his arm. 'Stop being a brat, Alice. As Raven said, we're in this together and we're all the same. Come on, you need a good night's sleep and you'll see things differently in the morning.'

The hotel was little more than a shack with a wooden veranda and one large room downstairs, which was filled with tables and benches, and a lean-to kitchen tacked onto the back. A rickety ladder led to the first floor, which was partitioned off into small rooms, each containing a camp bed and a palliasse filled with something prickly and crunchy that might have been dried grasses or straw, it was impossible to tell. The smell of unwashed bodies and urine hung in the still air like a bad memory, but Essie was so tired that she fell on the makeshift mattress, fully clothed, and was asleep in minutes with Sadie curled up at her side like a warm puppy. How Lady Alice coped with such privations was not Essie's main concern, although she knew that she would hear about it for several days to come.

Next morning Essie awakened to find herself covered in flea bites and she clambered to her feet, rousing Sadie by the sudden movement. She too had been bitten and they stripped off their clothes, regardless of who might see them, giving each garment a good shake to dislodge their unwelcome lodgers. A scream from Lady Alice followed by hysterical babbling made Essie rush to her side, although she knew what the problem was even before she had seen the red marks on Lady Alice's white skin.

'It's only fleas,' Essie said in an attempt to calm her, but the hysterical cries grew louder, bringing Raven and Falco hurrying to the door.

'Stop that, Alice,' Essie said angrily. 'They'll think you're being murdered.'

Lady Alice's eyes widened with shock. 'How dare you speak to me like that? Did you hear her, Raven?'

'For God's sake stop behaving like a spoiled brat, Alice,' he said, backing away. 'It's only a few flea bites. They won't kill you.'

'No, but I might murder you,' Lady Alice said, choking back a sob. 'You dragged me here, Raven. You and that villain Falco forced me to stay on board when I asked – no, demanded – to be put ashore.'

'Get dressed, Alice. I've bought horses, at enormous expense, and we're going to set off for Ballarat.'

'No.' Lady Alice stamped her foot. 'I want a passage home. You promised me that, Raven. I insist that you keep your word. These girls must go with me.'

'There are no ships leaving for England,' he said wearily. 'This is a penal colony, not a stop on the grand tour.'

Essie held her breath, watching Lady Alice's reaction. She was silent for a few seconds, her face turning ashen and her lips tightening into a rigid line. Sadie curled her fingers around Essie's hand and Essie gave them a comforting squeeze, as she waited for the storm to break.

'You'll pay for this,' Lady Alice hissed. 'I hate you, Raven Dorincourt.'

'Five minutes,' he said coolly. 'If you're not ready then you'll be left to make your own way.'

Essie followed him to the top of the ladder. 'Is it far to Ballarat?'

'About fifty miles.'

'I've never ridden a horse,' Essie admitted reluctantly. 'I don't suppose that Sadie has, either.'

His expression softened. 'We'll take it easy, don't

worry, and we should be there in two days or so.'
He climbed onto the ladder and disappeared into
the depths of the building.

Essie hesitated before going to break the news of
the journey ahead. She could hear Lady Alice grumbling and Sadie's more childish voice attempting to
soothe her. If the sea voyage had been trying, Essie
suspected that by comparison their troubles had
only just begun.

It was still dark when they set off on the track that
Raven assured them led to Ballarat, with dawn yet
to break. They had not eaten since the previous
evening, and, after a couple of hours riding on a
rutted track, Essie's stomach was rumbling and she
was thirsty. Clouds had gathered soon after first
light and a steady drizzle soaked her clothes and
hair. They rode in silence until Raven called a halt.
The rain had ceased and he set about making a fire.
It was obvious from the way he worked that he had
learned the art of survival during his five years in
the penal camp, and soon the fire was hot enough
to heat a billycan of water filled from a leather-
covered canteen. He made damper, mixing flour and
water and cooking the dough in the ashes of the
fire. Even Essie, who was usually willing to try
anything, balked at this at first, but eventually hunger
got the better of her and she scraped off the burned
bits and found it quite palatable. Sadie copied her,

as she did with everything, but Lady Alice refused to touch any of the food, including the salt beef that they had for their midday meal and again at supper, with the inevitable chunk of damper.

They camped that night, sleeping beneath the stars, and thankfully the rain held off. Essie was so exhausted that she would have slept on a bed of nails, and the irritating clouds of sand-flies, with their painful bites, failed to keep her awake. Next morning she was stiff and every part of her body ached, but she was determined to make the best of things. Not so Lady Alice, who awakened in a bad mood and refused once again to eat the damper. She huddled round the fire, sipping tea, but when she stood up again she crumpled to the ground in a dead faint.

Essie rushed to her side and Sadie began to cry. Between them Essie and Freddie helped her to her feet. 'Are you ill, my lady?' Essie asked anxiously.

'She will be sick if she doesn't eat.' Raven eyed his cousin with an ominous frown. 'If you continue to act so childishly I'll leave you behind, Alice.'

'That's cruel,' Essie said fiercely. 'You're hardened to this sort of life, but Lady Alice isn't.'

'That's right.' Freddie helped his cousin to a place where she could sit, leaning against the trunk of a gum tree. 'Have a little pity, Raven.'

Raven shrugged and walked away to tend to the horses. 'We leave in half an hour. Make your choice, Alice.'

'I know something that might help.' Essie had seen a bag of oatmeal in Raven's pack and she helped herself to a cupful, adding the last of the boiling water and stirring vigorously. She handed it to Lady Alice. 'Try this. It's not like the porridge you're used to, my lady, but it will give you the strength to go on.'

Lady Alice seemed about to refuse but a glance from Raven made her spoon the sticky mixture into her mouth. She gulped and swallowed, but as she continued to eat the colour gradually returned to her face.

'I hate you, Raven,' she muttered, thrusting the empty mug into Essie hands.

'You'll change your tune when you get your first glimpse of gold dust,' he said, chuckling as he led her horse to within easy reach. 'Come on, Alice. We're almost there so you'd better make the best of things. You might even come to like the place, in time.'

'Never.' She rose somewhat unsteadily to her feet. 'Help me mount that beast, Freddie. I swear it's the worst-tempered brute I've ever ridden. I'd give anything for a horse from my own stables.'

Freddie tossed her up onto the saddle. 'All in good time, Alice my love.' He turned to Sadie, picked her up and set her gently onto the back of her small but sturdy pony. 'You're doing very well, considering you'd never ridden before yesterday.'

Sadie's cheeks flamed with colour and she giggled self-consciously. 'Ta, sir. You're very kind.'

'Forget the niceties, Sadie. You may call me Freddie. In fact I think we should all use Christian names, and that includes you, Alice. Titles seem out of place and even a bit ridiculous in this wild country.'

'I agree.' Raven nodded emphatically. 'It will be much better that way, particularly when we reach camp.'

'I hate it here,' Alice said, pouting. 'But I suppose it makes sense. Essie and Sadie, you may call me Alice, but when we return to London you will revert to the correct mode of address.'

'Well, I never,' Sadie murmured, holding on for dear life as her pony decided to move forward.

'We'll try to remember that, Alice.' Essie mounted without any help and urged her horse to catch up with Sadie's pony. 'Are you all right?'

'Yes,' Sadie said, grinning. 'Did you hear that, Essie? He said I was to call him Freddie and I'm to call her ladyship Alice. Who'd have thought that Sadie Dixon from Shoreditch would be calling one of the gentry by his first name?'

'Who indeed?' Essie sighed. Where would it all end? That was the question.

Chapter Ten

They arrived in Ballarat early that evening. The twilight was punctuated by dozens of campfires and the scent of eucalyptus and wood smoke mingled with the aroma of cooking.

'Pot luck stew,' Raven said, reining in his horse beside Essie's tired mount. 'They call it poverty stew when times are particularly challenging.'

Essie peered into the gathering gloom. The tented city spread across the land, looking ghostly in the half-light, and she could just make out a line of trees with hills rising steeply in the distance.

'This is where you've been living?' She turned her head to look him in the eye. 'It must be a very hard life.'

He nodded. 'It's not easy, even for men, and it's much tougher on the women.'

'So why did you insist on bringing your cousin here? You know she's used to better things.'

'You're right. I should have insisted on putting all three of you ashore in Gibraltar. The wind and weather made it too difficult to put you ashore in Cape Town, but I do regret that.'

'Are we to stay here for the next two years?' Essie asked anxiously. 'I'd like to know, and I'm sure that Lady Alice will insist on learning her fate.'

A wry smile twisted his lips. 'You make it sound dire, but I have business here, Essie. I'm what's called a fossicker. I haven't got a mining licence and what I do is considered unimportant in the grand scheme of things. As it happens I've been lucky. I was here almost at the start and I found a rich vein of ore as well as a large quantity of small nuggets. I'll keep going because I have to remain here, but there's trouble brewing amongst the miners.'

'Why is that?'

'It's political, Essie. They resent paying the British Government for their licences to operate their mines, and I can't say I blame them.'

Essie would have liked to know more, but she was prevented from enquiring further by the arrival of the others.

'Is this it?' Alice demanded as she drew her horse to a halt beside Raven's tired animal. 'You've dragged us to the other side of the world to live in a tent?'

'Not quite. I've built myself a nice little hut from

wattle and daub. It's the height of luxury – well, comparatively speaking.'

'I'm tired, Raven.' Alice stifled a yawn. 'I don't care where we sleep tonight just as long as it's under cover and free from vermin.'

He reached across to pat her on the shoulder. 'I know you are, and so are the girls. You'll be much more comfortable in my shack. Freddie and I will sleep on the stoop.'

The hut stood on a small hillock overlooking the creek. It was, as Raven said proudly, constructed entirely of wood cut from the acacia trees that were abundant in the area, their slender branches woven into wattle, which was covered with a daub of mud mixed with animal dung and whitewashed for additional strength and waterproofing. The sloping roof extended over a veranda that ran the full width of the building and inside there was one reasonably large room. There was a rope bed in one corner of the room and a table made out of a packing case and two stools.

There was no question as to the person who would occupy the bed. Alice laid her bedroll over the rope mesh, leaving Essie and Sadie to set theirs out on the floor. It was not the most comfortable way to sleep, but at least they were warm and dry, and it had started to rain. Essie could hear Raven and Freddie making themselves as comfortable as possible on the narrow veranda, aided by a bottle of rum that Raven had produced from a cubbyhole beneath the floorboards. They had all had a tot before turning in, and the unaccustomed alcohol had sent Sadie off to sleep without a murmur. Even Alice seemed more mellow under its influence, and Essie closed her eyes, feeling pleasantly relaxed for the first time since they had come ashore in Geelong.

Next morning Essie awakened early. The raw spirit had left her with a headache and a parched throat and she sat up. Everything looked strange in the dawn light, but the sound of Sadie's even breathing and the creak of the ropes when Alice turned in her sleep reminded her that they were the fortunate ones. She rose from her makeshift bed and dressed quickly. Her first thought was to wash away some of the dirt and dust that clung to her face and hair after two days on the road. She picked up a wooden bucket and stepped outside, taking care not to tread on either of the two bedrolls placed toe to toe along the length of the stoop. She could just make out a tuft of dark hair where Raven slept and she took care not to wake him.

It was still only half-light but there was already a buzz of activity in the camp. Spirals of smoke floated upwards, dissipating into the blue-grey dawn, and the clump of heavy boots and the clank of pails being filled from the creek were accompanied by the gruff grunts and subdued chatter of the miners as they made their way to their diggings. Essie went to the creek where another woman was also fetching water. She looked up, giving Essie a hard stare.

'You're new here, ain't you?'

Essie nodded. 'We arrived last night.'

'Where are you from?'

'You ask a lot of questions.'

'It's just my way. We don't get too many women here, at least, not your sort anyway.'

'My sort?'

A grim smile curved the woman's lined cheeks, exposing a missing front tooth. 'You know what I mean, luv. They're either loose women or convicts, often they're both. I can see that you ain't neither.'

'No, that's true.' Essie put her bucket down and held out her hand. 'I'm Esther Chapman from Limehouse, but everyone calls me Essie.'

The woman wiped her hand on her dirty apron. 'Leah Halfpenny from Bow, but that was some time ago. We come to Australia looking for a better life, and ended up here.' She shook Essie's hand vigorously. 'Welcome to Ballarat, girl.' She bent down to pick up the heavy pails and started off up the hill.

Essie filled her bucket and followed the older woman, quickening her pace until she caught up with her. 'Maybe you could give me a few tips,' she said breathlessly. 'I've never done this sort of thing before.'

'I can see that. You'll find it hard. New ones always do.'

'Would you show me how to build a fire?' Essie asked shyly. 'I need to wash.'

Leah came to a halt, her pale blue eyes scanning Essie's face in disbelief. 'The creek is back there.'

'I'd like some warm water.'

'You got soap?'

'Yes, we brought some with us. Why?'

Leah's eyes brightened, giving her a bird-like look. 'How much for a cake of real soap?'

'Surely you have something to wash with and do the laundry?'

'Old Tandy runs the store but he's a robber. He charges an arm and a leg for a lump of lye soap. I make me own, but I'd give anything for a bar of good soap.'

Essie thought quickly. The tablets of soap she had purchased in Gibraltar were disappearing fast, but one of them might prove to be worth even more than gold. 'If I give you a bar of scented soap will you teach me how to make a proper campfire and how to make damper?'

'I will,' Leah said solemnly. 'I'll help you settle in and tell you anything you want to know. Just come to my hut – it's the one with the rocking chair on the porch. Let me put the water on for a brew and then I'll come to yours and give you the benefit of me knowledge.' She picked up her buckets and continued on her way.

Essie washed her hands and face in ice-cold water while she waited for Leah to return, and was just beginning to think that the promise of a bar of soap had not been enough to tempt the old woman when she saw the small figure in the faded cotton print dress and homemade sunbonnet striding across the rough ground.

Leah came to a halt, standing arms akimbo. 'What are you on about, girl?' she said, pointing to what looked like a pile of bricks. 'That's an oven, silly. It hasn't been used since him what lives here went away, but I see he's back home now.' Leah jerked her head in the direction of the sleeping figures on the veranda. 'Ain't got much to say for hisself, that one, but he's always polite when he passes by. Struck it rich, so I heard, but you mustn't believe everything you hear. Gossip runs rife and there's always meetings and grumblings about this and that. I got enough trouble feeding my old man and three hefty sons to worry about such things.' She rolled up her sleeves. 'You'll need to fetch brushwood and plenty of it to get the fire going. I'll show you where it is, but I got a pot of porridge cooking so I can't leave it for long or it'll burn. Follow me, girl, and watch out for snakes and spiders – they'll give you a nasty bite and some of them will kill you, so be careful.'

Essie bundled up her skirts and followed Leah into the stand of trees, keeping an eye out for anything that looked remotely like a snake. The streets of Limehouse would seem quite tame compared to the wilds of Victoria. Leah showed her what would burn well and between them they gathered two armfuls of brushwood. Having started the fire going Leah returned to her home to finish preparing breakfast for her men.

Essie boiled water and made a pot of tea, feeling very proud of herself, and had just thrown a couple of handfuls of oats into a pan of water when Raven appeared. She handed him a mug of tea. 'There's no milk or sugar,' she said, sighing. 'But it's warm and wet, as Pa would say.'

'We can buy milk from Old Tandy. He's got a couple of cows and a few hens, so if you've got the cash you can live reasonably well here. Anyway, the tea is good and you've mastered the fire. Well done.'

Essie tried not to look too pleased, but it was the first time that Raven had said anything verging on a compliment. 'I had some help,' she admitted reluctantly. 'I met a woman down at the creek. Leah Halfpenny, she said her name was. Do you know her?'

'Yes, I've spoken to her on a couple of occasions. Poor woman, she always looks exhausted, and no wonder: she seems to work all the hours God sends looking after her menfolk, and not much thanks for it either as far as I can see.'

'Her husband should take better care of her.'

'It's hard on women here, but don't worry, I have plans to get you and Alice back to England as soon as possible.'

Essie eyed him curiously. She was constantly seeing different sides to Raven's character, not all of them good, but today he seemed to be in a conciliatory mood. 'What have you in mind?'

'I didn't want to raise Alice's hopes in case there was a hitch, but I did a deal with Falco.' Raven lowered his voice. 'Keep this to yourself, Essie, because it might not happen, but when Falco returns from Melbourne I've persuaded him to take you three back to England. I have to remain here until I've served my time, unless my appeal is successful.'

Essie shook her head. 'Why didn't you tell us this before? Do you get some pleasure from tormenting Alice?'

'Certainly not, and don't you breathe a word of this, Essie. If Falco, for any reason, can't oblige then I'll have to find another ship, but the only vessels returning home will be convict ships or those that bring immigrants to this part of the world. I wouldn't like to trust you three to their tender mercies. The *Santa Gabriella* is pure luxury compared to those hulks.'

'You are a strange man, Raven. I don't know what to make of you.'

'At least I always know where I stand with you, Esther Chapman. You aren't afraid to speak your mind.'

'No, and perhaps it's just as well.'

'You won't say anything, promise me?'

'I'll keep quiet about this until Falco returns. But how will you know what he's doing? It's fifty miles to Geelong, you said so yourself.'

'He'll come here when he is ready to undertake the return journey to England. That's all I can tell you. For now, you and the others will have to make the best of it. Who knows? Maybe you'll strike gold and you can go home a rich woman.'

'Raven.' Alice's voice from the veranda made them both turn with a start.

'Here we go,' Raven said, groaning. 'What's the matter now, Alice?'

She came towards them with her long golden hair loose around her shoulders and her gown crumpled, giving her the look of a bedraggled Aphrodite rising from the waves, although Raven's expression was one of impatience rather than admiration. She eyed him warily. 'I know I won't get any sympathy from you, but look at me. I'm in such a state that I don't know what to do with myself.'

Essie filled a mug with tea and handed it to her. 'You'll feel better when you've had something to eat. I'm making porridge for us all.'

'I'm starving.' Sadie came bounding down from the hut like an eager puppy. 'You've made a fire, too.'

Alice drank some tea, pulling a face. 'I'd give anything for a good night's sleep in my own bed and a cup of chocolate first thing in the morning. This tea is putrid.'

'Can I have some?' Sadie asked eagerly. 'When will the porridge be ready?'

'Not for a while,' Essie said, filling her own mug with tea and passing it to Sadie. 'And we need more mugs. I think a visit to Tandy's store is called for.'

With Alice mollified after a breakfast of porridge and tea, and a wash in warm water using one of their precious cakes of soap, Essie felt free to take Sadie to buy some necessities. Raven gave her some money and Freddie accompanied them. They had to make their way on foot through the miners' humpies and bark gunyahs. These, Raven had explained, were shelters made by fossickers who travelled from one area to another in an attempt to strike it lucky. The gunyahs could be dismantled easily or simply left to rot, and some of the inhabitants were best avoided, which Essie could quite believe, judging by a few of the characters they passed on the way to Tandy's.

The sun had risen and it was pleasantly warm. Spring flowers bloomed beneath trees that were bursting into leaf. Sadie skipped along, hardly able to contain her excitement and Essie enjoyed the feeling of the hard-packed mud beneath her feet. After months at sea it was a relief to be on dry land, and with the hint of spring in the air, and the knowledge that their return home was not too far away she felt free to enjoy the new experience. Living in camp was not going to be easy, but to a girl brought up in Limehouse nothing was impossible.

'There it is,' Freddie said, pointing to a timber building ahead of them. 'General Store' had been painted in straggling black letters on a sign pinned above the entrance, and the window was filled with a jumble of pots and pans, tin dippers and tools. Freddie hurried them past a large shack, where scantily dressed females loitered in the doorway and the smell of stale alcohol and tobacco smoke wafted through the open doors. Freddie doffed his hat to two of the older women. 'Good morning, ladies.'

It was an innocent remark but was acknowledged by a torrent of abuse. The elder of the two spat a stream of tobacco juice at him, narrowly missing his shoes.

'I think they misunderstood,' Essie said, chuckling. 'They thought you were mocking them, Freddie. They aren't used to gentlemanly behaviour.' She waved to the frowsy-looking pair. 'He meant no harm.'

Their reply was lost as Freddie hurried Essie and Sadie into Tandy's store.

'They was worse than them what hang about

outside the kip-shops in Seven Dials,' Sadie said primly. 'I never heard such language in all me born days.'

'Never mind them,' Essie said hastily. 'Let's get what we need and then we can set about making the cabin comfortable.'

The man leaning on the counter with a clay pipe clenched between his teeth watched them with narrowed eyes. 'You'll find everything you need here,' he grunted. 'But cash on the nail only. No credit, so don't ask for it.'

'Wouldn't dream of it, old chap,' Freddie said equably.

'Just warning you, mate.'

Essie moved on quickly. She did not like the look of Old Tandy, who could have been any age from forty to sixty, but his balding head and long grey beard were ageing, and his surly expression was far from welcoming. Freddie ignored the implied threat and wandered off to inspect the barrels of salt pork, molasses and flour. Sides of bacon hung from the rafters and strings of onions were draped around hooks screwed into the joists. The scent of tea and roasted coffee beans mingled with that of beeswax, lamp oil and candles. The shelves were piled high with tin mugs and plates, cooking utensils and gardening tools. Spades, hoes and larger implements were ranged around the walls and on the opposite side of the large square room were bolts of calico, cotton and broadcloth. Trays of cotton, needles and scissors were scattered about, and boxes of knitting needles and crochet hooks were packed together alongside spools of coloured ribbon. A dusty spinning wheel sat in one corner as if begging someone to take it home and set it working, and a baby's cradle was filled with seed corn, onion sets and seed potatoes. Essie had a good look round, mentally working out how much she should spend as she decided what they needed most.

Half an hour later, each of them laden with their purchases, they left the store, making a wide detour of the alehouse and brothel, and retraced their steps to the shack. They were halfway there when Essie's skirt caught on a thorn bush and with her arms full of parcels she was unable to free herself. The others were ahead of her and she was about to call for help when a creature slithered out of the shadows, crawling across the dried mud towards her. She held her breath, staring in horror at the misshapen body.

'Who are you?' she asked nervously.

'What's yer name, girl?' The bald head did not look up as a bony hand reached out to grab her skirt.

She was too scared to cry out, but she managed to whisper her name. 'Essie Chapman.'

'I won't hurt you, Essie Chapman.'

The gnarled fingers worked quickly to free her,

and although she was tempted to run away something made her hesitate. 'Thank you,' she murmured. 'What's your name, sir?'

He looked up and she realised that her rescuer was an old man, whose crooked body and crippled legs made him look monstrous. His clothes were torn and filthy, and he smelled worse than the Thames at low tide.

'They say I'm mad,' he said, cackling with humourless laughter.

'Who says such a cruel thing?'

'Everyone. They shun me because I'm a cripple, but I wasn't always like this.'

'How did it happen? Did you have an accident?'

'The pit prop gave way and rocks fell on me. They thought I was dead, but I survived.'

Essie looked into his eyes and realised that he was blind, or at the very least partially sighted. 'I'm so sorry,' she said softly. 'Is there no one to care for you?'

'I don't need no one. Mind your own business.' Suddenly aggressive, he shuffled away, disappearing into the shadows like a wild animal.

'Come on, Essie,' Freddie shouted. 'What are you doing back there?'

'Just coming.' Essie hurried on.

'What were you doing?' Sadie demanded when Essie caught up with them.

'My skirt snagged on a thorn bush, and then a

weird old man crawled out of the trees and grabbed my skirt. He released me and then he disappeared.'

'You're shaking,' Freddie said, frowning. 'Did he hurt you, Essie? If he did—'

'No, not at all. He scared me, but only because he looked so odd. He said he'd been injured in a rock fall, but he didn't tell me his name.'

'Raven will know.' Freddie gave her an encouraging smile. 'I'd give you a hug if I could, but let's get you back to the hut, and I'll cook us a meal.'

They arrived to find Alice receiving a lesson in sweeping the floor from Leah. She turned at the sound of their approach and threw down the broom. 'There, I've done my bit, Mrs Halfpenny. Sadie can take over now.'

Leah shook her head. 'We all have to do our bit here, miss. Those what don't find themselves in a pretty pickle, and you don't have to take my word for it. If you're not careful you'll have poisonous spiders, cockroaches and all manner of ants and creepy crawlies taking over. You need to sweep at least once a day and keep the place spotless.'

'That's what servants are for,' Alice said wearily. 'I was just humouring you, madam. Now, thank you for your advice, but I'm sure you have things to do in your own shack.'

Essie put the packages she had been carrying on the deck. 'That was unkind,' she protested as Leah pushed past her and ran towards her home. 'That woman has a hard life and she was just trying to help.'

Freddie dumped the pots and pans, mops and scrubbing brushes in a heap, wiping his hands on the seat of his trousers. 'You'll have to mend your ways here, Alice. You can't treat these people as if they were your servants.'

'I should be doing that, my lady,' Sadie murmured shyly. 'It ain't your place to sweep floors.'

'No, it is not.' Alice tossed her head. 'It was Raven's idea, and he called that woman in to show me what to do. It was humiliating, to say the least, and then, to cap it all, he went off to do whatever it is that keeps him busy all day.'

'Do stop moaning, Alice,' Freddie said crossly. 'We've got to survive in this place, so he's right. You'll have to do your bit, and the sooner I learn how the mining business works the better, and then we can go home and start putting things to right at Starcross Abbey.'

Alice eyed him curiously. 'You've never shown any interest in that stately pile. Why now?'

'I've had five long years to think about it,' Freddie said simply. 'I wasn't just amusing myself daubing paint on canvas and romancing the local girls.'

Essie had had enough of their squabbles and she began sorting through their purchases. 'I think Leah is right. We have to work together or go under. I'll do my fair share and so will Sadie.' She met Alice's mutinous gaze with an unblinking stare. 'What about you?'

'I see that I'm outnumbered,' Alice said stiffly. 'All right, I'll do what I can, but don't expect too much of me. I've been waited on all my life and I don't know how to scrub a floor or wash clothes.'

'We'll teach you.' Essie waited a second or two, expecting to be cut down to size by a furious aristocrat, but Alice merely nodded.

'All right. I agree, but don't ask me to cook anything unless you want to risk being poisoned.'

Whether it was the threat of an invasion of poisonous spiders and other bugs that had constrained Alice to join them in keeping the hut clean and making it more comfortable, Essie did not know, but now they were equals, at least in theory. Alice Crozier, the earl's daughter, was making an effort, even if she slipped back into her old ways at times.

Freddie joined Raven at the diggings each morning and Essie learned to cook simple meals. She went to Leah for advice on how to make bread, setting the dough to rise overnight and baking it in the brick oven that Raven had constructed outside. In return she helped Leah on her vegetable patch, and created one of her own, aided by Sadie. Sometimes, when Leah seemed particularly tired, Essie took over, making her friend sit in the shade of a gum tree while she did the hard work.

One afternoon Sadie had accompanied Alice to Tandy's store and Essie was weeding between the rows of beans and onions. Leah had almost fainted while pegging out lines of washing and Essie had insisted that she went to lie down. Leah agreed, but only when Essie promised to finish what she had started. Essie was hard at work when a shadow fell across the warm soil. She looked up and found herself staring at a giant of a man.

'Where's Ma?'

Essie scrambled to her feet. She knew that Leah had three sons, named from the Bible. 'You must be Shem?'

He shook his head. 'Nah!'

'Ham?' she said, guessing again.

'Japheth. I'm the baby of the family.' He took her hand and shook it, pumping her arm up and down, his mouth stretched into a wide grin, revealing a row of stained and broken teeth.

'Japheth,' she repeated breathlessly. 'I'm Essie.'

'I know who you are. I seen you often.'

'Well, I haven't seen you, except maybe in the distance. I'm pleased to meet you, Japheth.'

'They call me Big Joe on account that I'm so large.' He released her hand to push his wide-brimmed hat to the back of his head. 'Why are you doing Ma's work?'

'She wasn't feeling too well, Joe. I think she does too much.'

He shook his head and his tow-coloured hair flopped over his brow. 'Ma's as strong as an ox. She's never tired.'

'You're wrong there. Why did you want her, anyway? Is there anything I can do?'

'I dunno. You're new here, and you're with the toff who's good with his fists. I seen him lay out three men, one after the other.'

Essie was suddenly seeing Raven in a new light. 'That's as maybe, Joe, but if there's anything I can do to help your ma, then I'd be pleased to help. She's been good to me since I arrived here.'

'That's Ma, all right. But it's not for her, it's Beasley, the creeping man, as they call him. She takes him bread and biscuits when she's done some baking. Pa built her an oven, just like at home in Sydney.'

'The creeping man.' Essie shuddered as she remembered the badly crippled person who had untangled her skirt from the thorny bush. 'His name is Beasley?'

'That's right. He got caught in a rock fall. Crippled his mind as well as his poor body. Ma is the only one who takes care of him.'

'Can't you do it for her sometimes?'

His brown eyes widened in horror and his wide mouth sagged open, as if she had said something shocking. 'Me? No, that's woman's work, miss. My brothers would think I had a screw loose if I was to do anything like that.' He put his hat straight and turned away. 'I'm going to find Ma and tell her that Beasley is sick and can't feed hisself.'

Essie hurried after him, sending a shower of grit off her skirts as she moved. 'No, don't do that, Joe. I'll take some food to Beasley. I know where he hides out.'

'He built hisself a humpy amongst the trees.'

'I know,' Essie said, nodding. 'I'll find him. You just let your ma rest and leave Beasley to me. I owe him a favour anyway.'

The hut was empty and it was easy for Essie to help herself to a small loaf and some cold salt pork that they had roasted for supper the previous evening. She wrapped the food in a clean cloth and set off to find Beasley, retracing her steps to where she thought they had met. The camp was bursting with noise and bustling with activity. The sound of sawing and the crash of trees falling to the ground was accompanied by the roar of the steam engine that powered the giant ore crushing machine. Essie had learned something of the process by listening to Freddie and Raven chatting after supper each evening. They were still finding small nuggets, although nothing like the large one that had made Raven's fortune. Nevertheless, it was profitable enough to continue and they talked of moving on to Bendigo. There was unrest amongst the miners due to the rise in the cost of mining licences. Tempers were reaching boiling point, and trouble was coming. Leah was also worried and had warned Essie to keep away from the tented community, but she put all this out of her mind as she went to find Beasley. The image of the poor man starving in his gunyah was too much to bear, and she was in a hurry to get to him before Alice and Sadie returned from Old Tandy's store.

She had reached the thicket of tall slender trees when she almost trod on something that moved with terrifying speed. She came to a petrified halt as the deadly brown snake raised its head, preparing to strike . . .

Chapter Eleven

Frozen to the spot and unable to move a muscle, Essie gazed into the cold eyes of the snake, convinced that she was about to die. Then, just as it was preparing to strike, a hand reached out to grab it by its tail. With surprising strength Beasley cracked the reptile like a whip and tossed the inert body into the scrub.

'Are you all right, missy?'

Essie leaned against the trunk of a gum tree, gasping for breath. The pungent scent of its bark would always remind her of the moment when she narrowly escaped death. 'I'm fine, Mr Beasley.' Even to her own ears her voice sounded thin and shaky.

He subsided onto the ground with a ragged groan and she hurried to his side.

'What can I do? How far is it to your hut?'

'Give me a minute.' He raised himself on his bony elbow, his eyes suddenly alert as he sniffed the air. 'What you got there? Do I smell meat?'

Essie sat down beside him and started to unwrap the parcel of food, but he grabbed a chunk of salt pork, biting into it like a ravenous hound. He demolished the piece, even though he appeared to have lost all his teeth, and he finished by stuffing the bread into his mouth.

'You were hungry.' Essie rose to her feet. 'What can I do to help you, sir?'

He cocked his head on one side, eyeing her with a twisted grin. 'No one's ever called me "sir". Are you in your right mind, missy?'

'My name is Esther, but everyone calls me Essie. What do your friends call you?'

'Beasley,' he muttered, wiping a stream of saliva from the corner of his mouth. 'I ain't got no other name. Born in the penal colony and left to run wild, I never knew what it was like to have a family.'

Essie stared at him, horrified by the casual way he spoke of his past. 'But your mother must have loved you.'

His hollow laughter echoed eerily through the stand of trees, disturbing a flock of colourful rainbow lorikeets. They flew up into the air shrieking and chattering as if complaining at the disturbance. 'I dunno. I don't really remember her.'

'Your father?' Essie asked tentatively, although she could guess at the answer.

'I don't think she knew, and if she did she kept it to herself. It don't matter now, anyway. She died of consumption when I was a nipper. I got no one and that's how I like it.'

Essie reached out to touch his hand but he snatched it away. 'I'm sorry.'

'You are, aren't you?' He peered at her beneath bushy grey eyebrows. 'Why should you care?'

'I wouldn't treat a dog like the people here have treated you,' Essie said angrily. 'Except for Leah, that is. She's a good woman and I know she's been bringing you food, but surely there are others who could at least see that you have proper shelter and something to eat?'

He shuffled backwards, moving on his belly. 'I don't need charity. I can look after meself.'

'You need a wash and some clean clothes.' Essie followed him as he slithered towards his makeshift home, and for the first time she saw his gunyah. It was made entirely from sheets of bark, which were laid over wooden props, creating a tent-like shelter.

He crawled inside. 'Ta for the food. Now go away. If they sees you here they'll throw stones at you as well as me. The fools think I'm cursed.' He collapsed onto the dirt floor, laying his head on his arm.

Essie could see that it was useless to argue and she walked away, but she had no intention of abandoning him. Beasley's story had touched her heart and had made her realise just how lucky she was. With good health and good friends nothing was impossible, and grumbling about the privations they suffered seemed futile and childish when compared to the life that the poor cripple was forced to endure.

She did not mention his plight to the others, but she owed her life to the creeping man and she was determined to do something to make his existence a little easier. There was only one person in whom she could confide and that was Leah. Early next morning she timed her trip to fetch water from the creek to coincide with Leah's. It was a cool, clear spring day and the scent of the gum trees filled the air, together with the fragrant smell of burning wattle and coffee.

'Are you feeling better today, Leah?' Essie asked, dipping her bucket into the creek.

'A bit, luv, although I get so tired these days.'

'You work too hard. Those boys of yours ought to do more for themselves.'

'Tell them that,' Leah said, wincing as she hefted the second bucket from the water. 'They're good boys, but they can't look after themselves. Goodness knows what would happen if I wasn't there to cook their meals and wash their clothes.'

'That's what I was going to talk to you about,' Essie said earnestly. 'I went to see Beasley yesterday. D'you know he saved my life – he killed a brown snake. Snapped its neck with a flick of his wrist. I've never seen anything like it.'

'You was lucky, dear. A bite from one of them brutes will kill you.'

'I know, and I'm truly grateful to him, but it's obvious that he isn't well. I gave him some food, but he's filthy and his clothes are in tatters. I want to do something for him.'

'He's a proud man, Essie. I take him grub when I can spare it, but he's used to me. He won't accept charity.'

'I know that, but perhaps if I gave him some old clothes of Raven's to wear while I wash and mend his tatters, maybe he'd allow that.'

Leah started off back in the direction of her hut. 'Good luck, that's all I can say.'

Essie said nothing. Her mind was set on helping Beasley, although she had seen grey faces like his in the back alleys of Limehouse and she had a feeling that time was running out for the creeping man. She took the water back to the hut and filled the kettle. Raven and Freddie were awake, demanding warm water for shaving, and she told them curtly that they would have to wait. Raven shrugged and went down to the creek to wash, but Freddie held back.

'What's the matter, Essie? You've been quiet since last evening.'

'I almost stepped on a brown snake yesterday afternoon.'

'You have to be more careful. Those things are extremely venomous.'

'I know, I wasn't thinking and it would have struck if Beasley hadn't intervened.'

'The creeping man?'

'Yes, the old man who helped me when my skirt got caught on a thorn. He killed the snake, but that's not what's worrying me. He's sick, Freddie, and in desperate need of clean clothes.'

Freddie gazed at her, frowning thoughtfully. 'I suppose you want me to give him some of mine.'

She smiled. 'That's the general idea. I didn't like to ask Raven, because I thought he'd tell me to leave well alone.'

'I dare say he would, but I'm not my brother. I know what it's like to have nothing.' He put his hand in his pocket and took out a few coins. 'Take this to Tandy's store and get what you think Beasley needs, and for heaven's sake keep a look out for snakes and spiders.'

She smiled and nodded, touched by his concern. 'I will, don't worry.'

'And don't stop to talk to anyone. The miners are up in arms and looking for trouble – you don't want to get involved.'

'Thanks, Freddie. You're a toff. I will be careful, I promise.' She glanced round to see Raven striding back from the creek. His hair was wet and drops of water glistened on his unshaven chin. His damp shirt clung to his broad chest and she was suddenly aware of the rippling musculature beneath the thin material. She turned away quickly and hurried into the hut.

Alice was just stirring but Sadie was still sound asleep, curled up in her bedroll. Alice swung her legs over the side of the bed, yawned and stretched. 'Another beastly day in this hellhole. My hands are ruined and I've caught the sun. I'll never be able to show my face in society again.'

Sometimes it was hard to be patient with Alice's self-obsession, but Essie knew that life in camp was hard for her and she made an effort to be patient. 'The tan will fade in time and when you return to your life of luxury your hands will heal.'

'It feels as though we'll be stuck here for ever,' Alice sighed. 'Falco promised to take me home. He gave me his word.'

'Then I'm sure he'll turn up, or maybe Raven will take us back to Geelong when he's satisfied that there's nothing left to find in his diggings.' Essie picked up the sack of oats. 'By the way, I have an errand to run after breakfast. Will you be all right here with Sadie?'

'Where are you going?'

'I have a debt to pay. Don't worry about me.'

'I worry that if anything happens to you, I'll be left to do your work as well as my own,' Alice said with a hint of a smile. She stood up and stretched. 'My friends in London would be dumbfounded if they could see me now.'

'I'm sure they would be impressed.' Essie picked up the sack of oatmeal and took it outside to measure scoopfuls into the big, soot-blackened saucepan.

Later that day she made the excuse of going to Tandy's to purchase some lamp oil. The store was quiet in the early afternoon, when the women in camp were busy with their endless round of chores while the men were at work. Essie had time to look through the rack of work clothes and found a flannel shirt and a pair of loose-fitting canvas trousers. They looked about the right size, but the fit was immaterial considering the physical deformity of the wearer, and she spent the rest of the money on bread, cheese and a bottle of rum to ease the creeping man's pain. She paid Tandy, wondering if he ever smiled or had a good word to say to anyone, but obviously it was not her turn to benefit from any sociable instincts he might possess and she left the shop feeling almost sorry for him. To live in such a joyless state must be an unhappy existence. She set off to find Beasley, but he was not in his gunyah, and although she called his name there was no response. She decided to leave the food and drink in his shelter, wrapped in what passed for a bedroll. There was little else she could do, and if he had had the strength to go foraging for food it must be a good sign. She made her way back to the hut but her feeling of relief was short-lived. Sadie met her with an anxious look on her small features.

'Leah is taken poorly again, Essie. Big Joe come to tell you, but you wasn't here.'

'Really!' Alice said, throwing down the sweeping brush. 'Are you the only person here who can help these people? What did they do before you arrived in camp, Esther?'

Ignoring Alice's petulant outburst, Essie hurried over to the Halfpennys' shack where she found Leah prostrate on the bed.

'She come over faint again,' Joe said anxiously. 'It was lucky I was the last to leave for the mine, but I got to go now or Pa will fetch me a clout that'll knock me into next week.'

'You go,' Essie said firmly. 'I'll take care of her.' She spoke with more confidence than she was feeling. It was obvious that Leah was in need of proper medical attention as her breathing was shallow and her face a colourless mask. Essie waited until Joe was out of earshot and she knelt by the bed.

'How are you feeling, Leah?'

'Not so good, luv. Me old ticker is racing like the favourite at the Derby.'

'Is there a doctor in the camp?'

'There's Ebenezer Pardon, but he served time for killing a patient. He's a ticket-of-leave man.'

'What does that mean?'

'He's free to work and earn his living but he can't return to England, and if he gets into trouble he goes back to the penal colony.'

'Where am I likely to find him?'

Leah closed her eyes. 'Ask Joe. He'll take you to him.'

Essie caught up with Joe, although she had to make her way through the diggings to the mine shaft where the huge crushing machine was thundering away, making conversation almost impossible. By means of sign language she managed to get him to a place where she could make herself heard.

'Your ma needs a doctor, and she said you might know where to find one.'

He shook his shaggy head. 'I dunno, Essie. Pa don't hold with Ebenezer Pardon. Says he's a quack.'

'Your ma is very sick, Joe. I can patch up cuts and help to bring down a fever, but I can't help her. She needs a doctor and if that man knows anything at all about medicine he's our best bet. Take me to him, please.'

'What's going on?' Shem, the eldest Halfpenny son, strode towards them, glowering at his brother. 'Get back to work.'

'Ma's sick again,' Joe said warily. 'Essie's come to ask for help.'

Shem towered over Essie, his brows meeting over the bridge of his hawk-like nose. 'We can take care of our own. Mind your own business, girl.'

'That ain't polite,' Joe protested angrily. 'Ma thinks the world of Essie.'

'And I think the world of her,' Essie said defiantly. 'She needs to see a doctor, Shem, and as far as I can tell there's only one in the camp.'

'I ain't giving Ma into the charge of a murderer. All she needs is rest, and we'll see that she gets it.'

'What's going on? Why have you two stopped work?' Ham, the middle son walked up to them, eyeing Essie speculatively. 'What's she doing here?'

By this time Essie had had enough of the Halfpenny brothers. She faced them, arms akimbo. 'Now you listen to me, you lazy lumps. Your ma is killing herself trying to look after you and you're all big enough and ugly enough to take care of yourselves.'

There was a stunned silence as all three gazed down at her in amazement.

'You may well look ashamed,' Essie continued. 'Your ma is a sick woman and she needs proper medical attention. I'm going to find Ebenezer Pardon with or without your help, but you all need to start taking care of your ma or the next thing you know you'll be burying her. Do you understand what I'm saying?'

All three bowed their heads like naughty school-boys. Shem was the first to recover and he nodded.

'Maybe you're right. But she's a stubborn woman. She won't let us help her.'

'We could try harder,' Joe said cautiously. 'I could fetch water.'

'Is she really bad?' Ham asked, his bottom lip trembling. 'She ain't going to die, is she?'

'Only a doctor can tell you that. We're wasting time, so do you know this man? If so where is he?'

'You boys get back to work.' Shem reached out to take Essie by the hand. 'I'll take the girl to find Pardon. He'd better make Ma better or he'll be sorry.' He led Essie away from the din of the crusher, and she had to run in order to keep up with his long strides.

Ebenezer Pardon was very drunk. He was unshaven and reeked of rum and stale tobacco. Shem had to hold his head under water in an attempt to sober him up, but eventually they managed to make him understand his mission. One look at Shem's set jaw was enough to convince Ebenezer to make a house call, but once outside his tent he tried to make a run for it, moving in a curious crab-like manner. Shem caught up with him in two long strides, seized him by the collar and the seat of his pants, and frog-marched him through the camp to the amusement of the onlookers, letting go only when Ebenezer promised to do as he was told.

Shem accompanied them all the way home. 'Right

then, you,' he growled, leaning close to Ebenezer. 'Look after my ma or you'll regret the day you was born. Understand?'

Ebenezer nodded, rolling his eyes like a scared cur. 'Yes, mate.'

'I ain't going in,' Shem said in a low voice. 'She'll know there's something wrong if she sees me here at this time of day.'

Essie patted him on the arm. 'Don't worry. I'm sure the doctor can prescribe something that will help, and if you all do your bit to take some of the work off her shoulders, she'll be fine.'

Shem nodded mutely and strode off in the direction of the diggings.

Essie went in first to prepare Leah for the doctor's visit. 'There's someone to see you,' she said gently. 'Dr Pardon is going to take a look at you, Leah.'

Ebenezer moved swiftly to Leah's bedside. 'Good day to you, madam. And how are you today?'

Leah pulled the sheet up to her chin. 'I don't need the likes of you to tell me that me ticker is old and tired.'

'Now, now, madam. You're not a medical person so you cannot possibly know what's wrong with you. Allow me, if you will.' He prised the material from her tightly clenched fingers and began his examination.

Essie stood back, saying nothing, but her heart

was racing. She had grown fond of Leah and the plucky little woman did not deserve to suffer.

After what felt like a lifetime, Ebenezer pulled up the sheet and tucked Leah in. 'There now, madam, that wasn't too bad, was it?'

Leah gazed up at him, her eyes round and wide with fear. 'Am I dying, doctor?'

'Yes, madam, but not for a good while, I hope. Your heart beats as strongly as that of a ten-year-old, but you are plainly undernourished and exhausted. You must eat better, and stop feeding your menfolk like turkey cocks. They can look after themselves and it's high time they started looking after you. I'll tell this to your husband and leave it to him to bring your sons into line.'

'My boys are good boys,' Leah said faintly.

'Said like a true mother.' Ebenezer rose from the edge of the bed where he had perched and picked up his felt hat, ramming it on his head. 'I'll make you up a tonic and give it to that big brute, Shem. Take a teaspoonful three times a day and try to improve your diet. I see hens scratching around outside so a lightly boiled egg and a glass of goat's milk will work wonders, and share the chores around.'

'Thank you, Doctor,' Leah said sleepily. 'I feel better already.'

Ebenezer surged out onto the veranda, taking deep breaths. 'I don't suppose you have anything to drink, do you?'

'I can make you a cup of tea,' Essie said, deliberately misunderstanding him. 'Or the water in the creek is cool and clean.'

'Thank you, no. I think I'll decline your kind offer.' He stepped off the veranda, doffing his hat. 'Good day, miss.'

Essie hurried after him as he walked off. 'Is what you said true? She's just tired and needs rest and good food?'

'As far as I can tell, yes. I've seen these women worn to the bone by child-bearing and hard work. Their menfolk either don't see what they're doing, or they don't care. It's a brutal existence out here, especially for the female of the species.' He came to a sudden halt, looking down at her. 'Take my advice and get away, miss. Go back to wherever you came from before it's too late.'

'It's not that easy.'

He shook his head. 'It never is, but you'll end up like her if you remain here and get tied up with one of the fossickers. You'll be old before your time.'

'Thank you for your advice, but I don't intend to stay here any longer than I have to.'

He was about to move on but she barred his way.

'Do you know Beasley? The creeping man, as they call him.'

'Everyone knows about the wretched creature. Has he been bothering you?'

'No, certainly not. In fact he saved my life by killing a snake with his bare hands.'

'The men think he's cursed by an evil spirit. Poor superstitious fools.' He gave her a searching look. 'If you're going to ask me to treat him – forget it. There's nothing I can do and I doubt if he'd welcome my intrusion anyway. Now move out of the way, please, young lady. I have a bottle of rum that urgently needs my attention.' He staggered away, swaying from side to side as if on the deck of a ship in a stormy sea.

Essie shook her head. She was relieved to think that Leah's condition was not serious, and she could only hope that her conversation with the Halfpenny brothers would make a difference. As to their father, she had heard him shouting and swearing, coming home at night the worse for drink, and she suspected that his sons were secretly scared of him, as was Leah. Life in the mining camp was hard.

Essie made her way back to the hut to find Sadie on her hands and knees, scrubbing the floor while Alice was on the veranda, struggling with the wooden dolly, twisting and twirling it in the washtub as she attempted to beat the dirt out of the clothes. The smell of lye soap and sweat wafted skywards in a damp cloud.

'Where have you been?' Alice demanded, wiping the sweat from her forehead on the back of her hand.

'I had to get the doctor for Leah. She's not at all well.'

'Not the man who killed his wife?' Alice stared at her in horror.

'You shouldn't listen to gossip,' Essie said severely. 'We don't know the full story.'

'D'you mean to say you brought that man here? We might all be murdered in our beds.'

'Nonsense. He's just a pathetic drunk, but he was good with Leah, and even if he was wrong about her condition, he made her feel better.'

'Just keep him away from me, that's all.' Alice abandoned her task. 'Some of this is your washing, Essie. I'd be grateful if you would take over, and that's an order.' Alice spoke severely, but there was a twinkle in her eyes.

Essie smiled and pushed her out of the way. 'If only your friends could see you now, Lady Alice Crozier. They wouldn't believe their eyes.'

Alice dried her hands on her apron. 'No, I don't suppose they would. I'd like to see them put in our position. I doubt if many of them would survive.'

Sadie emerged from the hut carrying a bucket filled with dirty water. She emptied it on the ground and it pooled in the dust. 'It feels like rain,' she said, sniffing the air. 'Your washing won't dry.'

'Let's hope the rain keeps off until it is.' Alice picked up the wicker basket filled with wet clothes and went to peg them out on the line that Freddie had put up for them.

'What you said is true.' Sadie watched her with a wide grin on her pert face. 'Who would have thought that Lady Alice would turn out to be one of us?'

'Who indeed?' Essie plunged her hands into the rapidly cooling water. 'I'll just rinse these through. What have we got to cook for supper this evening?'

'Big Joe brought round two dead possums. He'd skinned them ready for the pot. Said it was to thank you for what you're doing for his ma.'

'That was good of him. So it won't be poverty stew tonight then. We'll eat well.'

Later that day, when the stew was simmering on the fire, Essie took a bowlful to Leah and sat with her while she ate, but when she had supped the last drop Leah made to get up.

Essie laid a hand on her shoulder. 'What d'you think you're doing?'

'I feel better now, Essie. I have to get the fire going and start making supper for my men.'

'No, you don't. You'll stay in bed for the rest of the day, and let them look after you.'

'But I can't . . .'

'Yes, you can. I'll see to the fire and I'll fetch some vegetables from your patch to make some soup.'

'I can't put you to all that trouble, Essie.'

'You'd do the same for me, I'm sure. And after that your boys can take over some of the chores. I think you'll find they're more than willing to help.'

Leah relaxed a little, but her fingers plucked nervously at the thin counterpane. 'They've never had to do anything for themselves.'

'Then it's about time they started pulling their weight.' Essie patted her hand. 'Try to sleep and stop worrying. You heard what the doctor said – you have to rest.' She left Leah in bed and set about lighting the fire.

For the next few days Essie made sure that Leah rested, although it was impossible to keep her confined to her bed. She rose late, her only concession to taking things easy, but she found there was less to do, thanks to a sudden burst of co-operation from her sons. Leah said it was a miracle, but Essie knew better and she was satisfied that her dire warning had hit home. Noah Halfpenny carried on as usual, spending all day in the mine and most evenings drinking with his workmates.

Raven and Freddie worked their diggings every day, returning with tiny nuggets and paper pokes filled with gold dust they had panned from the creek.

Raven was satisfied with their finds, but Freddie was despondent. 'I'd hoped to strike it rich like you did, brother,' he said one evening after supper when they were all seated on the veranda enjoying the sunset. 'As it is I'll be living off your charity for the rest of my life.'

'Nonsense.' Raven sat back in one of the chairs he had constructed from roughly hewn timber, a mug of coffee in his hand. 'What's mine is ours, Freddie. You know that. Even if I don't strike it rich again I've left enough money in Coutts Bank to keep us in comfort for the foreseeable future.'

'It's all very well for you two,' Alice said crossly. 'But what about us? We're waiting on you hand and foot, living in a shack no bigger than the potting shed at Starcross, and we have no control over our lives whatsoever. I don't call that fair.'

'You're one of the wealthiest women in England, Alice. You don't need gold dust to make you happy.'

'No, but I want to go home, and so do the girls.' Alice waved her hands to include Essie and Sadie. 'What do they get out of this? Sadie will return to working in the kitchen and Essie will be at her father's beck and call.'

'That doesn't seem right,' Freddie said thoughtfully. 'I'll marry you, Essie, and take you away from life on the river.'

'Will you adopt me as your nipper?' Sadie asked, grinning. 'I wouldn't mind living in a castle.'

'Who knows?' Freddie drained the last drop of coffee and stood up. 'I'm going for a walk. Are you coming, Raven?'

'Yes, I need to stretch my legs.' Raven rose to his feet and the brothers walked off towards the heart of the camp.

'I can guess where they've gone,' Alice said, sighing. 'They'll be downing pints of ale with the rest of the men in the grog shop, leaving us to kick our heels here. They really do have the best of things.'

'I'll take the mugs down to the creek and wash them.' Essie gathered them up and strolled down to the creek. The sun had plummeted below the horizon, leaving purple bruises and streaks of crimson slashed across the azure sky, and the last of its rays glinted like molten gold on the rippled surface of the water.

Essie rinsed the mugs and was about to return to the hut when her attention was caught by something shining in the pebbles. At first she thought it was a trick of the light, but as she plunged her hand into the cool water her fingers closed over the walnut-sized lump of metal. Even as she plucked it from the creek bed she knew that her luck had changed, and the weight of the nugget convinced her that this was gold. She scrambled to her feet and raced back to the hut, forgetting the mugs in her haste. 'Alice, Sadie. Look what I found.'

Ignoring the bites from a myriad of sandflies, Alice and Sadie hurried down to the creek, hitching up their skirts and wading into the water as they turned over stones, hoping for similar finds, but darkness fell and they were forced to give up. They returned to the hut and Essie made cocoa, having remembered at last to retrieve the mugs. They sat on the veranda, sipping their hot drinks to the background sounds of cicadas and the scuffling of nocturnal creatures.

The daytime noise from the mine and diggings had ceased, but there was a constant drone of voices, sometimes raised in anger and the occasional burst of laughter. The odd shot rang out, but they had grown accustomed to hearing these as miners fired their weapons to warn off would-be marauders. On such a beautiful night it was easy to forget the danger that went hand in hand with gold fever, but as night enveloped them in a velvet cloak of darkness the animal kingdom took over.

'I'm going to bed,' Alice said, yawning. 'I've had enough excitement for one day, but your find has made me think, Essie. Tomorrow morning I'm going to have words with Raven. I want him to take us back to Geelong, and if Falco isn't there we'll book our passage home on any ship bound for England. What do you girls say?'

Chapter Twelve

For once Raven was in agreement with his cousin. 'The Diggers' Rights Society is growing in numbers,' he said, frowning. 'Things are going to turn nasty and I'd be happier if you were in Geelong. Falco should be returning soon, and he'll take you back to England.'

'I really don't know why we had to come here in the first place.' Alice tossed her head. 'You put us through this, Raven. I think you did it on purpose to amuse yourself.'

'That's not fair,' Freddie protested. 'What else was he supposed to do? Anyway, you've had an experience you can dine out on for years to come. You'll be invited to all manner of events just so that people can hear about your time in the goldfields. You'll be a celebrity, Alice.'

'Yes, I dare say I will,' Alice conceded. 'But what about you, Freddie? Why don't you come home? Gilfoyle should have the appeal well in hand by now. You might even have a pardon. That goes for you, too, Raven.'

Raven shook his head. 'I dare not risk it again. I've less than two years before I'm a free man.'

Freddie hesitated. 'Then I'll stay here, too. I've got off easily compared to you, Raven, and I was the one at fault. I should have gone to prison or been transported, not you.'

Essie left them to talk it over. This was something the family had to decide and it was none of her business, but to her surprise the thought of returning home was not as pleasing as she might have anticipated. For all his faults, she missed her father, but life in Limehouse was just as hard, if not harder, than living here in Ballarat.

She went into the hut and wrapped some bread, cheese and slices of meat in a cloth, which she intended to take to Beasley. If he had been grateful for the new clothes he kept his opinion to himself, but she had caught glimpses of him wearing them when she went to take him extra food.

Essie put on her cotton sun bonnet and went to find her basket. It was her turn to go to Tandy's store for eggs, milk and bread. An enterprising baker, who was a ticket-of-leave man, had built an oven and had set up in business. His bread was not perfect but it was more palatable than damper, and it was the last couple of slices from yesterday's loaf that she was taking to Beasley. She set off, heading for his gunyah, taking care where she trod. The episode with the snake had made her even more aware of the wildlife she might encounter. She did not know the names of half the creatures that abounded in this wild land, but she had seen all manner of insects and lizards. She was familiar with possums and walla- bies and the mobs of kangaroos she had seen moving at incredible speed across the open plain, but they usually kept their distance from the noisy campsite. It was the plagues of flies that made life most uncom- fortable, and biting insects created more problems than snakes. Essie knew she would have some regrets on leaving Australia but she would not miss the creatures that aggravated both man and beast.

She reached Beasley's hideaway in record time. 'Beasley, are you there? It's Essie. I've brought you some bread and cheese, and a couple of slices of mutton.' She waited for a few seconds, giving him time to wake up if he should be taking a nap. 'Beasley, it's Essie.'

A movement inside the gunyah confirmed his pres- ence and she lifted the bark flap, peering inside. The sight that met her eyes made her take a step back- wards. He was lying curled up with his head resting on his arm, but it was the wound on his head and his bloodstained face that made her cry out in horror.

'What happened?' she gasped. 'What have they done to you?'

'They was looking for me gold.' The words came out in a hoarse croak, and she could see that his lips were cracked and bleeding.

She had brought water in a leather canteen and she held it to his lips. He drank thirstily. 'I'm done for, Essie.' His breathing was ragged and his eyes dull and cloudy.

'No, you're not.' She stroked his bald head, trying not to recoil at the sticky feel of the blood that oozed from a long gash. It could only have been caused by a blow from a machete such as the miners used to clear the scrub. 'I'll fetch Dr Pardon.'

'No use. Too late, I'm going to me Maker, girl.'

'Don't say that. You'll feel better if I clean you up and get some salve for your wound. Perhaps you could eat something.'

'I'm dying, Essie.' With a huge effort he moved his cramped limbs, reaching for something tucked underneath his belly. 'This is yours. Take it and go home to England, girl. Don't stay here.' He produced a small bundle wrapped in a piece of filthy cloth.

'What is it?' Essie eyed it warily.

'It's what they was looking for, girl. I want you to have it. Take it and get away from this godforsaken place.' Exhausted and gasping for breath, he fell back onto the earth floor.

Essie peeled off the material and was almost

blinded by the glare of the fist-size nugget. 'It's gold. It must be worth a fortune, Beasley. I can't take this.'

'Yes,' he whispered. 'It's yours. You deserve it.' He closed his eyes and was suddenly still.

Essie shook him, panic-stricken. 'Beasley, say something. Speak to me.' She leaned over and kissed his rapidly cooling cheek. 'I'm so sorry you had to suffer like this. Don't die, Beasley.' She put her arms around his crippled body and held him.

'It's no use, Essie. He's gone.'

The sound of Raven's voice made her look up. 'They murdered him for his gold,' she said on a sob. 'They attacked him and left him to die like a wild animal.'

He helped her to her feet and wrapped his arms around her, stroking her hair, as if he were comforting an unhappy child. 'That's how it is here,' he said softly. 'The goldfield is a brutal place and I was at fault bringing you here.'

She drew away. The temptation to lay her head on his shoulder and allow him to comfort her was overwhelming, but self-preservation made her retreat, salvaging a little of the dignity she had almost completely lost. 'He wanted me to have this, but it seems too much.' She bent down and retrieve the gold nugget, thrusting it into Raven's hands.

He stared at it, shaking his head in wonder. 'You know, this is worth a small fortune.'

'That's why I can't keep it. He must have someone somewhere who needs it more than I do.'

'He was a loner, Essie. Men like Beasley are always on their own. You showed him compassion and he wanted you to have his treasure, so take it. Go home and build a new life for yourself. It's what he would want you to do.'

'He died because of that lump of metal,' Essie said, shuddering. 'It's tainted.'

'He was dying anyway. He knew he hadn't got long to live but he obviously intended that you would be his beneficiary. As to the gold being tainted, that's superstitious nonsense.' He thrust it back at her. 'Take it and put it to good use, as he would have wished. You owe him that at least. Falco should return shortly and Alice is desperate to go home. Return to London, Essie, and live like a lady.'

'It seems that I have no choice, but how will you manage on your own?'

'The same way I've coped with what life has thrown at me for the last five years,' he said with a wry smile. 'Not that I haven't appreciated the comfort of having my meals cooked for me and clean clothes, as well as female company, but I'll manage.'

She tucked the heavy nugget beneath the food in her basket, but the knowledge that Beasley had died hungry and unloved still haunted her, bringing fresh tears to her eyes. She turned away so that Raven would not see how much the death of a relative stranger had upset her. 'I have to go to the store,' she said hastily.

'Are you mad? You can't walk round with that lump of gold in your basket.' He took her by the shoulders and started her back on the path toward their hut. 'Hide it with the nugget you found yesterday. You can't trust anyone when such a large fortune is at stake, even those close to you.'

'Are you talking about yourself?'

'I might have been, before I struck it rich. I want you to profit from this venture, Essie. You were dragged into it by my headstrong cousin, and you've borne it all bravely and without complaint, which is more than I can say for Alice and Freddie.'

She turned to look him in the eye. He seemed to have been part of her life for ever, and it was hard to believe that she had known him only a few short months, but the feeling that this was the beginning of the end engulfed her like a London particular. She would return home and never see him again.

'I didn't choose to come here, it's true,' she said slowly, 'but I wouldn't have missed a moment of it – not the sea voyages, nor the difficulties we met on the way. I've had the time of my life and I'll never forget any of it.' The desire to cry was almost too much to bear, but she thrust her hand into the basket and lifted out the heavy nugget. 'Perhaps you'd hide this for me. I have to go to the store to get the things we need or the others will want to know why I came back empty-handed.'

'You trust me with this?'

'I've trusted you with my life so far. What's a lump of yellow metal compared to that?' She walked away, knowing that he was standing very still, staring after her. She could feel his presence whenever he was near – it was a sixth sense she had developed without even realising it was happening. And now it was all coming to an end. The great adventure for a girl from Limehouse would soon be over and she would have to return to the river and her loved ones. But the truth was that the people she truly loved were here, in Ballarat. If Sadie was like a little sister then Alice was an older cousin; spiky and difficult but beautiful and charming, and good company when she was not in one of her moods. Then there was Freddie – she loved Freddie, but not in a romantic way. He was like a second brother – he could never replace George in her heart, but she felt close to Freddie, for all his faults, or maybe because of them. Then there was Raven – handsome, clever, unpredictable and strong. It was only now, with the threat of being parted looming ever closer, that she realised how much he had come to mean to her. Even with her newfound wealth they were still worlds apart, and soon there would be many thousands of miles separating them. Her steps were heavy and her heart ever heavier. She was in mourning for the poor, tortured creeping man, and for the hopes and dreams she was about to leave behind in Australia.

It seemed that once Raven had made up his mind there was no stopping him. That evening after supper he announced that they would be leaving for Geelong first thing in the morning. There was no argument, and no questioning his decision. Freddie was to remain in camp to make sure that squatters did not move into the hut, and all that was left to do was to pack their few belongings and be ready to set off at dawn.

Essie slipped away, leaving Alice and Sadie in a frenzy of excitement at the thought of going home. She knew she ought to feel the same, but it was difficult to be enthusiastic about parting from people she cared for deeply, and Leah was one of them. She found her on her own, seated in the rocking chair that Joe had made especially for her. There was no sign of Noah or his sons, but that was to Essie's advantage.

'You've come to say goodbye,' Leah said calmly.

Essie sank down on the stoop, dangling her legs over the edge of the wooden platform. 'How did you know that?'

'You was never going to stay long, Essie. And with all the goings-on here, it's probably best that you go now. Nothing has been the same since the murder at the Eureka Hotel and the riots that followed. Goodness knows how it's going to end. Noah and the boys bolted their meal in order to get to a meeting this evening, and I'm afraid they're going to get drawn into the troubles.'

'Will you be all right, Leah? You could come with us.'

Leah shook her head. 'Ta, love, but my place is here with my family. I wouldn't leave them even if I could, but you got to go, for your own sake.'

'I don't like to leave you.'

'I'll be fine. The boys seem to realise that I need a bit of help now and again. They've been very good since I was took sick, especially Joe.'

Essie reached out to hold Leah's hand. 'You deserve to be treated well, Leah. I don't know how I would have managed here without your help.'

'It's been a pleasure, love. If I'd been blessed with a daughter I'd have wanted her to be just like you.'

Essie gulped and swallowed. Tears were only a blink away since Beasley's death, but with an effort she managed a smile. 'Thank you. That means a lot to me.'

'And don't fret about the creeping man. He's gone to a better place than this.'

'You know about poor Beasley?'

'It's all round the camp, Essie. They caught the men who attacked him. There's a sort of rough justice amongst the miners – they're not all brutes and bad men.'

Essie raised herself and leaned over to kiss Leah's leathery cheek. 'I'll try to remember only the good things when I get home, but I will miss you.'

'And I'll miss you, too.' Leah squeezed Essie's fingers with an encouragingly strong grip. 'Get along with you now, or you'll have me crying me eyes out. Take care of yourself, Essie, and have a good life back in England.'

Parting from Freddie next day was just as painful, if not more so. Essie's cheeks were wet with tears as she rode away with all her worldly goods, including the gold nuggets, wrapped in her bedroll. Raven rode on ahead with Alice close behind and Essie and Sadie bringing up the rear. It was the middle of spring and the temperature was rising steadily, but it was not yet hot enough to make the journey uncomfortable. They camped at night, as they had done when they travelled to Ballarat, and Essie was surprised to find how quickly the time passed compared to their outward journey. Then they had been travelling into the unknown, but now they were returning to what had become familiar. The prospect of many weeks at sea being tossed about in the confines of Falco's screw steamer was not exciting, but at least she did not suffer from seasickness, unlike Alice, who was openly dreading the voyage. Sadie seemed to have forgotten that she too had suffered on the outward voyage, and she was looking forward to seeing London again, although she admitted to being nervous about returning to her old way of life.

They were waiting on the jetty for the lighter to arrive and take them out to the *Santa Gabriella* at her moorings. Alice had changed into the gown that Essie had made for her on board ship, and had insisted on wearing her one and only straw bonnet. 'I am not boarding the ship looking like a drudge from the mining camp.'

There had been no point arguing, although Essie and Sadie still wore their simple cotton frocks and sun bonnets, but Alice was rapidly becoming Lady Alice, and Essie was afraid that, once aboard ship, they would slip back into the old ways.

'I don't know how I'll get on in the big house,' Sadie whispered. 'Her ladyship will forget how we've been in camp when we was all equals, but the servants in London will want to know everything. They won't half tease me.'

Essie gave Sadie's small hand a squeeze. 'I wouldn't worry about that just now, but I think we're all going to find it difficult to fit in again. I know I'm not the same person I was when we left London. Being here has changed me for ever.'

'You won't abandon me, will you, Essie?' Sadie gazed at her with anxious eyes.

'Never. We're sisters, aren't we? I won't allow anyone to bully you.'

'Do stop nattering, you two,' Alice said crossly. 'And don't raise the child's hopes, Essie. Life will go on as it did before when we reach London. It will be hard for all of us, even me.'

Raven raised his hand, beckoning to the lighterman who was bringing his craft towards the jetty. 'I see that Falco himself has come to greet you, Alice. That's good; it saves me from an added journey. I need to speak to him before you set sail.'

Alice turned to him with a bright smile. 'I'm not going to thank you for arranging our passage home, because we should never have been here in the first place, but I will miss you, Raven. And as soon as I get back to London I'll contact Gilfoyle to find out how things are going with the appeal. I hope to have good news for you before too long.'

Raven leaned over to plant a kiss on her cheek. 'I fully expect to work out my sentence, Alice. It's Freddie who concerns me. He's been in exile long enough for what was a youthful folly.'

'A mistake that is costing you seven years of your life, cousin.' Alice shielded her eyes against the sun, looking down at the sparkling water and the approaching lighter. 'I wish you and Freddie could come with us.'

'As do I, but it's not to be, and, you never know, we might strike gold again.' He turned away to greet

Falco, who had just climbed onto the jetty. They embraced like old friends and were soon deep in conversation.

'Why do men treat us like children?' Alice said crossly. 'I'm sure we have just as much intellect as they do, and yet we aren't allowed to participate in matters that concern us.'

'Maybe it's not about you or me.' Essie brushed the hair from her eyes as the wind freshened and tugged playfully at her bonnet strings. 'It's probably about money.'

'Raven is paying for our passage home whether he likes it or not.' Alice glared at him, but if he was aware of her mood he took no notice and continued his conversation with Falco. She stamped her foot. 'Raven, we're getting cold standing here. It's time we went on board.'

Falco came towards them, with an apologetic smile. 'It thrills my heart to see you again, most beautiful lady.'

Essie was amused to see Alice's expression change. She held out her hand to Falco, smiling and blushing. 'It seems that we will be together for the next few weeks, Captain.'

'An honour, my lady.' Falco bowed over her hand, raising it to his lips.

'I know I can trust you with my ladies,' Raven said casually. 'Take good care of them, Falco, and I'll see you when you return.'

'I will guard them with my life.' Falco struck a dramatic pose.

At any other time Essie would have found his antics funny, but her gaze was fixed on Raven. He glanced at her and then turned away to embrace Alice. 'I'll see you in two years' time, my dear. Look after Starcross Abbey for me.'

'I will, don't worry.' Alice laid her hand on Falco's arm. 'Goodbye, Raven.'

Essie held her breath, waiting for him to acknowledge her. The least he could do would be to wish her a safe journey, but Raven turned on his heel and strode back along the jetty. It was not the happiest of partings and her spirits felt heavier than the gold nuggets she had carried all the way from Ballarat. She was a wealthy woman, but as she climbed down the ladder and was helped into the lighter, she knew that she had lost something that she might never get back. She was going home, but she had left a small sliver of her heart in Australia.

That evening, they were seated around the small table in the saloon after supper, which was better than Essie had expected, when Falco produced his mandolin and began to sing. In the past Essie had thought his sudden bursts of song were amusing rather than touching, but there was something sad and yet beautiful in the melody. Even though he sang in his native language, the emotion in his voice transcended the need for words. Essie was deeply moved and Sadie sat with her elbow on the table and her chin cupped in her hands, eyes closed as she swayed in time to the music. But Alice sipped her coffee, apparently devoid of emotion, and when the song ended she patted Falco on the shoulder.

'That was very nice, Captain. Now could we have something a little livelier? I think we could do with cheering up.'

Falco leaned towards her, his brow puckered in a frown. 'You are sad, my lady?'

She shook her head. 'Not really, but I've just left my cousins to fend for themselves. I don't know how they'll get along without me to look after them.'

Essie and Sadie exchanged meaningful glances. Alice had exerted herself very little during their stay in Ballarat, although she had made an attempt to wash her own clothes and had occasionally picked up the broom to sweep the floor. For someone brought up to a life of ease and luxury this was a huge concession, and Essie had a sneaking admiration for her.

As if sensing their amused reactions, Alice turned on them, frowning. 'Isn't it time you were in your bunk, Sadie?'

Essie rose to her feet. 'I think I'll turn in, too. It's been a long day and I'm tired.'

'Good night,' Sadie said meekly as she followed

Essie from the saloon. Out of earshot she subsided
into giggles. 'I think the captain loves Lady Alice.'

'It's going to be an interesting trip,' Essie said,
trying not to laugh. 'I think Alice likes him, too.
Although she'd never admit to such a weakness. She
likes to be independent.'

'She can afford such a luxury.' Sadie pursed her
lips, scowling. 'It don't seem fair that some have lots
of money and others have none.'

Essie thought of the gold nugget that Beasley had
given his life to protect. If they arrived home in one
piece she would make certain that the money it
raised was put to good use. 'Come along, Sadie.
Let's get settled for the night. You can have the
bunk, but tomorrow it will be my turn.'

The *Santa Gabriella* took the Great Circle route that
was followed by the clipper ships, crossing the Pacific
and rounding Cape Horn, in order to take advantage
of the prevailing winds. Falco explained this in great
detail although Alice was only interested in how
quickly they would reach home.

The next few weeks were uneventful and the
weather reasonably good. There were squalls and
high winds, but the Pacific Ocean was relatively
calm. They developed a daily routine that involved
going to great lengths to preserve personal hygiene.
Fresh water was strictly rationed and washing in
sea water did nothing for the skin and hair. Clothes

came out clean but stiff with salt and scratchy on the skin, but anything was better than being dirty. Essie's experience of fleas and lice was enough to make her grateful for simple cleanliness. Falco did his best to keep his passengers entertained, although Essie knew that his efforts were mainly directed at Alice, who seemed impervious to his charms, although she was not above flirting with him when the mood took her. The crew were mostly the same as on the outward voyage, with the exception of Hooper, who had married his sweetheart and set up home in Sydney. Without him to act as interpreter it was difficult to make herself understood, but Essie set about learning as much Italian as she could, and by the time they rounded Cape Horn she was able to converse in simple sentences. Falco encouraged her in this, but his attempts to teach Alice were met with a marked lack of interest.

Christmas was spent at sea and they exchanged small gifts. Alice gave Sadie and Essie a bar of scented soap each, which was a huge sacrifice as these were the last of the store that Essie had purchased in Gibraltar. Essie had made hankies from scraps of material left from her dressmaking efforts, which Falco had stowed in a locker and apparently forgotten. She made one for Falco, too, but he decided to wear it as a bandana and sang them a comic song with it tied around his head, pirate fashion. His gift to Alice was a pearl necklace, which he had apparently bought during one of his trips to the South Seas, although Essie suspected that he had gone to great lengths to purchase it with Lady Alice in mind. His gift for Essie was a single pearl, shaped like a teardrop, and he gave Sadie several bars of white sweetmeat scented with orange and honey, and studded with almonds, which he said was an Italian favourite called Torrone. At dinner that evening the cook produced a dish of pasta in a spicy sauce, sprinkled with parmesan cheese, and Falco opened a bottle of his favourite wine, which they shared equally, although Sadie's was topped up with water. Even so, it went straight to her head and when she had finished eating she climbed onto the bench and sang a few carols in a sweet, clear soprano.

The memory of Christmases at home brought tears to Essie's eyes. George had made sure she had at least one present to open on Christmas morning. She still had the wooden doll with articulated arms and a painted face that he had carved in secret. Pa had never been particularly generous, even on birthdays, but at Christmas he always made a bowl of rum punch, which he invited Miss Flower, Josser and Ben to share. When he was flush with money, which did not happen very often, he would treat her to a pie and eel supper.

'Put her to bed before she falls down and does herself some harm.' Alice's sharp words interrupted Essie's reverie and she stood up, holding out her

arms to catch Sadie before she tumbled to the deck.
'That was lovely, Sadie,' she said, giving her a hug.
'Very Christmassy.'

Falco clapped his hands. 'I see I have a rival. We
will sing a duet tomorrow, *mia cara*.'

Sadie gave him a tipsy smile as she flung her arms
around Essie. 'Merry Christmas, Essie. I love you.'

'And I love you, too.' Essie led her from the saloon,
supporting her faltering footsteps.

'Next Christmas I'll buy you a lovely present,'
Sadie said, hiccuping. 'A big beautiful something or
other.'

'That will be nice.' Essie opened the cabin door
and guided Sadie to the bunk. 'Sit down, dear, and
I'll take your boots off.'

'But it's your turn for the bunk, Essie.'

'It's Christmas, Sadie. You can have the bunk.'

Sadie collapsed onto the bed. 'I wonder where
we'll be this time next year.'

'Who knows?' Essie undid the laces on Sadie's
boots and made her comfortable. The sound of her
even breathing confirmed that she was asleep even
before Essie had left the cabin, but instead of
returning to the saloon, where she could hear Falco
singing his heart out, Essie braved the weather on
deck. It was cold and clear, and the sea and sky
seemed to merge into one huge cavern of darkness.
A brisk wind whipped her cheeks and tossed her
hair into a mass of salty curls, but she took deep

breaths and scanned the sky for the North Star, which Falco said would guide them home. Ragged clouds scudded across the moon, obliterating its light, but there were clear patches where stars sparkled like diamonds against a black velvet gown. She was on her way home, but part of her longed to be back in Ballarat with Raven. 'Merry Christmas, Raven,' she said out loud. But Sadie's words echoed in her head. Where would they be this time next year? The future had never looked brighter, and yet Essie's heart was aching with loneliness.

Chapter Thirteen

Essie had expected the *Santa Gabriella* to dock in London, or at least to anchor in Limehouse Reach, but Falco, it seemed, had other ideas. She awakened one cold January morning to find the ship bobbing gently on its moorings, and when she looked out of the porthole she saw red cliffs at the mouth of what appeared to be a wide estuary. She dressed quickly and went to find him.

He was in the saloon drinking coffee and he greeted her with a wide smile. 'You are back in England.'

'But where are we? This isn't the Thames.'

'No, it is not.'

'Then where is this? Why aren't we in London?'

'Lady Alice wanted to go home first.'

'I don't know where she lives.'

Falco shrugged. 'Neither do I, *mia cara*. No doubt she will tell us in her own good time.'

'I'll soon find out.' Essie left him and went to rap on Alice's door. She entered without waiting for an answer.

Alice opened her eyes, staring blankly at Essie. 'What's the matter?'

'Where are you taking us?' Essie demanded crossly. 'Don't you think you should have consulted me?'

'Go away, Essie. Can't you see that I'm still half asleep? I'm not going to argue with you when I'm in my nightgown.'

Essie folded her arms across her chest, glaring at Alice. 'I'm not moving until you tell me where we are.'

'Oh, all right,' Alice sat up, yawning and stretching as if to make a point. 'It's the Exe estuary. We'll go ashore here and it's only a mile or two to Daumerle.'

'Daumerle?' Essie was intrigued. 'What and where is that?'

'It's the ancestral home of the Croziers,' Alice said, flinging back the coverlet. 'I need to rest and make myself presentable before I return to London. I can't be seen looking like a gypsy.'

'But I want to go home. My pa probably thinks I'm dead.'

'I'm not stopping you,' Alice said carelessly. 'This isn't the back of beyond – we're connected by the railway nowadays, so you can travel by the train.

I'll pay your fare and Sadie's, but I suggest you take a look at yourself in the mirror before you make any rash decisions. If you turn up looking like that your father will probably toss you out on the street.'

Essie glanced down at her patched and stained gown, and her hand flew automatically to pat her tousled hair into place. It felt sticky with salt and brittle to the touch. 'All right,' she conceded. 'Just a few days, if you'll be good enough to let us stay with you.'

'After everything we've been through together, it's the least I can do. And I need to visit Starcross Abbey to make sure that the servants are continuing to do their job while Raven is away. I've kept an eye on the place for the past five years so they know exactly what's expected of them.' Alice met Essie's gaze with a wry smile. 'Anyway, I'm sure you'd like to see where he was born and raised. You two were quite close at one point, I think.'

Essie turned away to hide her blushes. 'He barely noticed that I was alive.'

'Nonsense. A woman always knows if a man is interested in her, and it was obvious that he had a soft spot for you. I know my cousin so well.' Alice rose to her feet. 'Although, of course, nothing could come of it. Anyway, never mind him. We're here now and I can't wait to have my own clothes and a proper bath and all the comforts of home. You and Sadie will be my guests. There's no question of either you or the child being treated like servants.'

'Thank you.' Essie had nothing more to say and she backed out of the cabin in a daze. If Raven had told her he loved her she would have stayed in Ballarat for the rest of her life as long as he was there, but he had made her believe that he did not care and she would have to live with that. Now she would never know the truth, although it was obvious that the Earl of Starcross would never consider marriage with a commoner like herself. Alice had spoken the truth; it had hurt, but she was right – their worlds had met briefly, or perhaps they had collided, but now it was over.

Essie went to her cabin to wake Sadie and make ready to disembark.

An hour later, as they stepped onto the jetty Essie was surprised to find a carriage waiting for them.

'I sent a message on ahead,' Alice said smugly. 'I want to get home as quickly as possible.' She summoned the footman with an imperious wave of her hand and he leaped from the box to open the door, proffering his hand to help her into the vehicle.

'Thank you, James. See that our luggage is stowed carefully.' Alice climbed into the coach, followed by Essie and then Sadie, who seemed overawed by the whole experience.

Falco stood watching them, and Essie was struck

by his bereft expression. 'I think Falco wants to speak to you,' she said, nudging Alice, who was apparently oblivious to anything but her desire to return to her ancestral home.

'I've said goodbye to him.' Alice stared straight ahead. 'Drive on, Tully.'

The carriage ride to Daumerle took about half an hour, but Essie barely noticed the time as she was intent on gazing out of the window at the trees reaching up to the azure sky. The rolling hills were dotted with woolly white sheep and herds of cows, grazing on the lush grass. The lanes were frighteningly steep and narrow as they meandered between the fields, with high banks swagged with ivy. Even in the middle of winter there was greenery enough to make the Devonshire countryside appear lush and verdant, and clumps of snowdrops gave hope of spring to come. It was all such a complete change from the wide open spaces of Australia, not to mention the dark canyons of Limehouse, that it took Essie's breath away.

The carriage drew to a halt outside a pair of ornate wrought-iron gates, and the gatekeeper emerged from his lodge to throw them open. An avenue lined with trees stretched out in front of them, leading to a magnificent Palladian mansion.

'Welcome to Daumerle,' Alice said, as the carriage drew to a halt and a footman rushed to open the door and help them to alight.

The double doors were flung open and a stately looking butler came down the steps to greet his mistress, followed by another footman and a procession of uniformed maids, who lined the steps, headed by a woman in black with a chatelaine at her waist. She was plump with rosy cheeks and a gentle smile, and looked a lot less intimidating than Mrs Dent, the housekeeper in Hill Street. If the servants were shocked to see their mistress and her companions looking like gypsies they were too well disciplined to allow their astonishment to show.

'Welcome home, my lady.' The butler bowed low and the housekeeper bobbed a curtsey.

'Thank you, Garner,' Alice said graciously. 'It's good to be home.' She mounted the steps, coming to a halt beside the housekeeper. 'Good morning, Mrs Yelland. As you see I have two friends with me. Miss Chapman and Miss Dixon. Please see that rooms close to mine are prepared for them.'

'Yes, my lady, of course.' Mrs Yelland stood back, folding her hands primly in front of her as Alice entered the great hall followed by Essie and Sadie.

Essie looked round in awe. If the house in Hill Street was grand, Daumerle was palatial. She could imagine the Queen herself gliding down the wide sweep of the staircase, where Lady Alice's ancestors gazed out from their gilded frames, frozen in time for everyone to see and marvel at their splendour. The high ceiling was covered with frescos depicting scenes from antiquity with fat cherubs and scantily clad females in thrall to muscular heroes. Essie almost tripped over her feet as she gazed upwards, enchanted by the colour and beauty of the paintings. Sadie clutched her hand, looking around as if she expected to be pounced on and dragged off to the scullery where she would be put to work.

Alice hesitated as she was about to mount the stairs. 'Mrs Yelland will take you to your rooms.' She looked them up and down, shaking her head. 'You are in desperate need of new clothes. Come to my room when you're settled and I'll get Merrifield to sort out some of my things for both of you.' She ascended the stairs with a spring in her step. 'Home at last.'

'Come along, ladies,' Mrs Yelland said briskly. 'I'll show you to your rooms, and the maids will bring hot water so that you may take a bath, should you desire to do so.'

'Oh, definitely,' Essie said eagerly. 'You can't imagine how much I've longed for a bath during our time abroad.'

'No, indeed, miss. I doubt if I could stretch my imagination to that extent.'

'She talks like a toff,' Sadie whispered as she followed Essie upstairs.

'Hush, she'll hear you.'

Mrs Yelland turned her head to give them a wide smile. 'My hearing is very acute, young lady. But I take it as a compliment.'

Their rooms were adjacent and overlooked the parterre garden, where, in the mild Devon climate, spring flowers were bursting into bloom, and beyond to sweeping lawns separated from the deer park by a ha-ha. Sadie stood in the doorway, gazing round wide-eyed and for a moment speechless.

'It's a lovely room,' Essie said encouragingly. 'Do you like it, Sadie?'

'It's too grand for the likes of me,' Sadie whispered. 'How many of us have to share it?'

'Good gracious, child,' Mrs Yelland said with a gurgle of laughter. 'How quaint you are. This is your room, Miss Dixon, and Miss Chapman will be next door, so you will have company should you feel uneasy in a strange house.'

Essie gave her a grateful smile. 'Thank you, Mrs Yelland. I'm sure we'll both be more than comfortable. Daumerle is the most beautiful house I've ever seen.'

Mrs Yelland puffed out her chest and beamed with pride. 'It is a very fine building and we work hard to keep it at its best.' She stepped outside and moved along the corridor to open the door to Essie's room, which was even more impressive than Sadie's bedchamber. Furnished with dainty chairs and a small sofa upholstered in blue and silver striped damask with matching curtains, the room was large and winter sunshine flooded in from tall windows. Essie ran her fingers over the highly polished top of the burr walnut dressing table. There was also a wash stand and an impressive clothes press – it was a room fit for royalty.

'I'll have fires lit in both your rooms,' Mrs Yelland added hastily. 'A maid will bring hot water to fill the baths.'

'Thank you,' Essie said gratefully. 'We've been at sea for what seems like forever, and a bath in fresh water would be such luxury.'

'It will take a little time to fill the tubs as the maids have to carry the ewers some distance from the kitchen, but I'll show you to Lady Alice's room as she requested.'

Luncheon was taken in the morning parlour, which overlooked the paved terrace where stone urns were filled with early narcissi, nodding and swaying in the sea breeze. Alice was fashionably dressed in a blue and green plaid silk afternoon gown with pagoda sleeves, and Essie felt equally stylish in one of Alice's full-skirted grey tussore gowns trimmed with black fringing. It was last season's fashion, so Merrifield informed her with a disapproving sniff, but to Essie it was the height of luxury. Sadie was too small to wear any of Alice's clothes, even if they were considered to be unfashionable, so Merrifield had been sent, albeit rather unwillingly, to the attics and had searched through trunks packed with garments worn by Alice when she was much younger.

As a result Sadie had a whole new wardrobe, and if the clothes smelled rather strongly of camphor and lavender she did not complain. Merrifield had taken everything to the laundry room to hang on racks to air, but regardless of the cloying odour intended to keep the moths at bay, Sadie had insisted on wearing a red woollen gown with a white broderie anglaise collar and cuffs.

James, the footman, stood to attention behind Alice with Betsy, one of the senior housemaids, at his side. Essie was slightly unnerved by their presence, but, having served the first course, they stared straight ahead, their expressions impassive as if they were mentally elsewhere.

Alice picked up her knife and fork. 'Before we begin our meal I think I ought to point out that we don't eat off our knife, Sadie. It might be considered the done thing in Ballarat, but that doesn't apply here. Not only is it considered to be bad manners, but one would be in danger of cutting one's tongue.'

Sadie blushed and hung her head.

'Maybe we should eat in the servants' hall,' Essie suggested tentatively.

'There's no need to go to extremes, and I think you'll find that Garner is even more particular about table manners than I am. However, should you be invited to dinner parties you will find that there are some who set out to break all the rules, especially when the wine is flowing.'

'I'm not sure I understand,' Essie said frowning.

'We have to know the rules of etiquette, and also when it is acceptable to break them. Polite society is not always so polite, as you will discover, Essie.'

'I doubt if I'll ever be invited to such parties. Polite society doesn't exist in Limehouse.' Faced with a bewildering display of cutlery, Essie shot a surreptitious glance in Alice's direction, waiting to see which of them she used first.

'Do as I do and you won't go far wrong.' Alice looked from one to the other. 'You are my guests and it will be my pleasure to entertain you both for as long as you wish to stay.'

'Thank you, Alice, but I ought to go home as soon as possible.'

'Another week or two isn't going to make any difference. I suggest you send a letter to your father, letting him know that you are safe and well. If you turn up out of the blue he might drop dead from heart failure, so a prior warning would be in order.'

'What are you planning?' Essie asked suspiciously. 'Why do you care what happens to us?'

'Because we've been together for months – we've suffered the same privations – and more importantly because you are now a very wealthy young woman, Essie. Your life will be changed by the fortune you'll have, and you won't be able to pick up where you left off. If you return home too soon you'll be cheated out of your gold or robbed of it before you've been in London for more than twenty-four hours.'

Essie met Alice's earnest gaze and knew that she was speaking the truth. 'I hadn't thought of that,' she said slowly. 'I was going to sell the nuggets and buy a small house near the docks, but in a better area. I thought I could look after Pa and I'd put advertisements in the newspapers asking for information about my brother. If he saw them he might come home.'

'I think Alice is right.' Sadie pushed her plate away. 'Except about this stuff. I'm sorry, but I don't like fish nor never will. I'll puke if you make me eat it.'

'We don't speak about puking or throwing up at table,' Alice said severely. She signalled to James and Betsy to clear the table, before turning to Essie. 'Think about what I've just said. You need someone honest to advise you how to invest your money, and a bullion dealer who will give you the best price for the gold. Will you allow me to help you?'

Essie nodded. 'I'd be grateful, but I don't understand why you want to help me.'

'I've grown fond of you both, and if you must know, the last thing Raven said to me was, "Look after Essie, she's an innocent and I'd hate to see her cheated out of the gold that Beasley gave his life for." So you see, my cousin is concerned for your welfare.'

THE RIVER MAID

'What do you suggest?' Essie said eagerly. 'I really haven't given it a lot of thought.'

'I want to spend some time here. I employ a land agent to run the estate, and I need to see him and discuss any problems that might have arisen during my absence. I'll visit Starcross Abbey and make sure that all is well there, and when I'm satisfied that everything is running smoothly I'll return to London. There's still the matter of the appeal. Obviously I've lost contact with our solicitor, so I don't know how things are proceeding.'

Momentarily forgetting her own problems, Essie leaned forward eagerly. 'Do you think Raven and Freddie will be pardoned?'

'Who knows? But let's hope so, and in the meantime, if you're agreeable, I'll set about making a lady of you, Esther Chapman. With your looks and money you'll take society by storm.'

'What about me?' Sadie whispered, her eyes filling with tears. 'What's to become of me?'

'You'll be with me, of course,' Essie said hastily. 'I'll take care of you.'

'Of course she will, Sadie. Don't be silly.'

'Will I go back to being a scullery maid?'

Essie shook her head. 'Certainly not. I told you before, I think of you as my little sister.'

'Really?' Sadie's lips trembled and tears ran down her cheeks. 'Do you mean it, Essie?'

'I'm sure she does,' said Alice sternly. 'But you

249

have even more to learn than Essie, so you can start by taking your elbows off the table. As my old nanny used to say, "no uncooked joints on the table". You will have to learn manners and speak only when you're spoken to. I doubt if you can read and write.'

'Indeed I can.' Sadie faced Alice with a defiant stare. 'We learned our lessons in the orphanage. I ain't ignorant.'

'I am not ignorant,' Alice said patiently.

'I know you ain't,' Sadie added quickly. 'I was talking about meself.'

Alice rolled her eyes heavenward. 'You have your work cut out there, Essie. In fact, I think I'll send for Miss Potts, my old governess. She's retired now, but I think the two of you could benefit from her teaching, and no doubt she will be glad of a little extra money. I'll get word to her this afternoon and see what she says.'

Essie and Sadie exchanged wary glances, saying nothing as the next course was brought to the table. They finished their meal in silence and without any further criticism from Alice, who seemed to be lost in her own thoughts. She rose from the table and was about to leave the room when Betsy reappeared, looking flushed and flustered.

She bobbed a curtsey. 'I'm sorry to interrupt, my lady, but Mr Garner sent me to tell you that there's a strange foreign gentleman creating a fuss outside the gates and demanding to be let in.'

Alice eyed her thoughtfully. 'Describe him for me.'

'I haven't seen him, my lady. The gatekeeper sent his son with the message. The foreign gent refuses to go until he's spoken to you.'

Essie rushed to the window, followed by Sadie. The avenue leading to the road was long and straight, but Essie would have recognised him anywhere. 'I think it's Falco,' she said, chuckling. He's riding the strangest horse I ever saw.'

'Tell the gatekeeper to admit him,' Alice said hastily. 'I believe I know the gentleman. I'll see him in the drawing room.'

Betsy curtseyed again and hurried from the room. Essie could hear the maid's small feet pitter-pattering on the marble floor as she hurried to pass on the message.

'I wonder what he wants,' Essie said slowly. 'I thought the *Santa Gabriella* was due to sail on the tide.'

Alice shrugged casually, but Essie was quick to notice the bright spots of colour on her pale cheeks, and she seemed to be slightly breathless. Essie had long suspected that Lady Alice Crozier was not immune to Falco's charms, and his feelings for her had been obvious to anyone who had seen them together. But it was a relationship that seemed doomed to failure from the outset. The Earl of Dawlish's daughter and the renegade Italian sea captain was not a match made in heaven, and a happy ending seemed unlikely.

'The boy is passing on the message,' Sadie said excitedly. 'And the gates are being opened. Look, Essie, come and look.' She pointed a finger, jabbing at the windowpane as she jumped up and down, chortling with laughter. 'Where did he find a horse such as that?'

Essie hurried to the window, followed by Alice, and the sight that met her eyes made her chuckle. Falco was not an expert horseman, which had been obvious in Italy when they rode to the monastery, and the mount he had procured was a swayback piebald creature that looked to be on its last legs. Essie expected the poor animal to collapse as it broke into a lumbering trot, coming to a halt at the foot of the steps and almost unseating Falco.

'Good heavens, what a spectacle.' Alice backed away from the window. 'I'll see him and send him on his way, but someone must do something for that poor nag. Sadie, run and tell James to have it taken to the stables. The beast should be out at pasture and I shall tell Falco so in no uncertain terms.' Alice swept out of the room.

'I'll come with you,' Essie said as Sadie hurried into the hall. 'I want to see the gallant captain.'

They reached the main entrance at the same moment as Falco. James took his hat and boat cloak and passed them to Betsy. 'Lady Alice will see you in the drawing room, sir.'

'It's Captain Falco.'

'Yes, Captain. Come this way, if you please.'

Essie stepped in between them. 'Captain, this is a surprise. I thought you were in a hurry to leave our waters.'

'We needed to take on supplies and missed the tide, and unfortunately we developed engine trouble, so while repairs are being carried out I thought I would like to visit the home of Lady Alice.'

'I see. Well, I'm sure Lady Alice will be delighted to see you.'

Falco's smile faded and he leaned closer, lowering his voice. 'Do you really think so?'

'Why don't you go with James and find out?'

'I will. Lead on.' He followed James with a hint of his old swaggering gait, but Essie was not fooled. She sensed that Falco was nervous and she could only guess at his real reason for coming all this way.

'What do you think he wants?' Sadie whispered. 'We all said goodbye on the ship.'

'I don't know. I suppose we'll just have to wait for Alice to tell us.' Essie hesitated, not knowing what to do next.

'There's a fire in the morning parlour.' Betsy scurried past with Falco's outer garments clutched in her arms. 'You'd be more comfortable there, miss, if you don't mind me saying so.'

'Thank you,' Essie said gratefully. 'It's Betsy, isn't it?'

'Yes, miss. But please don't tell James or Mrs Yelland that I spoke first. I'll be in for it if you do.'

'I don't understand.'

'That's the way it is with servants, miss. I'd have thought a young lady like you would know how it is in big houses such as this.'

'I'm learning,' Essie said slowly. 'Thank you, Betsy. We'll be in the morning parlour if Lady Alice needs us.' Essie was about to head in that direction when James reappeared.

'Lady Alice requests your presence in the drawing room, miss.' He turned on his heel and walked off at a measured pace, leaving Essie and Sadie little alternative but to follow him.

Alice greeted them with a wide smile. 'I've invited Captain Falco to dine with us this evening, and he would like to see the grounds, so I thought you two might like to join us. Merrifield is sorting out some warm clothes for you, so perhaps you'd like to entertain the captain while I go and make myself ready to brave the chill of the English winter.' Alice swept out of the room without waiting for their answer.

Essie met Falco's twinkling eyes with a steady stare. 'Did your engine really break down, Captain? Or was that an excuse to spend more time with Alice?'

'My crew need a rest,' he said casually. 'We've been at sea for many months with very little time ashore.'

'But I thought you were afraid you'd be arrested if you landed in England.'

'I doubt if the police in this part of the country have ever heard of Enrico Falco, or the *Santa Gabriella*. But the matter is now settled. I made reparation to the person who was trying to sue me.'

'What did you do wrong?' Sadie asked bluntly.

Essie shot her a warning glance but Falco merely grinned. 'I was what you English call a privateer.'

'Are you a pirate?'

'Hush, Sadie,' Essie said hastily. 'You don't ask questions like that.'

'It is quite true.' Falco struck a pose. 'Although perhaps "pirate" is too harsh a word. I was involved in privateering, and then my vessel was set on fire while it was in Brindisi harbour by a rival. We, in turn, took their ship and changed the name to the *Santa Gabriella*. It was, as you English say – tit for tat, but the owner did not see it that way.'

'But if it was in Italy, why were you wanted in London?' Essie was even more puzzled by his explanation.

Falco shrugged. 'The owner was English, although not a good man. Anyway, the matter, as I said, is now resolved.'

'Does Alice know you were a criminal?' Essie asked.

'I could not allow her to think I am a better man than is true. I told her everything.'

'Will you be returning to Australia?' Essie asked wistfully.

He shook his head. 'I don't know, *mia cara*. I have yet to decide what I will do next. For myself I would like to give up the sea and settle down on shore, but my crew depend upon me, and I have no money of my own. Who would want to marry a man like me?'

'Who indeed?' Alice breezed into the room, dressed in a fur-lined cape with a matching fur hat, Cossack-style on her head, and blonde curls escaped cheekily as if to taunt and tease her admirers. Behind her Merrifield appeared carrying cloaks and bonnets for Essie and Sadie.

'Come along then, everyone,' Alice said briskly. 'Let's take a walk round the estate and work up an appetite for dinner this evening. I'm afraid we dine early in the country, Falco, but then after the slop your cook serves up you'll find the cuisine here unparalleled.'

That night, exhausted by the early start and the long walk, Essie was settling down in the luxurious feather bed when she heard someone tapping on the door. She snapped into a sitting position. 'Who is it?'

'It's me, Sadie. Can I come in?'

'Of course you can.' The words had barely left her lips when Sadie burst into the room and leaped onto the bed. 'What's the matter?'

Sadie clung to her, shivering. 'I'm scared in that big room all on my own. Can I sleep with you? I'll lie on the carpet, I don't mind.'

Essie gave her a hug, trying not to laugh. 'You are a silly, of course you can. This bed is big enough for both of us with space to spare, but if you kick me you'll have to sleep on the floor.'

'I don't mind,' Sadie said in a small voice. 'And I don't think I want to have lessons. I ain't a lady and never will be.'

'Don't worry about it. We'll give Miss Potts a fair trial, and if we don't like her I'll tell Alice to send her away. Does that satisfy you?'

A gentle snore from Sadie was her only answer. Essie had spoken confidently, but she too was worried. Her life, which had once seemed set in a pattern of working the river and marriage to Ben, had been upturned in the most cataclysmic manner. She was now a wealthy woman and she needed to learn how to live with her newfound wealth – but how would it affect those nearest and dearest to her? That was the burning question. It was a long time before sleep claimed her at last.

Chapter Fourteen

According to Alice, the schoolroom was apparently exactly the same as when she had taken lessons from Miss Potts. Alice strolled round the room, picking up small objects and putting them down again. 'Goodness gracious, I'd completely forgotten these things,' she said, smiling. 'I haven't been in this room for years.' She turned to the tall, thin woman who had entered behind her. 'You had a hard time trying to din mathematics and Latin into my head, Emmeline.'

Miss Potts nodded gravely. 'You were not always the most attentive pupil, my lady.'

'Sad but true.' Alice turned to Essie and Sadie, who were standing to attention by the door. 'This is Miss Potts, who will be your tutor for the next few weeks. She'll assess how much or how little you know, but her main task will be to correct your grammar and to teach you etiquette, deportment and whatever social graces she thinks might be necessary. We've agreed that she will come here every morning from nine o'clock until midday. Does that sound reasonable to you, Essie?'

'Yes, Alice.' Essie's initial reaction when Alice had broached the subject had been to refuse politely but firmly. However, since then she had given the matter a great deal of thought and she had to admit that it made sense. Her new fortune would only benefit her and those she loved if she knew how to handle it, and how to mix with people from all walks of life. She was no longer simply Essie Chapman, the boatman's daughter, she was the wealthy Miss Esther Chapman, who had yet to decide how she would spend her money or where she would reside, but she also knew that there were plenty of people who would try to part her from her riches, and she must keep one step ahead of them.

'I'll leave you to your work, Emmeline,' Alice said, smiling sweetly. 'I'll be out this morning, riding round the estate with Humphries, and I believe that Captain Falco has decided to accompany us. We'll meet up at luncheon, Essie, and this afternoon I thought we'd take the carriage to Starcross Abbey. I'm sure you must be curious to see Raven's ancestral home.' She left the room, closing the door behind her.

'Now then, ladies. Please be seated and we'll make

a start.' Miss Potts took off her black bonnet and hung it on a peg together with her black cape. Essie noted her black bombazine dress that was threadbare in places and wondered how long the lady had been in mourning, but it was not the sort of question she could ask. She waited for Miss Potts to take her seat behind the large desk before sitting down next to Sadie.

'I hope you don't use the cane too often if I gets things wrong, miss,' Sadie said in a low voice, her eyes filling with tears. 'I ain't too quick at learning.'

Miss Potts folded her wrinkled hands together as if she were about to say a prayer. 'I never use corporal punishment, Sadie. You are not in school now, but I am here to help you, so why don't you tell me a little about yourselves. Let's start with Esther, shall we?'

Stumbling at first, Essie told Miss Potts about her home in Limehouse and how she kept house for her father as well as helping him with his work on the river. Growing in confidence, she went on to talk about their time on board the *Santa Gabriella*, and how they had found Freddie living in the ruined monastery. Sadie seemed to forget her nerves and she added bits that Essie omitted. There was so much to relate, and although Essie spoke at length about their time in Ballarat, she did not choose to mention Beasley or the gold nugget that he had bequeathed to her. Sadie added graphic accounts of the hardships endured by the miners, adding vivid descriptions of the wildlife and the dangers they had faced daily from strange creatures, poisonous snakes and stinging insects. Miss Potts listened avidly, interrupting from time to time to correct their grammar, but apart from that she made no comment until they reached the end. She clapped her hands and rose to her feet.

'That was excellent. I can see that you need just a little polish, Essie, and Sadie will soon learn to speak correctly. That was a most enjoyable session and I look forward to seeing you both tomorrow morning at nine o'clock, sharp.'

Essie stared at her in astonishment. 'We can't have finished yet. Surely it's not time.'

Miss Potts took a half-hunter watch from her reticule. 'This belonged to my late father, the Reverend Marcus Potts, vicar of this parish. It keeps perfect time and it tells me that it's twelve noon.' She slipped the watch back into the velvet bag and stood up. 'It's been a most interesting and informative morning. I look forward to tomorrow.'

'But we haven't learned anything,' Essie said, frowning.

'I think you'll find that you've learned a great deal.' Miss Potts slipped on her cloak and bonnet. 'But if you want to continue your education, I suggest that you visit Lady Alice's library. Her father was a keen reader and you'll find many wonderful books there. Now I really must go. I have some errands in the village.' She hurried from the room, leaving a waft of lavender and peppermints in her wake.

Essie shook her head. 'I don't know what I've learned this morning, other than the fact that there is a library crammed with books somewhere in the house. Let's explore, Sadie. It's almost an hour until luncheon so we have plenty of time.'

Hand in hand like two schoolchildren who had escaped from class and were on the lookout for mischief, they went from room to room, marvelling at everything they saw. Essie lost count of the elegant bedchambers, which, without exception, were furnished in the height of luxury and good taste. The carpets, curtains and bed linen were of the finest quality, in colours and designs that Essie could barely have imagined. However, when they reached the attic rooms on the top floor it was another story. They had found the servants' quarters which, although adequate, were a complete contrast. The Spartan accommodation was not designed to make the staff want to linger in bed or spend any more time than strictly necessary in their quarters. Feeling like an intruder, Essie hurried down the back stairs with Sadie close on her heels.

'It's very odd,' she said breathlessly. 'In fact it's like two completely different worlds.'

'I thought you knew that already. It was like that in Hill Street, so it don't – I mean it doesn't surprise me.' Sadie cocked her leg over the balustrade and slid down the banisters, landing at the butler's feet.

Garner did not look amused. He took a deep breath, as if struggling with self-control. 'That's not a good idea, miss. Perhaps you'd be more comfortable in your part of the house.' He looked up as Essie hurried down the stairs. 'This is the servants' quarters, miss. It's not the place for young ladies to play games.'

Essie drew herself up to her full height. 'Thank you, Garner. It won't happen again.' She dragged Sadie to her feet. 'Come along, it must be almost time for luncheon.'

Garner stood aside, nodding. 'Her ladyship and the captain have just returned from their ride. Luncheon will be served in ten minutes.' He stalked off, twitching his shoulders in an outward display of annoyance.

'Now we've upset him,' Essie said ruefully. 'Oh, well, it can't be helped. Let's see if we can find our way to the dining room without offending any more servants.' Taking Sadie by the hand she set off along the maze of corridors, and eventually they arrived at the green baize door that separated those above stairs from the people who looked after their every need. Essie was suddenly nervous. On which side of that dividing door did she really belong? She pushed her doubts to the back of her mind as James descended upon them.

'Her ladyship and the captain are in the dining room, miss.'

Essie inclined her head. 'Thank you, James. I think I can remember the way. Come, Sadie.'

Sadie ran after her as Essie quickened her pace, hurrying in what she hoped was the right direction. 'What's the matter? Why were you huffy with James? He was only trying to help.'

'He's a servant and we're guests. We're supposed to keep them in their place. I don't like it, but it's what they expect,' Essie said sadly. 'Maybe someday things might be different, but for now we have to do what everyone else does.' She opened the door and entered the dining room, prepared to apologise for their lateness, but Alice and Falco were laughing at some shared joke and they did not seem to notice.

'You are a bad man, Enrico.' Alice fanned herself with her hand. 'Some of the things you say are quite outrageous, but very amusing.' She turned to Essie with a bright smile. 'And how was your morning? Did Miss Potts come up to scratch?'

'I hardly know,' Essie said honestly. 'She seemed pleased with us, but Sadie and I did all the talking.'

'This lady sounds very clever,' Falco observed, raising his glass of wine in a toast, but his gaze was fixed on Alice and she blushed prettily.

Essie took her seat at the table. 'Are we still going to Starcross Abbey this afternoon?'

'Of course.' Alice turned to Falco. 'I was thinking, Enrico . . .'

'A dangerous pastime, my lady.'

'Joking aside,' Alice continued seriously, 'the last time I visited Raven's home I was not entirely satisfied that it was being run properly. I had the feeling that the butler was taking advantage of his absence, and I had a quick look at the housekeeping accounts. There seemed to be rather a lot of food and wine consumed during his master's absence, and I warned him that such behaviour had to stop or he would be seeking employment elsewhere.'

'That's awful,' Essie said, shocked. 'That's stealing.'

'Taking advantage of his master's absence is wrong,' Falco agreed, nodding. 'How may I help you, my lady?'

'I thought you might like to stay there for a while, Enrico. You would be in sole charge of the household and the estate. You would be doing Raven a great service.'

Falco stared at her, his smile fading. 'But, my lady, I am a seafarer. I have my ship and my crew depend upon me.'

'You said yourself that your vessel needs overhauling,' Alice said tartly. 'Now would seem to be a very good time to put the ship into dock and give your crew some well-deserved shore leave.' She sat back as James proffered the tureen of watercress soup and she helped herself to a small portion.

'That is so, and the offer is very tempting.' Falco waited until James had left the room. 'I hope you can trust your servants to be discreet, my lady. I wouldn't want them to get the wrong idea.'

Essie almost choked on her soup. The relationship between Alice and Falco seemed to have deepened in a shockingly short space of time, but Alice remained impassive. 'I can and I do,' she said calmly. 'But you haven't answered my question.'

'I used all the money I earned in Australia to pay off my debts,' Falco said humbly. 'I have been at sea since I was a boy. I know nothing else.'

'Raven will fund the refit of the *Santa Gabriella*, and in return you can do him an invaluable service, Enrico,' Alice insisted. 'When you see Starcross Abbey you will fall under its spell, as everyone does. I'm not asking you to take up residence permanently, but you can't stay here. As you inferred, it might cause tongues to wag, and damage my reputation.'

'I cannot allow that, my beautiful lady.'

'I am not your lady, Enrico. We are just friends.'

'I would hope so, my lady.'

'Then it's settled,' Alice said, nodding. 'I'm sure that Raven would approve, and I think he owes you something in return for the risks you took on his behalf. You could have refused to bring him home.'

'I was well paid for my trouble. Raven owes me nothing, my lady.'

'Maybe, maybe not – but you brought us back to England, and for that I will be eternally in your debt.' Alice fixed him with a persuasive smile. 'Say you will stay a little longer, Captain, if only for my sake.'

'Very well, my lady. I will give you my answer after I have seen this place.' Falco dipped his spoon in his soup and sipped. 'This is good. I like it.'

Wrapped up well against the cold, the temperature having taken a tumble and dark clouds threatening rain, they set off after luncheon. The carriage was luxurious and copper foot warmers filled with hot coals kept their feet warm during the journey to Starcross Abbey. Falco kept them amused with outrageous accounts of life on the high seas, which Essie did not believe for a moment, but they were entertaining and he was a good raconteur. Outside the carriage the skies grew darker and sleety rain began to lash the windows. The coachman slowed the four-horse team to a walk as they negotiated the narrow lanes and when descending the steep hills, but eventually they arrived at their destination.

Alice glanced out of the window. 'Where are the servants?' she demanded angrily. 'The place looks deserted and there was no one in the gatekeeper's lodge.' She waited impatiently for James to open the door and put the steps down, and for a moment Essie was afraid that Alice would leap to the ground, but she contained herself and allowed James to help her to alight, followed by Sadie and Falco. Essie was last to climb out of the vehicle and she paused, gazing up at the uncompromising edifice constructed from granite. With four crenellated towers, Starcross Abbey stood guard on the cliff top overlooking the English Channel. It was protected on either side by woodland, with a wide gravel carriage sweep leading to the main entrance, which was guarded by two large stone lions.

Alice walked up to the front door and knocked. The echo resounded throughout the house, and they could do nothing other than wait in the bitter cold. 'There must be someone at home,' Alice said angrily. 'Raven kept all the servants on, regardless of cost. I'll want to know why we're being kept waiting.'

Essie clutched her cape around her. It was easy to imagine Raven and Freddie growing up in this place. It looked like a castle from a storybook and she longed to see inside. 'They weren't expecting us, Alice,' she said reasonably.

Alice rapped on the door again. 'I'll send James round to the servants' entrance. They will answer to me if they—' She broke off as the door opened with a screech of unoiled hinges and a blowsy woman stared stupidly at them.

'What d'you want?'

Alice pushed past her. 'Where is Smeaton? And

who are you?' She peered at the woman, whose dirty mobcap had tilted over one eye, and her ill-fitting blouse was stained with snuff.

'I'm Dottie. Who are you?'

Alice recoiled, glaring at the woman. 'You're a drunken slut, and I'm Lady Alice Crozier. I demand to see Smeaton.'

Dottie backed away, bowing and scraping like a cur that expected a beating. 'I dunno, my lady. I was just doing them below stairs a favour by seeing to the door. It ain't my job.'

'I don't know what you're doing here, but your position is terminated,' Alice said angrily.

'I dunno what that means, ma'am.' Dottie cringed visibly.

Feeling almost sorry for the drunken creature, Essie stepped forward. 'Lady Alice means that you're services are no long wanted.'

'Fetch Smeaton immediately,' Alice said imperiously. 'I don't care what he's doing. Bring him here right away. This is a disgrace.'

Falco moved to Alice's side. 'Would you like me to fetch the fellow, my lady? He won't gainsay Enrico Falco.'

'And he won't gainsay me.' Alice ran her finger across a carved oak monk's bench, pulling a face when she examined the tip of her glove. 'Filthy. This place hasn't been cleaned for weeks – months even. It's almost colder inside than it is outside. I'm not waiting for Smeaton to come up here with excuses. I'm going to the servants' quarters and I'll give him a piece of my mind.'

'I'm coming with you,' Falco said firmly.

'Me, too.' Essie followed them with Sadie close behind.

'They might turn nasty,' Sadie whispered.

'I grew up amongst dock workers and drunken sailors,' Essie said grimly. 'And the gold miners were a rough lot, too. I think we can handle a few idle servants between us.'

As they went deeper into the house the neglect became more apparent. Cobwebs hung from the ceilings and the air was thick with dust. Alice obviously knew her way around and she headed for the back stairs, which spiralled down to the basement. The cold was even more intense and Essie covered her nose with her hand as noxious smells assailed her nostrils.

'What a stench,' Sadie muttered.

Alice said nothing as she hurried on, arriving in the kitchen and throwing the door open so that it crashed against the wall. 'What the devil is going on here?' she demanded furiously.

Essie looked round in astonishment. There was litter everywhere and the floor was covered in grease and filth. A fire burned in the range and a blackened pan bubbled away, but what it contained was a mystery she would rather not fathom. The stench of it was enough to turn the strongest stomach and for a moment Essie thought she might be sick. But Alice did not seem to notice and she stormed across the floor, treading through the heaps of rotting vegetable matter mixed up with straw. She came to a halt in front of a man who was sprawled on a chair, his shirt open to the waist and his trousers unfastened. Instead of fainting or looking away, Alice snatched the wine bottle from his hand and hurled it at the wall, where it shattered and fell to the floor in a pool of red wine and broken glass.

'You're drunk, Smeaton, and so is the slut who opened the door to us.'

Smeaton staggered to his feet, grinning stupidly. 'Just a tot or two to keep out the cold, my lady.'

'You're sacked, Smeaton, and so is she, whoever she is. I don't recall seeing her here before today.'

Smeaton reached out to hook his arm around Dottie's shoulders, steadying himself by using her as a prop, although she was only slightly the less drunk of the pair. 'You can't sack me, and Dottie is me wife – all legal and above board.'

Alice looked past him to the woman who was trying to make herself invisible in the corner of the room. 'Is that you, Mrs Grimes?'

'Yes, my lady. I'm not responsible for all this.' Mrs Grimes waved her hands in a feeble attempt to distance herself from the mess around her. 'I'm only the cook – it's Mr Smeaton who's taken charge since you left for London, and things have gone from bad to worse.'

'It's not Ma's fault.' A young maidservant hurried in from the scullery. 'We done our best, my lady. But Smeaton and his woman have taken over and they do nothing but drink and do things that they should only do in their bedchamber. We don't hold with any of it, do we, Ma?'

Mrs Grimes nodded until her mobcap fell off. 'That's right, Jenifry. We done our best, my lady.'

'Shut your trap, you silly bitch.' Smeaton turned on her in a fury, but Falco stepped forward and grabbed him, twisting his arms behind his back.

Dottie screamed, cowering against the wall, and Sadie backed away from the flailing arms and flying fists. Essie watched in horror as Falco struggled with Smeaton, but Falco had the advantage of height, and was stone-cold sober. Smeaton was quickly overcome and Falco forced him down on his knees in front of Alice.

'Apologise to her ladyship,' Falco said grimly. 'And you'd better mind your manners if you don't want your bones broken.'

'You and that woman will leave this house immediately,' Alice said coldly.

'But I've worked here for years, my lady.' Smeaton's manner changed abruptly. He cowered before her. 'Where will we go and what will we do? It'll be dark soon.'

'Nonsense,' Alice said briskly. 'You've both drunk enough of my cousin's wine to keep you warm until you get to Newton Abbot. I'll give you ten minutes to pack your bags and if you're still here then you will be thrown out physically. Now give me the keys and get out of this house.'

'But we're owed money,' Dottie sobbed. 'We got nothing.'

'Where is the housekeeper?' Alice demanded.

'Mrs Wills left last week, my lady.' Mrs Grimes pointed her finger at Smeaton. 'That man made her life a misery and she could stand it no more.'

'Where did she go? Does she live in the village?'

'She do, ma'am.'

'Send a stable boy or a gardener with a message asking her to come and see me immediately.'

Essie laid her hand on Alice's arm. 'Are you going to stay here for a while? You won't get this mess sorted out in one afternoon.'

'You're right,' Alice said frowning. 'Falco, see these two off the premises. I'll be in the drawing room when you've done. Jenifry will show you where it is.'

Falco nodded and ushered Smeaton none too gently from the kitchen, with Dottie running after them, pleading for forgiveness.

Sadie sank down on a three-legged stool by the range. 'What a to-do.'

'There's no fire in the drawing room, my lady.'

Jenifry ventured shyly. 'We've not lit fires in the family rooms since the beginning of winter.'

'Why wasn't I told how things were?' Alice said angrily.

'Begging your pardon, my lady, but you wasn't available.' Mrs Grimes eyed her nervously. 'Word was sent to Daumerle, but nothing come of it.'

'I was abroad for a few months.' Alice paced the floor, wringing her hands. 'How could I have allowed this to happen? What will Raven say when he finds out?'

'I'm sure we can put matters right.' Essie glanced round at the chaotic state of the kitchen, hoping that she sounded more positive than she was feeling. 'Do you intend to remain here for a while?'

'Heavens, no. I wouldn't dream of spending a night in this place now. I'm sure the beds are damp, and goodness knows what state the bed linen is in. The housekeeper will sort it out when she returns.'

'But will you be here when she does?'

'Are you being deliberately difficult, Essie? Can't you see that this has been a terrible shock for me? I promised Raven that I would oversee matters at Starcross Abbey and I've let him down.'

Essie turned to Mrs Grimes and Jenifry, who were standing helplessly looking on. 'Might we have a fire in the drawing room, or is there a smaller room that would be more comfortable?'

Jenifry bobbed a curtsey. 'The blue parlour will get warm quicker, miss. Shall I set a fire in there?'

'That sounds much more sensible,' Essie said, smiling.

'I'll do it right away.' Jenifry moved to the fireplace, picked up a bucket of coal and a bundle of kindling and hurried from the room with a purposeful set to her thin shoulders.

Essie turned to Mrs Grimes. 'If you would put the kettle on, ma'am, I'm sure a cup of tea would help the situation, and if Smeaton hasn't drunk all the brandy, perhaps a tot would make her ladyship feel a little better.'

Mrs Grimes nodded eagerly. 'Of course, miss. Without that woman here watching everything I do, and making trouble for me and my girl, I can get back to normal, but I will need help from the village. Smeaton sacked all the maids except Jenifry, and I believe he pocketed the wages that would have gone to the other servants, although I can't prove it.'

'I should have him arrested,' Alice said angrily. 'He's nothing but a criminal. Do you know what has happened to the outside staff?'

'Much the same, my lady. But work is hard to find and I'm sure they'd be only too pleased to have their jobs back. That's if you want them to return.'

'I most definitely do.' Alice headed for the door. 'I'll leave you in charge for the moment, Essie. Sadie can bring a lamp and accompany me to the blue parlour. I want to make a list of things I'll require you to do.'

'What have you in mind?'

Alice hesitated in the doorway. 'I think it would be useful for you to remain here for a few days, if you will, Essie. You have a talent for organising things, and I've always left everything to my servants, but you know exactly what to do. Will you stay here and sort things out so that Raven will find his old home as it was when he left it?'

'I will, but only if everyone here understands that I have your authority to make any changes that I think necessary.'

Alice turned to Mrs Grimes. 'You're my witness, Cook. I give Miss Chapman my permission to do whatever she deems necessary, and if Mrs Wills decides to take up her old post I'll say the same to her.'

'I understand, my lady.' Mrs Grimes bobbed a curtsey. 'But what will we do if Smeaton returns?'

'I'll leave instructions with the head groom. You may call on him to use physical force, if necessary.'

'I'm sorry to tell you this, my lady, but Smeaton didn't pay the outside staff either, and most of them had to leave to find work elsewhere.'

'Raven would be furious if he knew what had been going on. Please don't tell me any more, Mrs Grimes. It will be sorted out, I promise you. Essie, come with me, we will have to work together.' Alice stormed out of the kitchen, almost bumping into Falco.

'What's wrong?' he asked anxiously. 'Who has upset you, my lady?'

'Your presence here is needed even more than I thought was possible. That man has created havoc in my cousin's home, and heaven knows what else he's done. I need your help to get Starcross back to what it was when Raven and Freddie left.'

'What about me, my lady?' Sadie clutched Essie's hand. 'You won't send me back to London, will you?'

Alice stared at her blankly. 'Of course not. You will remain here with Essie.' She gave Essie a straight look. 'I'm giving you a lot of responsibility for one so young. Am I making a mistake by leaving things to you?'

Chapter Fifteen

That night it snowed. Next morning Starcross Abbey was marooned in a white world and the old house was eerily silent when Essie awakened. She had shared her room with Sadie, mainly in an attempt to keep warm, and, although Jenifry had lit a fire, the bedding still felt damp. White light filtered through the curtains and Essie shook Sadie by the shoulder. 'Wake up, sleepy head, we've got a lot of work to do.'

Sadie opened her eyes and yawned. 'Just a few more minutes, Essie. It's nice and warm where I am.'

Essie pulled the covers off her. 'Get up and look out of the window. It's a sight worth seeing.'

Sadie scrambled out of bed, wrapping the coverlet around her as she crossed the floor to look out of the window. 'Snow,' she cried excitedly. 'Isn't that a pretty sight?'

'It is,' Essie said slowly, 'but the lanes are steep and narrow and even if they got the message last night the servants might not be able to get here.'

'Maybe it won't last long.' Sadie rested her elbows on the windowsill, gazing out longingly. 'I wish I had someone to play snowballs with.'

'I keep forgetting that you're just a child.' Essie slipped her arm around Sadie's shoulders and gave her a hug. 'If we get a lot of work done I'll come out with you and maybe we'll challenge the captain to a snowball fight.'

Sadie dissolved in giggles. 'That would be funny.'

'I'm going downstairs,' Essie said, reaching for her shawl. 'We need to get an early start.'

Sadie opened the window and leaned out. 'I've never seen so much whiteness – it's beautiful.'

'And it's cold. Please shut the window,' Essie said, laughing. 'Come on. We've lots to do today and it doesn't look as though we'll get much help.'

'Wait for me. I don't want to get lost.' Sadie closed the window. 'I'll get dressed quickly and come with you.'

Falco and Mrs Grimes were in the kitchen, which on first glance looked remarkably tidy. A fire burned in the range and the kettle was bubbling away on the hob. The scent of bacon frying masked the terrible odours that had filled the room the previous day, and Mrs Grimes was kneading bread dough. She looked up and smiled.

'How do you like waking up to a world white over, miss? Doesn't happen too often in these parts.'

'It's cold but very pretty.' Essie moved closer to the fire. 'What time did you get up, Captain?'

'I haven't been to bed.' Falco handled the frying pan with the ease of someone who was at home in the kitchen. 'At sea you get used to keeping watch at all hours and I wanted to make a start. Believe it or not, Essie, I like things to be shipshape. You can't live on board ship if things are in a mess.'

'And I always rise at six o'clock,' Mrs Grimes added cheerfully. 'It was so good to come downstairs and find the captain here instead of Smeaton and that trollop he brought into the house. You can't imagine what we've been through these past months.'

'No, I don't suppose I can,' Essie said thoughtfully. 'But it will be different now. Sadie and I will help to put things straight. We're used to hard work.'

'And a good breakfast will set us all up for the day.' Mrs Grimes gave the dough a final thump with her fists. 'There's enough here for two loaves and some small rolls, which will cook quickly, and if Smeaton's whore hasn't eaten it all there's some of my homemade raspberry jam in the cupboard. We have – or rather we had – a very productive vegetable garden, although goodness knows what state it's in now.'

Falco glanced over his shoulder, grinning broadly. 'I can command a ship and I sing like a nightingale. I can also cook bacon, but I don't know anything about gardening.'

'You'd better concentrate on what you're doing, Captain,' Mrs Grimes said grimly. 'Put this tray in the oven, will you, please? The first batch should be ready now so we'll have hot rolls to go with the bacon, providing it isn't burned to a crisp.'

Minutes later they were joined by Jenifry, who struggled into the kitchen carrying two wooden buckets filled with water. She knocked the snow off her boots and it plopped onto the tiles, dissolving into small puddles. 'I hope the pump don't freeze,' she said, shaking snowflakes from her hair. 'We're going to need lots of hot water.'

'Sit down and have some breakfast, maid.' Mrs Grimes began dishing out the bacon. 'There should be eggs in the henhouse, but someone will have to plough through the snow to reach them.'

'I'll go,' Sadie said eagerly. 'I can look for eggs.'

'What do you know about hens?' Mrs Grimes stared at her in surprise. 'You being a townsperson and all that.'

'There was chickens at the first place they sent me from the Foundling Hospital. Us nippers had to learn how to look after them, and I used to milk the goat on board the captain's ship. Lorenzo showed me how.'

'Lorenzo will feel the toe of my boot when I go back on board,' Falco said grimly. 'He's a lazy fellow.'

'Even so, Sadie has acquired a useful skill.' Essie took the rolls from the oven and tipped them into the wooden bowl. She set it down in the middle of the table. 'Are there any goats on the estate, Mrs Grimes?'

'There might be some in the home farm.' Mrs Grimes reached for the butter. 'Not that I venture over there. I don't like cows and sheep – nasty smelly things. But again, someone will have to go for supplies soon. Smeaton used to take the dog cart and drive to the farm several times a week.'

'That could be a job for you, Captain,' Essie said, taking a seat beside Falco. 'That is when the snow clears. Can we last that long, Mrs Grimes?'

'We'll have to, miss. Although things might get difficult if these conditions last for a week or more.'

After the meal was finished and everything cleared away, it was time to start work clearing the detritus left by Smeaton. According to Jenifry, he had taken Raven's study for his own use and the smell of stale spirits and tobacco smoke still lingered in the room. Empty wine bottles were littered on the floor; the carpet was badly stained, and there were burn marks where cigars had been stamped out. Ashes had spilled out of the fire basket to cover the hearth, and the furniture was coated in a thick blanket of dust. Essie backed out of the room and closed the door. 'We'll leave this for later. It's Raven's private place, but he's not here, so we'll start on the drawing room, then the dining room and so on.'

'It's been left for months, miss,' Jenifry said sadly. 'It will take forever and a day to clean all the rooms.'

'Well, we have to start somewhere.' Essie turned to Sadie, who was standing behind her, clutching a mop and bucket. She could see that the child was longing to go outside and it seemed unfair to keep her from enjoying the newly fallen snow. There would be plenty of time for working. 'Why don't you get a basket from Mrs Grimes and go to the henhouse to collect eggs?'

'May I really?'

'Wrap up warm,' Essie said, smiling. 'Maybe the captain could help you. I can't imagine him wielding a broom or a mop.'

Sadie needed no second bidding and she raced off in the direction of the kitchen, calling for Falco.

'So it's just you and me, miss,' Jenifry said, shaking her head. 'We'd best make a start.'

'One room at a time, that's the best we can do – and you can call me Essie. I'm not one of the gentry, I'm just an ordinary person.'

'I don't think so, miss. You're not like us, but that ain't a bad thing,' Jenifry added hastily. 'We'll rub along well enough, I'm sure.'

'Maybe we'd best begin in the drawing room.'

Essie waved a duster at Jenifry. 'Lead on, you know this house much better than I do.'

'If I didn't know different I'd think you be one of the family, miss.'

Essie chose to ignore this remark. Even so, Jenifry's innocent observation stirred memories of brief moments with Raven when they seemed to teeter on the brink of something more intimate than mere friendship. She squared her shoulders, pushing such thoughts from her mind as she followed Jenifry through the maze of corridors.

They had barely scratched the surface when Sadie burst into the drawing room, pink-cheeked with excitement. 'Look out of the window, Essie.'

'I've seen the snow, and I'm too busy to admire the view,' Essie said impatiently.

Sadie grabbed Essie's arm and tugged her towards one of the tall windows. 'Look out and see for yourself. You, too, Jenifry.'

Essie leaned on the windowsill and her hand flew to her mouth. 'Well, I never!'

Jenifry joined them and she emitted a long sigh. 'Thank goodness. They've come.'

'Who are they, Jenifry?' Essie asked, although she already knew the answer. The long procession of men and women who were plodding ankle-deep in snow, were those whom Smeaton had sent packing. The army of maidservants, stable boys, under grooms, footmen, gardeners and cleaning women were headed by a determined-looking woman, who could be none other than the redoubtable house-keeper, Mrs Wills, who was accompanied by a small man dressed in tweeds.

'Thank the Lord,' Jenifry whispered. 'Mrs Wills and Mr Havers, the steward. We're saved.'

Managing the staff at Starcross Abbey was, Essie decided, like commanding an army, but fortunately she had Havers to work with the tenants and oversee the work in the grounds, and Mrs Wills could have given the Iron Duke a few tips when it came to getting the best out of her staff. They lacked a butler, but Falco seemed to enjoy captaining the indoor servants in the same casual manner that he had employed on board the *Santa Gabriella*. He sat at the head of the table during meals in the servants' hall, with Mrs Wills on one side and Essie on the other. However, this arrangement found little favour with Mrs Wills, who insisted that Essie should dine apart from the servants. As someone who was favoured by both the Earl and his cousin, Lady Alice, Miss Esther Chapman was set apart from those below stairs and ought to be treated as if she were a member of the family. Sadie's position was equally ill-defined, and, although not related by blood, she might as well have been Essie's younger sister, but Sadie seemed to see herself as one of the maids. Essie solved the dilemma by insisting that they were all part of the Starcross family and they worked together, therefore it was logical that they should also dine together.

Even so, and as the days and weeks went by, Essie's position in the household became more like that of mistress of the house, with Falco spending much of his time going between Starcross and Daumerle, keeping Alice informed of their progress. Mrs Wills deferred to Essie on most things and it fell to Essie to check the accounts and agree the menus each day. She found herself with more time on her hands and she used it to explore the house and grounds. She spent hours in the library, studying the history of Starcross. The original medieval building had started out as an abbey, and during the dissolution of the monasteries had only narrowly escaped being razed to the ground. Sir Raven Dorincourt was created the 1st Earl of Starcross by Henry VIII and there the dynasty began. Successive generations built onto the house and it was interesting to see how Starcross had changed over a period of several hundred years. There were secret doors concealed cunningly as bookcases or wall panels, and hidden staircases used by the servants so that they did not disturb the family or guests.

The snow melted and spring was just around the corner. As the weather improved Essie explored the garden, chatting to the gardeners who were pleased to share their knowledge and years of experience with her. Havers charged the head groom with finding her a suitable mount, and Essie discovered that the bay mare he had chosen was a delight to ride, and much easier to handle than the animals they had ridden in Italy and Australia. Havers took her on a tour of the estate and they visited the home farm and the tenanted farms. The days passed all too quickly and Essie was beginning to feel so much at home that she suffered from pangs of conscience. She had written to her father several times, but had received no reply. This in itself was not a concern as she knew that he disliked putting pen to paper and the only printed matter he ever read was the occasional newspaper. Books and learning were not part of his daily life, but she worried about him and planned to return home at the first opportunity.

Alice visited every so often, and she made it clear that she had no intention of going to London until she was completely satisfied that Daumerle was in good order, and that everything at Starcross was running smoothly. She was delighted with the progress that Essie and Falco had made, and at the beginning of April she decided to spend a few days with them in order to catch up with some old friends who lived close by. Essie was alarmed at first when Alice announced casually that she had invited some of their neighbours for dinner the next day, but a quick consultation with Mrs Wills confirmed that the housekeeper was used to this sort of thing and

Cook was pleased to show off her culinary expertise. Essie breathed a sigh of relief and left them to work out the menu, but she was still nervous, and she waited until she had a few moments alone with Alice.

'I don't really fit in here,' Essie said as the door closed behind Cook, who had just handed a draft menu for Alice to approve. 'I'm neither a house guest nor a servant. Perhaps it would be best if Sadie and I took our meal in the servants' hall tonight.'

Alice stared at her in astonishment. 'Whatever makes you say that? You're as much a guest here as any of my friends. You've done more for Starcross than you can possibly imagine. It's lacked the hand of a mistress for so long that I was afraid the old place might crumble into dust.'

'That's hardly true,' Essie said, chuckling. 'I've only ever kept house for my pa in Limehouse. You can't compare that to managing a household such as this. The credit goes to Mrs Wills and Cook.'

'Utter nonsense,' Alice said firmly. 'You're a natural, only you don't realise it. Servants are only as good as the mistress who handles the reins. Raven left everything to Smeaton and you saw how that turned out. Mrs Wills and Cook were powerless to do anything other than obey him. Had he been left in charge much longer I fear he might have done irreparable harm.' Alice lowered her voice, glancing over her shoulder as if she were afraid of eavesdroppers.

'In fact, I have a feeling that he was the one who tipped off the revenue men. I've always suspected that it must be someone close to the family who had discovered that Freddie was involved with the smugglers.'

'What would he gain by that?'

'I've been trying to work it out,' Alice said seriously. 'Perhaps he held a grudge against him – I don't know – but he certainly took advantage of Raven's absence.'

'Didn't you suspect that something was wrong?' Essie asked, mystified by Alice's admission. 'You said you visited here quite often.'

'I did, and Smeaton was either clever, or crafty as a fox. Everything appeared to be running smoothly and nobody told me anything to the contrary. He must have made dire threats to silence Mrs Wills and Cook or they would have said something. So you see, Essie, you've brought about a small miracle and for that I'll be eternally grateful, and so will Raven when he hears what you've done. Don't worry about your position here – you are a dear friend and you will sit at table with us this evening with as much right to be there as I have.'

Wearing a gown borrowed from Alice for the occasion, Essie sat by the fire in the drawing room awaiting the arrival of Sir Robert Lawson, his wife, Priscilla, and her younger brother, Oscar

Bankes. Alice had warned Essie that Oscar was a ladies' man, and not to be taken seriously. Essie said nothing, but she remembered only too well the unwelcome advances of Diggory Tyce and many others on the river who had attempted to seduce her and failed. Falco declared that he would challenge any man to a duel who dared to take advantage of either of his ladies, receiving a sharp rebuke from Alice, who told him to mind his own business.

Falco retreated to a side table to pour himself a tot of brandy, leaving Alice seated on the sofa with an embroidery hoop in her hand, although Essie knew that it was just for show as Alice was no needlewoman. It suited her, however, to be seen carrying out a ladylike pursuit, although Essie doubted if her friends were fooled by this affectation. Sadie was absent even though she had been invited to join them for dinner, but she had begged to be excused. Essie knew that it would have been an ordeal for the twelve-year-old and she had not pressed the point. Alice had accepted Sadie's refusal with good grace, or maybe it was relief; Essie did not know and she did not pursue the matter. Now it was her turn to suffer from nerves and she turned with a start as the door opened and James ushered the guests into the room.

Alice rose to her feet and the embroidery hoop slid onto the carpet, unnoticed. She glided across the floor, her hand held out in welcome. 'Prissy, Rob and Oscar, how lovely to see you.'

Essie went to stand beside Falco and they waited in silence while Alice greeted her friends as if they had been separated for years. Eventually Alice turned to Essie with a beaming smile. 'Come, my dear. Allow me to introduce you to my oldest friends.'

Suddenly the room seemed twice as large and the distance between them might as well have been a mile rather than just a few feet. This would be her first test in polite society and Essie was nervous. Her mouth was dry and she was afraid her hands were sweating as she crossed the floor to meet them, but, even if they suspected her lowly background, Alice's friends were too polite to be anything other than friendly and charming. When the introductions were over and everyone was seated sedately sipping sherry, Essie knew that she was being scrutinised carefully and everything about her person, from her coronet of dark curls to her hazel eyes and shapely figure, was being noted. She hoped that Lady Lawson did not recognise her gown as one of Alice's cast-offs, and she wished that Oscar Bankes would stop ogling her. Then, after a moment of awkward silence when conversation flagged, Falco took centre stage. Quite what their guests thought of a foreign gentleman who liked to talk about himself was concealed beneath a mask of good manners, but Essie suspected that they were dying to discover how Lady Alice Crozier had become involved with such a colourful character.

After a long monologue Alice cut Falco short before his stories became too risqué. She enquired about the Lawsons' children, reeling off a list of names that left Essie puzzled as she tried to imagine a child called Beltane, and then it became obvious that they had gone on to discuss the wellbeing of the Lawsons' animals. It seemed that both Sir Robert and his wife paid more attention to their dogs and horses than they did to their five children. Falco was looking bored and it was a relief when dinner was announced.

Mrs Grimes had excelled herself and Falco had seen to the wine himself, having spent some time in the cellar sorting out the best vintages and a suitable wine for each course. The result was that they were all in various stage of intoxication by the time the meal ended. Essie had felt light-headed after one glass of sherry and she had just sipped her wine, but the others had quaffed theirs with obvious enjoyment. The volume of sound had risen with each course and the silliest joke seemed utterly hilarious, resulting in gales of laughter. Essie's sides ached by the time the ladies retired to the drawing room for coffee, leaving the gentlemen to enjoy their brandy and cigars. Essie had been waiting for Falco to burst into song, but he was well away with stories of derring-do on the high seas when she left the dining room.

Sir Robert and Oscar were happily drunk when they rejoined the ladies, and Falco was tottering slightly but was still able to enunciate without slurring his words. Lady Lawson tried to reprimand her husband, but she seemed to have trouble in finding the right words and she was reduced to giggles, which ended in a bout of hiccups.

'Fresh air,' Falco said boldly. 'That's what we need. A breath of air will cure you, my lady.'

'No, r-really.' Lady Lawson covered her face with her hands. 'I – I'm all right.'

'Capital idea, Falco.' Sir Robert grabbed his wife's hands and pulled her to her feet. 'Come along, Prissy. Best foot forward. The cold night air will set you right.'

'I know, Rob. Let's go the secret way.' Oscar grinned stupidly, tapping the side of his nose and winking.

'What are you talking about?' Alice demanded. 'You're drunk, Oscar.'

'So am I,' Oscar said stupidly. 'You're squiffy, Alice.'

His brother slapped him on the back. 'You're stewed to the gills, man. Let's show the ladies how we used to escape from the house when the old earl was angry with Raven and Freddie.'

'What is this?' Falco wagged his finger. 'I hope you're not taking my ladies into danger.'

Alice leaped to her feet, swaying a little, but

sobering rapidly. 'Shut up, Falco. You have no say in this.' She peered up at Sir Robert, studying his face in close detail. 'What are you talking about, Robbie?'

'Shhh.' He held his finger to his lips. 'Don't let the others hear you. It's a secret passage down to the beach. Smugglers,' he added, nodding his head. 'That's how the Dorincourts made their money.'

Alice stared at him, frowning. 'What a lot of rot you talk, Robbie.'

'Honest,' he said, crossing his heart. 'Hope to die.'

'Come on then.' Falco glared at him. 'Show us, or as Lady Alice said – shut up.'

'You can't speak to my husband like that.' Lady Lawson staggered to her feet, her hiccups seeming to have been cured. 'He's a magistrate, you foreign gentleman.'

'I'm Italian, my lady,' Falco said with dignity. 'If there's a secret passage – let's see it.'

Oscar chortled with laughter. 'Follow me. I've been longing to do this again.'

The entrance to the secret passage was in Raven's study. Despite his inebriated condition, Oscar knew exactly which panel to press and a door opened in what had appeared to be a solid wall. A gust of musty air wrapped itself around them and Essie shivered apprehensively.

'Hold on, Oscar,' Sir Robert said, clutching his

brother-in-law's coat sleeve. 'We can't take the ladies down there. They'll break their ankles.'

Alice pushed past him. 'Nonsense, Robbie. I had no idea that this was here. I'm going with Oscar. You can follow us or stay here, it's immaterial to me.' She gave Sir Robert a shove that sent him staggering backwards, narrowing missing treading on his wife's toes. 'Hold my hand, Oscar. I can't see a thing.'

'Wait for me, my lady.' Falco dived into the passage, his voice echoing off the narrow walls and low roof as he begged her to take care.

'At least give me a chance to fetch a lantern.' Essie was suddenly sober. 'This is madness.'

'I'm going, too.' Lady Lawson stepped into the passage. 'Give me a candle, Robert.'

Reluctantly he picked up a candlestick. 'All right, Prissy. Go ahead. I'm right behind you.' He turned to Essie with an apologetic smile. 'I'd stay here if I were you.'

'I wouldn't miss this for anything.' Essie followed him into the passage, holding her skirts above her ankles. Water seeped through the sandstone, trickling down the walls to form deep puddles in the uneven ground. Further on there were shallow steps leading downwards into what seemed to be the bowels of the earth. No one spoke but their laboured breathing echoed off the low roof, and the occasional hiccup was followed by an exclamation of annoyance from Priscilla.

3

The quality of the air changed suddenly, becoming fresher with the tang of salt, and Essie could see a faint glimmer of light ahead. A waft of cool air grew in intensity and the sound of waves crashing against rocks grew louder as the passage opened out into a cave. There was just enough headroom to enable the men to stand upright, and, for a moment there was silence, and then Oscar hallooed as if he were on the hunting field.

'This is amazing. I'd almost forgotten the secret passage, Robbie. We had some larks down here.'

'That was a long time ago,' Sir Robert said primly. 'We've grown up since then, Oscar.'

'You might have done, but Raven and Freddie must have been using it to store contraband,' Oscar said slyly. 'Pity they didn't let me in on the secret. I could have done with the money.'

Alice turned on him, her eyes glinting in a shaft of moonlight. 'Shut up, Oscar. You don't know what you're talking about.'

'Be fair, Alice,' Oscar said plaintively. 'They were caught in the act. Smuggling is still a crime.'

'Freddie got himself mixed up with a local gang.' Alice faced him angrily. 'Someone informed the revenue men and they were caught red-handed. Freddie was implicated simply because he happened to be on the beach at the time, and Raven had nothing to do with it, although he took the blame.'

'We know the story, Alice,' Sir Robert said calmly.

'I can't condone their behaviour. Raven should have let Freddie take his punishment. As it is I think they both got off lightly.'

'I think, sir, you do not know what you're talking about.' Falco's tone was measured but Essie knew him well enough to be wary. One wrong word from Sir Robert could bring a storm of abuse on his head.

'Falco is right,' Essie said quickly. 'You have no idea what being transported to the other side of the world means.'

'That's enough, Essie. This isn't the time or the place to discuss such matters.' Alice reached out to lay a hand on Essie's arm, but she brushed it away.

'No, let me speak. I've listened to your small talk all evening and I'm surprised at you, Alice. We know what life was like in the goldfields at Ballarat, and we saw how ill Freddie was in that tumbledown monastery.' Essie was too angry to worry about offending these people who knew nothing, but thought they knew everything. 'If you don't think that transportation and exile are hardships, Sir Robert, you are living in a very different world.'

'I'm glad to say that is true,' Sir Robert said stiffly. 'You should keep your opinions to yourself, Miss Chapman.'

'That's your answer to everything, isn't it? You people, with your big houses and fleets of servants, have no idea how the rest of us live. I doubt if you've ever been so hungry that your stomach aches and you barely have the energy to move. Have you ever been to the East End and seen the poor souls they call creepers dying in shop doorways for lack of food and warmth? Have you seen small children barefoot even in midwinter, their skin covered in scabs and their limbs bowed with rickets?'

'How dare you talk to us in that manner?' Lady Lawson said angrily. 'Robert, say something.'

Sir Robert turned his back on Essie. 'Oscar, take your sister back into the house. You go, too, Alice. I don't know where you found this girl, and why you foisted her on us, I can't imagine.'

'I beg your pardon?' Essie said angrily. 'Don't talk about me as if I weren't here. You are the one with no manners, sir.'

'And you are the type of person who ends up in court, having wheedled your way into the good books of a well-meaning wealthy person with intent to walk off with their valuables.'

'That's enough, Robert,' Alice cried angrily. 'How dare you insult Essie in that manner?'

'I can stand up for myself, thank you, Alice.' Essie glared at Sir Robert, her eyes narrowed. 'You think you're so far above everyone that you can say what you like.'

Falco stepped forward. 'That's where you're mistaken, my friend. No one speaks to a lady like that in my presence.' He took a mighty swing and knocked Sir Robert to the ground with one blow of his fist. 'Take on someone your own size next time.'

Lady Lawson uttered a feeble groan and collapsed onto the wet sand in a dead faint, and Essie stared at Sir Robert's inert body, at a loss for words.

Alice covered her mouth with her hands, and for a moment Essie thought she was crying, but she realised suddenly that Alice was laughing. Oscar leaned against the wall of the cave, chuckling. 'You deserved that, Rob.'

'Oh my goodness,' Essie said urgently. 'I can see a lantern bobbing up and down along the beach. Someone's coming.'

Chapter Sixteen

It had not been difficult to convince the revenue officers that the party was simply a drunken spree enjoyed by the rich and privileged, which ended in an argument getting out of hand. Essie could see that the revenue men were accustomed to such behaviour amongst the gentry. They had taken Alice's word for the fact she and her guests had left the great house and negotiated the steep cliff path to the beach, and the officers left the cave without further investigation. It was as well that both Sir Robert and Lady Lawson were unconscious for most of the short interview, and Oscar was so eager to corroborate Alice's account of events that Essie wondered if he had something to hide. Falco had said little throughout, and Essie had chosen to remain silent.

Sir Robert was groggy and bad-tempered when he came round and Lady Lawson was tearful, but they managed to get back to the study without mishap and everyone retired to bed except Oscar and Falco, who had opted to finish off a bottle of brandy before turning in.

Next morning the atmosphere at breakfast was frigid and the Lawsons left as soon as the meal was over, taking a hungover Oscar with them. Alice and Essie saw them off, but the goodbyes were brief.

'I'm worried,' Alice said as they re-entered the house. 'Robert is a magistrate and I'm afraid he might decide to press charges against Falco.'

'He didn't mention it at breakfast.' Essie eyed her anxiously. 'After all, if he admits that he knows of the secret tunnel he'll place himself in a difficult position.'

'That's true, but I think it best if you and Falco return to London today. We've set things straight here, and I know I can leave Havers to run the estate and Mrs Wills is absolutely trustworthy. Now that Smeaton is gone everything should go back to normal, although I'll make sure I visit more often than I did before.'

'You're right, Alice,' Essie said reluctantly. 'I should go home. I've written to tell Pa that I'm safe and well, so it won't be too much of a shock when I turn up, and I need to take my gold to a bullion dealer.'

'No. Don't do that.' Alice shook her head emphatically. 'You must stay in Hill Street until matters are settled. You know where to find Watkin Gilfoyle, Raven's solicitor. He's absolutely reliable and you can trust him to handle your affairs. He'll see that you get the best price for your gold, and he'll give you advice on making investments. He has contacts in the City and he'll make sure you aren't cheated.'

'But what about my pa?'

'Go and see him by all means, but it might be sensible to keep your finances to yourself. From what you've told me I don't think your father is a man of business, and he might expect you to hand over a large part of your fortune to him. In my opinion that would be a huge mistake.'

'You're right,' Essie said slowly. 'Pa would expect me to keep him in beer for the rest of his life.'

'It's your money, Essie, but you won't have it for long if you allow others to take it off you for their own selfish needs. Anyway, Tully will take you and Falco to the station and he can come back for me. I'll return to Daumerle today and I'll come to London when I'm satisfied that everything is running smoothly.'

'What about Sir Robert and his wife?'

'Don't worry about them. I'll let them cool down for twenty-four hours and then I'll ride over to Atherton Hall and make my apologies.'

'Will he be prepared to forget about last night, do you think?'

'Robert has had his eye on one of my hunters for a long time, and I think if I offered it to him at a good price he would be prepared to forgive almost anything. As to Prissy, she'll do what Robbie tells her, and she'll soon forget. She's a bit silly at times but she has a good heart. Now you'd best go upstairs and pack and I'll tell Falco he's to take you to London.'

'But what about the *Santa Gabriella*? Surely Falco will want to return to his ship?'

'Leave him to me,' Alice said smugly. 'You'll be in London by this evening, I promise you.'

'There's only one problem with your plan,' Essie said, slowly. 'I can't just turn up at your house in Hill Street. The last time we were there, Sadie and I were servants. Fielding will have us thrown out.'

'You're right, of course. I hadn't thought of that. Perhaps you ought to go home, but remember what I said, and take the gold to Gilfoyle at the first opportunity. You can trust him absolutely.'

'I'm sure I can, but it's not fair to ask Falco to come to London with me, and Pa would be sure to get the wrong idea if I turned up with a foreign sea captain in tow.' Essie had a sudden vision of her father with his sleeves rolled up, making dire threats on Falco's life if he refused to make an honest woman of her.

'I don't know,' Alice said doubtfully. 'It's a long

journey for you to undertake without an escort, especially with that lump of gold in your possession.'

'I don't think anyone would suspect that I was carrying a fortune in my luggage, and Sadie will be with me. We've been round the world and back again – I think I can get to London without an armed guard.'

'All right, if you're sure, and I dare say Falco will want to return to his ship, so perhaps it's for the best. But I'll send word as soon as I arrive in Hill Street and I want you and Sadie to join me there. Your life is about to change, and you can say goodbye to Limehouse.'

White's Rents looked even shabbier than Essie remembered. The train had passed through glorious countryside on a perfect spring day with trees and hedgerows bursting into leaf and fields filled with placid cows or dotted with sheep and lively lambs, but in Limehouse the sun never managed to force its way between the tall warehouses and manufactories that lined the narrow streets. Above her, mare's-tail clouds wafted across an azure sky, teasing the inhabitants with false promises of balmy, sun-soaked days yet to come, but at pavement level it was still winter.

It was late afternoon and washing lines straddled the street with grimy clothes dangling limply, gathering yet more dirt from the sooty air. The smell from the brewery wrapped itself around Essie like a damp cloth. A young woman came towards them, her attention focused on the toddler who clung to her skirts and the two older girls running on ahead. Essie recognised her as Marie, Saul Hoskins' wife, but her greeting fell on deaf ears as Marie scolded the twins and the little boy began to howl. It was obvious from her bloated belly that there would soon be an addition to the family, and another mouth to feed.

Sadie covered her nose and mouth with her hand. 'It stinks round here, Essie. I wish we'd stayed in the country.'

Essie was feeling much the same, but she managed a tight little smile. 'It's not so bad when you get used to it. Anyway, we won't be here for long. Just don't tell anyone.' She came to a halt outside number seven and tried the handle. It turned easily and the door swung open. 'Pa, are you there? It's me, Essie.' She stepped inside, coming to a sudden halt as she was faced by a large woman wearing an ill-fitting dressing robe and apparently little else. 'Who are you?' Essie stared at the blowsy creature whose hair was an unnatural shade of fiery copper, darker at the roots.

'Never mind me – who the hell are you?' The woman demanded. 'How dare you come busting into my house without knocking?'

'Your house?' Essie's voice rose an octave. 'This is my house. Where's my pa?'

'Essie?' Jacob's bare feet slapped on the bare

boards as he crossed the floor. 'What are you doing here? Why didn't you let me know you was coming?'

'Who is this, Pa?' Essie dropped her heavy valise on the doorstep. 'What's she doing in our house?'

'I live here, sweetheart.' The woman's manner changed subtly and she stretched her full lips into a sickly grin. 'I suppose it don't look good, but it's all honest and above board.' She held out a plump left hand. 'It's all legal, dearie. I'm your new ma.'

'You should've warned me you was coming, girl,' Jacob said gruffly.

'You're married to this woman?'

'I can't deny it,' Jacob said, nodding.

'I've only been gone a few months, Pa. How did this happen?'

'You left me to fend for meself. When they found the boat missing I thought you was dead and gone. I had to have someone to look after me, then Annie offered to cook me dinner one evening, and we went on from there.' He slipped his arm around Annie's plump shoulders. 'It was me lucky day when she got sacked for having a little tipple or two while she was working behind the bar.'

'Let me get this straight,' Essie said slowly. 'You married this woman when you were supposed to be in mourning for your only daughter.'

'So what?' Annie demanded, sticking out her chin.

'You wasn't dead and you run off and left the poor man in the lurch. Sick he was, sick and in need of loving care, which I offered.'

Sadie tugged at Essie's sleeve. 'Are we to stay here, or not?'

Jacob opened his mouth to speak but was silenced by a searing glance from his wife. 'There ain't room for two women in this house,' Annie said, nudging him in the ribs. 'Ain't that so, my dear?'

'I thought you was a goner, Essie,' Jacob said with an apologetic smile. 'You must see how it is with me now.'

Essie made a move towards the staircase. 'I see exactly how it is, Pa. I'll collect my things and we'll leave.'

With surprising agility for a large woman, Annie barred her way. 'You won't find nothing of yours upstairs. I had to clear the room for me own use.'

'You had no right to touch my things,' Essie said angrily. 'What have you done with my clothes?'

'They wasn't up to much. They barely fetched enough for a bottle of blue ruin.'

'You sold my possessions?' Essie could hardly believe her ears.

'That's wicked.' Sadie gave Annie a shove, catching her off balance. 'You're a bad woman.'

Recovering her balance, Annie took a swing at Sadie, catching her a blow on the side of her head that knocked her off her feet. 'Get out of my house.'

307

Annie's voice rose to a screech. 'Jacob, tell that girl of yours to take the brat and go.'

Essie helped Sadie to stand. 'I wouldn't stay here if you paid me,' she said furiously. 'As for you, Pa, you're welcome to this harpy.' She moved swiftly to the door and picked up her valise. 'Come on, Sadie. We're leaving.'

Jacob followed them, ignoring a tirade from Annie. 'Don't go like this, love.'

'I'm sorry, Pa, but you can see how it is.'

'Where will you go?'

'Don't worry about me.' Essie stood on tiptoe to plant a kiss on her father's whiskery cheek. 'Take care of yourself, Pa, and don't let her ruin your life.' She stepped out into the street, following by Sadie.

'I heard that,' Annie shouted. 'Good riddance, that's what I say.'

'Shut up, Annie.' Jacob slammed the door, but Essie could still hear her stepmother berating him. As they walked away the sound of Annie's shrill voice mingled with the general hubbub of the street.

'Where will we go?' Sadie asked tearfully. 'Will we have to sleep in a doorway?'

'Certainly not. I've got enough money to pay for a night's lodging. We'll just have to find a respectable inn, but first I want to see an old friend.' Essie set out purposefully, intent on finding Ben, although she was not sure what sort of welcome she would receive. The discovery that she had a stepmother had been a shock.

Somehow she had never imagined her father remarrying, and his choice of bride was questionable, but for the moment she had more pressing problems to deal with. She led the way to Fore Street and Duke Shore Dock, where she hoped to catch Ben in between trips, but there was no sign of Diggory Tyce's lighter. Essie realised that she was getting curious looks from men who, in the past, would have greeted her with a grin and a wave, and she felt like a stranger in a place she had once thought of as her home.

'Do I look so different, Sadie? I can't think why they're staring at me as if I were a foreigner.'

Sadie blew her nose on a ragged scrap of handkerchief. 'It's the duds, Essie. We're both used to dressing up smart like Lady Alice, and that's what makes them stare.'

'I'm the same person as I ever was.' Essie wrapped her shawl a little tighter around her shoulders as a cool east wind rattled up the river, ruffling the surface, and the incoming tide grappled with the tea-coloured waters of the Thames as it surged towards the coast. 'I wonder where Ben is. I need to speak to him.'

'Is he your sweetheart?' Sadie asked innocently. 'Do you think he's missed you?'

'We were friends,' Essie said firmly. 'Just friends, although I think he wanted more of me than I was prepared to give. You'll understand when you get a bit older.'

'There's a big fellow coming towards us. Looks like he knows you.'

Essie turned to see Diggory Tyce striding towards them.

'If you're a ghost, you're a very solid one.' Diggory came to a halt, looking her up and down. 'And you've done all right for yourself, I see by the duds you're wearing.'

'It's a long story,' Essie said casually. 'But, as you say, I'm still very much alive and I'm looking for Ben.'

'Poor boy, broke his heart when he thought you was drowned. Dunno what he'll think when he sees you dressed up like a toff.'

'Where is he?' Essie asked urgently. 'I want to see him.'

'I'm sure you do, but I sent the boy downriver and he won't be back for an hour or more.' Diggory made a move towards her but Essie backed away.

'I'll find him. There's no need for you to say anything.' She walked away with Sadie at her side.

'I don't trust him,' Sadie whispered.

'Quite right. Neither do I. We'll take a room at the White Hart, just for tonight, and tomorrow morning I'll visit Lady Alice's man of business. We need a home of our own, Sadie, and that will be at the top of my list.'

They walked on in silence. It had been a long day. Essie was tired and her legs were aching, as were her arms. The valise was heavy, weighed down by the gold nuggets, and getting it to a place of safety was her main concern.

They arrived at the pub without incident and the landlady, Mrs Steptow, showed them to a room beneath the eaves.

'We don't let rooms as a rule,' she said, eyeing Essie curiously. 'But my husband knows your pa quite well. He's a regular, or he was until he took up with Annie Ginger. She worked for us for a while, but a fondness for a nip or two got the better of her, and my old man had to let her go.'

'Yes, I met her for the first time today,' Essie dropped the valise onto the only bed in the room, creating a dent in the flock-filled mattress.

'Heavens above! Have you got bricks in that bag?' Mrs Steptow said, chuckling.

'I've got all my worldly goods packed in it, including my flat iron. I never could abide wearing a creased gown.' Essie tried to sound casual. The last thing she wanted was to arouse the woman's curiosity.

Mrs Steptow handed her a key. 'Well, love, whatever you got in there will be safe. You can lock the door and no one will bother you up here. It's just the one night, is it, for you and your little sister?'

Essie nodded, sending a warning look to Sadie. 'Yes, at the moment, anyway. We might need the room for a little longer. It all depends on how quickly I can find somewhere permanent.'

'Throw you out, did she? That sounds like Annie
Ginger. She'd not be one to share her good fortune.
I pity your pa, and that's the truth. Give me a shout
if you need anything, my dear. And you're welcome
to share our supper, if you're hungry. I'll send my
daughter up with a tray when it's ready. You don't
want to mix with the sorts we get in the bar – they're
not fit company for two young ladies.' She left the
room, closing the door behind her.

'I wish I was your sister, Essie.' Sadie slumped
down on the bed. 'I can't walk another step today.'

'There's no need for you to go out again, but if
you don't mind being on your own for an hour or
so I'll go back to the wharf and look for Ben. I
don't want him to hear of my return from someone
else.' Essie opened the valise and unpacked her nightgown. 'We'll be busy tomorrow, and I hope that Mr
Gilfoyle can find us somewhere to live. Wouldn't it
be lovely to have a house of our own?' She turned
to find Sadie curled up on the end of the bed, sound
asleep.

Essie pulled the coverlet over Sadie before stowing
the valise in a cupboard. She let herself quietly out
of the room and left the pub by the back stairs.
Daylight was fading fast and she quickened her pace.
Several times she was accosted by drunken men,
offering her money for her favours, but she managed
to evade them and arrived back at Duke's Wharf to
find that Tyce's lighter was already at its moorings,

and there was no sign of Diggory or Ben. She made
her way to the wharfinger's office in the hope of
catching Riley before he went home for his supper,
but the door was locked and it was unusually quiet.
Essie walked on, hoping that she might meet Ben on
the way to his lodgings, but there was no sign of
him. Darkness was rapidly claiming the city and
flickering gaslights shimmered on the surface of the
river, playing with the ripples like mischievous fireflies.

Essie had spent most of her life in Limehouse and
was accustomed to being out alone in the dark, but
she sensed that she was being followed and she
hurried towards the next set of steps that would
take her back onto the relatively safe area of Fore
Street. Her heart was racing and she fought down
a feeling of panic as the footsteps drew near and,
at last, unable to bear it any longer, she stopped and
spun round.

'It's you,' she gasped. 'I might have known it.
Leave me alone, Diggory Tyce.'

He lunged forward, seizing her in a hold that
almost crushed the breath from her lungs. 'You've
played fast and loose with me for years, and it's
time you was taught a lesson.'

'I don't know what you're talking about. Let me
go, or I'll scream.'

'There's no one to hear you, so scream away. I
like it when women shriek their silly heads off.'
Diggory pinned her to him with one muscular arm,

ripping her blouse open with his free hand. 'I've waited a long time for this, Essie Chapman.'

Essie opened her mouth to cry for help but he clamped his lips over hers, his tongue probing hers until she thought she was going to choke. She kicked out with her feet, but he thrust her against the brick wall. The taste and smell of him revolted her and every move she made seemed to excite him even more. She fought with all her might, but she was no match for a man of his size and strength. His weight pressing her against the wall made it hard to breathe and she was in danger of losing consciousness when he was dragged away from her with such violence that she crumpled to the ground. In the darkness she could make out the shape of the two men in a grim struggle. Fists flew and booted feet kicked out, accompanied by loud grunts and groans as blows hit home. Essie scrambled to her feet, holding her torn blouse together with a trembling hand. Her first instinct was to run for safety, but the man who had come to her aid was not getting it all his own way, and she looked round for a weapon of some sort that would bring an end to the uneven conflict. Tyce seemed to be winning, but even as Essie bent down to seize a broken pick handle, he was floored by a punch that knocked him senseless. Essie backed away, brandishing the stick.

'Don't come any nearer.'

'Essie? I heard that brute call you by name. Is that really you?'

The weapon slipped from her nerveless fingers. 'George?' Suddenly she was in an embrace that took her back to her childhood and tears flowed down her cheeks. 'It is you. I'd know you anywhere, even after all these years. I can't believe it.'

He held her at arm's length. 'It's too dark to see you properly, Essie, but you look and sound just like Ma.' He glanced down at Diggory's inert form sprawled on the ground. 'He'll come round in a minute or two. Let's get you away from here and you can tell me what you're doing wandering around the docks on your own at this time of night.'

Unprotesting, Essie allowed him to lead her up the steps to Fore Street. She came to a halt beneath a street lamp, gazing up at the brother she had not seen for so many years. 'It's a miracle,' she said slowly. 'You saved me, George. You appeared from nowhere.'

'Not exactly,' he said smiling. 'I've been working on the dock since I came ashore two months ago.'

'Why didn't you go home?'

'You know the answer to that as well as I do, but I hung around hoping to see you.'

'But you came to my rescue.'

'I saw Tyce manhandling a young woman, and I wasn't going to stand by and do nothing. Then he spoke your name and I saw red.' He took her by the arm. 'Come on, Essie. We can't stand about here. Where are you staying?'

'I booked a room at the White Hart.' Essie's hand flew to her mouth. 'And I left Sadie there on her own. She'll think I've met with an accident.'

'You could call Tyce an accident, I suppose. I know that man of old. He's a bad 'un and always has been.'

'I didn't encourage him, George.'

'Of course not. I never thought you had for a second.' George quickened his pace. 'Who's this Sadie, then?'

'Oh, George, I've got so much to tell you – I don't know where to begin.'

'Start at the beginning then. I've always found that's best.'

Essie squeezed his arm. 'No, for once you can answer me a few questions. Where have you been all this time, and why didn't you try to contact me?'

'I went to sea, Essie. It's as simple as that. After that set-to with Pa I went down to the dock and got into conversation with the mate on a ship bound for New Zealand. He took me on board and the captain signed me up as ship's boy.'

'Did you come back to London often?'

'Now and again, but I couldn't bring myself to visit the house. I missed you, of course, but I thought it best to keep away. I'll never forgive the old man for the way he treated Ma, but you'd be too young to remember it.'

'I always hoped you'd come back, but I didn't think it would be like this.'

'We'll make up for lost time. I'm going to stay ashore now. I saved a bit of money while I was away on long trips and I was careful not to squander it when I did go ashore. I thought I'd buy myself a business of some sort, although I haven't quite worked out what it will be.'

They came to a halt outside the White Hart and he took her hands in his. 'I'd best let you get some rest. You look exhausted, girl.' He stared at her, frowning. 'Did he hurt you? If so I'll go back and finish him off.'

She shook her head. 'No, George, you came in the nick of time. I was never so glad to see anyone in my whole life, and now I know it's you that makes it even better. I can't believe you're really here.'

'The same goes for you.' He held her at arm's length. 'Who'd have thought that skinny little child would grow up into a beautiful young woman?'

'I loved you dearly and it broke my heart when you left.'

'We'll make up for it, Essie love. Go inside and get some sleep. We'll spend the day together tomorrow, and you can tell me all about yourself. I'll come and call for you, first thing in the morning.'

'I have got such a lot to tell you.'

He grinned, looking suddenly boyish. 'Tell me one thing. Why are you staying at an inn when you've got a home down the road, such as it is? Did the old man throw you out, too?'

'No, but it's a long story, George. I've been away for months and when I got home I found that Pa has remarried, and she's not the sort of stepmother I'd wish on anyone.'

George nodded, giving her a sympathetic smile. 'I can imagine the type.' He leaned over to kiss Essie on the cheek. 'Good night, poppet. Sleep tight.'

'Don't let the bed bugs bite,' Essie finished the sentence with a chuckle. 'Good night, dear brother. I can't tell you how happy I am to see you again.'

Essie was awakened by the sound of someone tapping on the bedroom door. She sat up in bed, still drugged with sleep. 'Who is it?'

'It's Mrs Steptow, miss. There's a gentleman downstairs who says he's your brother.'

Essie leaped out of bed. 'Thank you, Mrs Steptow. Would you be kind enough to ask him to wait? I'll be down in a second or two.'

'Yes, miss.' Mrs Steptow did not sound too pleased, but Essie was too excited to care. She leaned over to shake Sadie by the shoulder.

'Wake up. There's someone I want you to meet. I've got a feeling that it's going to be a wonderful day.'

Chapter Seventeen

George took them to a coffee shop for breakfast and he listened in silence while Essie recounted the adventures that she and Sadie had shared with Lady Alice and Raven.

'My time at sea sounds quite tame compared with what you two have been through,' he said admiringly. 'I can't believe that my little sister has grown up to be such an enterprising and brave young woman.'

'I had Sadie with me all the time,' Essie insisted. 'She's part of the family now, George.'

He smiled and nodded. 'Of course, and you're more than welcome to join us, young Sadie.' His expression darkened. 'But I don't know how I'm going to provide for you both. I've been living in cheap lodgings since I came ashore, and I don't earn enough to rent a decent house in a better area. Limehouse isn't the best of places.'

Essie hefted her valise onto the table. 'I have the answer, George.'

'What have you got in there? It seems to weigh a ton.'

Essie glanced round nervously, but at this early hour there were few customers and they were chatting to each other over steaming cups of coffee, too involved in their own affairs to bother about anyone else. 'I told you about poor Beasley,' Essie said in a low voice. 'Well, this is his legacy. He gave it to me before he died, the poor man, and I'm taking it to Lady Alice's solicitor in Lincoln's Inn. The sooner I get there the better.'

'Are you saying what I think you're saying?'

'Gold,' Essie whispered. 'A large nugget, worth a fortune, and a smaller one that I found in the creek at Ballarat.'

George stared at her, disbelief written on his even features. 'You're joking.'

'I'm not going to show you now, but you'll see it soon enough, if you'll come with us to the solicitor.'

George downed the last of his coffee. 'I most certainly will.'

Watkin Gilfoyle held the larger gold nugget in both hands, and let out a low whistle between his teeth.

'This must be worth a fortune, Miss Chapman. You're a rich young woman.'

George bristled visibly. 'I'm here to see that my sister doesn't get fleeced.'

'I can assure you that won't happen while I handle her affairs,' Gilfoyle said stiffly.

'My brother didn't mean any disrespect, sir.' Essie shot a warning look at George. 'But where we come from it's hard to know who is honest and who would steal the shirt off your back.'

'Quite so.' Gilfoyle eyed them, frowning. 'That will be my responsibility from now on, should you wish me to act on your behalf.'

Sadie shifted from one foot to the other. 'What's he saying, Essie?'

Essie hushed her with a finger to her lips. 'I do, Mr Gilfoyle. I want you to handle my affairs, and most important, we need somewhere to live and we must find it quickly.'

'I see.' Gilfoyle looked from one to the other. 'Does that include you, sir?'

George turned to Essie, eyebrows raised. 'That's up to my sister. We've been separated for a long time due to circumstances that I won't go into now, but she knows that I've always loved her and I want to look after her to the best of my ability.'

'You are not in employment, I take it?' Gilfoyle scrutinised George carefully, as if putting every detail of his face to memory.

'I recently came ashore, sir, and have been working in the docks for the last two months, but I have some money saved and I intend to go into business for myself.'

'With the help of your sister, no doubt.'

Essie winced at the implied suggestion that her brother would take advantage of her position, but George answered before she had a chance to defend him. 'I've only just found out about Essie's stroke of good fortune, and I don't intend to take a penny piece from her.'

'I'm glad to hear it,' Gilfoyle said with a hint of a smile. 'It seems that we both have her best interests at heart, Mr Chapman.'

George nodded. 'Most assuredly.'

'Then we understand each other.' Gilfoyle picked up a sheaf of papers and leafed through them. 'Ah, here it is. I have a property for rent that might suit your requirements at present. It's fully furnished and well within your means, Miss Chapman. It belongs to one of my clients who has entrusted me to find a good tenant, and I think you would both be well suited.'

'Really?' Essie could hardly contain her excitement. 'Where is it, Mr Gilfoyle?'

'It's a charming house in Curzon Street, off Park Lane. It's only a short distance to Hyde Park and not very far from Lady Alice's town house in Hill Street. I think you might be very comfortable there.'

'Really?' Essie said eagerly. 'Is it big enough for all of us? I mean is there room for my brother as well as Sadie and myself?'

Gilfoyle nodded, smiling. 'I think you'll find it quite commodious, Miss Chapman. I take it that you will want to keep the servants on? The present owner died abroad, leaving everything to a niece who has an estate in Yorkshire and little or no interest in what goes on in London.'

'I'm not sure if I can afford to pay staff, sir,' Essie said doubtfully. 'Will I have enough money for that?'

'Money is the least of your worries, Miss Chapman. I will see that you are kept fully informed as to your assets, and maybe you will allow me to advise you on making investments?'

George cleared his throat noisily. 'You'll pardon my asking, sir, but how do we know you'll give Essie the best advice? No offence meant.'

'None taken, Mr Chapman. I see your dilemma, and all I can say is that Lady Alice Crozier has trusted me to handle her affairs since she came of age and inherited a fortune. Maybe you ought to have a word with her before you come to any decision.'

Essie shook her head. 'No, sir. Thank you, but I am happy to leave everything to you. I know Lady Alice trusts you, and that's good enough for me.'

'Splendid. I'm sure you would like to inspect the house before you agree to take on the tenancy.'

Sadie tugged at Essie's sleeve. 'May we? Please.'

'Of course.' Essie was about to stand up, but she hesitated, eyeing Gilfoyle warily. 'There's only one problem, sir.'

'What is that, Miss Chapman?' Gilfoyle leaned forward, fixing her with a penetrating stare. 'What can I do to assist you further?'

'I'm a bit short of readies, sir.' Essie glanced at George.

'I'll look after you,' he said firmly. 'I told you that I've got money saved.'

'There's no need for that, sir.' Gilfoyle reached for a brass bell and rang it. 'I'll tell my clerk to advance you enough to get by on, Miss Chapman. Will fifty do?'

'Fifty shillings will be a great help, sir,' Essie said, stifling a sigh of relief.

'Fifty pounds, Miss Chapman. You will have expenses now that you're moving up in society.'

Essie stared at him in amazement. Fifty pounds was a fortune – she had never had that much money in her whole life. 'I wasn't planning to live like a lord, Mr Gilfoyle.'

He laughed. 'You'll discover that the gentry have a different attitude to money from the rest of us mortals, Miss Chapman. But, in any event, you will need cash for incidentals; gloves, fans, ribbons and furbelows, items that ladies seem unable to live without.'

'What's a furbelow?' Sadie whispered. 'Can you eat it? Because I'm starving and it's a long time since breakfast.'

Essie was about to answer when the door opened and Gilfoyle's clerk sidled into the room. 'You rang, sir?'

'Miss Chapman is considering the property in Curzon Street, Phipps. Send a messenger on ahead to warn the servants of their arrival, and give her fifty pounds from the safe.' Gilfoyle glanced out of the window. 'And tell the boy to find a cab. It looks like rain.'

They arrived in Curzon Street in the middle of a thunderstorm. The sky was heavy with rainclouds and the air was sultry and sulphurous. The cab had pulled up at the kerb outside a five-storey terraced house. With an imposing columned portico and wrought-iron balconies it looked so grand that Essie wondered if they had come to the wrong address. George opened the door and stepped onto the pavement, holding out his hand to help Essie alight. Sadie leaped to the ground unaided.

'There must be some mistake,' Essie said anxiously. 'This is as grand as Lady Alice's house.'

'That'll be a shilling, guv.' The cabby leaned down from his perch, holding out his hand.

'Are you sure this is the right place?' Essie counted out the pennies. 'I think there must be a mistake.'

The cabby snatched the money and pocketed it. 'No mistake, lady. This is Curzon Street. Servants' entrance down the steps.' He flicked the whip and the horse ambled off in the direction of Park Lane.

Essie stared at the elegant façade and her heart sank. 'Maybe we're to rent rooms here, George. This looks far too big and grand for us.'

George marched up to the front door and rapped on the brass knocker. 'There's only one way to find out, girl. If you're going to be a lady, you'd better start acting like one.' He held out his hand. 'Come on, you're my brave little sister. I remember when you was faced by a big black rat in the back yard, and you only five years old. You picked up a broom and chased it off.'

Even as he spoke the door opened and they were faced by a stern-looking butler, dressed in black. The memory of the rat was fresh in her mind and Essie braced her shoulders. 'We've come to view the property. Mr Gilfoyle sent word.'

The butler's stony expression relaxed a little. 'We were expecting you, Miss Chapman. Please come in.' He stepped aside and ushered them inside.

Essie's first reaction was one of awe, quickly followed by dismay. At the far end of the wide, marble-tiled entrance hall an elegant staircase swept up to the first floor. This was an imposing mansion, far too large for three people, and her practical mind warned her that the running costs would be exorbitant. 'Is the whole house for rent?' she asked tentatively. 'Or are we to have just a few rooms?'

The butler's eyebrows shot up to his hairline. 'The whole house, of course, ma'am.'

Essie came to a halt. 'What's your name, sir?'

'It's Parkinson, miss.'

'Well, Parkinson, I think there's been a mistake. I think we had better leave now.'

'You don't approve of the accommodation, miss?' Parkinson's mouth drooped at the corners and for a terrible moment Essie thought he was going to cry.

'No, no. I mean, yes, I do. It's beautiful, but it's very grand and extremely large. There's only me and my brother and Sadie. We'll rattle round like peas on a drum.'

Parkinson coughed into his hand, or maybe he was trying not to laugh, Essie was not sure, but he seemed to relax. 'Allow me to show you around, Miss Chapman. It's true that there are many rooms, but not all are in use, and the servants are afraid they might lose their positions if a new tenant isn't found soon. I believe there was talk of selling up.'

George stepped forward. 'Well, we can't have that, can we, Essie? Lead on, Parkinson. We'll certainly take a look.'

Sadie clutched Essie's hand and they followed

Parkinson into the reception rooms on the ground floor. The morning parlour overlooked Curzon Street, and Parkinson described it as being small and on the poky side, although it seemed very spacious to Essie. He was more generous about the dining room, which to Essie looked like a banqueting hall, and he waxed lyrical about the billiard room and the study. The drawing room was on the first floor and was sufficiently large to merit favourable comments, and the library was situated across the landing. There were two bedrooms on that floor and four good-sized bedchambers on the second and third floors, with a nursery suite tucked away at the back of the house. The servants' quarters were situated on the top floor, but Parkinson did not offer to take them up the narrow flight of stairs, and Essie did not like to ask. She would have liked to inspect the rooms, just as she would have been interested in seeing the kitchen and servants' hall below stairs, but she had learned enough at Starcross Abbey to know that the lady of the house rarely bothered herself with such details.

Parkinson took them back to the morning parlour where a tray of coffee and small cakes had materialised, as if by magic. 'I thought you might like some refreshment,' he said stiffly.

'Thank you, Parkinson,' Essie said, taking a seat nearest to the silver coffeepot. 'This is most welcome.'

Sadie slumped down on a chair and her hand shot

out to snatch a cake. 'I'm sorry,' she said defiantly, 'but I'm really hungry.'

George perched somewhat awkwardly on the edge of the dainty sofa. 'Nice house you've got here, Parkinson.'

Parkinson stared straight ahead. 'Do I take it that you might consider taking up the lease, sir?'

'That's up to my sister,' George said, reaching for a cake and popping it into his mouth.

'It is a very nice house, but it's much too large for us.' Essie handed a cup of coffee to her brother, giving him a warning look. George seemed to be carried away by his surroundings, but, in her opinion, this mansion was not for the likes of them.

Parkinson backed towards the door. 'I'll leave you to discuss the matter, miss. Ring the bell if you require anything more.'

Essie waited until the door closed on him. 'What do you really think, George? It is splendid, but the rent is likely to be more than we can afford, and I hate to think how much it would cost to run such an establishment. We ought to look for something smaller and a bit more homely.'

George sipped his coffee. 'It seems to me that you'll be a wealthy woman when the nugget is sold. Why not live up to it? Who knows, you might snare a rich husband and then you'd be set up for life.'

'George Chapman! What a thing to say.' Essie

gazed at him in a mixture of amusement and dismay. 'I'm not interested in marriage.'

He shrugged. 'I thought that was all females talked about. What else would you do?'

Sadie stuffed another cake into her mouth. 'I don't want to get married.'

'Neither do I,' Essie said firmly. 'At least, not yet. I want to do something good with the money. Maybe I could help the poor, or cripples like Beasley.'

'Lord help us.' George shook his head. 'Don't tell me you're going to be a missionary.'

'There's no fear of that,' Essie said, chuckling. 'I intend to enjoy life, but I won't forget where the opportunity came from and I will try to do something to help others.'

'Pass me another cake, Sadie.' George placed his cup and saucer back on the tray. 'Is there any more coffee in the pot, Essie?'

She refilled his cup. 'What do you think, George? Should I take this house? Or should I ask Mr Gilfoyle to find us something more modest?'

'I say take it, Essie. Your friend Lady Alice lives nearby. If she decides to introduce you to her circle you'll need to live as they do.'

'But that's not what I want,' Essie protested. 'I don't wish to live in a social whirl. I met some of her friends in Devonshire, and I wasn't impressed. I thought they were smug and shallow.'

'But you like Raven and Freddie.' Sadie licked the

sugar crystals off her fingers, one at a time. 'We all got on well in Ballarat.'

'That was different,' Essie said quickly. 'We were thrown together in difficult circumstances, and we had to survive. Besides which, I doubt if I'll ever see Raven or Freddie again.'

George and Sadie exchanged knowing glances.

'Why are you looking like that?' Essie asked crossly. 'What have I said?'

'You've made your feelings clear, love.' George took her hand and squeezed it. 'You're involved with that family and I don't see that coming to an end. Take the house. You deserve to have a good life after what Pa put you through. Live like a lady and enjoy yourself for a change.'

'I like it here,' Sadie said, swallowing a mouthful of cake. 'It's nicer than Limehouse and it smells better.'

Essie chuckled. 'That's true, but I need to speak to Mr Gilfoyle before I make a decision. But what about you, George? You said something about starting a business. If it's to do with the river perhaps we ought to think again, and look for something closer.'

'The future is steam, Essie. Sail is all very well, and still has a place, but steam is king. I'm having talks with a chap who owns a vessel and is looking for a partner.'

'Does that mean you'd go back to sea?' Essie asked anxiously.

'Not necessarily. I'd like to have a spell ashore.'

'Who is this person?' Essie asked suspiciously. 'And how did you meet him?'

'His name is Jack Manning and he's interested in the purchase of a second screw steamer so that he can expand his business. He's already made a success with one ship and he's a go-ahead sort of fellow.'

'But he wants your money,' Essie said flatly. 'Are you sure he's reliable?'

'You are a suspicious girl, Essie. But don't worry, Jack's family have money. His father started the business years ago and when he died he left everything to his only son. Jack did a spell at sea when he was younger and he's well respected.'

'And have you enough money to invest?'

George nodded, grinning. 'I'm not asking for a loan, little sister. I've saved enough to finance this venture. I was going to meet Jack when I saw that oaf manhandling you.'

'I'm sorry,' Essie said sincerely. 'Does that mean you've missed the opportunity?'

'I caught up with him in the Bunch of Grapes after I left you, last evening. He's as keen as I am to conclude our business, and I'm meeting him at six o'clock to finalise the deal.'

'So you've made up your mind.' Essie eyed him thoughtfully. 'Do you think I ought to take this house?'

'What would Lady Alice say?' George said seriously. 'You seem to think a lot of her, Essie.'

Sadie jumped to her feet. 'I know she'd agree. Lady Alice made us take lessons in deportment and manners and all sorts of stuff like that. And,' she added slyly, 'won't it be a surprise for Raven when he comes home a free man?'

They moved into the house in Curzon Street next day. Essie had toyed with the idea of paying a final call on her father, but she had a feeling that his new wife would make a nuisance of herself if she discovered that her stepdaughter had come into money. At least she had found George, and, although he had declined financial help, she was determined to assist him in any way she could. They were a family at last and she could not wait to introduce her tall, good-looking brother to Alice, who had not yet returned from Devonshire. What George lacked in town polish he made up for with natural charm and personality. She wished that she could introduce him to Raven and Freddie, and, despite her good fortune, she sometimes found herself wishing that she was back in Ballarat where life was simple and basic. She hoped that Leah's health had improved, and that her sons were looking after her.

After the first couple of weeks, during which time Essie had been kept busy settling into her new home and getting to know the servants, she woke up one morning wondering how she was going to fill the day. The housemaid had lit the fire and had brought her a cup of hot chocolate, returning minutes later to fill the china jug on the washstand with warm water. This left Essie with nothing to do other than recline on a mountain of pillows and sip her drink. She sighed, watching the flames lick around the glossy black coals in the grate. The chocolate was sweet and rich, and when she went downstairs to the dining room she knew there would be a mouth-watering selection of food in the silver salvers. It was all so different from her life in Limehouse, when she would be lucky to have a slice of bread and dripping for breakfast, and more often than not she had gone to work hungry. She smiled as she recalled the food they had cooked over the campfire in Ballarat. Lumpy porridge had seemed like a luxury and she had been grateful for the damper cooked on the embers, even if it was burned and chewy.

Even so, the morning stretched out before her. There would be the inevitable meeting with Mrs Jackson, the housekeeper: a decent enough woman, if a little starchy. Essie would discuss the menu for the day and that would be an end to their conversation. After that, time was her own to fill as she pleased, unless she had a fitting with her dressmaker. Essie was in desperate need of a complete new wardrobe, as was Sadie. Gilfoyle, with surprising knowledge of such matters, had recommended a young widow who lived in lodgings not too far away, and Essie had found her to be an excellent choice.

However, these distractions took up very little time and what to do with such leisure was her main problem. Essie replaced her empty cup on the table at her bedside, stretched and yawned as she considered her options. Boredom was her enemy and the luxurious house was beginning to feel like a prison.

George had come to an agreement with Jack Manning, and he left for Wapping early each morning, returning late in the evening. Sometimes he arrived in time to dine with her and Sadie, but more often than not they had retired to bed before he came home. But George appeared to be happy and that was all that mattered to Essie. He had found something at last that suited his nature and temperament and he was exercising his abilities to the full. She could not but he glad for him: he had found his calling in life, she had yet to find hers, and it was no good moping in bed.

Today, she decided, would be different. She had a fluttery feeling in her stomach, as though something exciting was in the offing, and she leaped out of bed, washed, dressed and went downstairs to the dining room.

George was seated at the table finishing off a plate of bacon and devilled kidneys. He half rose from his chair but Essie shook her head, smiling. 'Don't get up, George.'

He sat down again. 'You're up early. I wasn't expecting company.'

'I always have breakfast at this time every day, but you're such an early bird these days. I hardly ever have time to speak to you.'

'I've a late start this morning. Manning has found a ship that he's interested in and I'm going to take a look at it.'

'How exciting. I wish I could see it.' Essie went to the sideboard and helped herself to buttered eggs and a rasher of bacon. She smiled and nodded to the parlour maid. 'I'd like a fresh pot of coffee, please, Biddy.'

'Yes, miss.'

'I hope your cold is better today,' Essie added, smiling.

Biddy picked up the coffee pot and sketched a curtsey. 'Yes, miss. Thank you, miss.' She hurried from the room.

'Should you be so familiar with the girl?' George asked as Essie sat down beside him.

'She's a person, just like us,' Essie said calmly. 'And she looked terrible yesterday.'

'Even so, I've seen the expression on Parkinson's face when you chat to the servants. I don't think it's the right way to behave.'

'This is my house – I mean, it's our home, George. I'll treat the servants as I see fit. Now tell me about this new ship.'

George eyed her speculatively. 'You're bored, aren't you, Essie? And don't deny it, because it's obvious. You weren't brought up to be a lady of leisure, so why don't you come down to the docks with me today? I'll introduce you to Manning and maybe you could look over the ship with us. After all, you've been round the world in a steamship, so you know what you're talking about.'

Essie paused with her fork halfway to her mouth. 'That would be so exciting. I never thought I'd feel this way, but I miss the river and life on the water.'

'You're not sorry you struck it rich, are you, Essie?'

She glanced at the polished mahogany table and the silver place settings; the fine bone china and the silver epergne laden with fruit and flowers. 'Sometimes I feel that I don't deserve all this.'

'I think you need a day out, and hopefully your friend Lady Alice will return to London soon. I know you've missed her company.'

Essie nodded. 'I have. I know I've got Sadie and she's a dear, but it's not the same as having a friend closer to my age.'

'Would Sadie like to come with us?'

'I'm sure she would. I'll send Biddy to wake her up and tell her to hurry or we'll go without her. It will be a lovely day out.'

They arrived at the wharf in time for George to open up the office. Essie and Sadie inspected the premises, although that did not take long as there were only two rooms. The front office was furnished simply, with a desk and two chairs, and the general purpose room at the back had a small fireplace with a blackened kettle resting on a trivet, as if waiting for someone to light the fire. There was a wooden table littered with dirty cups and plates, old newspapers and empty beer bottles. The walls were covered in tide tables, charts and official documents relating to working on the river.

'It's cold in here,' Sadie said, shivering. 'Shall I light the fire for you, George?'

He poked his head round the office door. 'Later, nipper. The ship we're going to look over has hauled into sight, and I've just seen Jack striding along the wharf. You'll like him, Essie. He's a good fellow. Anyway, step outside and take a look at our prize.'

Essie and Sadie followed him out onto the wharf. A chilly east wind tugged at their bonnets and slapped their cheeks. Essie gazed at the ship and her heart lurched against her tightly laced stays.

She clutched her brother's arm. 'George, is that the vessel you're thinking of buying?'

He followed her gaze. 'That's the one, but Jack has put up most of the money. I'll only have a small stake in it, but that's better than nothing. Here he comes, now. I'll introduce you.'

Essie nodded absently, but her attention was firmly focused on the familiar figure who stood on deck, waiting for the lighter to get close enough to allow him to board.

Chapter Eighteen

'Falco.' Essie and Sadie spoke in unison.

'Who the devil is Falco?' George stared at them as if they had gone mad.

'He's the captain of the *Santa Gabriella*,' Essie said, smiling. 'I can't think why he would bring his ship upriver.'

'Here's someone who can explain everything.' George turned to greet the man who strode up to them. 'Jack, come and meet my sister. Essie, this is Jack Manning, my business partner.'

'Good morning, Miss Chapman.' Jack doffed his hat with a courtly bow.

'Good morning, sir.' Essie eyed him curiously, liking what she saw. He had a friendly smile and pleasant features, and, although she would not have described him as handsome, there was something attractive about him that she could not quite define. A little above medium height and solidly built, he gave the impression of being dependable and trustworthy, like an English oak tree.

'What about me?' Sadie demanded crossly. 'I'm here, too.'

'Shame on you, George,' Jack said severely. 'Where are you manners, sir? Won't you introduce me to your lovely younger sister?'

Essie could see that her brother was at a loss and she stepped in quickly. 'This is Sadie Dixon, Mr Manning. I suppose you might call her my ward, although I do think of her as my sister.'

'How do you do, sir?' Sadie took his hand and shook it, pumping Jack's arm up and down enthusiastically.

'How do you do, Sadie?' Jack acknowledged her with a bow and a smile. 'I'm delighted to make your acquaintance.'

'Now the pleasantries are over, let's get on with the important business,' George said impatiently. 'That is the vessel you're thinking of purchasing, isn't it?' He pointed to the *Santa Gabriella*.

'Yes, indeed. I gather that the owner wants a quick sale, so we might get a bargain.'

'The captain is coming ashore in the lighter. It's a strange coincidence but Essie knows him and his ship.'

Essie nodded. 'It's Captain Falco. We sailed to Australia and back in the *Santa Gabriella*, but when

I last saw Falco he was intent on staying in Devonshire with Lady Alice. I'm surprised to see him here.'

'There is Lady Alice,' Sadie cried, pointing to a fashionably dressed figure standing on deck.

'How lovely.' Essie could hardly contain her delight. 'I've missed them both. I can't wait to see them again.'

'You say you sailed halfway round the world in that tub, Miss Chapman?' Jack said incredulously.

'It's not a tub,' Essie said sharply. 'It took us to Australia, crossing the Pacific and we rounded Cape Horn on the way back. It's a good ship and Falco is an excellent captain, but I find it hard to believe that he's selling the *Santa Gabriella*. I thought he loved that boat.'

'Ship,' George said sternly.

'Boat or ship, it makes no difference to me. The *Santa Gabriella* might creak a bit and it could do with a lick of paint, but it took us across oceans and brought us home safely.'

'That's all I need to know.' Jack moved to the top of Hermitage Stairs, gazing down at the lighter as it bobbed its way across the turbulent water. 'Captain Falco looks like a reasonable man, George. Perhaps it's providence that led him to us, especially with your sister's experiences in mind.'

'What would you say, Essie?' George asked seriously. 'Did the engine ever break down during your voyage?'

'No, George. The accommodation could be made

more comfortable, but we sailed through some bad weather and there was never any doubt as to our safety. I was never afraid on the *Santa Gabriella*.'

'Neither was I,' Sadie said proudly. 'Captain Falco kept us safe.'

'You will take us on board, won't you, George?' Essie asked eagerly. 'I want to see Alice.'

'Yes, if it's all right with Jack.'

Jack turned his head and smiled. 'Of course it is. I'd value your opinion, Miss Chapman.'

'It's Essie,' she said firmly. 'Thank you, Jack.' She moved to his side and waited while the lighter ploughed its way towards them, fighting wind and tide until it reached the bottom of the steps.

Falco stepped ashore, his face wreathed in smiles as he reached the wharf, and he wrapped Essie in a warm embrace. 'What a surprise. I looked up and thought I saw the face of an angel – then I realised it was you, Essie. But you're the last person I was expecting to find waiting for me.'

'I knew nothing about this, Falco. It's as much a surprise to me as it is to you.'

'I don't understand,' he said, frowning. 'I thought I was to meet a prospective purchaser. It's not you, is it?'

'No, of course not.'

Jack cleared his throat. 'Welcome ashore, Captain Falco.' He shook Falco's hand. 'My name is Jack Manning, and I'm the party interested in purchasing your vessel, providing she meets my criteria and the terms are satisfactory, of course.'

George stepped forward. 'And I'm Jack's business partner, Captain. George Chapman.'

'Chapman?' Falco turned to Essie with a questioning look.

'George is my long-lost brother,' she said proudly. 'He turned up out of the blue and it seemed like a miracle, and it was just this morning that I discovered he and his partner are interested in purchasing the *Santa Gabriella*. Why do you want to sell her?'

Falco shook his head. 'Time for questions later – it's too chilly to stand about here. Come on board. I know Alice would love to see you – she's talked about nothing else since we set sail from Exmouth.'

'A good idea.' Jack proffered his hand to Sadie. 'Allow me to help you down the steps, Miss Dixon. They're slippery and I wouldn't want you to fall into the filthy water.'

Sadie's cheeks were rosy already but darkened to crimson in the radiance of his charming smile. Jack caught Essie's eye and winked.

With an unusual display of emotion, Alice threw her arms around Essie and hugged her. 'My dear, what a lovely surprise. How did you know that we were arriving today?'

'I didn't,' Essie said breathlessly. 'It's one of a set

of amazing coincidences.' She turned to George, holding out her hand. 'There's someone I want you to meet, Alice. This is my brother, George.'

George left Falco and Jack, who were deep in conversation, and he bowed over Alice's hand. 'My lady, Essie has told me so much about you, I feel that I know you already.'

Alice stared at him, wide-eyed. 'Good heavens! So you're the errant brother, returned to the fold.'

'I can't tell you how much being reunited with Essie means to me. Leaving her all those years ago was the hardest thing I've ever done in my life, but now I intend to make up for lost time.'

'I don't suppose her good fortune has anything to do with your enthusiasm, does it, Mr Chapman?'

George recoiled as if Alice had slapped his face. 'No, my lady. I didn't know about the gold, and even if I had learned of her good fortune I'm not the sort of fellow who would live off a woman.'

'I should hope not. Anyway, I expect we will get to know each other better now that I am back in London.'

'That would be my pleasure, ma'am,' George said gallantly.

'Yes, maybe.' Alice turned her back on him. 'I've sent word to Fielding and Mrs Dent, Essie. The house in Hill Street should be ready for my return. I decided to spend some time in London with you, my dear.' She treated Sadie to a brilliant smile. 'And you, of course, Sadie. How grown-up you look in that delightful outfit.'

Essie glanced at George, sensing his chagrin. 'You'll want to inspect the ship. I hope you'll find it to your liking.'

'Of course. If you'll excuse me, my lady?' George gave Alice a curt bow and crossed the deck to rejoin Jack and Falco.

'What did he say to upset you, Lady Alice?' Sadie demanded crossly. 'Essie's brother is a nice kind man, and you were mean to him.'

'Really, Sadie. You forget yourself.' Alice wrapped her cloak tightly around her slender frame. 'Mind your manners, my girl.'

'Sadie meant no harm,' Essie said sharply. 'You were rather abrupt with my brother and he didn't deserve such treatment.'

'If I offended him, I'm sorry, but it does seem strange that a young man should disappear for years, only to return at the precise moment his sister inherits a fortune.'

'It might seem so,' Alice said stiffly, 'if he had known about my good luck, but he didn't. George was stunned when I showed him the gold nugget. He has money that he saved while he was at sea, which he's invested in Jack's business venture. Anyway, that's by the by. Why is Falco selling up? I thought the *Santa Gabriella* was his life?'

Alice shrugged and turned away. 'You'll have to

ask him that. Why do men do anything? Anyway, it might be spring but it's still chilly and I'm getting cold. Let's go below and wait until they've completed their transactions.'

'You must come and see our new house, Lady Alice,' Sadie suggested shyly. 'It's not as grand as the one you own, but it is very nice.'

'Yes, of course,' Essie added hastily. 'I hope you will visit us, Alice. Mr Gilfoyle found me a splendid residence in Curzon Street, complete with servants. I feel as though I've lived there for years.'

'Gilfoyle is a good man. I intend to visit him tomorrow. Did he say anything about Raven's appeal?'

'No, he didn't, and it wasn't my place to enquire.'

'I thought you would want to know, as I do.' Alice headed towards the companionway.

'Of course, but I'm not a relative and I doubt if he would share such information with me.'

Alice glanced over her shoulder. 'My goodness, you are so very proper, Essie. It puts me to shame. You must come with me to see Gilfoyle. We went through so much together on our travels that I think of you as part of the family. Come along, and that includes you, too, Sadie. Best foot forward, as Miss Potts would say.'

Essie and Sadie followed Lady Alice as she went below, and Falco, Jack and George joined them in the saloon. One look at her brother's face was enough to convince Essie that the talks were floundering.

'Well?' Alice looked from one to the other. 'Have you reached an agreement?'

Falco shrugged. 'The gentlemen think the price is too high, but they don't understand what the *Santa Gabriella* means to me.' He clutched his hands to his heart. 'Parting with her is like losing a loved one.'

'Oh, come on, Falco,' Jack said sharply. 'There is a lot of work to be done before this vessel is seaworthy again.'

'We have just sailed from Exmouth without mishap.' Falco eyed him warily. 'The weather was not good.'

'You're asking too much.' George shook his head. 'It won't do, sir. I've sailed in old tubs like this, and I know what I'm talking about.'

Falco drew himself up to his full height. 'The *Santa Gabriella* is not an old tub. I am insulted, sir. If you were not Essie's brother I would call you out.'

'Don't be ridiculous, Falco,' Alice said crossly. 'Acting like a spoiled child is not the way to conduct a sale.'

Jack patted him on the shoulder. 'You're right, Falco, but the trouble is that our finances are limited. We would like to do a deal, but I can see that you do not wish to go ahead. I respect that.'

'I cannot give my ship away,' Falco said angrily.

'But you want to sell her, Falco,' Alice said firmly. 'You promised me that you would give up the sea.'

He gave her a baleful look. 'But it's in my blood, *mia cara*.'

347

'Go back to your old ways or return to Italy and face arrest. I really don't care.' Alice snatched up the cape she had discarded and wrapped it around her shoulders. 'I, for one, wish to go ashore now.'

'Then we'd best board the lighter,' George said hastily. 'I expect Essie and Sadie would like some luncheon and I'm pretty peckish, myself.'

Jack nodded. 'Good idea, George. However, perhaps the captain would like to accompany me to a tavern. I think we might talk more easily over a bowl of punch. I can smell the hot rum and lemon peel as I speak.'

'That sounds eminently sensible, sir.' Falco picked up his hat and rammed it on his head. 'Very civilised, if I might say so.'

'As you wish.' Alice marched out of the saloon. 'Come along, Essie. We'll leave the gentlemen to sort out their differences and get drunk, while we deal with the important things in life, as usual.'

George saw them safely ashore and found them a cab. Alice hesitated as he was about to hand her into the hackney carriage. 'I'm sorry if I was a trifle curt with you, George. I'm very fond of Essie and I wouldn't want anyone to take advantage of her good nature.'

'My sentiments exactly, my lady.'

'I expect we will be seeing more of each other, so you may call me Alice.' She settled herself in the corner seat, holding a handkerchief to her nose. 'This cab smells disgusting. The last passenger could not have bathed for a year or more. Hurry up, Essie, and you, too, Sadie. I can't wait to get home.'

George helped Essie into the cab. 'I'd better keep an eye on Jack and the captain. A bowl of hot rum punch might bring them closer to an agreement, or it could end in fisticuffs.'

Essie squeezed his hand. 'Good luck. I think you might need it. Just don't ask Falco to sing. He does so at the slightest excuse.'

'I'll remember that.' George lifted Sadie into the cab. 'There you go, dumpling. Look after Essie until I get home.'

'Men!' Alice drew her skirts around her as if afraid that there might be vermin lurking in the footwell. 'They really do think they are indispensable.'

Essie sat back against the squabs as the vehicle lurched forward. 'Why do you have such a poor opinion of men, Alice? You love Raven and Freddie, don't you?'

'I suppose so. But they're my cousins; I have to love them.'

'The Queen married her first cousin,' Sadie said seriously. 'Prince Albert is very good-looking, and Raven is handsome. At least,' she added, blushing, 'I think so.'

'I have no intention of marrying my cousin or anyone else at the moment,' Alice said firmly. 'I gave my heart to someone a long time ago and that ended badly. I'm not going to make the same mistake again.'

Essie sat forward. 'Tell us, Alice. Who was it and what did he do?'

'I suppose there's no harm in admitting it after all these years. He was one of our under footmen.' Alice gazed into space as if conjuring up a vision of her lost love. 'I was sixteen and he was seventeen. William was handsome and daring, and he made me laugh. We met in the rose garden every evening after dinner when the warmth of the sun lingered and the smell of roses was like the most expensive perfume. When he kissed me I thought I'd died and gone to heaven.' Alice heaved a sigh, closing her eyes and puckering her lips.

Essie stared at her in surprise. This was not the Lady Alice she had come to know and love like a sister. She was transformed into a lovelorn sixteen-year-old.

'Go on,' Essie said softly. 'What happened then?'

'We were discovered.' Alice opened her eyes and her lips trembled. 'One of the servants had been spying on us. William was dismissed without a character and I was sent to live with my aunt who owned the house in Hill Street.'

'Didn't you try to find William?' Sadie asked innocently. 'I know I would have done so.'

'That would have been impossible. For one thing I didn't know where he lived, and the servants who might have been able to help me had been threatened with dismissal if they divulged his whereabouts.'

'How sad.' Sadie's eyes filled with tears.

'It was tragic. I had to endure a season in London, when I was introduced to eligible bachelors, but none of them matched up to my William. Then, when eventually I was allowed to visit Daumerle, I learned that he had married a village girl and she was expecting their first child. I knew then that he was lost to me for ever. He had betrayed me with another and I couldn't forgive him for the pain he caused me.'

'But surely you can't hate all men because of a failed romance?' Essie said slowly. 'You were so young then.'

'What do you know about it?' Alice snapped. 'I'm sorry I told you.'

'Falco must think a lot of you. He shows no sign of wanting to leave, and he's willing to sell his ship. Don't you think that proves something?'

Alice stared at her as if she had said something quite shocking. 'What are you saying? Do you think I would want a man like him? My father—'

'Was an earl,' Essie finished the sentence for her. 'Yes, we know that, Alice. But if you want to find a man who's devoted to you, I think you could do worse than Falco. And he has a lovely singing voice,' she added mischievously. 'I think he would do well in the opera buffa, and I will tell him so.'

'What's the opera buffa?' Sadie demanded.

Alice glanced out of the window. 'Hill Street, at last. I'll alight here, Essie. You may call on me tomorrow morning at eleven o'clock, and we will visit Gilfoyle together. My main concern is for Raven and Freddie. Falco can handle his own affairs.'

George returned home that evening, slightly tipsy, but in good humour. 'We've settled things, Essie.'

'Really, George, that's wonderful.' Essie put down the gift she had been wrapping. 'Sit down and tell me about it.'

George sprawled in a chair by the fire, resting his feet on the brass fender. 'We couldn't afford to buy the *Santa Gabriella* outright, but Falco agreed to remain as captain, taking a share in the profits. That way he doesn't lose his vessel, and everyone is satisfied.'

'But surely it means that the profits have to be shared three ways?' Essie said thoughtfully. 'That doesn't seem like a good deal to me.'

'It's better than nothing, and Falco is an experienced seafarer. He might act the fool at times but he's astute when it comes to business matters, even if he has wavered on the wrong side of the law – but that's all going to change. Falco knows that and he's promised to reform.'

'I'm very glad to hear it,' Essie said, reaching for

a piece of ribbon. 'I'll just finish wrapping this gift and then I'm going to bed.'

The following morning Essie accompanied Alice to Gilfoyle's office in Lincoln's Inn Fields. Outside the sun was shining and birds were nesting in the gardens, but inside the building was as gloomy as ever and the musty smell of old books and dusty documents was only partly disguised by the rank odour of tallow candles in the clerk's office. A small meanness on Gilfoyle's part that Essie was quick to notice. They followed the bent figure of the clerk along the dark corridor leading to Gilfoyle's office at the back of the building, and he ushered them in and retreated hastily.

Gilfoyle rose to his feet, emerging from behind piles of leather-bound books and heaps of documents tied with red tape. 'Good morning, my lady, and good morning to you, Miss Chapman. Please take a seat.'

Alice settled herself on the most comfortable chair. 'I've come about Raven's appeal.' She folded her hands in her lap. 'What news, Gilfoyle?'

He shook his head. 'I was going to send word to you today, as it happens, although I didn't know whether you were residing in London or Devonshire.'

'I am here, as you see.'

'Yes, precisely so. I'm afraid it's not good news. The appeal was rejected. Raven will have to serve the rest of his sentence.'

'And Freddie?'

'The warrant for his arrest still stands. If he returns to England he will be committed for trial, and there is nothing I can do about that.'

'What, in your opinion, would be the outcome of such a trial?'

'It would definitely be a custodial sentence, and possible transportation.'

Alice uttered a mirthless laugh. 'Freddie is in Australia as we speak. It seems ironic that if he came home he might be sent back there as a punishment for something so trifling. It's not as if he benefited from his brief association with the smugglers.'

'Quite so, my lady, but that is the law.' Gilfoyle reached for a sheaf of papers and spread them out in the space available. 'Might I have a few words with Miss Chapman, my lady?'

'I suppose so, since our business seems to have come to a halt.' Alice pursed her lips, frowning. 'But I'm not giving up so easily.'

'Quite so, my lady. I admire your fortitude.' Gilfoyle turned to Essie, curving his thin lips in a semblance of a smile. 'I have more cheerful news for you, Miss Chapman. You are a very rich young woman.'

Chapter Nineteen

'I can't believe it,' Essie said, leaning back against the luxurious velvet squabs in Lady Alice's barouche. 'I had no idea that the gold was worth so much.'

'You're a wealthy young woman. You already knew that.' Alice stared out of the window as the carriage drove through the rookeries of Clare Market. 'Really they should raze these slums to the ground. The people live like sewer rats.'

'That makes it all the more difficult for me to accept the fact that Beasley's gold nugget fetched such an enormous sum of money. To profit from the poor man's death seems wrong.'

'He was born into the criminal class and his life was blighted from that day onwards. The accident you told me about was bad luck, but he obviously wanted you to benefit from the one good thing that had happened to him.'

'Yes,' Essie said slowly. 'I know you're right.'

'And if you're thinking of giving large sums to charity or founding a home for the poor and destitute, there are already places like that. You've moved up in the world, and you need to take your place in society.' Alice put her head on one side, giving Essie a calculating look. 'In fact, I'm going to take you in hand once again. I will introduce you to the right people and take you to the places where one should be seen – art galleries, theatres and the opera. You will receive invitations to balls and soirées and I will be at your side to guide you.'

'Thank you, Alice.' When Alice was in this mood there was no point arguing with her. Essie had learned that long ago. They lapsed into silence. Alice might be visualising glittering social events with Essie as her protégée, but Essie was thinking of something quite different.

'You will need a diary in which to keep a note of all your appointments,' Alice said as Essie was about to alight from the carriage outside the house in Curzon Street. 'I will draw up a list of places to visit and I think the opera would be a good start. I know that Falco would enjoy that, although I don't think your brother would be very interested. I'll send word to you when I've organised something.'

Essie allowed the footman to hand her to the pavement. 'Goodbye, Alice.'

'*Au revoir*, my dear. And keep tomorrow afternoon free. I intend to take you to the fabric warehouse. You'll need a whole new wardrobe.'

'As a matter of fact I have ordered a new dress and I'm due for a fitting this afternoon.'

'You still need my advice when it comes to fashion, Essie. I'll see you tomorrow. Drive on, Clifton.'

The footman leaped onto the box to take his place beside the coachman and the horses moved forward at a sedate pace, breaking into a brisk trot. Essie breathed a sigh of relief. No doubt Alice meant well, but her idea of the future did not correspond with Essie's vision. She mounted the steps and the door opened as if by magic. Parkinson stepped aside to allow her to enter.

'Thank you, Parkinson. Is my brother at home?'

'He left about an hour ago, Miss Chapman.'

'And Miss Sadie?'

'I believe you will find her in the morning parlour, Miss Chapman.'

'I'll be going out again directly. Please send someone to find me a cab.' Essie waved aside the young housemaid's offer to take her outer garments as she hurried to the morning parlour.

Sadie was seated at the table poring over a copy of the *Englishwoman's Domestic Magazine*. She looked up and smiled. 'Parkinson said you'd gone to the solicitor with Lady Alice. What did he say?'

'Run upstairs and get your outdoor things, Sadie. We're going for a drive. I'll tell you everything on the way.'

Sadie jumped to her feet. 'Why the hurry?'

'If I don't do this now, I might never do it. You'll understand when I explain.'

The cab rattled over the cobbled streets, coming to a halt outside the office in Wapping. 'Wait here, please, cabby.' Essie alighted with difficulty. Hansom cabs were not designed to make it easy for women wearing long gowns and crinoline petticoats. 'Stay in the cab, Sadie. I'll only be a couple of minutes.' She picked up her skirts, stepping over the slushy puddles as she crossed the pavement.

As she had hoped, George was seated at the desk. 'What are you doing here, Essie? This isn't the sort of place for a lady to visit without an escort.'

'Have you forgotten where we came from, George? This part of London is more home to me than Mayfair, and that's partly why I'm here.' She opened her reticule. 'I've just come from Gilfoyle's office. This is for you.' She took out a leather pouch and placed it on the desk with a thud.

'What is this? I don't understand.'

'I'm a rich woman. Gilfoyle secured a huge amount for the gold nugget, and he's invested it so that it's making even more money. This is for you to use as you please.'

'You don't have to do this, Essie. It's yours by right.'

'Yes, I do. My conscience won't allow me to live like a duchess while you are struggling to build up a business. Anyway, I must go now. I have things to do and a cab waiting outside.'

George weighed the pouch in his hand. 'I don't have to count this to know it's too much. I walked out on you when you needed me. I don't deserve to share your good fortune.'

'You did what you had to do, but you're here now, and that's all that matters. I really must go, George.'

He stood up. 'You're going back to Curzon Street, I hope.'

She smiled. 'Yes, I have an appointment with Lady Alice's dressmaker. Sometimes I wish we were back in Ballarat where life was so much simpler.'

George tucked the pouch into his pocket. 'I'd better take this straight to the bank. You can drop me off on the way home, Essie.'

Despite Alice's attempts to introduce her to society, Essie was often restless. George's new venture took up most of his time, and in between visits to the dressmaker, dancing lessons, shopping and attending social functions, Essie found herself with little to do. Spring had given way to summer and, although George seemed able to forget their father, Essie could not. Once again cholera was rife in the slum areas and Essie could not rest until she knew that her father had escaped the dreaded disease.

One hot summer morning, with Sadie at her side Essie hailed a cab. 'White's Rents, Limehouse, please.'

'Are you sure you want to visit your pa, Essie?' Sadie asked anxiously as Essie climbed in and sat beside her. 'He wasn't very nice to you when we saw him last.'

'Pa behaves badly when he's been drinking, but he's still my father. I want to make sure that he's all right and I don't trust that woman, Annie Ginger. I don't believe that Pa would have married her, even though she showed me her ring. It could have been brass, for all I know.'

'Do you think he deserves to be forgiven? After all, he wasn't to know you had money. We might have had to sleep rough when his woman threw us out.'

'The one thing I've learned recently is that everyone deserves a second chance. If he's just the same as he ever was then at least I'll stop worrying about him. And there's Ben; he was my sweetheart when we were younger. I owe him an explanation for leaving so abruptly.'

Sadie shook her head. 'I dunno, Essie. I think they'll find you very changed. You're a lady now and you've left Limehouse far behind.'

'Not really,' Essie said sadly. 'It will always be a part of me, no matter how much money I have or how much town polish I acquire. Deep down I'll always be the girl who worked on the river, but I need to say goodbye to my childhood and I want to make sure that Pa is all right.' She sniffed the air and sighed. 'This is the stench that greeted me every morning when I opened our front door. One day perhaps someone will do something about it, but for now people simply have to live with it, and die from foul water and bad air.'

'You can't alter it on your own,' Sadie said wisely. 'You could give all your money away and still nothing would have changed.'

Essie smiled. 'When did you grow up, Sadie? Yesterday you were just a child and now you're talking like a wise old woman.'

'I'll be thirteen in July, although I never knew the exact date.'

'Then we must make a special day. You can choose the date you would like to have as your birthday and we'll have a party and cake and presents.'

'That would be lovely.' Sadie glanced out of the window as the cab drew to a sudden halt. 'We're here. I remember this place.'

Essie alighted first and paid the cabby. They set off, plunging into the gloom that was White's Rents. When she reached her father's house, Essie took a deep breath and knocked on the door. She was expecting the brazen creature with the flame-coloured hair to open it, but it was her father who eventually came to the door. He looked ill. That was her first impression, and he had lost weight. His clothes were filthy and hung off him in tatters. He stared at her blankly. 'Who are you?'

'Pa, it's me, Essie. Don't you recognise me?'

He shook his head. 'Essie ran away, just like her brother. You got the wrong house, lady.' He was about to close the door in her face but Essie put her foot over the threshold.

'I am Essie, Pa. What's happened to you?' Her hand flew to cover her nose as she stepped into the living room, which looked as though a tornado had swept through it, leaving behind a trail of debris and destruction. The only piece of furniture left was the sofa and its upholstery had been slashed so that the horsehair spilled out in long hanks. 'Who did this, Pa?'

Sadie covered her face with her hands. 'It's disgusting. I never seen such a mess.'

Jacob teetered on his feet and Essie led him to the sofa. 'Sit down and tell me who did this? Where is that woman who claimed to be your wife?'

'Annie's husband come for her. Big brute, he was, and he left his mark. Dragged her off screaming and kicking, but good riddance, I say. She took every penny I had and more. She run up debts everywhere but I can't pay them.'

'Let her husband worry about that.' Essie glanced

round. 'You can't stay here, Pa. When did you last have anything to eat?'

'I dunno, girl. Miss Flower brought me some soup, but I can't remember when. Josser bought a bottle of ale last evening, but I got no money and I can't work since I lost me boat.' He glared at her. 'That were your fault. You let it sink.'

'You nasty old man,' Sadie said angrily. 'We nearly drowned that night.'

'Who are you?' Jacob demanded. 'I don't know you, girl. Go away.'

Essie stepped over the broken furniture and empty beer bottles as she made her way across the room to investigate the kitchen. As she had suspected, the devastation was not limited to the living room. The table had been overturned and one of its legs had been wrenched off. All the crockery had been smashed, as had the window, and the back door hung on its hinges, allowing the cold air to fill the room with the putrid smells from the back yard. The cupboards were bare and there was not a scrap of food to be found. There was nothing she could do other than return to the living room.

'Get your things, Pa. You're coming with me,' she said firmly. 'You can't stay here.'

'This is me home, Essie. I ain't leaving.'

'You're ill, Pa. You need proper food and rest, and most of all you need a bath.'

'I ain't had a bath since I was a nipper. A wash

down with lye soap was good enough for my ma and pa and it suits me, too.'

'Stay with him, Sadie. I'll go upstairs and get him something warmer to wear.'

'I need a drink, Essie,' Jacob moaned. 'Go to the pub like a good girl and fetch me a jug of ale, or a bottle of rum, if you've been paid this week.'

'No, Pa. I'll get your coat and we'll get a cab to my house. You'll like it there.'

'What?' Jacob leaped to his feet. 'Do as I say, daughter. You're not too big to put across my knee. I need a drink. D'you hear me?'

Sadie shrank away, hiding behind Essie. 'Shall I run to the pub and get what he wants?'

Essie nodded, taking a coin from her reticule. 'All right, but hurry and don't stop to speak to anyone.' She waited until the front door closed behind Sadie. 'She's gone to fetch a bottle of rum, Pa. Sit down, please.'

Jacob sank back onto the sofa. 'I'm a sick man, Essie.'

'Yes, Pa. But I'm here to look after you now. You can have a tot of rum when Sadie returns and then I'm taking you for a cab ride. You'll have a warm bed and a good meal with as much rum as you can drink, but only if you do as I say.'

'All right, Essie.'

Jacob capitulated like an obedient child and lay back, closing his eyes. Essie breathed a sigh of relief, but he sprang back to life when Sadie returned with the rum. Essie had been unable to find a cup or a glass left intact and there was no alternative but to give him the bottle. Almost immediately she realised that she had made a grave error. Jacob became aggressive when she tried to take it away from him. He drank until he collapsed insensible on the sofa.

'What do we do now?' Sadie asked anxiously. 'Will you leave him here?'

Essie shook her head. 'I can't. Look at the state of him.' She stared at him, frowning. 'He's harmless at the moment. I'm going to see if I can find Ben or one of Pa's old workmates to get him into a cab.'

'You're never going to take him back to Curzon Street,' Sadie said aghast. 'What will Parkinson say?'

Essie had a sudden vision of Parkinson's shocked expression and she laughed. 'I hate to think, but I can't leave him here. Anyway, I'll be as quick as I can, I promise.' She slipped her cloak around her shoulders and pulled up the hood as she left the house, heading for Duke Shore Dock. She wanted to see Ben and explain her new circumstances, although the chances of finding him were slim, but there were others who would be willing to help – she only had to seek them out.

The first person she saw had known her since childhood, but he failed to recognise her and he hurried past, even when she called him by name. In desperation she went to Riley's office, but he was not there, and then she came face to face with the last person she wanted to see, and as luck would have it he knew her instantly.

'Well, if it isn't young Essie Chapman, rigged out like a lady. You must have done well Up West, missy.'

The inference was clear but she chose to ignore the insult. 'I'm looking for Ben.'

'I could tell you where he's living now, but I don't think his woman would be too pleased to see her man's old girlfriend on the doorstep.'

'What are you saying?'

'I thought I'd made meself clear, darling. Ben took up with Nancy Styles. I reckon he gave up waiting for you to get off your high horse and give him what he wanted. But I'm still available, sweetheart.' He lunged forward and grabbed Essie round the waist. His face was close to hers and the stench of his sweaty body and bad breath made her gasp for air.

'Let her go, Tyce.' George's voice echoed off the dock buildings.

Tyce twisted Essie round, holding his arm around her throat in a suffocating grip. 'One move and I'll break her pretty little neck. I've been waiting too long for a bit of satisfaction from this tease.'

Daylight was fading fast and the shadows were deepening but through a mist of pain Essie saw two figures hurl themselves at Tyce. Jack dived for his legs and George dragged her to safety.

'Are you hurt, Essie?'

'No. I'm all right, but how did you know where I was?' she asked breathlessly.

A loud splash made her turn her head to see Diggory Tyce flailing about in the water. Jack came towards them, grinning.

'I enjoyed that. I don't know the fellow but I recognise the type.' His smile faded. 'What were you thinking of, wandering around this area on your own?'

'Come on, Essie. Let's get you away from here.' George tucked her hand in the crook of his arm. 'Jack and I arrived in Curzon Street to see you drive off in the cab. You'd been worrying about the old man for days, so I guessed where you were going and we followed you to White's Rents. I couldn't allow you to face the old man on your own.'

'How did you know I was here?'

'You'd just left when we got to Pa's house. Sadie told us you'd gone looking for Ben. The rest was easy.' He glanced at Tyce, who was thrashing about and yelling at the top of his voice. 'It doesn't look as though he can swim.'

'Hard luck,' Jack said grimly. 'I'm not jumping in after him. Perhaps the rats will recognise one of their own and save him.'

'He's an old lecher but you can't stand by and watch him drowning.' Essie stared anxiously at the man, who appeared to be going down for the third time.

'Riley is over by the cranes. I saw him as we came to your aid. He'll throw a spar or something for the old devil to cling on to. Tyce will live another day, but you've got to keep away from this place. We've moved on, Essie. Limehouse is no longer home.'

Essie leaned on his arm. 'You're right, and we've got to get Pa away from here, too.'

'You can't mean to take him to Curzon Street in the state he's got himself into?' George said, quickening his pace.

'What else can we do, George?'

'Look, I don't wish to interfere.' Jack fell into step beside them. 'I don't know Mr Chapman, but I've had experience with this sort of thing. Drink took my father at a relatively young age, which is why I'm careful not to overindulge . . . Anyway, that's not your problem. I have a large house overlooking the river, and I've lived there alone since my sister married and moved away. We can take him there and hire a woman to nurse him through the worst stages. It won't be easy and you shouldn't have to put up with it, Essie.'

Essie came to a halt, gazing at Jack as if seeing him for the first time.

'That's very kind of you, Jack,' she said slowly, 'but I couldn't impose on you like that. He's our father and it's up to us to look after him, but I would be grateful if you could help us get him into a cab. We'll take him home.'

*   *   *

Parkinson was clearly not amused and Mrs Jackson managed to convey her disapproval of their guest without saying a word. Her tight-lipped, disdainful expression spoke volumes, and the maids acted as if a wild animal had escaped from the zoological gardens and been locked away in a bedchamber close to George's room. Despite her appeals, George refused to have anything to do with their father.

'I'm sorry, Essie. I know we couldn't leave him in the old house, but you shouldn't have brought him here. He'll be as mad as fire when he sobers up, and who knows what he'll do.'

'I know, but what was I supposed to do, George? I've sent the under footman and the head groom to undress Pa and do the necessary. They're young and strong and they won't stand for any nonsense.'

'But, Essie, we can't keep him prisoner here. He'll go mad for want of a drink, and if we give in and let him have what he wants he'll be even worse. We should have taken Jack up on his offer.'

'Pa is our responsibility and it wouldn't be fair to foist him on Jack. I can't think why he would want to take Pa on, anyway.'

'I think he had an ulterior motive,' George said, grinning. 'That was a cracking dinner, Essie. We've certainly fallen on our feet with this establishment. I could get used to living like a lord.'

Essie put down the cup of coffee she had been sipping. 'What do you mean by ulterior motive?'

George stretched his booted feet out in front of the fire with a sigh of contentment. 'What do you think I meant? You're a lovely girl and you're worth a fortune. What man in his right mind wouldn't want a wife like you?'

'A wife?' Essie shook her head. 'What nonsense, George. I hardly know Jack Manning and he certainly doesn't know me.'

'I've seen the way he looks at you. He's smitten, or I'm a Dutchman.'

Essie rose from her chair. 'You're talking nonsense, and I'm going to bed. We'll talk about Pa in the morning, and he might be more receptive to suggestions when he's sobered up.' She headed for the door. 'Good night, George.'

Essie slept badly. She was exhausted, but worrying about her father's future kept her awake until the small hours. It seemed that she had just fallen asleep when she was awakened by the housemaid who came to light the fire. She returned with a cup of hot chocolate and a jug of warm water, and went through the routine of plumping up Essie's pillow so that she could sit up in comfort. Essie drank the chocolate, barely appreciating the velvety sweetness as her thoughts returned to the problem of her father. She knew him well enough to realise that he would hate Curzon Street. Jacob Chapman would never settle away from the river, and that in itself gave her an idea. She put her cup down, swung her legs over the side of the bed and was about to ring for Miss West, the lady's maid that Mrs Jackson had assigned to her, when she changed her mind.

Miss West was not the sort of person who would smile easily or with whom Essie could share a joke, and having a relative stranger to help her with her toilette was unnerving and embarrassing. Essie washed, dressed and sat down at the dressing table, smiling at her reflection in the mirror as she picked up a silver-backed hairbrush. It was a small rebellion against the life she had been compelled to live, but a significant one, and she brushed her long hair until it gleamed like satin, and secured it in a chignon at the back of her neck. Miss West was useful when it came to a more elaborate coiffure, but Essie was in a hurry. She had allowed herself to drift, but now she was determined to take charge of her affairs.

Her father's door was unlocked and she went in without knocking. He was still asleep with his mouth hanging slack and a dribble of saliva running down his chin. The room stank of stale alcohol, sweat and his desperate need for a bath. She drew back the curtains, allowing the sunlight to flood the room. The fire had not yet been lit, but the servants had been told to await her instructions.

She shook him gently. 'Pa, wake up. It's me, Essie.'

Jacob opened one bloodshot eye. 'Go away.'

She shook him harder this time. 'No, Pa. Wake up, please.'

'What's the matter?' Jacob snapped into a sitting position, groaning loudly. 'My head is pounding.'

It was impossible to be sympathetic, but Essie managed to restrain herself. 'I'll have a seltzer brought to you, Pa. But first I need to talk to you.' She perched on the end of the bed. 'I don't suppose you remember anything that happened last evening?'

He squinted at her as if finding it difficult to focus. 'Where am I? This ain't my home.'

'No, Pa. It's my house. I live here now.'

'You must have taken up with a wealthy toff, or else how could a girl like you end up in a house like this? You was a good girl once, Esther Chapman.'

'I'm not dependent on anyone, Pa.' Essie tried to explain how she came by her money but Jacob seemed to have it fixed in his mind that she had sold herself to a rich man, and nothing would convince him otherwise. In the end she gave up. 'Never mind what you think, Pa. You couldn't be more wrong, but the important thing is what are we going to do with you? You're in a terrible state. You can't work and your house is wrecked.'

'Get off the bed, girl. I'm going home.'

'I've just told you that's impossible. You haven't any money and you're ruining your health with drink.'

Jacob swung his legs over the side of the bed, grimacing with pain. 'That's my business, not yours.

You run away and took me boat. You're a bad girl, Esther.'

She could see that this conversation was going nowhere and she stood up. 'All right, Pa. You can go home, but first you have to have a bath and I'll have to find some clothes for you.'

'What's this?' Jacob gazed down at the nightshirt that Mrs Jackson had found for him, it having belonged to a servant who had run off with a set of silver spoons and never been seen again. 'How did I get this garb?'

'It doesn't matter, Pa. Get back into bed and I'll send the servants up with the bath and hot water, and a glass of seltzer. When you're ready you can have some breakfast and I'll get a cab to take you back to Limehouse, if that's what you really want.'

'Of course I do,' Jacob said crossly. 'I'm going home and you can't stop me.'

Chapter Twenty

Once again Essie had to call on the services of the burly footman and the under groom in order to persuade her father to take a bath. Jacob's roars of fury and the sound of splashing, cursing and thumping on the sides of the tub echoed throughout the house. Essie was halfway down the main stairs when George appeared on the landing above her. His hair was tousled and he was still wearing his dressing robe.

'What the devil's going on, Essie?'

'Pa is taking a bath.'

'It sounds as though all hell has been let loose. Maybe we should do what he wants and leave him in Limehouse.'

'Go and get dressed,' Essie said wearily. 'I'll be in the dining room if you want me.'

'Did you hear what I said?'

'Yes, George, but I'm not listening to you. I'll find a way to help Pa, whether he likes it or not.' Essie continued down the stairs, but she paused when she reached the main hall. Someone was rapping on the door and she was curious. She waited for Parkinson to open the door, which he did at a leisurely pace, taking a step backwards as Falco pushed past him.

'Essie, you look beautiful this morning.' Falco tossed his hat and gloves to the housemaid.

'What are you doing here so early in the morning, Captain?' Essie asked curiously.

He crossed the floor in long strides and raised her hand to his lips. 'Lady Alice asked me to tell you that she will be here at midday. She intends to take you to her modiste.'

'But I have plenty of new gowns,' Essie protested. 'I don't need more clothes.'

Falco held his hand to his heart. 'Never say that, *mia cara*. A lady can never have too many beautiful things. You should allow Lady Alice to guide you in such matters. She has superb taste.' He hesitated, cocking his head on one side. 'What is going on upstairs? It sounds as if someone is being murdered.'

Essie sighed. 'Come into the dining room, and I'll tell you.'

Falco needed no second bidding. 'I didn't have time for breakfast.'

In the dining room Essie sent the maid for a pot

of coffee and she motioned Falco to take a seat. 'That is my pa,' she said, sighing. 'George and I brought him here last evening.'

'I don't understand.' Falco eyed the silver serving dishes on the sideboard. 'Do I smell bacon?'

'You can have what you like, but first I need your advice.' Essie pulled up a chair and sat down beside him. 'When I came home I found that Pa had taken up with a dreadful woman who took everything he had, leaving him destitute, and he has turned to drink. He used to be a good boat handler and was well respected, but now he's a wreck of a man and I don't know what to do with him.'

'I would like to meet him, but first I will take advantage of your kind offer.' He stood up and sent to the sideboard. 'I am very hungry.'

Essie helped herself to a small amount of buttered eggs, in complete contrast to Falco, who heaped his plate with food and proceeded to demolish it as if he had not eaten for days. He barely noticed when George entered the dining room, followed by the maid with a silver coffee pot and a jug of cream.

'Falco. This is a surprise.' George took his seat at the head of the table, a privilege that Essie had bestowed on him as her elder brother.

'I was just telling him about Pa,' Essie said hastily. 'I don't know what we're going to do, George. Please don't tell me to send Pa back to Limehouse, because my conscience wouldn't allow such a thing.'

George shrugged. 'You should have let Jack look after him. Pa would have been able to sit and watch the river all day.' He wandered over to the sideboard and began lifting the lids on the serving dishes.

'Yes, and drink rum or jigger gin while he was idling his time away.' Essie turned to Falco. 'What would you do in similar circumstances?'

He gulped and swallowed. 'This is excellent bacon. As to your father, did you say he was a waterman?'

'He's worked the river all his life.' Essie laid her hand on Falco's sleeve. 'Are you thinking what I'm thinking?'

'Maybe, but I would like to meet him first.'

George returned to the table with a plate of kedgeree. 'What's all this?'

Essie pushed her plate away, the food untouched. 'I'll go and see if Pa is ready.'

'Send the maid,' George protested, digging into his plate of food with relish.

Essie shook her head. 'I wouldn't dream of it. This is for me to do.'

The bedroom carpet was soaked and the two men who had been wrestling Jacob in an attempt to keep him in the bath were dripping with water. Jacob himself was wrapped in a dressing robe with a towel around his head. He glared at Essie.

'This was your idea, of course.'

'You certainly needed a bath, Pa. You only have

to look at what's left in the tub to see it's true. It looks like Limehouse Hole at slack water.'

A snigger from the footman reminded Essie of the task in hand. She turned to him, frowning. 'Did you find clothes that will fit my father?'

He snapped to attention despite his sodden livery. 'Yes, Miss Chapman. The items belonged to Briggs, the groom who was sacked for drunkenness.'

'I want to go back to Limehouse,' Jacob said gloomily. 'It ain't too much to ask. I've been man-handled and half drowned, so the least you can do is to allow me out of this bordello.'

'Pa, don't say such things. This is my home, paid for by my own money.' Essie glanced anxiously at the two servants who were staring straight ahead, although the groom's lips were twitching. 'Don't repeat any of this below stairs. You may go now and you'd best change out of those wet clothes.' Essie turned to her father, frowning. 'Get dressed, Pa. I'll wait for you on the landing.'

'Are you taking me home?'

'I want you to come downstairs and have some breakfast before you go anywhere,' Essie said tactfully. 'There's bacon and eggs, as much as you can eat.'

Jacob stood up, allowing the robe to fall to the ground. Essie hurried from the room – she had no wish to see her father naked as a newborn babe.

*   *   *

378

Falco had finished eating and was sipping his coffee when Essie ushered her father into the dining room. George sat back in his chair, eyeing Jacob critically.

'Well, Pa. I hardly recognise you.'

Jacob rubbed his newly shaven chin. 'I didn't ask to come here and be molested.' He glanced down at the coarse tweed trousers and jacket that had once belonged to a groom. 'And I don't normally wear duds like this.'

Falco eyed him critically. 'I hear you're a waterman, sir.'

'Sit down, Pa, and I'll bring you some food.' Essie guided her father to a seat opposite Falco.

'I was born and raised on the riverbank, cully.'

'Have you any experience of seafaring?'

'Who are you? Why are you asking me all these questions?'

Essie set a plate of bacon and eggs in front of her father. 'I'm sorry, Pa. I should have introduced you. This is Captain Falco of the *Santa Gabriella*. It was his ship that took me and Sadie round the world, quite literally.'

'Was it you who sunk me boat?' Jacob demanded, pointing his knife at Falco. 'If it was, you owe me.'

'Shut up, Pa,' George said impatiently. 'Falco is trying to help you. We had a chat when Essie went upstairs to fetch you, and we think we might have the solution to your problem.'

379

'I ain't got no problem other than you and your sister.' Jacob spoke with his mouth full, making it hard to understand what he was saying, but Falco nodded.

'You are an independent man. I respect that, which is why I'm offering to take you on as part of my crew.' Falco picked up the coffee pot and refilled his cup. 'I have agreed to go into business with your son and his partner, but I am still captain of the *Santa Gabriella* and part owner. I need a man with experience of the river. You could be very useful.'

Essie stared at him in surprise. 'Does that mean you're going away soon, Falco?'

He nodded. 'An idle ship costs money, and Jack has found us a cargo.'

'When do you plan to sail?'

'At the turn of the tide.'

'But what does Lady Alice say to that?'

'Why would she care?' Falco said casually. 'I kept her amused for a while, but the lady bores easily.'

'Just a minute, cully.' Jacob snatched a slice of toast from the rack and began mopping his plate. 'You ain't given me time to consider, nor told me anything about your vessel.'

'Finish your breakfast and we'll take a cab to Wapping where my ship is moored. You may look her over and meet the rest of the crew. No one is forcing you to do anything against your will.'

'Just think about it, Pa,' Essie said gently. 'You would be doing what you love most.'

George sat back in his chair. 'I'd be tempted to go myself if I hadn't gone into business with Jack. You could do worse, Pa.'

'But I got no gear to take with me,' Jacob protested. 'I can't go to sea in a tweed suit.'

'There's a ship's chandlers near the office, I saw it yesterday.' Essie patted his arm, smiling. 'I'll come with you and see that you're kitted out, Pa.'

Falco wagged a finger at her. 'Don't forget your appointment with Lady Alice.'

'This is far more important than fine clothes,' Essie said firmly. 'I'll send the footman with a message to ask her to make it another day.'

'She won't like that, Essie.'

'I'm sorry, but that's the way it has to be.' Essie turned to the maid. 'Send Thomas to me. I have a message for him to take to Hill Street.'

Essie waited in the office with Jack while George rowed his father and Falco out to the *Santa Gabriella* at her moorings.

'This could be the answer,' Essie said, gazing out of the window. The azure sky transformed the murky water to steel blue and the wharfs and docks were bathed in sunlight.

Jack closed the ledger he had been studying. 'They'll be gone for some time – why don't we take the short walk to my house? My housekeeper was busy baking jam tarts when I left this morning and she's an excellent cook.'

Essie hesitated. 'I need to be here when Pa returns.'

Jack stood up, holding out his hand. 'We can see him from the window of my front parlour. Come, Essie. I'd like to show you my home.'

The word 'home' sent a shiver down her spine. It seemed a long time since she could really call somewhere home. The house in Curzon Street was well appointed and luxurious but it did not belong to her, and someone else had chosen the contents, which might be elegant and fashionable, but were not entirely to her taste. She laid her hand on Jack's arm.

'Thank you. I'd like that very much.'

Jack had not exaggerated. It was a short walk to his house, which overlooked the Upper Pool. It was set amongst a jumble of buildings that appeared to have been thrown together in a random fashion, none of them seeming to follow any particular architectural style. There were wooden structures teetering on stilts above the Thames mud, and sturdier brick buildings plastered with advertisements for the traders who had occupied them at one time or another. A ship's chandler, a candle maker, a marine architect and a boat builder lived cheek by jowl with a sail maker and an undertaker.

Jack took Essie's hand to help her up the steep wooden steps to the entrance of one of the more permanent-looking dwellings. It was certainly the largest and most imposing of all the houses in the row, with bow windows and a balcony on the top floor, which would undoubtedly be a wonderful vantage point.

'What a fascinating house,' Essie breathed, entranced by the sheer oddity of the building and its closeness to the river she loved.

'I thought you'd like it,' Jack said proudly. 'It's known as the Old Captain's House because it was built by a retired seafarer who couldn't bear to be more than a few yards away from the water. He made his fortune importing timber from the Baltic and he spent his declining years here.' Jack opened the door and ushered her inside.

The rich aroma of baking wrapped itself around her like a warm blanket, as if the house itself were welcoming her. The walls of the oak-panelled hallway were covered with paintings depicting the river in all its moods. There were sketches of every type of craft from the humble lighter to the sturdy Thames barges, their dark tan sails in contrast to the billowing white canvas of stately tea clippers. Essie could have spent all day admiring the collection, but Jack took her bonnet and shawl and hung them on a set of wall pegs amongst reefer jackets, oilskins and a variety of head gear. It was all very informal and homely.

'I allowed the butler and the housemaids to have the day off,' Jack said solemnly.

Essie was about to respond when she realised that he was teasing her, and the twinkle in his dark eyes was irresistible.

'I'm sure they appreciate your generosity,' she said, chuckling. 'To be perfectly honest I find it much more comfortable this way.'

'You don't like being waited on hand and foot?'

'In some ways I do, of course, but sometimes I long for the freedom of doing things for myself. Does that make sense?'

'Perfectly. I'm sure I'd feel the same.' Jack showed her into the front parlour, which had a comfortable, lived-in look, with an eclectic mix of furnishings.

The view from the bow window took Essie's breath away and she clapped her hands in delight. 'This is wonderful. I could sit here all day and watch the ships.'

'It's tempting, I must admit, and I can understand why the old sea captain wanted to end his days here. Take a seat, Essie, and I'll let Mrs Cooper know we're here. Would you prefer tea or coffee?'

'A cup of tea would be lovely,' Essie said, smiling. 'This is such a cosy room, Jack. No wonder you love this old house.'

'I do. It's not to everyone's taste and it's not a patch on your mansion in Curzon Street, but it suits me well enough.'

He left before she had a chance to protest, and she walked slowly round the room, taking in each homely detail with a feeling of intense pleasure. The floor was covered in a patchwork of oriental and Middle Eastern rugs, some of them old and faded, while others still retained their bright hues. The wooden mantelshelf was crowded with small objects that Jack or his father must have collected on their travels. A brass carriage clock was wedged between a china spill jar and a carved wooden elephant with a howdah on its back. Exotic shells and tiny fragments of coral nestled together like a memory of a sea voyage to far-off lands, and a telescope lay on a table next to a set of tide tables. The armchair by the fireplace had faded upholstery and threadbare patches, but Essie could imagine Jack seated there at night, sipping a brandy or a mug of cocoa, with a fire blazing up the chimney and his feet resting on the brass fender. She turned away, angry with herself for allowing her imagination to run away with her. This was Jack's private world and she was merely a visitor.

She went to sit on the window seat where she had a clear view of the wharfs and the busy traffic on the river, including the *Santa Gabriella* at her moorings. She could only hope that Falco managed to persuade her father to consider his offer. As part of the crew Pa would have little or no opportunity to drink himself insensible, and he would be among his own kind. Instinctively, she crossed her fingers, turning with a start at the sound of the door opening.

Jack entered carrying a tray of tea, followed by a small woman, dressed in black bombazine with her grey hair partially concealed by a spotless white mobcap. She placed a plate of tarts on the table, pushing the tide tables to one side.

'This is Mrs Cooper, Essie. She is my prop and mainstay. I don't know what I'd do without her, and she is a wonderful cook, as you'll find out when you sample one of her strawberry jam tarts.'

Essie rose to her feet. 'How do you do, Mrs Cooper? I'm very pleased to meet you.'

Mrs Cooper bobbed a curtsey. 'Likewise, miss. Mr Jack has talked about nothing else since he first met you, and now I see you I can understand why.'

Essie felt the blood rush to her cheeks, and she realised that she was blushing like a schoolgirl, which was ridiculous. Jack was George's friend and she barely knew him. 'It's a pleasure to meet you, ma'am,' she said hastily.

'Thank you, Mrs Cooper.' Jack held the door open. 'I think I smell something burning.'

'Oh, heavens, that will be the steak and kidney pie for supper.' Mrs Cooper hurried from the room, and Jack closed the door.

'She's a good sort, given to exaggerating at times. Of course I told her about you. She's been with my family since I was a boy, in fact she kept house for my father, myself and my two sisters after our mother died. We all love Mrs Cooper.'

'Your sisters?' Essie eyed him curiously. 'They don't live here now?'

'Lord, no. Cecelia and Maggie are both married with children of their own. I see them as often as I can.' Jack pulled up a chair. 'Shall I pour?'

'Please do.' Essie settled back on the window seat. 'Mrs Cooper is obviously very fond of you, and I think that's lovely. I don't think I'll ever get used to servants watching my every move, and rushing to tie up my boot laces, if you know what I mean.'

Jack filled a cup with tea and placed it on the windowsill within her reach. 'I do, as it happens, although most people would think it the height of luxury. Can I tempt you to a jam tart?'

'Thank you.' Essie took a bite, realising that he was eagerly awaiting her verdict. She smiled. 'Delicious. I've never tasted better. You're a lucky man, Jack. You have this interesting old house and a servant who is also a friend. I think that's wonderful.'

'Some people think the house is creepy – haunted by the old captain, but if he's a ghost, he's a friendly one.'

'I'd love to see the rest of it,' Essie said enthusiastically. 'If the captain truly loved this house it must be a happy ghost who haunts the place.'

'That's what I think, too. When you're ready I'll

show you round – that's if you don't mind the chaos of a bachelor's way of life?'

'To tell you the truth I find having everything just so is a little daunting. I think I was happier living in the miner's shack in Ballarat, where life was simple. Lady Alice is trying to introduce me to polite society, but I'm not sure I fit in.'

'But you get on well with Lady Alice and her cousins. George told me something of your travels.'

'Yes, I'm very fond of Alice.' Essie changed the subject. Her relationship with Raven, like her time in Ballarat, was in the past and she was desperate to move on. 'Enough about me, Jack. I'd really like to have the conducted tour before the others return from the ship.'

'Of course.' Suddenly formal, Jack rose to his feet. 'I hope you won't be disappointed now that I've built up your expectations.'

The moment of embarrassment passed as quickly as it had occurred. Jack showed Essie the small dining room, and the larger parlour, which he explained was used very little now that he lived alone. There were various other smaller rooms and then there was the kitchen, which he said was the heart of the house. Mrs Cooper was flushed and embarrassed, apologising profusely because she had not had time to sweep the floor and clear away the cooking utensils. Essie said she was sorry for the intrusion and complimented her on the lightness of her pastry, and the delicious jam she had used for the tarts.

'Homemade,' Mrs Cooper said proudly. 'My sister lives in Shoreditch and she has a garden where she grows all manner of fruit and vegetables.' She shook her finger at Jack. 'You should know better than to burst into my kitchen, catching me unawares. I'm sure Miss Esther would like to see the rest of the house.'

'I hope we didn't upset her too much,' Essie said as they left the kitchen and climbed the narrow staircase to the first floor.

'Not at all. You've made a hit with Mrs Cooper. She called you "Miss Esther" – that's a sure sign. It would have been "Miss Chapman" had she not approved of you.' He opened a door on the first floor. 'This is my room. It's directly above the parlour and, as you see, has a similar bow window, with an even better view.' He glanced round the room and apologised for the untidiness, edging an odd shoe under the bed with the toe of his boot, but to Essie the room had a charming lived-in look, and she said as much. There was a small box room, filled with trunks and baggage of all descriptions, and another bedroom at the back of the house. The second floor was a similar layout and Mrs Cooper occupied the whole of the third floor. Above that were two small attics beneath the roof, and the dormer window of the largest room opened onto the balcony. They stepped outside at Essie's request, and stood side by side in the small space. She was instantly aware of the warmth radiating from his body and a masculine scent that was strangely exciting.

'How lovely to be high above the rest of the world,' she said softly. 'I feel like a bird.'

'That's why I love it up here. Sometimes I come up at night and look out across the river at the twinkling lights and the stars in the heavens.' He turned to give her a searching look. 'You're shivering and yet the sun is at its height.'

'Someone must have walked over my grave,' she said, smiling. But it was a shiver of anticipation that had made her spine tingle – she was far from cold.

'Perhaps we'd better go inside. Too much sun is as bad as feeling the ice-cold blast of winter.'

Essie was reluctant to leave, but she could see the small boat setting off from the *Santa Gabriella*. 'You're right, but I could spend all day here.'

Jack laughed and ushered her back to the relative coolness of the attic. 'You are a woman after my own heart, Essie.'

She shot him a sideways glance and saw that he was serious. 'It would seem so, Jack.'

For a long moment they stood there, inches apart and yet connected in a way that Essie could not quite understand. She had only recently become acquainted with Jack Manning and yet she felt as though she had known him all her life. A sudden gust of air fragrant with the smell of a good cigar wafted through the room.

'I think you must have a visitor, Jack.'

His serious expression melted into a warm smile. 'It's just Captain Oakes. It's his way of welcoming you to his home, Essie.'

'Thank you, Captain. I want you to know that I love your house. I can feel you must have been very happy here.'

The scent of tobacco faded away, leaving the air musty and still.

'I think the captain likes you, Essie,' Jack said, smiling. 'He's a benign old gentleman, but if he takes a dislike to someone he's been known to rush through the house slamming doors as a sign of his disapproval.'

Essie glanced round the empty attic, half expecting to see an apparition shimmering in the shadows, but there was nothing other than a few cobwebs. 'I'm not scared, which surprises me.'

'We'd best get back to the office or George will be there before us.' Jack held out his hand.

'Yes, of course. I almost forgot the reason for our visit today.' Essie ignored the gesture. If she allowed him to take her by the hand once more she feared the consequences. Her emotions were spiralling dangerously out of control. Maybe it was the influence of the romantic old house, but she was in danger of compromising her good name simply by being alone with an unmarried man. George would not approve and neither would Alice. 'You're quite right,' she said hastily. 'We must go at once, but if Pa refuses Falco's offer I don't know what I'll do.'

Chapter Twenty-One

Alice was in the drawing room at Curzon Street, seated on the sofa and bristling with anger, which she did not bother to conceal. 'I suppose you thought a jaunt to Wapping was more important than our engagement this morning, Essie.'

'I'm sorry, but in fact it was.'

'Then I'd better leave now before I say something I'll regret.' Alice rose to her feet, holding herself stiffly erect.

'Wait, please.' Essie slipped off her cloak and handed it to the maidservant, who was, as always, hovering in the background. 'It was an emergency. Please sit down and I'll send for some coffee, or something stronger if you prefer.'

'It's too late for that. In fact it's past midday and time for luncheon.' Alice hesitated and then, seeming to relent a little, she sat down again. 'Go on, explain.'

'I went to see my father and found him in a terrible state . . .' Essie's explanation was cut short by Falco who burst into the room.

'I saved the day,' he said modestly. 'I saw that our dear Essie was having trouble with her papa and I solved the problem. A few weeks at sea and he'll be a new man.'

Alice looked from one to the other. 'I don't know which one of you is the least maddening. Here am I, trying to introduce Essie to society, and you are both making my life more difficult.'

'*Mia cara.*' Falco went down on one knee before her. 'I am forever your humble servant, but I am no lapdog. I am a seafarer and therefore, with regret, I must leave you.'

Alice stared at him in dismay. 'What are you saying, Falco?'

'The *Santa Gabriella* sails on the tide and I am taking command.'

'But I have arranged dinner parties and I accepted an invitation to a ball. I need an escort and I was relying on you.'

'I am sure that there are gentlemen queuing for the privilege, *mia cara.*' Falco turned to Essie, smiling broadly. 'Your papa will be in good hands. I will see that he earns his pay with hard work, and he will have little opportunity to indulge in drink.'

Essie rushed over to embrace him. 'Thank you, Falco. I am truly grateful, but we will miss you.'

'And I will miss my beautiful ladies. But I will see you both again soon.' He blew them a kiss as he left the room.

'Well!' Alice stared at the closed door. 'I can't believe that he would desert me this way.'

'I'm sorry.' Essie could understand Falco's desire to escape from the rigid confines of society, but she could also sympathise with Alice, who seemed genuinely shocked by his sudden departure.

'Let him go, I say.' Alice stood up, brushing imaginary creases from her silk skirts. 'Men are totally unreliable and untrustworthy. We will go to Brown's for luncheon and afterwards we will visit my modiste.'

Essie shook her head. 'Luncheon would be nice, Alice, but I don't need any more gowns.'

'Yes, my dear, you do. This evening we will be attending a soirée at the home of Sir Henry Bearwood. My maid has selected a gown for you, but to be seen wearing my cast-offs is not good for you or for me.'

'But Sir Henry tried to rape you, Alice.'

'Rape is such an ugly word. Henry is a passionate man and I could have handled him perfectly well on my own, but Raven had to act the hero. It was sheer luck that neither of them died that night. Anyway, Henry came to call on me the moment he knew that I was back in town. He apologised profusely and I believe he is a changed man, although you may judge for yourself.'

'He knows that I was a servant. He'll remember me.'

'All that is in the past, Essie. Sir Henry recovered from his wound, as did Raven, so there's an end to it. Anyway, we're going and that's that.' Alice looked her up and down, frowning. 'My maid will see that you're properly attired. I'm sure she will find something that will suit you.'

'I really would rather stay at home this evening. I have things to do.'

'Nonsense. I won't allow you to mope here on your own. You are my companion, Essie, and you will learn to behave as such. It's a pity that Falco has decided to leave me in the lurch like this, as he was to escort us tonight.' Alice eyed her curiously. 'How is that brother of yours shaping up, Essie? He's a handsome fellow, even if he lacks polish.'

'George? He came home to change and then, I suppose, he'll return to Wapping with Falco and Jack.'

'Jack Manning?' Alice tapped her cheek with the tip of her finger. 'I remember him. He's another fine-looking specimen. I wonder if they have evening dress. Two handsome escorts are better than one.'

'Oh, I don't think they would like to come,' Essie said quickly.

'Why not? All they need to do is to stand behind us and look pleasant. They don't have to converse with the other guests, and quite honestly it would be better if they kept silent. I'll send a messenger with an invitation. There are few who can resist me at my most persuasive.'

Sir Henry's palatial home in Piccadilly was lit by so many candles that the heat in the vast entrance hall was as intense as it was outside. Essie had expected there to be half a dozen or so guests and with that in mind had managed to persuade George to accompany them. Jack had encouraged him, laughing and telling him that it would be an experience of a lifetime, which slightly unnerved Essie. She was unaccountably nervous to find herself in a large gathering of fashionable society, but Jack patted her gloved hand as it lay on his sleeve and gave her an encouraging smile.

'Cheer up, Essie,' he said softly. 'They won't bite, and if they do, I'll bite them back.'

She stifled a giggle. 'I don't know how you can be so calm.'

Jack encompassed the gathering with a casual wave of his hand. 'These people might have money and breeding, but take away the titles and the trappings and they're just like the rest of us mortals.'

'I don't think they'd appreciate being compared to street sweepers and dollymops, but I know what you mean.' Essie came to a halt behind Alice and George, wondering why they had stopped and then she spotted Sir Henry himself as he ploughed his way through the assembled guests. He seized Alice's hand and raised it to his lips.

'How delightful you look this evening, my dear.'

Alice inclined her head graciously. 'May I present my partner, George Chapman?' She nudged George, who reacted like an automaton, inclining his head in a bow and shaking Sir Henry's hand.

'How do you do, Chapman?' Sir Henry's glance flickered past him, coming to rest on Essie.

'And this is Miss Esther Chapman and Mr Jack Manning. Very good friends of mine,' Alice said firmly.

'A pleasure to meet you.' Sir Henry gave them a vague smile and then turned away. 'Come, Alice, there are people I want you to meet.' He slapped George on the back. 'I'm sure you can spare her for a while, sir.' He proffered his arm and, to Essie's surprise, Alice accepted with a smile, abandoning George.

'I knew I shouldn't have come,' he muttered angrily. 'What am I supposed to do now?'

'Mingle,' Essie said hastily. 'We'll do what everyone else seems to be doing, except that we don't know anyone, so we'll have to chat amongst ourselves.'

Jack took her by the hand. 'Excellent plan, Essie. Let's enjoy Sir Henry's hospitality while keeping an eye on her ladyship. That man is a ladykiller if ever I saw one.'

'I thought you said that Raven shot him,' George said in a low voice as they edged their way through the crowd, following the general drift of the other guests.

'I'm not sure what happened.' Essie kept a tight hold on Jack's hand. 'But, whatever it was, Sir Henry doesn't seem to hold a grudge.'

Carried along by the general surge towards the ballroom, like so much flotsam on a sea of bejewelled ladies and their dashing escorts, they passed between double doors flanked by two liveried footmen. Tables and chairs had been set out at intervals, some of which were already occupied, and the air was thick with the scent of expensive perfume, pomade and hothouse flowers. Champagne flowed and the volume of conversation rose in competition with the orchestra and a rather large lady, dressed in apple-green satin, who entertained them with snatches from the operas in an amazing coloratura soprano that made the crystal drops on the chandeliers tinkle like silver bells.

'I don't think I was cut out for this sort of life.' George downed a glass of champagne in one gulp.

'We came to support Alice,' Essie said hastily. 'But I don't think she needs us. She seems to be doing very well on her own.'

Jack sipped his champagne. 'I'd prefer a glass of ale or a tot of brandy, but I have to hand it to Sir Henry, he is a generous host.'

'I heard someone say that supper is being served soon,' Essie added, stifling a yawn. 'I wonder how long this will go on.'

'Don't tell me you're bored.' George stretched out his legs, almost tripping up a footman who was balancing a tray of champagne on one hand. 'Sorry, old chap. Here, let me take a couple and reduce your load.' He winked at the footman as he snatched two brimming glasses.

'George, really.' Essie frowned at him, but it was almost impossible to keep a straight face. 'Behave yourself.'

He glanced round at the company where respectable matrons were openly flirting with unattached gentlemen while their spouses played cards for what looked like enormous stakes. 'Seems to me we're the only ones who are observing decorum,' he said, grinning. 'Maybe I should try my luck with one of those bored beauties whose husband is neglecting her.'

'Don't you dare,' Essie said severely.

'It's lucky for you that duelling has been outlawed, George,' Jack added cheerfully.

'Heaven knows what it will be like later.' Essie held her hand to her forehead. 'I'm sure that singer has a lovely voice, but she's giving me a headache.'

'I can't wait for supper to be served.' George gulped champagne, pulling a face. 'D'you know, I

don't really like this stuff. Like you, Jack, I'd rather
have a glass of ale.'

Essie sighed. It was going to be a long evening.

Supper had been served and even George could find
no fault with the food. The orchestra had taken a
well-deserved break and the opera singer had taken
her final bow. The gamblers seemed to be too intent
on the cards to leave their tables for anything other
than their most pressing needs, but some of the
furniture had been moved back to form a dance
floor, and the orchestra re-formed and began to play
a waltz. Sir Henry led Alice out to start the dancing
and they moved together in perfect harmony. Essie
was startled and yet not surprised by Alice's change
of heart. Sir Henry had a rakish charm and his
reputation as a lady's man posed a challenge to any
woman. With his dark good looks and devil-may-
care attitude to life, he put Essie in mind of a tiger:
handsome but dangerous. She was afraid that Alice
might imagine she could bring him to heel, in a
similar manner to the way she had managed Falco,
and no doubt many others.

'May I have this dance, Essie?'

She looked up with a start to see Jack standing
in front of her, holding out his hand. In a moment
of panic she was about to refuse, but then she
remembered the brief instructions that Miss Potts
had given her and Sadie when she was teaching

them to behave like young ladies. Essie rose to her feet and allowed him to lead her onto the floor. Luckily it was a waltz, and the steps came back to her as she followed Jack's lead. It might have been the effect of the champagne and the shimmering candlelight, but Essie felt as though her feet hardly touched the ground as they whirled around the polished floor. When the music stopped they did not separate immediately, and she met Jack's steady gaze, finding it impossible to look away. They were marooned in a pool of golden light, and everything around them had faded into a misty nothingness.

'Oh, Lord! There you are, Essie.' Alice's voice shattered the moment into shards like broken glass. 'I've been looking for you.'

'We were dancing,' Essie said weakly.

'I can see that.' Alice looked from one to the other, frowning. 'You may go home, if you wish. I intend to stay for a while longer.'

'But you need me to act as your chaperone.'

'I am perfectly capable of looking after myself, Essie. I intend to beat Henry at cards and I don't need any distractions. I've sent for my carriage to take you home. Now go, please. I don't need you any more tonight, or should I say this morning. I haven't had such an entertaining evening for months.'

Alice glided away to join Sir Henry and his friends

at one of the card tables and Essie realised that they had been dismissed.

'Don't worry about Lady Alice.' Jack gave Essie's hand a gentle squeeze. 'I have a feeling that she's a match for any man.'

'I don't know why she wanted me to come.' George swayed on his feet. 'That woman uses people, Essie. She'll toss you aside when she's had enough of your company.'

'It's the drink talking,' Essie said crossly. 'You're just piqued because she prefers Sir Henry's company. At least she's put her carriage at our disposal and I, for one, am ready to go home.'

Next morning Essie was awakened by Sadie bursting into her room. 'Essie, wake up.'

'What time is it?'

'It's half-past eight.'

'We didn't get home until one o'clock. I think I'll sleep for a while longer. Go away, Sadie, there's a good girl.'

'No, you don't understand. Lady Alice sent an urgent message for you to go to Hill Street. The carriage is waiting.'

Essie sat up in bed, suddenly wide awake. 'What did the message say? Who brought it?'

'One of her footmen. He said there's been a fire at Starcross Abbey and Lady Alice wants to see you right away.'

All thoughts of sleep were wiped away as Essie leaped out of bed. 'Help me to get dressed, Sadie.'

Essie had expected to arrive at Hill Street to find Alice pacing the floor, but her ladyship was sitting up in bed, sipping a cup of coffee. Essie's stomach rumbled and her mouth was dry. She had not stopped to have breakfast and now she regretted her impulsive reaction to obey Alice's command.

'I was told you wanted to see me urgently,' she said crossly. 'You don't appear to be distressed by the news of the fire. How bad was it?'

'Of course I'm upset.' Alice replaced her cup on its saucer. 'And that's why I sent for you.'

'What can I do?'

'I want you to go to Devonshire right away. Heaven knows how the servants are coping without anyone other than the housekeeper to organise them.'

'I don't see how I could help, Alice. I have no authority to make decisions at Starcross.'

'I had thought that Falco might stay on and run things until Raven returned from Australia, but I should have known that the captain would let me down.'

'Falco will always be a seafarer at heart, and he had no reason to stay on at Starcross.'

'He said he would do anything for me, which was patently untrue,' Alice said, pouting. 'He deserted me in my time of need.'

'But Starcross Abbey wasn't his responsibility, nor is it mine.'

Alice put her head on one side, giving Essie a searching look. 'I had the impression that you were rather fond of my cousin. All that time in Ballarat I had the feeling that there was something going on between you two. Was I wrong?'

'Even if that were true I can't make decisions on his behalf.'

'I'm tired of this conversation. I will pay for you to travel first class on the train today. You may take George and Sadie if you wish, but I need to know the full extent of the damage, and then I can decide what course of action should be taken in my cousin's absence.'

Essie was about to refuse, but memories of her time in Ballarat with Raven and Freddie came flooding back. But for Raven she would never have travelled to the other side of the world and found her fortune. At one time she had imagined herself to be in love with him, but now she was not so sure. Whatever her feelings for him they were friends and she could do this one thing for him.

'All right, Alice. I'll go to Starcross Abbey and see what can be done.'

George had grumbled, but he had agreed to accompany Essie to Devonshire, and Sadie had been eager to return to Starcross Abbey. They had travelled by train and had hired a cab at the station.

'I can see smoke,' Sadie said excitedly, peering out of the carriage window as they approached Starcross Abbey.

'Surely it can't still be burning.' Essie leaned forward as the vehicle swung round the steep bend in the lane and drove through the open gates. Her hand flew to her mouth as she stifled a cry of dismay. Smoking piles of rubble were strewn over the carriage sweep in front of the house, and the roof on the east wing was missing. Exposed timbers reached up into the summer sky like blackened fingers.

George studied the devastation, shaking his head. 'That must have been some conflagration. I wonder how it started.'

'That's what I hope to find out.' Essie waited impatiently for the carriage to come to a halt. George opened the door and helped her to alight.

'This is so sad,' she said, gazing up at what was left of the old house with tears in her eyes.

'It looks to have burned itself out, which is a good thing.' George helped Sadie to the ground and picked up their cases. 'Knock on the door, there's a good girl. My hands are full.'

Sadie obliged without hesitating and moments later the door was opened by a tearful Mrs Grimes. She flung her arms around Essie's neck in an uncharacteristic show of emotion. 'I'm so glad you came, miss. I'm at my wits' end to know what to do, and that be a fact. Mrs Wills is away visiting her sick brother, and Mr Havers is in Plymouth on estate business.'

'I'm so sorry, Mrs Grimes.' Essie extricated herself from the cook's grip. 'Let's go inside. Lady Alice sent me to assess the damage.'

'The whole of the east wing has gone – burned to the ground overnight. But there were a sudden storm, as if the Good Lord hisself had opened the heavens in order to save Starcross Abbey from the work of the devil. Although we know the name of the fiend who did this evil thing.'

Essie stepped over the threshold, followed by Sadie, and George came last, carrying their luggage. The smell of charred wood hung in a pall, covering everything in the entrance hall with a thick layer of soot. Mrs Grimes led the way to what had once been the billiard room. She opened the door and they were enveloped in a gust of smoke-laden air and dust. Essie blinked at the sight of the utter devastation. The outer walls were standing but the upper floors were missing, as was the roof. Open to the sky there was nothing left of the east wing other than smouldering rubble.

'Close the door, Mrs Grimes. I've seen enough.' Essie stepped back into the part of the building untouched by the flames.

'Come to the kitchen, miss. It's the only tidy room in what's left of the house.' Mrs Grimes headed off, leaving them to follow.

'We'll need to stay for a night or two,' Essie said worriedly. 'Two rooms will do. I don't want to put you to unnecessary trouble.'

'There's only Jenifry and Beattie to help me. With most of the rooms under Holland covers, we haven't needed much help in the house, but we'll manage, miss. I've never let his lordship down and never will.'

The kitchen appeared to have escaped the flames and, apart from the cloying sooty smell, everything look exactly the same as when Essie was last there.

'Jenifry, put the kettle on and make us a pot of tea. Where's that silly girl?'

'Beattie's in the yard drawing water from the pump, Ma.' Jenifry shot a shy smile in Essie's direction. 'It's good to see you again, miss. We need someone to tell us what must be done.' She glanced at George and bobbed a curtsey. 'Begging your pardon for being so forward, sir.'

'Don't mind us,' Essie said hastily. 'This is my brother, George Chapman, and of course you know Sadie. Lady Alice asked us to come and see the damage for ourselves. We're here to help.'

'Take a seat, please do.' Mrs Grimes pulled up a chair and sank down. 'I'm sorry, but this has fair upset me. I'm too old to deal with suchlike.'

George pulled up a chair for Essie and one for himself, and Sadie perched on a stool.

'What did you mean when you said you know

the name of the person who did this, Mrs Grimes?' Essie said gently. 'Was it a deliberate act of arson?'

'It were Smeaton, miss. He must have hid in the still room. He bided his time and then when we was all abed he set the fire going.'

'How do you know this?' George eyed her doubtfully. 'He surely didn't stay around to watch the flames take hold.'

'That's where you're wrong, master. Smeaton was drunk. He'd taken a keg of brandy from the cellar and drunk some of the contents before tipping the rest over the furniture and settling light to it. Trouble was that the old fool caught hisself on fire at the same time and he run out into the stable yard screaming blue murder. That's how us was alerted and we all got out before us was burned alive.'

'How terrible. I can't believe he would do such a thing.' Essie stared at her in disbelief. 'Where is he now?'

'The constable arrested him and took him away. I don't care what happens to him now. I hope as how he suffers the torments of hell for what he's done, especially after what he said when he thought he was going to his Maker. He confessed to his sins in the hope of being forgiven. God might be that generous, but I never will.' Mrs Grimes covered her face with her grimy apron and began to weep.

Essie looked to Jenifry for clarification. 'What did he say?'

'Smeaton told the constable that he'd smuggled the brandy they found in the cellar that night, years ago. I were only a tiddy little maid then, but Ma told me all about it.'

'That's true.' Mrs Grimes nodded vigorously. 'Master Frederick got the blame, but he suffered for his act of bravery.'

'That doesn't make sense,' George said impatiently. 'He must have been implicated in some way.'

'Master Frederick was a bit on the wild side, sir. He liked to share a jug of ale with the local boys at the inn. It just happened that he was walking home along the strand one night when he saw them trying to land their boat in rough weather, and he waded into the sea to help.'

'The revenue men was waiting in the cove,' Jenifry added excitedly. 'Smeaton confessed that he was part of the gang, and that he knocked Master Frederick senseless in the struggle to get ashore.'

'That's what he told us.' Mrs Grimes eased herself out of the chair and reached for the milk jug. 'Smeaton convinced the revenue men that he'd been the one who went to the aid of the floundering vessel and he swore that Master Frederick had been on the boat with the gang.'

'But surely Frederick denied the accusation.' Essie looked from one to the other. 'Why didn't anyone speak up for him?'

'We wasn't asked, miss. Smeaton spoke for all of

us and Master Frederick had often been seen drinking with the Pascoe boys and Jan Hawkes. They were all arrested and sent for trial, but Master Frederick was too poorly after the knock on the head. We all thought he'd been injured when the boat hit the rocks, until Smeaton told us different.'

Essie accepted a cup of tea from Jenifry but she was still puzzled. There were elements in the story that did not make sense. 'Where was Lord Raven in all this?'

Mrs Grimes pursed her lips. 'He was with his lady love. It was the night they were attempting to elope. Quite a scandal, it were at the time.'

'He was engaged to be married?' Essie stared at her in disbelief. Raven had never mentioned a fiancée, but now she came to think of it he had rarely spoken about anything that related to his past.

'It were all a secret.' Mrs Grimes topped her tea up with a generous helping of milk. She set the jug back on the table with a thud. 'The young lady's father had other plans for her. He wanted her to marry a widowed duke who owned a huge estate up north. That was why Master Frederick was out so late at night in a terrible storm. He'd gone to warn Sir Raven that the young lady's father had discovered their plan to elope.'

'I still don't understand how Raven was involved in the smuggling,' Essie said, frowning.

'He wasn't, miss. We all knew that, but Lord Crozier

came to the house in a fit of temper such as you've never seen, and Master Frederick went to warn his brother.'

Essie stared at her in disbelief. 'She was Lord Crozier's daughter? No, surely not?'

Chapter Twenty-Two

Mrs Grimes put her teacup down with a sigh. 'It was a love match if ever there was one, but I don't think you knew the lady in question.'

Sadie had been listening wide-eyed. 'Then it couldn't have been Lady Alice.'

Essie was at a loss for words. There had never been anything in the least romantic in the way Alice treated her cousin, and he had never shown any preference for her company.

'Certainly not,' Mrs Grimes said firmly. 'Whatever next? No, the young lady in question was Lady Alice's younger sister, Lady Cordelia.'

'Was?' Essie caught her breath. 'I didn't know that Lady Alice had a sister. What happened to her, Mrs Grimes?'

'Lord Crozier headed them off and forced his

daughter to return home. No one knows whether it were an accident or whether she threw herself into the sea, but her body was washed ashore on Red Rock sands the next day,' Jenifry said in a low voice. 'I remember the shock of it all.'

Mrs Grimes nodded earnestly. 'It isn't spoken of much round here, miss. Folk reckon it was her loss that killed the old earl. He died of a heart attack some days later and Lord Raven gave hisself up to the magistrate, taking the blame for a crime he thought his brother had committed. Not that us knew it at the time.'

Essie's hand trembled as she picked up the cup and held it to her lips. She took a sip, giving herself time to think. 'What was Lady Cordelia like?'

'Very pretty and a nice young lady, miss.' Mrs Grimes put her head on one side, studying Essie's face with a critical eye. 'Not unlike yourself in some ways, but a complete opposite to Lady Alice, who was always very wayward, although I wouldn't say that in her hearing.'

George downed the rest of his tea, stood up and stretched. 'It seems to me that the past is best forgotten. We have to deal with the problems on hand.'

'I think it is a very sad story.' Sadie wiped tears from her cheeks. 'Poor Raven.'

'Yes,' Essie said slowly. 'It is a tragic case. But Smeaton's confession means that Freddie and Raven can prove their innocence. Raven has served more than five years of a seven-year sentence for a crime he didn't commit, and Freddie has been in exile even though he's done nothing wrong.'

'That's very true, miss.' Jenifry turned to her mother. 'Who would have thought that Smeaton was such a wicked man? I never liked him, but how could he stand by and see someone else take the blame for his evil deeds?'

Mrs Grimes shook her head. 'There's no accounting for some folk.'

'Was he very badly burned?' Essie asked anxiously. 'Because he's the only person who can clear the family name.'

'I can't say, miss. He certainly made enough fuss about it.'

'Are there any horses left in the stables, Mrs Grimes?'

'Yes, miss. The head groom and his boy stayed on, but Whiddon, the coachman, found work at Daumerle, seeing as how there was no call for his services here, at least until the master returns.'

'What are you going to do, Essie?' George asked anxiously.

'I'm going to have a word with the police constable who arrested Smeaton.' Essie rose to her feet. 'We need Smeaton's testimony if we're to clear Raven's name and Freddie's, too.'

'But what about the house, miss?' Mrs Grimes followed Essie to the door. 'What shall us do?'

'You'd best shut off the east wing and get some extra help with the cleaning,' Essie said, picking up her cloak and muff. 'I'm going to the stables.'

George caught her by the hand. 'Wait a minute, Essie. You can handle a craft on the river, but you can't ride a horse.'

She snatched her hand free. 'You'd be surprised what I can do,' she said with a wry smile. 'I'm a very good horsewoman, as it happens.'

The village constable was seated behind the desk in the police station, which consisted of one room and a lock-up at the rear. He listened attentively while Essie explained her mission, with George backing her story with more enthusiasm than accuracy.

'So you see,' Essie concluded, 'I must talk to Smeaton and persuade him to repeat what he said in front of the magistrate or a lawyer. Is he here?'

'He was badly burned, miss. I took him straight to hospital.'

'Then I must go there right away.'

The constable shook his head. 'I doubt if the doctor will allow you to see him at present.'

'But you won't let him go free?'

'He's still under arrest, miss. Smeaton will go to prison if he recovers, although I wouldn't hold out too much hope of that.'

Essie turned to George. 'We must send for Gilfoyle. He'll know what to do.'

'Do you think he'd drop everything to travel all the way to Devonshire?'

'I know one person who could make him do whatever she wanted.' Essie turned to the policeman with a grateful smile. 'Thank you for your help, Constable. I assume you made a note of Smeaton's confession?'

He patted his pocket. 'As always, miss. Everything has to be written down and used as evidence in court.'

'You're very efficient. Goodbye and thank you again. I'm going to London and I hope to return with my solicitor. I'm going to prove once and for all that Lord Starcross and Mr Frederick Dorincourt are both innocent.'

The constable rose to his feet. 'Amen to that, miss.'

It was early afternoon when Essie and Sadie arrived back in London. George had been reluctant to allow them to travel unaccompanied, but Essie insisted that he was needed at Starcross and she promised to return next day, with or without Gilfoyle. She doubted whether she had enough powers of persuasion to make him undertake the journey at such short notice, but it was quite literally a matter of life and death. They took a cab to Hill Street only to be informed by a disapproving Fielding that her ladyship had accepted an invitation to luncheon with Sir Henry.

Essie dragged Sadie down the steps and hailed a passing hansom cab. 'Bearwood House, Piccadilly, please, cabby.' She bundled Sadie inside and climbed up after her. 'What a palaver, but time is short and I have to get a signed affidavit from Smeaton. If he should die without leaving something the law recognises all this will be in vain and Raven and Freddie will be branded as criminals for the rest of their lives.'

Sadie leaned back against the worn leather squabs. 'It's like being in one of Mrs Radcliffe's stories. I feel like a heroine.'

'I wish I did,' Essie groaned. 'I'm afraid that Alice will refuse to help. Now that she's set her cap at Sir Henry, who knows what will happen? I neither like nor trust that man.'

She knotted her fingers together in an attempt to stop her hands trembling as the cab trundled at an alarmingly slow pace through the traffic, but it was not far to Piccadilly and Essie leaped from the vehicle as soon as it came to a halt. She tossed a coin to the cabby and hurried up the steps to rap on the door knocker.

The footman eyed her suspiciously but Essie held her ground, refusing to be fobbed off by excuses. 'I know that Lady Alice Crozier is here. I insist on seeing her and I'm not leaving until I have.'

'If you would kindly wait there, miss, I'll make

enquiries.' The footman was about to close the door but Essie was too quick for him. She slipped into the vestibule followed by Sadie.

'We'll wait all day if necessary. Please tell Lady Alice that it's of the utmost urgency.'

'I'm with you, Essie,' Sadie whispered. 'We won't let them push us around.'

'No, indeed,' Essie said with more certainty than she was feeling, but to her relief the footman returned quickly.

'Lady Alice will see you now. Follow me, if you please.'

The drawing room was on the first floor with tall windows overlooking Green Park. Alice was seated decorously on a sofa with Sir Henry standing at her side. He did not look pleased.

'State your business, Miss Chapman,' he said abruptly.

'I would like a word with her ladyship, in private, please.'

His dark eyebrows snapped together in a frown. 'This is my house. I don't take kindly to be ordered about by a servant.'

Essie drew herself up to her full height. 'It was a polite request, sir. And I am not a servant.'

'Neither is she, Henry,' Alice said crossly. 'Go away and leave us alone. This won't take long.'

Sir Henry hesitated for a moment and then he shrugged. 'Have it your way, my dear.' He left the room, allowing the door to swing shut of its own accord, as if to underline his displeasure.

'Don't take any notice of him,' Alice said, smiling. 'He likes to think that he is master of all he surveys, but he will soon learn.' She leaned back against the silk cushions. 'Now, take a seat, both of you, and Essie you must tell me about Starcross. What state is it in?'

'Very poor. The whole of the east wing was burned to the ground.' Essie remained standing but Sadie plumped down in a wingback chair by the fire. 'The rest of the house is untouched, although everything is covered in soot.'

'I see. Well, thank goodness for small mercies. I'll authorise any work you think necessary, but just to make it safe, you understand.'

'I've left George to organise the clean-up and make sure it's done in an orderly manner, but don't you want to see the damage for yourself?'

'It's not my home, Essie. I'm sure that any restoration work can wait until Raven is a free man.'

'And that's why we're here,' Essie said eagerly. 'It seems that the butler, Smeaton, was the fire raiser, and he suffered severe burns in doing so. I think he must have feared for his eternal soul because he made a confession that will clear both Raven and Freddie.'

'Really?' Alice sat forward, giving Essie her full attention. 'What did he say?'

'That he was the person involved with the smugglers and Freddie was merely a bystander who helped them drag the boat ashore when it was in danger of capsizing.'

Alice stared at her in disbelief. 'But that makes no sense. Why didn't Freddie tell the judge what really happened?'

'Smeaton knocked him unconscious and it seems that when Freddie recovered from the blow he had no memory of anything that happened. Perhaps Raven assumed that he was guilty, it's impossible to say, but Smeaton is in a serious condition. If he dies the truth will never be known.'

'I was in Paris when it happened,' Alice said slowly. 'Losing my sister and my papa in such a short space of time came as a terrible shock. It was all over by the time I returned home. Freddie had fled the country and Raven was on his way to Australia.'

'It must have been awful for you.'

'It was, but I survived. Had I known the truth I might have done something about it, but it's too late now.'

'No, it isn't. Raven still has two years before he's a free man, and Freddie will never be able to return home unless Smeaton makes a full confession. That's why I'm here, today, Alice. Mr Gilfoyle will know what to do, but I doubt if he would see me.'

'Are there no solicitors in Devonshire? I'm sure I must number a justice of the peace amongst my acquaintances, although I cannot recall a name at present.'

'I'm sure there are, but Smeaton is seriously ill and he might die. We simply can't delay. You do want to clear the family name, don't you?'

'Of course, I do.' Alice rose from her chair and tugged on an embroidered bell pull. 'Henry won't appreciate a change in plans, but you and I are going to visit Gilfoyle's chambers.'

'Me, too.' Sadie leaped to her feet. 'Don't leave me here.'

'Come, if you must,' Alice said impatiently. 'I'll send for my carriage.'

Faced by a determined Lady Alice Crozier, Gilfoyle eventually crumbled and agreed to travel to Starcross after he had seen his last client and had been home to pack a bag. He promised to meet Essie and Sadie on the station platform at six o'clock that evening. Alice thanked him graciously and Essie sighed with relief.

'Henry will be grumpy for at least an hour.' Alice waved to attract the attention of her coachman, who had been waiting on the far side of the square. 'He was going to take me to tea at Gunter's and he hates having his arrangements altered in any way.'

'Why are you seeing him again, Alice? You know his reputation.'

'Of course I do, silly. That's what makes him so

exciting. Beneath it all he's just a spoiled little boy, and a very wealthy one, too. If I accept his proposal, and yes, he has proposed more than once, I will be one of the wealthiest women in England, and life will never be dull.'

'What would Raven say to such a match?'

'My dear, I really don't care. I love my cousin dearly, but he has no control of my life. I want the best for him and Freddie, but there's a small part of me that can never quite forgive him for what happened to my sister. She was young and impressionable, and if I'd been at home I would have tried to talk her out of an elopement.'

'But he wanted to marry her.'

'He knew that my papa would never consent to such a match. Royalty may marry first cousins, but Papa was firmly against it. He said that interbreeding, if you'll forgive the expression, created simpletons and weakened the lineage. I don't know if he was right, but that was his firmly held belief, and Raven knew how Papa felt. He should have walked away and left Cordelia to marry the man that Papa had chosen for her. The Duke would have treated her well and she would be alive today.'

'I'm sorry,' Essie said earnestly. 'I didn't mean to upset you.'

Sadie tugged at her sleeve. 'Here comes the carriage. Are we going back to Bearwood House, Essie?'

'I think not,' Essie spotted a hansom cab that had just dropped a gentleman off outside one of the chambers. She raised her hand to hail it. 'I want to see Jack. I need to let him know that we'll be away for longer than I expected.'

Alice was about to climb into her carriage, but she hesitated. 'You seem to be getting very close to that person, Essie. You could do better.'

'That's funny – I was just thinking the same thing about you.' Essie had the satisfaction of leaving Alice speechless. 'Wapping High Street, please, cabby.'

Jack was seated at his desk when Essie and Sadie walked into the office. He stood up, greeting them with a warm smile. 'This is a pleasant surprise, Essie. I thought you were in Devonshire.'

'We had to come to London on urgent business, but we're returning this evening.'

'I'd offer you a cup of tea, but, as you might guess by looking at my attire, I've been on board ship all afternoon going over the bill of lading with the first mate. Captain Kitchen has been taken ill, so I'm looking for another master to take command.' Jack crossed the floor to pick up the poker and prod the dying embers of the fire. 'I'm afraid it would take a long time to boil a kettle.'

'It's all right,' Essie assured him. 'We're on our way to Curzon Street and then we'll be leaving for

Waterloo Bridge Station to meet Mr Gilfoyle at six. He's the reason we came to London.'

Jack glanced at the white-faced clock on the wall above the fireplace. 'It's only three o'clock. I'm closing up early anyway, so why don't you come to my house, and you can tell me everything over a nice hot cup of tea?'

'And a jam tart?' Essie said, smiling.

Jack nodded. 'Of course, or maybe a slice of cake. Mrs Cooper has been baking today.'

'Do you think the old sea captain will smoke his pipe while I'm there?' Sadie asked excitedly. 'Essie told me all about your house.'

'I'm sure he'll oblige for a young lady like you, Sadie.' Jack opened the door and ushered them out onto the wharf, and by the time they reached the Old Captain's House, Essie had given him a brief account of what had occurred at Starcross Abbey.

Mrs Cooper hurried out of the kitchen to greet Essie as if she were an old friend, and she enveloped Sadie in a warm hug.

'My dear, you look as though you could do with a mug of my homemade lemonade. Come into the kitchen and you can help me to decorate the cake I've just made.'

Sadie glanced at Essie and she nodded her approval. 'Of course, but remember to save a slice for me. Mrs Cooper is an excellent cook.'

Mrs Cooper shepherded Sadie towards the kitchen

and Jack ushered Essie into the front parlour. 'You'll have a friend for life there,' he said, chuckling. 'Mrs Cooper loves cosseting people. I'm afraid she's given up on me, but she will spoil young Sadie and take pleasure in doing so.'

Essie went straight to the window seat and sat down. 'I could spend all day here, just watching the river,' she said, sighing. 'But there is so much to do at Starcross, and most importantly we have to get Smeaton to sign a document that will prove once and for all that Raven and Freddie were not involved with the smuggling gang.'

'You've taken a lot on,' Jack said seriously. 'It should be up to Lady Alice to sort out her family's affairs.'

'You obviously aren't very well acquainted with her ladyship. Alice does whatever she wants and I think that Sir Henry has met his match. They are totally unsuited and I'm sure there will be fireworks, but in an odd sort of way I think they will get along very well.'

Jack opened the door to admit Mrs Cooper, bearing a tray of tea, followed by Sadie with a plate of strawberry tarts and a chocolate cake studded with raspberries.

'Thank you, Mrs Cooper,' Essie said, smiling. 'You're very kind.'

'Not at all, miss. It's so nice to have company. I hope you and Sadie will come often.'

'I will,' Sadie said, swallowing a mouthful of the

sweet-smelling drink. 'I'll come and see you every day if you'll teach me how to make this lovely chocolate.' She sniffed the air. 'I can't smell tobacco smoke. Do you think the old captain will come today?'

'I'm sure he knows you're here, Sadie,' Mrs Cooper said, nodding. 'But he's reserving judgement. The captain was a bachelor and he didn't have any children, so he's not used to young ladies like you.'

'I'm very well behaved.' Sadie looked to Essie for confirmation. 'I am, aren't I, Essie?'

'Indeed you are.' Essie accepted a cup of tea from Jack, who winked at her. She smiled up at him. 'Thank you, Jack. This is delightful, but we mustn't get too comfortable. We have a train to catch at six.'

At ten to six that evening, Essie and Sadie were waiting on the platform at Waterloo Bridge Station. They had called in briefly at Curzon Street but it was of necessity a brief visit as they had spent far too much time in the Old Captain's House with Jack and Mrs Cooper. Sadie had blossomed under the benign influence of the kindly housekeeper and had been reluctant to leave.

Essie glanced at the station clock.

'I hope Mr Gilfoyle hasn't changed his mind,' she said anxiously. 'It will ruin everything if he doesn't turn up.'

Sadie stamped her feet. 'I'm tired, Essie. I wish we

could have stayed in the Old Captain's House. I loved it there, and Mrs Cooper is so nice. If I had a grannie I would want her to be just like Mrs Cooper.'

'Yes, she's a kind lady and a very good cook. Jack is lucky to have her.' Essie stood on tiptoe. She thought she had recognised a man pushing his way through the crowd. 'There's Gilfoyle. Thank goodness! I was beginning to think he wasn't coming.' She waved and he responded. She opened the carriage door and was about to climb in when she saw someone else hurrying toward them. 'Sadie, look who's come to see us off. It's Jack.'

Sadie turned and uttered a cry of delight. She ran to meet him and returned, dragging him by the hand. Gilfoyle caught up with them just as the guard blew his whistle. He tossed his case into the carriage and proffered his hand to Essie.

'After you, Mr Gilfoyle,' Essie said hastily. She turned to Jack. 'It was good of you to come, but, as you see, we have to leave now.'

Jack put down the packages and the small valise that he was carrying, and he lifted Sadie bodily into the carriage. 'I couldn't let you do this on your own, Essie. I'm coming, too.'

Too surprised to argue, Essie took her seat. She watched as Jack placed his luggage on the rack and the train slowly pulled away from the station with a loud burst of steam. 'I don't understand. I thought you had a lot of business on hand.'

'Some things are more important, Essie.' Jack sat down next to Sadie, so that he was facing Essie and Gilfoyle. I've taken a few days off, the first I've had in three years, so I think it's well earned.'

Gilfoyle cleared his throat. 'We haven't met, sir. My name is Gilfoyle. I'm Miss Chapman's lawyer.'

'I'm so sorry,' Essie said hastily. 'I should have introduced you. Mr Gilfoyle, this is Jack Manning, my brother's business partner.'

'And close friend, it would seem.' Gilfoyle sat back in his seat, folding his hands in his lap and turning his head to look out of the window.

Essie met Jack's amused gaze with a wry smile. 'What made you decide to join us? You won't find much comfort at Starcross Abbey.'

'I thought I might be able to help in some way. I'm quite handy when it comes to wielding a hammer, or even a mop.'

'It will be fun,' Sadie said excitedly. 'We'll be like a proper family.'

Gilfoyle cleared his throat. 'This is a serious business, Miss Chapman. I'm only doing this as a favour to Lady Alice, but, whatever happens with the man Smeaton, I intend to return to London tomorrow afternoon.'

'Yes, Mr Gilfoyle,' Essie said hastily. 'I fully understand.'

*   *   *

It was midnight when they arrived at Starcross Abbey. Sadie had fallen asleep during the uncomfortable ride in the only vehicle available, which happened to be a farm wagon. The farmer had been loading milk churns into the guard's van when Essie alighted from the train, and he had grudgingly agreed to take them to Starcross. It meant going a couple of miles out of his way, but a generous tip from Jack had clinched the deal. Essie was cold, tired and cramped from sitting hunched up on the wooden seat as the vehicle jolted and lurched its way through the country lanes.

The house stood eerily silent in the moonlight, and the gravel crunched beneath her feet as she walked up to the front door and rapped on the knocker. For a moment she was afraid that everyone had gone to bed, but then she heard footsteps and the door opened. George held up a lantern.

'I was beginning to think you'd stayed the night in London. Why are you so late?'

'Answers later, George. Mr Gilfoyle has been kind enough to accompany us. Did Mrs Grimes make a room ready for him?'

Gilfoyle followed her into the hall and George shook his hand. 'Good of you to come at such short notice, sir. I'll show you the way.' He glanced over his shoulder as Jack entered, carrying the luggage. 'What are you doing here, Jack? This isn't your problem.'

'I thought I might be of assistance,' Jack said cheerfully. 'And I admit I was curious, too.'

Sadie pushed past him. 'I'm hungry,' she said, sniffing. 'And I'm tired.'

'Come with me.' Essie took her by the hand. 'We'll see what we can find in the kitchen. Perhaps Mr Gilfoyle would like something to drink?'

'Good idea, Essie. Why didn't I think of that?' George started off across the entrance hall, heading for Raven's study. 'I know where there's a bottle of cognac. Will you join me in a nightcap, gentlemen?'

Essie watched Gilfoyle and Jack trail after George as if he were the Pied Piper. 'I'm sure a cup of cocoa will go down well, Sadie. What do you say?'

Sadie yawned and rubbed her eyes. 'Cocoa will be fine. Can we take it to bed? I don't think I can stay awake much longer.'

'Of course,' Essie said, giving her a hug. 'Tomorrow is going to be a very busy day.'

Sadie glanced at the huge grandfather clock. 'It's tomorrow now, Essie.'

'So it is.' Essie picked up a candlestick and led the way to the kitchen. 'We need to get some sleep, because so much hangs on what happens with Smeaton. If he's too unwell or unwilling to testify, all our efforts to free Raven and Freddie will have been in vain.'

Chapter Twenty-Three

Essie and Gilfoyle arrived at the infirmary early next morning, driven by the head groom from Starcross Abbey in the Dorincourts' governess cart, which was not the most comfortable of conveyances. It was a fine morning with a clear azure sky and warm sunshine, which made up for any discomfort during the relatively short journey. Gilfoyle made enquiries at the desk and they were sent to a small waiting room where they sat in silence. Essie clasped and unclasped her hands as she stared at the bare grey walls. It was not the most cheerful of places and the hard seats did not encourage a long stay. The smell of carbolic had enveloped her the moment she stepped into the hospital, and she was convinced that the cloying odour would cling to her hair and clothes long after they had left.

'I wonder what the delay is,' she said in a low voice. 'Surely he can't have many visitors.'

Gilfoyle took the pocket watch from his waistcoat and examined it, frowning. 'I need to leave before midday. Let's hope the fellow doesn't expire before I've had a chance to take down his statement.'

Essie subsided into silence. There was nothing she could say that would make up for the uncomfortable night that Gilfoyle had spent. He complained that the bed was damp and everything in the room had been tainted by soot and smoke. The porridge served to him that morning had been tepid and lumpy, and the coffee was cold. It was unfortunate that Mrs Grimes had developed a sick headache and had remained in bed, leaving everything to Jenifry and Beattie. Essie had attempted to help, as had Sadie, but the resultant chaos in the kitchen had caused the first lot of porridge to burn and the second attempt was little better. Jack had eaten his without complaint, but George had not come down to breakfast, having imbibed too much brandy before retiring to bed, and was suffering the aftereffects.

Just as Gilfoyle was growing even more restive the door opened and a police sergeant entered.

'I demand to see the patient now, Officer.'

'You may, of course, but I'm afraid you'd find him rather silent.' The sergeant stood in the doorway, an uncompromising figure. 'I'm afraid the prisoner, or perhaps I should call him the patient, passed away half an hour ago.'

Essie stared at him in dismay. 'Oh, no. That's terrible.'

The sergeant gave her an inscrutable look. 'He had no chance of surviving, miss. That's the doctor's opinion.'

'Then my time has been wasted,' Gilfoyle said angrily. 'There is nothing to be gained by remaining here.'

'Begging your pardon, sir,' the sergeant said smugly, 'but Smeaton made a deathbed confession, which is admissible in court in some circumstances. The constable who was posted at the door overnight noted it down and Smeaton signed the document.' The sergeant handed the slip of paper to Gilfoyle. 'It will be in my report.'

Gilfoyle scanned the contents. 'I suppose this will have to do.'

'Do you think that's enough to prove Raven and Freddie's innocence, Mr Gilfoyle?' Essie asked anxiously.

'This, together with the statements I've already taken from the servants to whom Smeaton made his first confession, should be enough to convince a judge, but one can never take these things for granted.' Gilfoyle tucked the sheet of paper into his briefcase and rose to his feet. 'We must hope for the best, Miss Chapman. I'll take the next train to

London and start the proceedings at the first possible opportunity.'

'Thank you, Sergeant.' Essie left the room, following in Gilfoyle's wake. She was disappointed, but she clung to the hope that a judge would consider Smeaton's admission of guilt was enough to exonerate Raven and Freddie.

They returned to Starcross Abbey where Gilfoyle collected his valise, said his goodbyes and left for the station, promising to take up the Dorincourts' case as a matter of urgency. He had been gone less than half an hour when Sadie burst into the kitchen where Essie was helping Jenifry to prepare luncheon. 'You won't believe this, but there's a carriage drawn up outside and there's a coat of arms on the door.'

Essie wiped her hands on her apron. 'Run and tell George and Jack that we've got visitors. They're in the east wing helping to shore up the damaged interior wall.' Essie hurried through the house to open the front door, and was astonished to see Sir Henry helping Alice to alight from the carriage. She went to greet them.

'This is an unexpected pleasure. What are you doing here, Alice?'

'We've come to inspect the damage,' Alice said, kissing her on the cheek.

Sir Henry's flared nostrils quivered. 'You can still smell the soot, and smoke damage is almost as bad as charring. Have you called in the experts, Esther?'

'We can go into that later, Henry.' Alice stepped across the threshold, turning to Essie with eyebrows raised. 'Where are the housemaids?' She held out her arms, waiting for someone to take her cape.

Essie took the garment and explained the servant situation, adding that Mrs Grimes was in bed. 'Jenifry and Beattie are preparing luncheon because Mrs Grimes is lying down with a bad headache.'

'No wonder she feels ill. It smells frightful in here.' Alice shivered dramatically. 'You were right, Henry. The house is uninhabitable in this state, but I want to see the east wing. Lead on, Essie.' Alice snatched her cape back and wrapped it around her shoulders. 'Even in summer this old house is like an ice cave. We won't be stopping and I don't want to leave you here on your own.'

'George is here with me,' Essie said over her shoulder. 'And Sadie, of course, and Jack came to help us put things straight.' She opened the door to the east wing and Henry stepped into the ruin. He looked round, shaking his head. 'You need builders to shore up that wall and make it safe.' He nodded to Jack, who was helping the gamekeeper and several local men to nail boards to the damaged wall. 'You people are wasting your time. This part of the house will have to be demolished. In fact, the old place should have been razed to the ground years ago.'

Jack stepped forward, wiping his grimy hands on a borrowed leather apron. 'Even if you're right, Sir

Henry, this is someone's home, and there are many years of history in these ancient walls.'

'You have no right to speak to me in that tone,' Sir Henry said angrily. 'Servants should know their place.'

'Jack is a good friend,' Essie said hastily. 'He's come all the way from London to help save Starcross.'

'If you want my opinion, it's a hopeless case.' Sir Henry glowered at Jack, who held his ground.

Essie could see that an argument was about to ensue. 'I think we should leave them to carry on the good work,' she suggested tactfully. 'Alice, why don't you take Sir Henry to the drawing room and I'll ask Jenifry to bring refreshments?'

'Come, Henry,' Alice said imperiously. 'Leave them to their labours. I can see there's very little we can do here, and I suggest you collect your things and make ready to accompany us to Daumerle, Essie.'

'Knock it down,' Sir Henry muttered as he followed her into the house. 'That's all there is to it.'

'Stay here,' Essie whispered to Jack. 'I'll deal with them.' She turned to Sadie. 'Please will you ask Jenifry to bring a tea tray to the drawing room?'

'I don't want to go Daumerle, Essie,' Sadie said urgently. 'Lady Alice will probably send me back to the schoolroom. I want to stay here.'

Essie patted her on the cheek. 'Don't worry, poppet. We're not going to Daumerle, but I'll try to persuade Alice to take Sir Henry away before he upsets anyone else.'

Sadie nodded and hurried off in the direction of the kitchen.

'Aren't you tempted to spend some time in luxury with Lady Alice and her swain?' Jack's lips curved into a mischievous smile. 'Think what you're missing.'

'That's exactly what I have in mind. A little of Sir Henry's company goes a very long way.'

'So you choose a draughty, burned-out pile over luxury and the company of the nobility?'

'Stop teasing me, Jack. You know the answer very well. Now I have to go and break the news to Alice.'

'Shall I send the men home, Essie?'

'I'm sure that Raven would want us to do all we can to save Starcross,' she said firmly. 'Keep them on for as long as they are willing to work. I'll foot the bill and Raven can repay me when he comes home.' Essie left him to pass on the message and she hurried to the drawing room where she found Alice pacing the floor while Sir Henry tried in vain to light the fire.

'Really, Essie. This is appalling.' Alice came to a halt, shivering dramatically. 'You can't stay here. The smoke will get into your lungs and the damp will give you a chill.'

'I'm truly grateful for your concern,' Essie said gently, 'but that's exactly what I intend to do. At least, we'll stay until Monday and do what we can to make the house habitable before we return to London. Jack and George have a business to run, or we would stay longer.'

Alice eyed her doubtfully. 'If you're sure, but I wouldn't want to remain here under these circumstances. Anyway, one of the reasons I came here today was to find out if Gilfoyle was successful in obtaining a signed affidavit.'

'We were too late. Smeaton died of his injuries, but he had made a full confession, which was noted down by the policeman on duty at his bedside. Gilfoyle has taken it to London, and he's hopeful that it will be enough to prove that neither Freddie nor Raven had anything to do with the smugglers.'

Alice's lips trembled and she brushed away a tear. 'I have a speck in my eye. It's the dust in this wretched house.'

'It's time we left, my love,' Sir Henry said firmly. 'You've done your duty here. I'll wait for you in the carriage while you say your goodbyes.' He strode out of the room and the door creaked on its hinges as it closed.

'That sounds very final,' Essie said curiously. It was obvious that Alice was not her usual self. 'Is anything wrong?'

'On the contrary, my life has taken a turn for the better, although I could not have imagined I would say so, even a short while ago.'

'How has it changed? I don't understand.'

'Sir Henry proposed and I accepted.'

'But I thought you disliked him intensely, Alice.'

'Henry is a challenge that I cannot resist. We are two of a kind, only it took me some time to realise it.'

'Are you sure? It seems so sudden.'

'A bolt of lightning, my dear. It hit me so suddenly that it took my breath away. We're to be married in the chapel at Daumerle on Monday. Henry has obtained a special licence.'

'I don't know what to say.' Essie stared at her, dazed by the announcement.

'I want you to wish me well, and even if you don't want to come with us now, I hope you'll attend our wedding.'

Essie enveloped her in a hug. 'Of course I will. We'll all come to wish you well, but I haven't brought anything suitable to wear to a wedding.'

'You will be the only guests. Henry fell out with his family years ago, and, apart from Raven and Freddie, I don't wish to involve any of my relations. They would be sure to disapprove and cast a cloud over the proceedings. I'll send my carriage to fetch you. Please say you'll come.'

'I wouldn't miss it for the world,' Essie said earnestly.

The chapel at Daumerle was decorated with flowers grown in the hothouse on the estate. The scent of lilies mingled with the scent of roses from the garden, and incense burning in the censer. Essie sat between Jack and Sadie. They were the only members of the congregation, and Sir Henry stood alone in front of the altar. At a signal from the vicar they rose from the pew and the organist began to play. Essie turned her head to see Alice, a vision in white silk lavishly trimmed with lace, walking up the aisle on George's arm. With no close relative to give her away she had, at the last minute, asked George to officiate.

Essie's eyes filled with tears as she watched her brother lead Alice to the altar, and when his part in the proceedings was done he came to sit beside Sadie, who was mopping her eyes with her handkerchief. Essie felt Jack's fingers close gently around her hand, giving it a comforting squeeze and she gave him a sideways glance, meeting his sympathetic look with a smile. He alone seemed to understand her worries for Alice's future happiness. As the vicar droned on, Essie found herself thinking of Raven and Freddie and wishing they were here to wish Alice well.

'. . . I now pronounce you man and wife.' The vicar's voice rose as he uttered the last words of the marriage ceremony.

With the formalities completed, the wedding party left the church to be greeted by a storm of applause from both indoor and outdoor servants. Rose petals were scattered in front of the happy couple and handfuls of rice were thrown. The small bridal party walked slowly to the house, and Sir Henry stopped at the foot of the steps to throw a pocketful of coins for the children to pounce upon.

A cold collation was set out in the dining room, after which Sir Henry rose to his feet and raised a toast to his new wife.

'Now, my dear. I really must ask you to change into your travelling costume. We must leave within the hour if we're to catch the tide.'

'You're honeymooning at sea?' Essie sent a questioning glance to Alice.

'It's news to me,' she said, shrugging. 'You might have consulted me, Henry.'

'It was to be a surprise. My yacht is moored in the Exe estuary, ready to take us to my plantation in Jamaica.'

'You made your fortune in sugar,' Essie said, recalling something that Alice had once told her.

'Yes, sugar.' Sir Henry eyed her with a cynical smile. 'And I have never employed slaves. Whatever your opinion of me, Miss Esther Chapman, I pay my workers a decent wage and they have free accommodation. I am in trade, but I'm not ashamed to have made my money honestly and without causing suffering to others.'

'Well said, sir.' Jack raised his glass to Sir Henry.

'We are also in trade. At the moment George and I have only two ships, but I hope soon to add another to our small fleet. Maybe one day, at a more opportune moment, we can talk business.'

'Maybe we can, Mr Manning. I am a great supporter of enterprise, particularly amongst young men such as yourselves.' He turned to Alice, his expression softening. 'My dear, I must hurry you if we're to catch the tide.'

Alice rose to her feet. 'Essie, will you come with me? With your help I can be ready all the sooner.'

Essie stood up obediently and followed her out of the room. They did not speak until they reached the privacy of Alice's bedchamber. 'Shall I ring for your maid?' Essie asked.

'No, thank you. As you can see, my cases are all packed and I have only to change into my travelling attire. Perhaps you could help me. I wanted to speak to you in private.'

Essie began undoing the tiny buttons at the back of Alice's wedding dress. 'What did you want to say?'

'It may seem as though I'm abandoning Raven and Freddie, but Gilfoyle will handle the legalities. I just want to know that you will keep an eye on things. Henry took me by surprise when he announced our bridal trip – I had thought we might travel to Italy or Switzerland, but I had no idea we were going on a long sea voyage. It sounds as though we will be away for months.'

'You could refuse.'

'No, I want to go. It sounds idyllic, but I have to be sure that you will do your utmost on my behalf.'

Essie helped Alice out of the wedding dress and slipped the elegant silk gown over her head. 'What are you asking of me, Alice? I know you only too well, so it's not just the occasional trip to Lincoln's Inn that you expect of me.'

Alice twisted round so that they were face to face. 'I want you to promise that if the court decides in Raven's favour you will take the news to him in person.'

'You want me to go to Australia? But why, Alice? Surely a letter would suffice?'

'You don't know Raven as well as I do. I could tell that he was very much at home in the goldfields, and I'm afraid he might decide to remain in Australia. But he has obligations to his tenants, and for the upkeep of Starcross Abbey itself.'

'Are you sure about that, Alice?'

'He never wanted to inherit the title and the estate, and I think his heart was broken when Cordelia died. Mine was, too, but I knew I had to live on. Maybe you could convince him to take up his responsibilities at home. Will you at least try?'

'Of course I will, if that's what you really want. But I doubt if he will listen to me.'

Alice clasped Essie's hands in hers. 'You almost made him forget Cordelia. I could see that he had tender feelings for you, but Raven has a stubborn streak and he seems unable to put the past behind him. If anyone can persuade him to return home it would be you.'

'I promise to do what I can.' Essie stood back to admire Alice's smart outfit. 'You look lovely. Sir Henry is a very lucky man.'

'Yes, he is, and I'll remind him of that every day.' Alice turned away to primp in front of the tall cheval mirror. 'I do look rather splendid. This shade of green matches my eyes.'

'You are a vain peacock,' Essie said, laughing. 'But I hope you will be happy with Sir Henry.'

'Whatever you think of him, he's really quite a dear when you get past the schoolboy swagger. I think we'll deal very well together.' Alice swung round to face Essie with a bright smile. 'The first thing I'll do when Henry and I return from our honeymoon will be to come and see you, Essie. Don't forget me.'

Essie enveloped her in a hug. 'As if I could.'

The party ended as those left behind waved off the newlyweds. Alice had put her carriage at their disposal and the drive home was uneventful, but after the luxury of Daumerle, Starcross Abbey seemed even shabbier and more uncomfortable than before. That evening, after supper, Essie, Jack and George huddled round a desultory fire in the drawing room. Sadie had opted to remain in the kitchen with

Mrs Grimes and Jenifry, who were agog to hear the details of the wedding at Daumerle.

It did not take much of a discussion to realise that they had done all that they could to restore some order at Starcross Abbey, and that there was little point in staying on. It would require Raven's permission and considerable funding to repair the fire damage, but, as George said, they had overseen the work to shore up the part of the house untouched by the flames, and it was safe for habitation, at least in the short term. Essie knew that she would be sad to leave, and yet she was eager to return to London.

'The first thing I'll do when we get home will be to visit Gilfoyle. I want to make certain that he is doing all he can to bring the case against Raven and Freddie to a satisfactory conclusion.'

'Don't you think you've done enough?' George said gloomily. 'It's really not our problem, Essie.'

'I promised Alice that I would see it through, and that's exactly what I intend to do.'

Jack eyed her thoughtfully. 'I applaud your loyalty, but it won't take all your time. Why don't you come to the office each day? You could be a tremendous help.'

'What could I do? I know nothing of shipping.'

'As I understand it, you were raised on the river. You must know the upper reaches as well as any waterman, and you could deal with the day-to-day enquiries as well as either of us.'

'I agree with Jack,' George added seriously. 'You know you would die of boredom if you had nothing to do other than spend your time shopping and gossiping with Alice's society friends.'

'That's the last thing I'd do with my time.' Essie looked from one to the other. 'Have you two been plotting together?'

'No!' Jack and George spoke in unison.

'It seems to me that you want me to abandon the Dorincourts' cause.'

George shook his head. 'No, Essie, of course not. I want you to do whatever makes you happy, but we could work together to make a success of the business.'

'I'll think about it.' Essie stifled a yawn. 'I'm going to bed. If we're to leave first thing in the morning I need to get a good night's sleep.'

Chapter Twenty-Four

The day after their return to London Essie's first task was to visit Gilfoyle's office. He assured her that he was doing everything in his power to bring the case before a judge, and with that she had to be satisfied, although she insisted on being kept informed of every twist and turn in the case, and he agreed. She returned home to find herself alone, apart from the servants. George had left for Wapping earlier that morning, taking Sadie with him as she had taken a real liking to Mrs Cooper, and was eager to see her again.

Essie sat in solitary state at the vast dining table and ate her midday meal, although she barely tasted the dishes that were set before her. Once, not long ago, she would have thought she had died and gone to heaven at the sight of such delicacies as potted shrimps, lamb collops and lemon syllabub. In the days when she had existed on bread and dripping, and quite often dry bread only, washed down with weak tea, she could not have imagined that there were people who ate like this every day. Now, when food was plentiful and appeared on her table without so much as lifting a finger, she had lost her appetite.

'Will that be all, ma'am?'

Essie looked up and smiled at the housemaid. 'Yes, that's all, thank you, Rose. You may clear the table, but first will you fetch my bonnet and shawl? I'm going out.'

Essie arrived at the office to find Jack and George deep in conversation. They gazed at her expectantly.

'This is a nice surprise,' Jack said, smiling.

'I don't suppose you'd like to look after things for an hour or two, would you, Essie?' George reached for his jacket, which he had slung carelessly over the back of a chair. 'We have business in Limehouse, but we'll be as quick as we can.'

'I haven't said I would,' Essie protested.

George kissed her cheek. 'But you will. You're a good sister as well as being a good friend. I know you'll help out.'

'Just this once,' she said, pretending to frown.

Jack gave her a beaming smile. 'Thank you, Essie. You must call in and see Mrs Cooper before you go home. She's been asking after you.'

'I will, and I can collect Sadie at the same time.'

'Come on, old chap.' George opened the door and held it, allowing a gust of cold air to rifle through the papers on the desk and snatch at Essie's hair.

'Sorry about this,' Jack said as he hurried past. 'Everything is very straightforward. If you get any enquiries you can't deal with tell them to return later.'

'Don't worry, Jack.'

'You might enjoy the challenge,' he said softly. 'The offer of a position with us is still there, if you'd like to think about it.'

Jack proved to be right. Essie did enjoy working in the office and she readily accepted his offer of a permanent position. Each day was a new and exciting experience, and she met old acquaintances and made new friends amongst the men who worked on shore and on the water. The traders were charmed to find a young woman who understood their desire for speedy service when it came to shipping goods up and down river, as well as to the Continent. Jack's vessel sailed regularly for France, Belgium and the Netherlands, taking cargoes of all types. The knowledge that Essie had acquired while helping her father on the river was invaluable, and she was keen to learn more and ready to listen and take advice, which made her even more popular. Jack and George were delighted with her progress, and within months Essie had almost doubled their business.

Sadie accompanied Essie to the office every day and was an avid student. She watched and learned and soon had a grasp of how things were done, so much so that Jack paid her a wage. When she was not needed by Essie, she spent time helping Mrs Cooper in the kitchen at the Old Captain's House. Sadie loved to cook and Essie was treated as the honoured guest when she found the time to visit. Perched on the window seat, Essie was waited on by Sadie, who plied her with the results of her cookery lessons – crisp, buttery biscuits, melt-in-the-mouth sponge cake or spicy seed cake – all were equally delicious. George often dropped in on the excuse of passing on a message to Essie, but everyone knew that he had a particular fondness for cake, and Jack would turn up unexpectedly, taking a seat next to Essie and insisting that Mrs Cooper should join them for a well-earned rest and a cup of strong, sweet tea.

Essie loved these impromptu tea parties in the oak-panelled room, with the fire roaring up the chimney and rain lashing on the windows. Sometimes the faint smell of tobacco smoke wafted around the room and everyone smiled and nodded, knowing that the old captain was happy to see them there. Essie was loath to admit it, but she was far more comfortable and at ease in the Old Captain's House than she was in her luxurious home in Curzon Street, and almost imperceptibly her relationship with Jack deepened with each passing day. They shared the same desire to make the business prosper and a similar sense of humour, which eased even the most frustrating situations.

Life was good and fulfilling, but Essie had never allowed Gilfoyle to become complacent, and had regularly attended his chambers, demanding to be kept up to date as to the progress of their latest appeal. Finally, just when she was beginning to think that the case would never come to court, Gilfoyle sent his messenger to inform her that the hearing was set for the middle of November. Essie was delighted, but apprehensive. If Smeaton's deathbed confession was discounted there would be no chance of a pardon.

Alice and Sir Henry had recently returned from Jamaica, but when Essie visited Bearwood House she found her friend lying on a sofa in the drawing room, looking pale and listless.

'I have some good news for you, Alice.'

'Really?' Alice turned her head away.

'Are you ill?' Essie asked anxiously.

Alice motioned her to sit down. 'I get these bouts of nausea every day. The doctor says it's quite normal for a woman in my delicate condition.'

'Are you in the family way, Alice?'

'I prefer the French word *enceinte*. It's so much

more genteel.' Alice reached for a glass of water and took a sip. 'I don't know how Her Majesty has gone through this ordeal eight times.'

'But surely you want to have children?' Essie took the glass from Alice's hand and put it down on the table. 'Is Sir Henry pleased?'

'Oh, him! Yes, of course he's delighted at the thought of producing a son and heir. This might be the first, but it will most definitely be the last. I am not going to lose my figure and suffer the agony of childbirth every year, no matter what he says.'

'I think you'll change your mind when you hold the baby in your arms.' Essie leaned over and dropped a kiss on Alice's forehead. 'You might feel poorly, but you look beautiful. Your skin has a lovely glow and your hair is like silk.'

Alice sat up. 'Really? I thought I looked like an old hag.'

'Why don't you get dressed and come to Gunter's with me? I'm sure you could manage a dish of ice cream or a slice of cake.'

'Perhaps I could,' Alice said doubtfully. 'Are you sure I look all right?'

'Never better. Shall I ring the bell for your maid?'

'Yes, do.' Alice put her head on one side. 'When you first arrived you said you had news for me. What is it?'

'The court hearing is next week, Alice. If it goes

in their favour both Raven and Freddie will be free men. Will you attend?'

'No, I think not, but you will, I'm sure.'

'Most certainly.'

'And you haven't forgotten your promise to take the news to Raven in person? He needs to return home as soon as possible and put things right at Starcross. It's not my responsibility.'

Essie reached for the bell pull. 'I always keep my promises.'

Essie attended the court accompanied by George, and Sadie was left in charge of the office with Jack close at hand in case she needed him.

Sick with nerves, Essie sat in the public gallery, clutching her brother's hand. Quite how long the proceedings lasted she could not have said, and the legal jargon was sometimes baffling, but eventually the judge uttered the longed-for words – 'NOT GUILTY'. Essie was too stunned to react, but George uttered a loud 'Hurrah' and was immediately threatened with expulsion by a stern-faced court official. They left the gallery and made their way out of the court building.

In the street Essie lifted her face to the pale November sun, closing her eyes and sighing with relief. 'They're free men, George. It's over.'

'Not quite. Raven and Freddie have yet to be informed.'

'And I promised Alice that I would take the news personally,' Essie said, thoughtfully. 'I have to travel to Australia right away, George.'

'Surely you could send a letter.' He stared at her, shaking his head. 'That's ridiculous. Let Lady Alice travel to the other side of the world, if that's what she wishes.'

Essie smiled. 'I don't think Alice will be travelling far for a while – she's in the family way.'

He let out a whistle between his teeth. 'Well, I never! I can't see Alice as a mother, wiping noses and patching up cuts and bruises.'

'She'll have a fleet of nannies and nursery maids to do all that. But she may surprise us all and become a doting mama. Who knows?'

George hailed a cab. 'Wapping High Street, cabby.' He helped Essie into the vehicle and climbed in beside her. 'Are you really going to Australia, Essie?'

'It seems so, George.'

It all happened so quickly that Essie had little time to reconsider her decision. One moment they had been in the courtroom and the next she was supervising the packing of a steamer trunk and various smaller items of luggage. The only thing left to do was to break the news to Jack. Essie waited until they were alone in the office, except for Sadie who was poring over a bill of lading.

Essie cleared her throat nervously. She knew he

would challenge her decision, but that brought out her stubborn streak. Even if what she planned was a foolhardy thing to do, she had made a promise and she was determined to see it through. 'Jack, I've been thinking.'

He looked up from the chart he had been studying. 'Is something wrong, Essie?'

'No, not at all.' She took a deep breath. 'The *Santa Gabriella* is moored in the Upper Reach and I want to charter her to take me to Australia.' She met his startled gaze with a persuasive smile. 'I can afford it, Jack. I gave Alice my word that I would take the news to Raven and Freddie in person.'

'But that's ridiculous, Essie. Surely it's unnecessary, and a waste of time and money.'

'Sadie is perfectly capable of helping in the office – she knows most of our clients and she understands how we do things. Besides which, the *Santa Gabriella* is a fast ship, and I only intend to stay long enough to persuade Raven to come home.'

'But we need you here, Essie,' Jack said, frowning. 'You're a born businesswoman, and I've come to rely on you.'

'You'll have Sadie to run errands and take messages, and I won't be away for more than a few months. You'll hardly notice I'm gone.'

Sadie had been sitting behind the desk, listening quietly, but she jumped to her feet clapping her hands. 'I can cope, Jack. If you'll let me stay with

you and Mrs Cooper at the Old Captain's House
I'll be on hand. I'm thirteen now, practically a
woman, and very capable – Mrs Cooper says so.'

'Of course you are.' Essie blew her a kiss. 'I have
complete faith in you, Sadie.'

Sadie opened her mouth to reply and closed it
again as her attention strayed to the person who
burst into the office. Her face lit up with a delighted
smile. 'Captain Falco.'

'How did the trip to the Crimea go, Captain?'
Jack's grim expression melted into a smile and he
greeted Falco with a handshake. 'You made good
time.'

'It went as well as can be expected.' Serious, for
once, Falco shook his head. 'I dislike taking young
men to face the horrors of the battlefield. I hope the
war will soon be over.'

'Amen to that,' Jack said, nodding. 'But you can
comfort yourself with the fact that the army have
enough troop ships now. That was a single trip.'

'I brought back many wounded. We set them
ashore in Portsmouth, as instructed, but I wouldn't
want to go through that again.'

Essie could see that Falco was genuinely upset
and she laid a comforting hand on his shoulder.
'Welcome home. It's good to see you safe and sound,
Captain. Did my father do himself proud?'

'He did, and not a drop of liquor has passed his
lips since we left port. You'll see him soon.'

'I'm so relieved, and I have some good news. Raven and Freddie have been exonerated of any wrongdoing,' Essie said eagerly. 'They're free men now, Falco. I want to charter your ship to take me to Australia so that I can tell them in person.'

Falco took her hand and raised it to his lips. 'Gladly, *mia cara*. When do we sail?'

'As soon as possible.' Essie turned to Jack, but his tight-lipped expression and stony silence spoke more than a thousand words. 'I have to do this, Jack. You do understand, don't you?'

'I thought you were happy here, Essie. Isn't all this enough for you? Or have you set your sights on being a countess?'

'That's unworthy of you,' Essie said, sharply. 'You know me better than that.'

'Do I? I see no reason for you to travel halfway across the world, unless you're desperate to see your friend again.'

'I can't talk to you when you're in this mood,' Essie said angrily.

Jack snatched his hat off a row of pegs. 'I have business to attend to.'

'That's right,' Essie said, throwing up her hands. 'Walk away. Don't stop to discuss things.'

The slamming of the door was her only answer.

'He'll come round in time,' Falco said gently. 'He thinks a lot of you, Essie.'

'And it's mutual, but he doesn't own me, Falco.

458

I'm an independent woman and I can do as I please. Raven and Freddie are my friends and I intend to bring them home.'

'I'd come with you, Essie.' Sadie rushed up to her and gave her a hug. 'But it's best if I stay here. Don't take any notice of Jack, he's just jealous.'

Essie buried her face in Sadie's golden curls, holding her close. 'You must look after him for me, and George, too.'

'I will.' Sadie broke away and did a twirl. 'I'll be in charge and I'll make sure they behave themselves while you're away.'

'I hope I'm doing the right thing, Falco,' Essie said in an undertone.

Falco gave her a sympathetic smile. 'We will bring them home together, *mia cara*. I've seen enough suffering to last me a lifetime, so it will be good to see old friends.' He cleared his throat noisily. 'How is Lady Alice? I would like to see her while I am ashore.'

Essie hesitated, unsure how to break the news of Alice's marriage. She had long suspected that Falco had deep feelings for her ladyship, and now she was certain. 'I'm afraid that might be difficult for you, Captain. Alice married Sir Henry Bearwood in June.'

His eyes darkened and he looked away. 'I wish her joy.'

'They are well suited, Falco.' Essie laid her hand on his arm. 'Alice is quite content and in a few months' time she'll be a mother.'

'I'll have the ship ready to sail in two days.' Falco's smile did not reach his eyes, but his tone was brisk as ever. 'You will be pleased with your papa, Essie. He's waiting on the wharf and he wants to see you.'

Essie snatched her shawl and wrapped it around her shoulders as she followed Falco out into the cold greyness of a November day. The river was in a benevolent mood as it snaked silkily towards the sea on the outgoing tide. Essie looked round for her father but she barely recognised the sturdy, upright man in seaman's clothing who was waiting at the top of the steps. He turned to face her and she hurried to meet him.

'Pa. Welcome home.'

His weathered features creased into a smile and he patted her on the shoulder. 'I'm pleased to see you, girl. You look like a proper lady.'

'And you're looking good, Pa.' Essie hesitated. 'I'm well and happy.'

'No thanks to me, girl. Your ma would turn in her grave if she knew how I'd treated you and George. I wouldn't blame you if you hated me.'

'I don't hate you and neither does George.'

'Where is my boy?'

'You'll see him at supper tonight, Pa. You will join us, won't you?'

'I don't remember much of what happened when I was a slave to drink, but I'm a changed man now.' Jacob shot a wary glance at Falco, who was standing behind Essie. 'I will take supper with you, Essie. If it's all right with the Cap'n?'

'Everyone has two days' shore leave and then we sail for Australia.' Falco winked at Essie. 'You'd better explain to your papa, Essie. I have business to discuss with Jack.' He strolled back to the office and went inside.

Essie was about to suggest that her father accompanied her to Curzon Street when she spotted her brother walking towards them. She waved to attract his attention and beckoned. 'George is coming, Pa. Now is as good a time as any to make your peace with him. He's a fine man and I'm sure he'll be more than willing to shake hands.'

That evening, over dinner, Essie could see that her pa was uncomfortable and ill at ease. The meeting between George and their father had gone reasonably well considering what had happened in the past, but it was obvious to Essie that it would take time for old wounds to heal. During the meal George did his best to keep the conversation flowing, but Jacob seemed at a loss for words, especially in the presence of the butler and parlourmaid. He toyed with his food and dropped his knife on the floor, followed by his table napkin. He bumped heads with Parkinson when they both bent to retrieve the knife and napkin, and he spilled his water when he reached for the salt. Jacob was clearly embarrassed by his clumsiness and he mumbled an apology to Parkinson, who mopped up the spilled liquid.

When dessert was served Jacob spooned the syllabub into his mouth as if it was his last meal on earth and when his plate was clean he stood up.

'I must go now, Essie. Ta for the grub, but I ain't accustomed to such high living.'

Essie leaped to her feet. 'Don't go, Pa. I've asked my housekeeper to make a room ready so that you can stay here. Why don't you come to the drawing room and we'll have coffee? I'm sure that you and George have a lot to talk about.'

Jacob shot a glance at his son, lowering his shaggy eyebrows. 'I think it's too late. I know me faults, George. I don't expect forgiveness, son.'

George rose from the table. 'We're still family, Pa. It will take time, but there's no reason to think we can't get along tolerably well. I've learned a thing or two since I left home.'

'Ta, son.' Jacob made a move towards the door. 'I'd best be going now.'

'Won't you stay the night?' Essie asked anxiously.

'It's kind of you, but I'm not comfortable here. This isn't for the likes of me. I'll walk back to the dock and find someone to take me out to the ship.'

'No, you won't,' George said firmly. 'We'll take a cab and I'll row you in our skiff.'

'I'll send for the carriage.' Essie raised her hand to tug at the bell pull, but George shook his head.

'Don't drag the coachman out at this hour. Pa and I will walk some of the way and enjoy a cigarillo together. We'll get a cab for the rest of the journey, so don't wait up for me, Essie. I might be a while.' He slapped his father on the back. 'Come on, guvnor. Let's go.'

They left together and suddenly the elegant dining room seemed like a prison. Essie sank down on her chair, gazing round at the trappings of wealth, which suddenly seemed worthless and tawdry. She understood why her father felt out of place, but his discomfort made her realise just how much she herself had changed. She was no longer the girl from Limehouse working the river for pennies, but neither was she entirely happy as the mistress of a mansion in Curzon Street. Essie Chapman had yet to find her rightful place in the world. Maybe she would discover it in Australia, or perhaps it was here at home? She could not forget Jack's adverse reaction when she told him about her proposed trip. His attitude had hurt her and had left her confused as to her own feelings.

Two days later, goodbyes were said and tears flowed freely. At the last minute Alice had sent a message wishing her '*Bon voyage*', and the time had come to board the *Santa Gabriella*.

Sadie threw her arms around Essie and had to be prised away by Mrs Cooper, who had come to wish Essie a safe journey and a speedy return home.

'I'll take good care of Sadie,' Mrs Cooper said with a watery smile. 'The old captain approves and he'll keep an eye on the girl, too.'

'As will I,' Jack added hastily.

'Me, too! So don't worry about anything, Essie.' George hugged her in an unusual show of brotherly love.

'I'll miss you all.' Essie glanced at Jack, who had so far shown a degree of reserve. He had said all the right things in the run-up to her departure, but she knew that it was just words, and she sensed his frustration. Whether it was anger or something deeper she had no way of knowing, although if he had begged her to stay she might have been persuaded to reconsider her decision. She hesitated, hoping that he might unbend for just long enough to wish her well, but he remained tight-lipped as he followed her down the steps and handed her into the wherry.

'Are you sure this is what you want?' he said gruffly.

There was a note of desperation in his voice and he held her gaze with an intensity that made it impossible to look away. His fingers closed over hers and he held her as if he could not bear to be parted. She was tempted to change her mind – she wanted to give in and throw her arms around him – but it was too late. She could not back down now.

'I have the official papers in my luggage, Jack.

I'm going to make sure that Raven and Freddie have them and then I'll return, with or without them.'

'I can see that nothing I say will make you change your mind.' He raised her hand to his lips and brushed it with a kiss as soft as a butterfly's wing. 'Safe journey, Essie. Come home to me.'

She sat down suddenly as the wherry cast off. The plash of the rower's oars and a series of hoots from steam whistles, accompanied by the grinding sound of a working crane, drowned Jack's final words of farewell. He raised his hand and then let it fall to his side.

Essie's throat constricted with unshed tears and she turned away, resolutely fixing her attention on the *Santa Gabriella*, which was to be her home for the next two months or more, depending on wind and weather. Falco and her father were already on board, but, for a moment, she had an almost irresistible urge to tell the waterman to turn back. She glanced over her shoulder and saw Jack standing on the edge of the wharf, and behind him were George, Sadie and Mrs Cooper, who was alternately dabbing her eyes with her hanky and then waving it frantically.

Leaving the people she loved most in the whole world was hard, but Essie owed a debt of gratitude to Raven, and she had made a promise that she must keep. There was no turning back now.

Chapter Twenty-Five

They had left London in the second week of November and arrived in Corio Bay in the middle of January, having made good time, even allowing for coaling stops and taking on fresh water and supplies on the way. They landed at Geelong and memories of that first trip came flooding back, but this time Essie knew exactly where she was going. They hired horses for greater speed and pack mules to carry the essentials needed for making camp. Falco opted to accompany her and it seemed natural to take Jacob, who was a good man in a fight. Essie had no illusions as to the dangers that might beset them from marauding gangs and escaped convicts.

It was the middle of summer but the nights were cool, and Jacob built huge brushwood fires every evening when they set up camp. This time they were well equipped and ready for anything that the weather, wildlife, sand-flies or desperate men could throw at them. The ride through what was now familiar country provided a welcome change from the long days spent at sea. Lacking female company, Essie had been thrown back on her own resources and she had kept a journal, filled with descriptions of the sights she had seen and the minutiae of daily life on board. She had made herself useful, helping in the galley or tending to the scalds, cuts and bruises and minor ailments suffered by the crew, but she was glad to be ashore and excited at the thought of seeing Raven and Freddie again.

The first sign of habitation was the familiar smell of eucalyptus and wood smoke. Then, as they reached the top of the rise the camp spread out before them. Huts, wooden shacks, tents and fossickers' humpies and bark gunyahs stretched as far as the eye could see. It was mid-afternoon and men were working at the diggings. The ground beneath them shook as the steam engine powered the huge rock crusher.

'I've never seen nothing like it in me life.' Jacob pushed his cap to the back of his head.

'The lust for gold,' Falco said, nodding. 'It consumes men and eats into their souls.'

'Never mind that. We've made it.' Essie urged her tired horse on with a gentle nudge of her heels against the animal's flanks. 'I want to find Raven and Freddie.'

She rode past Tandy's general store and the liquor shop as she headed to the far side of the camp. Dismounting outside Raven's wattle and daub hut, she looped the reins around a stunted tree and went to investigate. There was no one at home, which was hardly surprising, but then she spotted Leah, who was hefting buckets of water up the hill from the creek, and she ran down the incline, slithering on the mud in her haste to greet her old friend.

Leah dropped the buckets and threw her arms around Essie. 'I thought I was seeing things. It is you, Essie.' She held her at arm's length, tears sparkling on the tips of her sandy eyelashes. 'Let me look at you. How smart you are now, dear. You look a proper lady, and there's me in my old cotton frock and pinafore.'

Essie kissed Leah's lined cheek. 'It's so good to see you. How are you keeping? I hope those sons of yours are looking after you.'

'Yes, indeed. The boys have been ever so good since you told them what's what. Especially my baby, Joe. He's a good boy.'

Essie tried to imagine Big Joe as a baby and failed miserably, but he was definitely the nicest of Leah's three sons and he loved his ma.

'Yes,' she said, smiling. 'Joe is one of the best. Now let's get this water back to your hut and we can have a proper chat later.' She bent down and picked up one of the heavy buckets.

Leah did not argue. She carried her pail up to the shack and placed it on the stoop. 'Can you sit a while, love? We'll have a cup of tea and you can tell me why you've come back.' She paused, eyeing Essie with a puzzled frown. 'Beasley made you rich, so why return to this hellhole?'

'I have good news for Raven and Freddie. Do you know where I might find them?'

'No, love. Freddie could be anywhere, although it's lucky you arrived when you did because I heard that Raven is planning to move on, and he's gone to Bendigo, but no doubt he'll tell you himself when he returns to camp.' Leah glanced up at the sky. 'It's getting late and they'll all be packing up for the night.'

'You're right, of course. I'll go and tell Pa and Falco that I'll be a while.'

'Bring them over too.' Leah peered into the gathering gloom. 'So that's your pa, is it? I'd like to meet him.'

Essie had grown closer to her father during the long sea voyage and she wanted to put matters straight. 'He's a changed man since he stopped drinking. We've ridden a long way today and I'm sure they'd both be most grateful for a hot drink.'

'The kettle should be boiling. I always stop for a cup of tea before my men get back from the diggings. It's my quiet time of the day when I sit and watch the sunset.'

'I'll be back in two ticks.' Essie hurried to where Falco and Jacob were unsaddling the horses.

Falco glanced over his shoulder. 'You've met with an old friend, Essie.'

'Indeed I have and she's asked you both over for a cup of tea. I'd like you to meet Leah, she's a wonderful woman.'

'All in good time, *mia cara*. First we must see to the animals, and then we will join you.'

Essie retraced her steps and climbed onto the stoop to sit on the bench next to Leah's rocking chair. She had almost forgotten what it was like to live in camp. The reality was appalling, particularly when compared to the utter luxury of the house in Curzon Street, not to mention the splendid mansions belonging to Alice and Sir Henry. The tiny house in White's Rents was a palace compared to the one room shared by the Halfpenny family. The total lack of comfort and privacy was something she had chosen to forget, but now it came home to her and was all the more shocking.

Essie sipped tea from the tin mug that Leah passed to her. 'Have your boys had any luck at the mine?'

'Some,' Leah said, gravely. 'But not enough to retire on. I think the chances of finding nuggets like the one Beasley left to you are very slim. Maybe if we moved on to Bendigo or another site we might be lucky, but Noah is getting too old for such a hard life. He's crippled with rheumatics and sometimes he can hardly get out of bed.'

'I'm sorry to hear that, Leah. You deserve better.'

'We've got three fine sons who'll look after us in our dotage,' Leah said, chuckling. 'At least, that's what I keep telling them.'

'Joe will take care of you.'

'I'm not complaining.' Leah rose to her feet. 'Your pa and the other man are heading this way. I'll add some water to the pot.' She glanced over her shoulder with a wry smile. 'We have to be mean with the tea. Old Tandy charges what he likes for his goods, the villain.'

Essie stood up as Falco mounted the steps, followed by her father, and she made the necessary introductions. Leah was as gracious as any society hostess and her obvious pride in her home, humble though it may be, touched Essie's heart and made her choke back tears.

Falco was his usual charming self and Jacob was instantly at ease and was on excellent terms with Leah from the moment they met. He settled down over a mug of tea, recounting incidents during their sea voyage that made Leah laugh, even though they were at his expense. Essie was surprised and pleased to discover that her father had developed a sense of humour and had a genuine talent as a storyteller. But all too soon she realised that the sky was darkening and she could hear the tramp of booted feet as the men returned from the mine and the diggings.

'We'd best let Leah get on with supper for her family,' Essie said tactfully. 'And we ought to build up the fire ready to cook something for ourselves.'

Falco kissed Leah's hand. 'A pleasure to meet you, *signora.*'

'And you, sir.' Leah giggled like a schoolgirl. 'What lovely manners he has to be sure,' she said in an aside to Essie as Falco leaped off the stoop. 'Such a gentleman even though he is a foreigner.'

Jacob bowed from the waist. 'We recognise a lady when we see one, Mrs Halfpenny.'

'Thank you, Mr Chapman,' Leah said primly. 'Perhaps you'll have time to meet my Noah and our boys. It's always nice to speak to someone from home.'

'It would be my pleasure.' Jacob bowed from the waist. 'Maybe tomorrow, but now I must see what I can do about grub. I'm so hungry I could eat a horse.' He followed Falco, their figures merging swiftly into the deep shadow.

'Are you planning to stay long?' Leah asked anxiously.

Essie shook her head. 'No, I'm afraid not. I've come to give Raven some good news, and I hope that he and Freddie will return to England with me.'

'Then I'll just have to make the most of your

visit.' Leah gave her a brief hug. 'Now I'd better see to my men's supper or I'll have a riot on my hands.'

Essie returned to Raven's hut, arriving at the same time as Freddie. He enveloped her in a warm embrace.

'Essie, for a moment I thought I must be dreaming, but you're real and you're here. I can't believe it.'

She extricated herself from his grasp. 'Falco is here, too.' She held her hand out to her father. 'And this is my pa, Jacob Chapman. Pa, I'd like you to meet Freddie, or should I say the Honourable Frederick Dorincourt?'

Freddie grinned and shook hands with Jacob. 'Freddie will do nicely.' He turned to Falco, slapping him on the back. 'And it's good to see you again, Captain. But why are you here, Essie? Have you run out of money already?'

'No, it's nothing like that,' she said, smiling. 'I've missed you, Freddie.'

He threw back his head and laughed. 'You didn't travel halfway round the world to tell me that.'

'No, of course not, but I need to see Raven. Leah said something about him moving on to Bendigo.'

'That's right. He left over a week ago to put in for a licence to open up a mine at Bendigo.' Freddie held her at arm's length. 'Never mind him – it's wonderful to see you again, Essie. Life here wasn't the same after you left.'

'Will Raven be away for long?'

'I can't say,' Freddie said, frowning. 'It must be something very important to bring you all this way. What is it?'

She eyed him thoughtfully. 'I really wanted to tell you together, but I can't leave you in suspense. The good news is that you're a free man.'

Freddie grabbed both her hands in his. 'The appeal went well?'

'Yes, because we had new evidence, but I'm afraid your freedom came at a price. Starcross Abbey was badly damaged in a fire that Smeaton started.'

'Smeaton?' Freddie stared at her in surprise. 'I don't understand why he would do a thing like that. We've always treated our servants well.'

'He was sacked for allowing everything to go to rack and ruin. It must have been his way of getting his revenge, but he was caught in the flames and badly burned.'

'Great heavens! He should go to prison for arson.'

'He was arrested, but he died of his injuries, Freddie. He must have been afraid for his eternal soul because he made a deathbed confession and admitted everything. It's a long story, but it means that you are free men and I've come to take you home.' She tucked her hand through the crook of his arm. 'Falco and my pa are seeing to supper, so let's go and sit on the stoop and I'll tell you how it all came about.'

* * *

Freddie's reaction was exactly as she had imagined it would be. He was shocked and stunned and then elated to think that he was able to return home without a stain on his character. They ate the meal prepared by Falco and Jacob, washed down with a bottle of wine that Falco had secreted in his saddlebag, although Jacob opted for tea.

'Lady Alice will be pleased to see you again, Freddie,' Essie said earnestly. 'It was she who insisted that you must be told in person.'

'I can't believe that she married old Bearwood.' Freddie drained his mug and held it out for a refill. 'But if she's happy then who am I to say anything?'

'Quite right,' Essie said firmly. 'It's her business, and she seems content with her lot. But what about you, Freddie? Will you return to Starcross?'

He frowned thoughtfully. 'That's something I need to discuss with Raven. After all, he's the heir to the title and the estate. I'm just the younger brother.'

'Will he rebuild Starcross?'

'I certainly would, although I'm not sure about Raven. He was never particularly interested in the estate. In fact I think he considered it to be a bit of a burden, and he certainly didn't care about inheriting the title. He never used it, as far as I can recall.'

'But Starcross Abbey is beautiful, or it was before the fire. I'd hope that Raven has enough money to restore it to its former glory.'

'My brother will do his duty, but strictly between

us four, I've never seen him happier than he is here in Australia. You'd think the years of being a prisoner would have affected him, but I think in an odd way he's enjoyed the experience.'

'What will you do now, Essie?' Falco asked. 'It sounds as if Raven might be gone for days or even weeks.'

Essie glanced at each of them in turn. The flickering flames of the campfire threw their features into sharp relief and darkness folded its velvety arms around the small group. Each of them held a special place in her heart and she felt close to all of them.

'I'm going to set off for Bendigo in the morning,' she said, after a moment's reflection. 'Raven needs to know that he's a free man and it's up to him to decide whether or not he wishes to return to England with us.' She turned to Freddie. 'What will you do?'

He stretched lazily and grinned. 'Do you really need to ask? I'm going home.'

At daybreak next morning, Essie was getting ready to saddle up and set off for Bendigo when she heard the sound of approaching hoof beats. Despite the wide-brimmed hat that obscured most of his face, she knew who it was even before he drew his horse to a standstill and she ran to meet him.

'Good God, Essie.' Raven dismounted and seized her by the shoulders, peering at her as if he could hardly believe his eyes. 'What are you doing here?'

'I was just about to set off to find you,' she said breathlessly. 'How are you, Raven?'

'Never better.' He leaned over and kissed her on the cheek. 'I don't have to ask how you are, you're blooming. Being a rich woman suits you.' He released her abruptly. 'I must see to my horse and then you can tell me what you're doing back in Ballarat.'

'I'll stoke the fire and put the kettle on. We put some porridge in the hay box last night so it should be ready to eat, if you're hungry.'

'Starving,' Raven said, smiling. 'Ever practical, Essie. It's good to see you again.' He patted his horse's neck and led it down to the creek.

'Did I hear Raven's voice?'

Essie turned to see Falco standing on the stoop. 'Yes, he's seeing to his horse and then he'll join us for breakfast. Will you wake Freddie and my pa?'

'With pleasure. I must admit I am relieved that he's returned. I'm still saddle sore from our journey here and I wasn't looking forward to another long ride.' Falco disappeared into the hut, leaving Essie to make tea and take the porridge pot out of the hay box. She went to join Raven, who had watered his horse and was rubbing him down with a handful of straw.

He shot her a curious glance. 'Well, are you going to tell me why you're here? Surely you haven't spent all your fortune and come back in the hope of finding more gold?'

'No, of course not. I've come to tell you that you're a free man. Your name has been cleared and you can return home.'

He continued his task without a pause.

'I thought the appeal had gone against us.'

'It did, but the real villain was your butler, Smeaton.'

He paused, turning to look at her. 'What has he got to do with anything?'

The words came tumbling from her lips as she related the series of events that had taken place in his absence. 'So you see,' she concluded, 'it's over, Raven. You're exonerated and so is Freddie. You can come home.'

He straightened up, looking her in the eye. 'I'm truly grateful to you and Alice for everything you've done, but I intend to remain in Australia.'

She stared at him, momentarily at a loss for words. 'What did you say?'

'I know it must come as a surprise, but this is where I belong.'

'No, Raven. You're needed at Starcross Abbey. Didn't you hear what I said? The whole east wing was burned to the ground.'

'Go back to the hut and I'll follow in a minute. We'll talk about it then.' He led his horse back to the shelter of the trees, leaving Essie little alternative but to return to the shack.

Falco was making the tea, and Freddie emerged

from the hut, wiping soap off his newly shaven face. He came to a standstill, and Jacob sat on the stoop with one boot on and the other clutched in his hand. They all looked up expectantly.

'Well?' Falco said loudly. 'He seems to have taken the good news in his stride. What did he say?'

'He's going to stay in Australia. Raven doesn't want to go home.' Essie looked to Freddie for help. 'Talk to him, please.'

'I had a feeling he was going to do something like this.' Freddie looped the towel over the railing. 'I'll have a word, but I know my brother – once he's made up his mind, there's nothing anyone can say or do that will change it for him.' He strolled down the steps and went to join Raven.

'Well, what do you make of that?' Jacob shook his head. 'Not that I blame him. I wouldn't mind staying here myself.'

Essie stared at him in amazement. 'Really, Pa? You'd like to try your hand at mining?'

'Yes,' Jacob said simply. 'I would.'

Essie was about to follow Freddie but Falco laid his hand on her arm. 'Leave them, *mia cara*. Let them sort it out between them. It's family business.'

She wanted to get Raven on his own, but in the end she had to wait until Freddie, Jacob and Falco had gone to the diggings. Raven had helped himself to the last of the porridge and was sitting at the table. Essie pulled up a stool and sat opposite him.

'Why don't you want to go home, Raven? What will I tell Alice?'

'Tell her the truth. I've decided to stay in Australia. I've bought a licence to start up in Bendigo and I've purchased a plot of land where I intend to build a house.'

'But you're the Earl of Starcross. Surely you can't give that up? And what about your responsibility to your tenants and servants?'

'Titles mean nothing here.' Raven dropped his spoon into the empty bowl. 'I've given it a lot of thought, and I've decided to sign everything over to Freddie. He's always loved Starcross far more than I ever did and he'll settle down. He'll be as good a master and landlord as any man, and I'll see that he has enough money to rebuild the east wing. One day, when he's ready, he'll marry and fill the old place with heirs.'

'But you might marry and have children of your own.'

He met her gaze with a steady look. 'There was only one woman for me and she's dead.'

Essie looked away, unable to bear the pain in his eyes. 'I know, and I'm sorry.'

'I apologise if I led you to believe that there could be anything between us, but you're so much like her it took my breath away.' He paused, gazing into the distance as if seeing a vision of his lost love. 'For a while I thought I could love you as I loved her, but then I realised it would have been a cruel deception. It would have brought us nothing but pain and unhappiness.'

The temptation to deny the feelings that she had harboured for him was almost too great, but his candour deserved an honest answer and she nodded.

'I might have thought I was in love with you in the beginning, Raven. You are a very attractive man, and I find it hard to believe that you'll never marry, but you'll always have a special place in my heart.'

He reached across the table and clasped her hands in his. 'It would have been very easy to convince myself that we were meant for each other, but that would have been unfair. Cordelia's memory is etched into my soul and it was bound to come between us.'

Essie stared down at his hands, tanned and work worn as they rested on hers, which were now white and smooth like those of a lady. 'I hope that's not the reason why you're staying in Australia,' she said slowly. 'I wouldn't want that on my conscience.'

He shook his head. 'No – well, maybe a little, but I genuinely love this wild country. I want to make my way here on my own merit. To me my inheritance was always a burden because I knew that I had done nothing to deserve such wealth and privilege, other than being born to the right parents. Can you understand that?'

'I think I can. I was born to poverty because of

an accident of birth and I had a stroke of good fortune, which I didn't earn, but I intend to put it to good use.'

His eyes twinkled and his lips curved into a smile. 'How are you going to do that? I hope you're not thinking of investing in a gold mine.'

'Are you afraid of the competition, Raven?'

'Yes, if you were a business rival I think I might be very worried.'

'Rest easy, because I intend to buy shares in the *Santa Gabriella*. I'm already involved in a business venture with my brother and his partner, Jack Manning. This trip has convinced me that steam is going to take over from sail. Maybe we'll concentrate on trade with Australia and New Zealand. I believe these young countries are the future.'

He raised her hands to his lips. 'And so do I.'

'I'll be sorry to say goodbye, Raven.'

'You'll do well in London, Essie. That's where you belong.' He met her gaze with a wry smile. 'I've a feeling that there's someone waiting for you at home.'

She looked away. 'I don't know. Maybe.'

'He's a fool, whoever he is, if he lets you slip through his fingers.' Raven rose to his feet. 'I have work to do, if you'll forgive me for abandoning you, but I'll see you this evening.'

'Yes, of course, and I need to tell Leah that I'll be leaving again soon.'

'Don't worry about the Halfpenny family.' Raven

reached for his hat. 'I've a mind to take them with me when I leave for Bendigo. Noah is an experienced miner and so are his sons. I need men like that.'

'Leah is a good woman, but she's overworked and I fear for her health.'

'I'll need a housekeeper, and a maid or two. I'll make sure that Leah is all right.'

'And she'll take care of you, so I won't have any qualms about going home.' Essie rose to her feet. 'I'll walk with you, Raven. Falco will be relieved to hear that we're returning to England, and Freddie will, too. But I have a feeling that Pa would like to try his hand at prospecting.'

'He told me last night that he'd like to try his luck in the mine. Would you mind if he stayed behind?'

'If that's what he wants then I won't stand in his way, and if it doesn't work out he will always be welcome in my house.'

When Essie told them of her plans to leave next day, Freddie and Falco were eager to be off, but, as Raven had said, Jacob was keen to stay with him and move on to Bendigo.

'I'll make my fortune, Essie, love,' he said, puffing out his chest. 'Then I'll return to London a wealthy man. I'll show Diggory Tyce and Gaffer Wiggins what I'm made of. Riley will smile on the other side of his face when I turn up in the pub with a pocket full of readies.'

'I'll miss you, Pa,' Essie said, sighing. 'To be honest, I never thought I'd say that, but we've got to know each other better since we left London.'

'I've seen the error of me ways, love. I ain't the same man I was back in White's Rents. It's a pity I can't make it up to your ma, but she's in a better place.'

Essie kissed his whiskery cheek. 'I hope so, Pa. Which reminds me, I must tell Leah that we'll be leaving very soon. She's been like a mother to me and I want her to know that her future is secure. Raven said I might tell her about his plans.'

'He's a good man, Essie. You could do far worse, even if he ain't taking up his title and all that goes with it.'

She shook her head. 'My future is in London, Pa. I'm going home.'

Chapter Twenty-Six

Two months later the *Santa Gabriella* moored in the Upper Reach of the River Thames, and Essie stepped ashore on a wet March morning with the wind whipping at her bonnet and tugging at her skirts. She was so happy to be home that it was possible to ignore the greyness of the skies, with heavy feather-bed clouds threatening to spill rain on the turbulent River Thames. She barely noticed the putrid stench of the river mud and the foul-smelling smoke from the gasworks and the factories, and the mewling screech of the seagulls wheeling overhead was like a choir welcoming her home. The hoots of steam ships and the constant drumming of horses' hoofs on cobblestones combined with the shouts of stevedores and cries of the street sellers. Some might think that the noise and smells of the city were unlovely, but they were achingly familiar to Essie, and she was glad to be back in the place she loved most in the world.

'Essie.' A cry of delight made Essie turn to see Sadie rushing towards her, Next moment she was enveloped in a hug that threatened to topple them both over the edge of the wharf.

'Steady on.' Jack had come up behind Sadie and his arm shot out to save them from pitching into the seething, coffee-coloured water. 'Welcome home, Essie. You've been sorely missed.'

Freddie took the steps two at a time, followed more slowly by Falco and a seaman laden with their luggage.

'It's wonderful to be back in London,' Essie said, torn between tears and laughter. 'I've missed you all so much.'

'We haven't met, sir.' Freddie held out his hand. 'Freddie Dorincourt.'

'I'm sorry,' Essie said hastily. 'I was forgetting my manners. Freddie this is Jack Manning, my brother's business partner, and mine too, I hope.'

'I am?' Jack eyed her speculatively. 'That's the first I've heard of it, Essie. Although it sounds good to me.'

'Yes,' she said, taking his proffered arm. 'I've had months to think it over, Jack. I've got the money and I want to invest it wisely. Of course we'll need to talk it over with George, but I think I know almost as much about running the company as either of you.'

He patted her gloved hand as it lay on his sleeve. 'I have a completely different proposition to put to you, but I think we ought to discuss this properly when we are alone.'

Essie felt the blood rush to her cheeks and she dropped her gaze, suddenly shy. Her heart was thudding against her ribcage like a caged bird attempting to escape, but the tone of his voice and the look in his eyes held a promise for the future that took her breath away. Or perhaps she was imagining things. She withdrew her hand hastily and turned to Sadie, who was tugging at her sleeve.

'You must come to the Old Captain's House, Essie. I want you to take a look at my room. I've got new curtains and a matching coverlet – it's ever so pretty. Mrs Cooper will be pleased to see you, and I'm sure the old captain will be delighted that you've come home at last.'

Essie recovered sufficiently to smile and shake her head. 'All in good time, poppet. First of all I need to go to Curzon Street, and then perhaps we can all meet up somewhere for supper. What do you say, Jack?' She shot him a sideways glance and was rewarded by a smile.

'You must all come to my house. Mrs Cooper will be most offended if we go elsewhere.'

'We couldn't put her to so much trouble,' Essie said hastily.

'Nonsense. Sadie will go and warn her to expect

company and you're all welcome.' Jack included Freddie and Falco in a general sweep of his hand.

'Freddie is going to stay with me while he's in London,' Essie said firmly. 'But it seems unfair to burden Mrs Cooper with unexpected guests, and so little time to prepare.'

'She won't mind.' Sadie backed away. 'I'll go and tell her now, and I'll help her. I'm getting really good at cooking. Oh, do say yes, Essie. I want to hear about your travels. Did you see Leah and Big Joe? I want to know everything. Promise you'll come – please.' She hurried off in the direction of the Old Captain's House without waiting for a response.

'It seems as though it's all arranged,' Essie said dazedly. 'But first we need a cab to take us to Curzon Street.'

'I'll go and find one,' Freddie volunteered. 'It's wonderful to be free to do as I please without the fear of being arrested. You can't imagine how good it feels to be back home.'

'We've got business to discuss, Jack. I'll go to the office and wait for you there.' Falco doffed his hat to Essie and he and Freddie strolled off together.

'I meant what I said, Jack.' Essie fell into step beside him. 'I want to be more involved in the business, and I can help financially. I'd like to be a full partner.'

'I think it's an excellent idea.'

She came to a halt, staring at him in surprise. 'You do? I thought you might object because I'm a woman, and we're not supposed to interfere in business matters.'

'I think having a woman on board is a definite advantage, and I have the greatest respect for you, Essie.'

She met his gaze and realised that he was sincere, but that in itself was a worry. Perhaps, after all, he simply saw her as being a source of investment and valued her head for business above all. The brisk March wind suddenly felt like a blast of arctic air, laced with hailstones, and the sky seemed to darken, even though the sun was pushing its way through a bank of cloud. Bitterly disappointed and shocked by her own reaction she nodded. 'Oh, look. Freddie has found a cab. I'd better hurry, but we can talk later.'

The house in Curzon Street seemed even larger and more opulent than before. Parkinson was just as aloof and professional, but Mrs Jackson eyed Freddie suspiciously, although her attitude changed subtly when Essie introduced him using his title. Seemingly oblivious, Freddie was obviously charmed with everything he saw, but Essie felt even more uncomfortable and out of place than she had previously. The months spent on board ship had convinced her that a life of enforced idleness was not for her, and, oddly enough, there was only one person in whom she could confide. Alice had been her employer and had become her friend and mentor – they had shared the experience of living in a mining camp, and they both loved the Dorincourt brothers, each in her own way. Essie made up her mind to visit Bearwood House at the first possible opportunity.

She was up early next morning, taking the servants by surprise. Mrs Jackson apologised profusely when Essie found that breakfast had not yet been served, but her tight-lipped expression gave her away and it was obvious that she was extremely put out.

'Tea and toast will be fine,' Essie said calmly. 'I don't need a large breakfast, Mrs Jackson. Save that for Mr Dorincourt – I'm sure he will do it justice.'

'Yes, ma'am.' Mrs Jackson sketched a curtsey and was about to leave the dining room when Essie called her back.

'I'm going out as soon as I've eaten.'

'Shall I send for the carriage, ma'am?'

'No. I'll walk.'

'Then you'll want your maid to accompany you, ma'am.'

'No, thank you. I can look after myself, Mrs Jackson. I'll need my outdoor things, that's all.'

Despite the overt disapproval of the servants, Essie set off for Piccadilly at a brisk pace. Her welcome at Bearwood House was as guarded as the one she had received from her own servants. The butler seemed slightly affronted that she had arrived unaccompanied and on foot, but she insisted that she must see Lady

Alice and she refused to leave until he had announced her arrival. Essie moved closer to the elegant Carrara marble fireplace, where a coal fired blazed up the chimney, and she waited impatiently.

The butler returned minutes later, poker-faced and so rigid with displeasure that Essie wanted to giggle. 'Her ladyship is in her boudoir, miss. Follow me, if you please.'

He headed for the grand staircase, which was flanked by two life-sized bronze figures clutching candelabra. The flickering glow of the firelight created the illusion that the statues of nubile young women were moving very slightly, as if waking from a long slumber. Essie hurried past them.

Alice was still in bed, reclining against a mountain of pillows with a cup of chocolate balanced on her swollen belly. Her face lit up with a smile. 'Essie, I'm so pleased to see you.'

Essie crossed the floor to perch on the edge of the bed. She leaned over to kiss Alice's cheek. 'You're looking blooming.'

Alice placed the cup and saucer on a bedside table. 'When people say that they mean I'm fat and blowsy.'

'Nonsense. You look wonderful. When is the baby due?'

'Any day now. In fact I think he has been waiting for you to bring Raven and Freddie home. Where are they? No, let me guess, they're both still in bed sound asleep.'

'Freddie is, but Raven chose to stay in Australia.'

'No!' Alice's eyes widened. 'Why? He's a free man and he's rich. He should have come home and taken up his responsibilities. How like him to be difficult.'

'He's signed everything over to Freddie,' Essie said gently. 'And he's given Freddie the money to rebuild Starcross Abbey.'

Alice pulled a face. 'I suppose that's better than nothing, but I'm very angry with Raven. After all we've been through to get him pardoned and he decides to live like a convict for ever.'

'I don't think that's the case, Alice. He's bought a licence to dig a mine in Bendigo and he's planning to build a house there.'

'I thought perhaps you and he might make a match of it, Essie. But it seems I was wrong, as I have been in so many things, including my first impressions of Bearwood. Anyway, there's a much more suitable man for you, who's been waiting patiently for your return.'

Essie stared at her in surprise. 'What are you talking about?'

'Are you blind, Essie? Surely you've realised that Jack Manning is head over heels in love with you? It was obvious from the start, but you were too involved with my cousin to see it.'

'It's just business,' Essie said dazedly. 'I'm going there this morning to talk about becoming a full partner.'

Alice patted her on the shoulder. 'Follow your heart and not your head. I did, and I must say it's working out really well. Bearwood is a much better husband than I could have hoped for. I fully admit that I misjudged him in the past, but then I saw sense.'

'I'm confused,' Essie said, frowning. 'We had supper at his house last night – all of us, that is – and it was very jolly. Jack was an excellent host, but that was all. We're just business associates, Alice. I think you're wrong.'

'And you're happy to let things go on like that?'

Essie rose to her feet. 'I don't know exactly how I feel, but you have enough to think about so don't worry about me.' She leaned over the bed and kissed Alice on the forehead. 'I have to go now, but I'll call on you tomorrow, if that's all right.'

'Yes, please do. I'm frankly bored with all this lying around and I can't wait to have my figure back and be able to wear my proper clothes. I'm sure I'll love my child, but the nursery is prepared and the wet nurse and nanny are ready and waiting.'

Essie headed for the door. 'You'll made a wonderful mother, Alice.'

'Wait.' Stifling a groan, Alice clutched her belly, her face contorted with pain. 'Essie, fetch Bearwood. Fetch the midwife. I think the baby's coming.'

Essie had wanted to stay until Alice's baby was born, but Sir Henry was at his wife's side and the house was suddenly filled with nurses, midwives and physicians. There was nothing that Essie could do, other than to extract a promise that someone would send a message to her when the baby arrived.

A cab took Essie to Wapping and she arrived at the office to find Jack on his own. In the light of her conversation with Alice she was suddenly embarrassed and ill at ease. She could only hope he would put her heightened colour down to the chilly east wind.

'Good morning, Jack.'

He leaped to his feet and hurried round the desk to pull up a chair. 'Good morning, Essie. Won't you take a seat?'

She hesitated and remained standing as she peeled off her gloves. 'Where are the others? I thought Sadie would be here, and George, too.'

'I wanted to speak to you alone. They'll be here later.'

She fixed her gaze on the top button of his waistcoat, unable to look him in the eye. Alice's words had plagued her during the cab ride from Piccadilly and had unleashed a torrent of emotion that threatened to smother her with its intensity.

'I suppose the transaction should be done with a solicitor in attendance,' she said stiffly.

'That's not the way I want it to be, Essie.' He laid a hand on her shoulder, raising her chin with a gentle finger so that she was forced to meet his gaze. 'Last evening Freddie told me that his brother has chosen to remain in Australia, and he intends to build a life for himself there.'

'That's true,' Essie said breathlessly. Her heart was racing and her knees threatened to give way beneath her, but she held her head high. 'That was his decision and has nothing to do with me, Jack.'

'I was afraid that you might not return. I thought that you were in love with Raven and he with you.'

She shook her head. 'You might say that fate threw us together, but I'm not of their world. This is where I want to be.'

'Could you find a small space in your heart for someone who's loved you from the first moment he saw you, Essie?'

They were so close that she could feel his breath against her cheek and the look in his eyes was like a warm caress. 'Perhaps,' she murmured, making a feeble effort to push him away and failing as his mouth claimed hers in a kiss. 'Maybe,' she added dazedly. He kissed her again and this time she offered no resistance.

'I love you, Essie,' he said softly. 'I want you as my partner in life as well as in business. I thought I'd lost you, but I never want to go through that again. Will you marry me?'

All that had occurred in the past was erased by one softly spoken word. 'Yes.'

'I can't offer you a castle or a title. I'm only a common man.'

She laid her finger across his lips. 'Don't say such things, Jack. You're the reason I came home.'

'You can't imagine how much I've wanted to hear you say that.' He was about to kiss her when the door flew open and Sadie rushed in followed by George, Freddie and Falco.

'She said yes?' George took off his cap and threw it in the air. 'Congratulations, old fellow. My sister is a wise woman.'

'How romantic,' Sadie breathed, clutching her hands to her breast. 'I want to be a bridesmaid.'

'Of course,' Essie said, smiling. 'And tomorrow we'll order a pair of red boots to be made especially for you, in the finest leather that money can buy.'

'You haven't forgotten,' Sadie said, clapping her hands.

'Of course not. You're my little sister.'

'I am, and we must give Mrs Cooper the good news.' Sadie grabbed Essie by the hand. 'She knew that you'd say yes. She told me so last evening when I was helping her to clear away the dishes. The captain will be delighted – I'm sure he was there, too. We must go and tell him.'

'We can't leave the office unattended,' Essie said, laughing at Sadie's eagerness.

'Allow me to stay here.' Falco tossed his hat onto a wall peg and swept Essie into a warm embrace. 'I love you like a daughter, Esther. I wish you all the happiness in the world, *mia cara*.'

'Thank you, Falco. That means a lot to me.' Essie held her hand out to Jack. 'Shall we?'

'I think we must.' Jack nodded to Falco. 'Thank you – we'll celebrate later with the best champagne.'

'And I will serenade the beautiful bride to be.' Falco took his seat behind the desk. 'But I would not like to sit here all day. The deck doesn't move beneath my feet.'

Freddie took the opportunity to kiss Essie on the cheek. 'I couldn't be more pleased, Essie. My brother wasn't worthy of a woman like you.'

'My sister is a very special woman,' George added seriously. 'It's a pity the old man isn't here to share the good news. He'll approve, I know it.'

Sadie opened the door and held it for them to pass. 'Come on. There's some chocolate cake left in the larder. Maybe Mrs Cooper will cut us a slice.'

Jack proffered his arm. 'I can see we'll get no peace until we've broadcast the news, my love.'

'I'm so happy, I want to tell the whole world.' Essie stood on tiptoe to kiss him on the lips.

'Enough of that,' George said, laughing. 'Let's celebrate.'

Arms linked, Essie and Jack walked the short distance to the Old Captain's House.

Mrs Cooper was tearful with joy when she heard their news and insisted on opening the bottle of Madeira that she had been saving for Christmas.

'We should have Madeira cake,' she said apologetic-
ally, 'but chocolate is all I have.'

'I think we can cope with that, Mrs Cooper,' Jack
said, beaming at everyone as he passed round the
glasses. 'Let's drink a toast to my beautiful fiancée.
I'm the luckiest man in the whole world.'

Sadie sniffed the air. 'I smell tobacco smoke. The
captain agrees with you, Jack.'

After the toasts were drunk and all that remained
of the cake was a crumb or two, they were about
to leave the house when Falco arrived, waving a
sheet of expensive writing paper. 'A message from
Bearwood House. Sir Henry and Lady Bearwood
are proud to announce the birth of their daughter
– Esther Cordelia Bearwood. Mother and baby are
doing well,' he added grinning. 'The footman told
me to tell you that, Essie.'

'That was quick for a first baby,' Mrs Cooper
said, nodding. 'My sister was in labour for two days
with her Maudie.'

Essie clapped her hands. 'This is the happiest day
of my life. I was blind, Jack, but now I'm seeing
properly for the very first time. I really do love you
with all my heart.' She gazed into his smiling eyes
and saw a reflection of herself in their dark depths.
It was a magical journey she was about to embark
on, and, come what may, they would share it together.

THE END

Read on for an exclusive extract of the next book
in *The River Maid* series

The
Summer Maiden

Coming 14th June

Chapter One

Caroline Manning stood a little apart from the rest of the mourners who were preparing to walk away from her father's grave. The interment was over, the last words of farewell to a good man had been said, and his widow, Esther, had dropped a crimson rose onto the coffin. Her face was hidden behind the dark veil of widow's weeds, but Caroline sensed that her mother was crying. Tears stung her own eyes, but she was determined to be brave. She had loved her father dearly, but she knew that Papa would have wanted her to support the rest of the family and help her mother through the trauma of such a great loss. Max and James, her younger brothers, had been away at boarding school when their father had fallen ill and died, and Esther had travelled to Rugby with Sadie, her friend and companion, to bring them home. The boys had been brave throughout the interment, but Jimmy had broken down and sobbed when the first handful of earth fell on the coffin, and he was clinging to their mother, who was weeping openly. Caroline could see that fourteen-year-old Max was struggling and she placed her arm around his shoulders.

'Papa didn't suffer, Max. He just slipped away, so Mama told me.'

Max dashed his hand across his eyes. 'Yes, that's what she said, but I'm going to miss him.'

'We all are.' Caroline gave him a comforting hug. 'We'd best follow the others, Max. We have to get the train back to London.'

'We're going now, Carrie, dear.' Esther braced her slender shoulders and led Jimmy away from the yawning chasm of Jack Manning's last resting place.

'I won't be long.'

'The train will be here soon,' Sadie said firmly. 'Come on, Carrie, love. Best foot forward.'

'I said I won't be long.' Caroline could not help a note of impatience creeping into her voice. She had so far kept herself composed, but she was in danger of losing the cast-iron self-control that had helped her to get through the carriage ride from their home in Finsbury Circus to Waterloo Bridge Station, and the journey on the Necropolis Railway to Brookwood Cemetery. Mama had her standards and would not travel any other way than first class, even though Aunt Sadie was quite happy to use the omnibus and had even braved the Metropolitan Railway, which ran underground.

'Come with me, Max. We'll let Carrie have a minute to herself.' Sadie beckoned to Max and he allowed her to take him by the hand, something that he would never have done normally.

At any other time Caroline might have smiled to see her normally strong-willed brother acting so meekly, but this was not a normal day. Sadie was no relation, but she had been with the family ever since Caroline could remember, and had become a surrogate aunt with an enduring place in their affections.

The distant sound of a train's whistle jolted Caroline back to the present and she raised the tea rose to her lips, inhaling the delicate perfume before allowing it to flutter through the air, landing on the coffin with a gentle thud. Papa had loved tea roses and she had picked several from the garden with the morning dew still upon them, choosing the biggest and the best to bring with her on Papa's last, sad journey. She wiped her eyes and took a deep breath, raising her face to the cloudless azure sky. She wondered if Papa and her two baby brothers, who had been taken by whooping cough, were looking down on her, but that was childish and, at seventeen years old, she knew better.

She picked up her black silk skirts and trudged across the scorched grass as she followed her family to the station platform. It was a fiery June day and the ground beneath her feet was baked hard. The return train journey promised to be hot and sticky and less than cheerful, and she had a sudden urge to cry out that it was not fair. Papa had been in his mid-forties when he contracted pneumonia during a business trip to the Continent. Her last sight of him had been when she had waved him off, thinking that he would return soon with news of a profitable deal. Caroline bit the inside of her lip to prevent herself from bursting into tears as she caught up with her mother, Sadie and the boys.

'Are you all right?' Sadie whispered.

'Yes, of course.' It was a lie, but Caroline held her head high as she took her mother's mittened hand in hers. 'We'll be home soon, Mama.'

'Home.' Esther's voice was harsh and thick with tears. 'There is no future for me without Jack. My heart is broken and buried with him in that cold grave.'

Sadie sighed and shook her head. 'It's a sad time, but you'll feel better when you've had a cup of tea and something to eat.'

'Stop being so cheerful,' Esther said wearily. 'Leave me alone.' She broke away from Caroline's restraining hand and marched towards the station platform.

'When Mama cries it makes me sad, too,' Jimmy said, sniffing.

'It's all right to cry, Jimmy.' Max slapped his brother on the shoulder. 'Just don't let them see you're sad when we go back to school.'

'Come on, boys,' Sadie said briskly. 'We'd better get a move on, or we'll be left behind.' She quickened her pace, the others falling into step beside her.

The rest of the mourners, most of whom were employees of the Manning and Chapman Shipping Company, travelled second class, but Esther and the family had a first-class carriage to themselves.

'If only your uncle George were here.' Esther leaned back in her seat. 'I don't know if he received the cable I sent to the agent in New York, as there was no reply.'

'He'll be as upset as you are, Essie.' Sadie turned her head away to stare out of the window. 'It seems your family are only happy when they are sailing the seven seas.'

'*Our* family.' Esther took off her gloves and laid them on the seat beside her. 'How many times do I have to stress that you're as important to me as if we were related by blood?'

'I know you believe that, Essie, but that doesn't make it true.' Sadie shot her a sideways glance. 'Jack wouldn't want you to wear yourself out with grief. He was a good man, and you're a strong woman. You've seen hard times and you'll come through this, as always.'

'Yes, but I'm allowed to mourn in my own way.'

Esther brushed a tear from her cheek and her lips trembled ominously. 'Besides which, I thought that Alice might have taken the trouble to attend the funeral.'

'You know she sent her apologies,' Sadie said sternly. 'Sir Henry is taking part in an important debate in the Commons, and Lady Bearwood wanted to be there to support him.'

'I know. I'm being unreasonable. It's all too much. If Jack had remained in London he would still be alive today.'

Caroline glanced anxiously at her brothers, but Jimmy had fallen asleep in the corner seat and Max was gazing out of the window, seemingly in a world of his own. She moved closer to Sadie, lowering her voice to a whisper. 'What's going on, Aunt Sadie? I know that Mama is heartbroken, but there's more, isn't there? I'm not a child; I need to know.'

Sadie inclined her head so that the brims of their black bonnets were almost touching. 'It's business, Carrie. I don't know the ins and outs, but the loss of the *Mary Louise* was a blow, and between you and me, I don't think it was insured.'

'That was nearly a year ago,' Caroline said, frowning.

'That's right. All were lost as well as the cargo.'

'I'm grieving, but I'm not deaf.' Esther folded back her veil. Even in her tear-stained and emotional state, she was still a handsome woman. At thirty-nine she had kept her figure and her skin was smooth with only a few laughter lines crinkling the corners of her hazel eyes, and the hint of silver in her dark hair did nothing to detract from her good looks. 'If you have questions, ask me, Caroline. Don't mutter behind my back.'

Sadie leaned over to pat Esther's clasped hands. 'I'm sorry, but you shouldn't bottle it all up, Essie. We're here to help you, and Carrie and the boys have lost their pa.'

Esther's eyes swan with unshed tears. 'I know, and I'm trying to keep the worst from them. As if it isn't bad enough to lose the husband and father that we love, it seems inevitable that we will lose our home as well.'

'Surely it can't be that bad, Mama?' Caroline said dazedly. 'We've always been well off.'

'What happened to the fortune that you brought home from the goldfields in Australia?' Sadie asked, frowning. 'You must still have your investments, and the business seemed to be going well.'

'That's all you know.' Esther's full lips tightened into a pencil-thin line. 'Jack did his best to keep it from us, and I've only just discovered the true state of affairs. My brother must have known that the business was in a bad way when he sailed off for the Americas, but he didn't think to confide in me. It was only when I went to the office and demanded to see the books that I discovered the parlous state of our finances. George should have said something before he went away.'

'That's not fair, Essie,' Sadie protested angrily. 'George was only doing his job. When he's offloaded the cargo he'll find another one to bring home, doubling the profit. You know as well as I do that that's how it goes in business.'

Esther held up her hand, tears seeping between her closed eyelids. 'Please, that's enough. I don't want to hear any more. Just leave me alone. My head is pounding.'

Caroline sat back in her seat, staring out of the window at the sun-drenched fields and hedgerows as they flashed past. Dog roses, buttercups and dandelions made bright splashes of colour against the dark green of hawthorn leaves and the pale gold of ripening cornfields. Cows grazed on patches of grass beneath shady trees and woolly white sheep clustered together on the hillsides. It was all so serene and peaceful, but Caroline had a feeling that they were heading for trouble at home, and without the solid backing of her father the future loomed before her engraved with a huge question mark.